Hollington Homecoming

VOLUME ONE

SANDRA KITT

ESSENCE BESTSELLING AUTHOR

JACQUELIN THOMAS

Hollington Homecoming

VOLUME ONE

HARLEQUIN® KIMANI ARABESQUE®

HOLLINGTON HOMECOMING, VOLUME ONE

ISBN-13: 978-0-373-09131-7

Copyright © 2013 by Harlequin Books S.A.

This edition published August 2013

The publisher acknowledges the copyright holder of the individual works as follows:

RSVP WITH LOVE
Copyright © 2009 by Sandra Kitt

TEACH ME TONIGHT
Copyright © 2009 by Jacquelin Thomas

PLEASE RECYCLE · THIS PRODUCT IS RECYCLABLE

Recycling programs for this product may not exist in your area.

Printed in U.S.A.

HARLEQUIN®
™ www.Harlequin.com

CONTENTS

Dear Reader,

We hope that your college years were filled with fond memories—football games with tailgating parties; studying all night; and meeting your roommate for the first time. Aside from these remembrances, there might also be that one love that you left behind and wondered, what if…

This *Hollington Homecoming* collection presents four wonderful stories that take you on an exciting adventure back to homecoming weekend. You will be reminded of what it feels like to revisit your old stomping grounds and connect with friends and lovers. Your heart will beat with nostalgia as you read these sensual class reunion tales and are swept off your feet by the power of passion.

In Sandra Kitt's "RSVP with Love," event planner Chloe gets the chance to bond with the former Most Popular Guy on Campus. An opportunity she has been waiting for since she first laid eyes on him as an undergraduate. *Essence* bestselling author Jacquelin Thomas's "Teach Me Tonight" introduces Tamara Hodges, a magazine writer who is determined to make things right with the computer geek who turned into Mr. Fine and Successful.

Enjoy this escape down memory lane with *Hollington Homecoming Volume One* and look to continue the journey with *Hollington Homecoming Volume Two* available next month wherever books are sold.

Happy Reading,

Harlequin Kimani

RSVP WITH LOVE
Sandra Kitt

Dedicated to everyone who shared all those
fabulous college years with me.

Prologue

"Go on. Admit it. The last four years at Hollington have been exciting, enriching and challenging. None of us will *ever* forget those night-before-exam cram sessions fueled by potato chips, beer and desperation..."

There was a smattering of laughter from the young men and women seated in front of the band shell stage, uniformly dressed in caps and gowns. Chloe Jackson was sure, as she knew the faculty must be, that their four years had been stoked at times with far more than what she'd politely mentioned. But this was neither the time nor the forum for reminding her fellow classmates that they'd arrived at Hollington College, for the most part, as teenagers with a penchant for arrogance, and were leaving as adults who'd learned they still didn't know everything. There had been a lot of foolish mistakes, unforgivable behavior, triumphs, broken hearts and vendettas but also a unilateral determination to succeed.

Chloe glanced over the gathering of her classmates, detecting the rising hum of restlessness as they waited for the pomp and circumstance to be done, for her valedictorian address to end. The late afternoon sun was already shifting to the west. The next order of business for the graduates and the coming evening…some serious celebration.

"Even those crazy days and nights were part of our education, part of the process by which we learn to manage life, our uncompromising professors and bad diets. So, here we are at the tipping point. The scoreboard shows winning numbers all around. Hollington will soon be behind us and our futures straight ahead. We have been given all the necessary tools to make it bright and rewarding. Congratulations, class of 1999. We did it. Game on!"

Chloe gathered her notes and turned to leave the stage as enthusiastic and sustained applause broke out from the seated students. While she made her way back to her seat, the dean was already making final remarks, bringing the ceremony to a close. Chloe took her seat, and the young man in black-framed glasses sitting next to her leaned close.

"In training to be speaker of the house or a sports announcer?" Micah Ross whispered. "Impressive send-off."

Chloe acknowledged the comment with a smile but said nothing. Micah, a very smart but quiet young man, was probably her best friend at Hollington. They'd somehow managed to become each other's confidant in an environment that mostly cultivated couples and brief flings. Micah had been telling her in their last year that she would make a great senator, or congresswoman or anything. But she wasn't interested in working for someone else, least of all the government.

"...We are so proud of all of you. Once again, congratulations to the Hollington College graduating class of 1999."

With those words, it was done.

Chloe felt a chill of finality with the pronouncement. She stood along with everyone else as her classmates applauded each other. Most had decided on that time-honored tradition of tossing their mortarboards into the air and shouting with relief, joy and the freedom they'd earned along with their degrees and awards. She wasn't about to toss her mortarboard anywhere. It had to be returned along with the gown or she'd be held financially responsible. It was an added expense she couldn't afford.

Instead, after a brief hug from Micah, and cheek kisses from many around her with whom she'd spent four years, Chloe bent to retrieve from beneath her chair the three plaques and certificates she'd been awarded along with her diploma.

Then, she stood a bit dazed. Despite her speech heralding all her potential, she wasn't sure what to do next. The graduation rituals seemed anticlimactic. Four years of work culminating in ninety minutes of speeches and a sheet of paper in a faux leather presentation folder. For a moment she felt a flash of emptiness. Like...how did she get here in the first place? Now that she'd actually achieved her goal of an undergraduate degree Chloe fingered the folder and wondered if this was all there was.

She looked around for the only two people in the crowd of nearly two thousand students and guests who should be attending the commencement ceremony because of her. There were clusters of people everywhere. Chloe quickly realized that she was the only one who stood alone.

On the band shell stage where all the college officials and faculty had been seated they, too, congratulated themselves on successfully shepherding another enrollment of students from freshman through senior year without any incidents that made the local papers or embarrassed the school, themselves or the students. And she suspected that by the end of the evening, the responsibility for this latest graduating class would all have been forgotten by those who had guided and tried to teach them.

Chloe was suddenly caught completely off guard when a young woman, almost twice her size, grabbed her in a fierce bear hug. The sharp edges of her awards pressed into her through the fabric of her gown. Her mortarboard fell off her head and landed at their feet. The woman stepped on it.

"Girl, thank you, thank you, *thank* you! I would *not* be standing here if you hadn't helped me through that first year. Lord, I just knew I wasn't going to get through."

Chloe extracted herself and bent to retrieve her cap. "Darlene, you don't have to thank me." She carefully brushed loose grass and dirt from the cap. "You did all the work, and you worked really hard."

Darlene, a big woman with a big voice and laugh and exuberance, shook her head. "Uh-uh. Don't let it go like that. You kept me on point. All those times you helped me do research in the library. I couldn't face my grandmother if I had failed. I'm the first person in my family to go to college."

Chloe shrugged lightly. "Me, too."

Seeing Darlene's surprised expression she rushed on, not allowing her classmate a chance to ask questions, and sorry that she was so unguarded in her choice of words.

"Is your grandmother here?" Chloe asked.

"She sure is. Said she wouldn't miss today for anything. You know, she could never come on parents' weekends, so I want to show her around. The campus sure isn't like where I grew up." Darlene stopped suddenly, looking a bit embarrassed. "You know what I'm talking about, right? You were always alone on those weekends, too."

"I know what you mean," Chloe responded smoothly.

Darlene looked beyond her. "What about you? Did your…"

"They're here somewhere," Chloe spoke confidently. "It's crowded. They're probably wandering around right now trying to find me."

"Yeah. Right," Darlene murmured. "Well, I gotta go. My grandmother can't stand too long. I'll see you at the party later, okay?"

She rushed away before Chloe could answer, saving her the trouble of admitting she knew nothing about a party. She carefully placed the graduation cap back atop her head, straightened her gown and began meandering through the hundreds of milling people, looking for one couple in particular.

The great field in front of the band shell stage was beginning to empty. She'd walked the grassy area twice and was now wondering if anyone had shown up at all to see her graduate, to see her win the President's Award for scholastic merit, the Hollington Discovery Award for entrepreneurial spirit, a plaque recognizing her volunteer work tutoring kids living in shelters in Atlanta. There was also a check for five thousand dollars from an anonymous benefactor. It sounded impressive, but Chloe knew she would trade it all in a heartbeat for a look of love and pride from her own family.

She turned at the whoop of laughter behind her and found a sizable gathering surrounding Beverly Turner. People were taking endless digital pictures of Hollington's statuesque and pretty homecoming queen, and it was clear that, as always, Beverly was enjoying being the center of attention. But to her credit Beverly had always been understated about her God-given gifts of beauty and personality. She was well-liked, incredibly popular and in the top fifteen percent of the graduating class. Darlene had once said, not without a bit of envy, "I swear that girl lives a blessed life."

Chloe smiled tightly to herself. Beverly's pictures were sure to end up in the local paper the next day: "Hollington Homecoming Beauty Says Goodbye."

Chloe sighed and turned away, encroaching disappointment eating away at her early euphoria. There weren't many people left on the field. The custodial staff was already spread out, collecting the folding chairs and disconnecting the audio equipment on stage.

"Hey! How come you're still out here? I've been looking all over the place for you."

Once again Chloe found herself grabbed, this time from behind. She scrambled to hold on to her awards, but they all dropped to the ground.

She was pulled into someone's arms and kissed unceremoniously, catching only a glimpse of the man crushing her against his lean body. Once again, her mortarboard fell from her head. Caught off guard, Chloe was unprepared to ward off the assault and could only react instinctively. She kissed him back.

Her mouth was compliant and soft. He controlled the pressure and intensity and contact with her tongue, gently forcing it to dance with his. She inhaled his scent and found it pleasant, almost comforting. Somewhere in her mind Chloe knew this was inappropriate, a mistake. But she also sensed a familiarity that made the embrace nonthreatening. And very seductive.

Chloe's assailant seemed in no hurry to…hurry. But then he pulled back as swiftly as he'd grabbed her, releasing her so suddenly she stumbled backward, stunned…and giddy.

"Oh, *man!* I'm so sorry," the tall handsome graduate said, chuckling.

Chloe blinked silently at him. It was hard to take the apology seriously. He looked only mildly taken aback and more than a little amused. He was tall with a sinewy athletic leanness. He also had a cocky stance as if he hadn't really done anything so terrible and, of course, she wasn't going to hold his mistake against him.

He was also very good-looking, his skin a latte tone broken only by the devilish goatee that grew around his wide mouth. With teeth that were even and white, his smile made him look rakish. Chloe had the distinct feeling that he was totally aware of his appeal, and had no trouble playing on it. If the gossip on campus was half-true, Kevin Stayton, if not exactly a womanizer, was at the very least a seasoned heartbreaker.

Trying to catch her breath and her voice, Chloe stared at him. Of course she recognized him. It was certainly confirmed by the sudden roiling of her stomach and the heated ignition of her hormones. She struggled not to betray herself. She lightly placed her fingers over her lips, as if to seal the taste and feel of him. An unexpected bonus to the day was how she saw the encounter—an unexpected graduation gift.

"I think you've made a mistake," Chloe said the obvious.

A slightly wicked and totally noncontrite expression crossed his face as his gaze roamed thoroughly over her.

"Yeah, seems like it. Hey, I didn't mean to jump you like that."

Chloe pursed her lips, the implication creating an image for her of what *that* would be like. His voice, this close, was every bit as resonant and deep as she'd imagined. She knew more about Kevin Stayton than he could ever know.

"I see you like to act first and ask questions later."

Kevin grinned, a "what can I say?" look on his face.

"I swear, from the back you looked just like…anyway, I'm really sorry…"

A trio of young men hurried by in their gowns. They shouted greetings to Kevin, offering high fives and fist bumps to each other. They said nothing to her.

"I'm not in the habit of attacking unsuspecting women," Kevin said.

"Don't worry about it," Chloe said in as steady a voice as she could manage. "I guess I should be flattered."

He shrugged lightly, accepting the implied compliment. "Don't look at it like that. It's been that kind of day, you know? Hey, by the way, congratulations."

Kevin spread his arms as if to warn her that he was going to touch her again. He did so, grabbing her upper arms and leaning toward Chloe to chastely kiss her cheek.

Chloe briefly closed her eyes. He smelled so nice. She liked his sudden attack much better.

"I'm—"

"Kevin Stayton. I know who you are."

Again, he didn't seem embarrassed or nonplussed by her calm identification. Chloe realized that Hollington's resident babe magnet and popular man-about-campus was probably used to being recognized…and idolized.

"Chloe Jackson," she said with a little lift of her chin.

Kevin narrowed his gaze and stared at her. "Sounds familiar." Then, he snapped his fingers. "Right! You were up on stage. Valedictorian or something. Got a bunch of awards. Put me to shame."

She wondered if he was making fun of her—the brainiac and Goody Two-shoes who largely went unnoticed by Kevin and his crowd. And it's not like she was never invited to the parties, dances, rallies, clubs like any other coed. But she was the one most likely to sit alone along the sidelines and watch, super-careful not to do anything that would jeopardize her scholarships and the ultimate goal of getting her degree.

"I got a couple. I saw you go up to the stage, too," she murmured, bending to retrieve her cap and awards.

Kevin beat her to it, swooping up everything and handing them back to her.

"For economics and marketing. Not too shabby."

Chloe took her things from him. There was a moment's awkward silence. Then, she made it easy for him. "Er...I bet she's in the ladies' room. Hair. Makeup. Panty hose."

He shook his head and laughed quietly at her description. "Hadn't thought of that. So how come you're not in there?"

"I'm looking for someone, too. My...family," she rushed on, the word coming forth uncomfortably.

"Right. Mine are waiting for me somewhere, but..."

Kevin ran his hand over his hair, a very close cut defining the shape of his head. It emphasized his square chin and the clean, straight line of his nose. His bottom lip was wide and full. Lush and mobile. Suddenly recalling the movement of his mouth, Chloe inadvertently moistened her lips.

He frowned and studied her again. "I feel like I should know you from somewhere. Any ideas?"

She shrugged, calm again and poised. "We probably had some classes together."

He pursed his mouth, nodding. "Yeah, yeah...now I remember."

Chloe sighed inwardly. He didn't have a clue.

"You have promises to keep," she quoted, staying cool and not allowing the fact that, after four years of passing one another on campus, sitting side by side in world studies, that at the eleventh hour as they were about to go their separate ways forever, she'd finally gotten Kevin Stayton to notice her.

He smiled ruefully. "I have to be careful about that. I mean, making promises."

"Chloe! We made it. I know we're late…"

Chloe glanced beyond Kevin to the couple advancing across the field. She could tell by their breathlessness that they'd either not been able to find her in the crowds of students earlier or they'd just arrived.

The woman, short and stout and dressed in one of her Sunday church ensembles, took Chloe in a light embrace and kissed her cheek.

"We're so happy for you," the woman said.

"We know this was real important to you," said the man.

He was tall and broad. His dark suit was the only one he owned and was a tad too small for his frame. He, too, gave Chloe a brief hard hug and squeezed her shoulder.

"Sorry we don't have a gift or anything for you," he apologized.

"I'm glad you're here." Chloe smiled at him. Aware that Kevin Stayton stood watching this tableau she took a deep breath and turned to face him.

Kevin stepped forward and thrust his hand out to the man standing next to her.

"I'm Kevin Stayton. Congratulations, Mr. Jackson. Mrs. Jackson. I know you're proud of your daughter," Kevin offered with charm and a polished demeanor.

Silently the man and woman exchanged glances. Then looked at Chloe. She turned to Kevin.

"This is Mr. and Mrs. Fields. Harold and Nettie."

"We're Chloe's foster parents," Nettie Fields clarified with a calm smile.

"Oh," Kevin said, nodding. "Sorry, I..."

"No need to be sorry, son. We couldn't be more happy for this girl if she'd been one of our own. Right, Nettie? And today sure means a lot to Chloe."

There was an awkward silence. The Fields, being simple and honest people, thought nothing of Kevin's understandable mistake. Chloe, on the other hand, felt like she was falling down a rabbit hole, rushing back into a past that was undefined and blurred in her memory. By circumstances, she knew she shouldn't even be there graduating from Hollington. She quietly squared off with Kevin, their gazes meeting and holding. His darkening gaze told her he got it—no further explanation was needed. With an imperceptible nod of his head Kevin lifted a corner of his mouth.

"She's going to go far," he said to the Fields. "I can tell she's going to have a great future. Most likely to succeed."

"Thanks. Nice of you to say so," Chloe murmured.

As the four of them faced each other with nothing more to say, Kevin heard his name being called behind him. They all turned to the female voice and saw a young woman attempting to trot across the grass, unsteady in high heels. Her graduation robe hung open, and they could see her body swaying unsteadily but seductively in a pretty spring dress. The show was all for Kevin.

"That's my cue," Kevin said to them all, backing away toward the woman.

Chloe could not see how he could have mistaken the advancing alluring sight with her. Curve for curve, attribute for attribute, there was no contest. Like her, however, the young woman was tall and thin. Her hair was upswept in the back, while Chloe's was short and only seemed to be longer because of the way it was combed. Chloe could see that their complexions were similar. Medium-brown. Plus from behind, all you could see was their robes.

Kevin had made an honest mistake.

"Seems like a nice young man," Mrs. Fields said quietly. "Is he a good friend?"

Chloe shook her head, watching the couple walk away, their arms around one another. "This is the second time we've ever spoken."

Her foster mother looked incredulous. "In four years?"

"He seemed to have a lot to say when we walked up on you. Sure there's nothin' going on?" Mr. Fields cackled good-naturedly.

"Not a chance," Chloe responded caustically, despite an infuriating flash recall of Kevin kissing her.

"I'm so sorry we're late," Mrs. Fields said sincerely. "Harold got lost."

"Well, tell her how we got started late. Nettie couldn't find her good purse. It ain't all my fault," he groused.

"I'm glad you got here," Chloe said.

Mrs. Fields looked around. "Did we miss everything?"

"Just a lot of talking," Chloe answered kindly, not wanting to blame them or make them feel bad. The truth of the matter was the couple didn't have to come at all. It wasn't part of their agreement.

Mrs. Fields sighed, remorseful.

Chloe realized that she would have to rescue the afternoon and protect the memory of the day. She'd have to take responsibility for it to end on an up note.

"You've never been here before. Would you like to look around?"

"Sure is pretty," Mr. Fields commented as they fell into step together and headed back toward the quad, around which all the buildings were laid out. "Not like where we live, right, Nettie?"

"Well, we can't always help where we're born and raised," Mrs. Fields sighed. "But Chloe got lucky, thank the good Lord."

Chloe smiled warmly at Mrs. Fields. "I also got lucky and had you and Mr. Fields."

Nettie Fields brushed the compliment aside with an airy wave of her hand. "We didn't do much. Why, look at her now. Don't she look grown up, Harold?"

"Sure do."

Mrs. Fields gasped and stopped walking. "Honey, we didn't take you away from anything, did we? You know, maybe meeting friends later. Was that young man about to ask you to join him?"

Chloe shook her head, looking down at her feet and inexpensive pumps.

She wished.

"No, he wasn't. Kevin Stayton and I never hung out together. He's not really a friend."

She hoped that the longing and schoolgirl crush weren't obvious. It was one thing to hold out hope with such a ridiculous thought. It was another for anyone to know and only make fun of her.

Chloe knew exactly the direction Kevin and his girlfriend had walked. Covertly she let her eyes find them, standing in the shadows of a tree near the entrance to the student lounge. They were embracing and kissing, unmindful of anyone else walking by making comments about their open display of affection.

She hardly thought Kevin Stayton was going to remember her, let alone give her a second thought.

Chapter 1

"Hey, girl! It's good to see you."

Chloe was in midstride to shake hands with the gregarious petite young woman who greeted her but was never given the chance. Kyra Dixon ignored her outstretched hand and, instead, reached out her arms. She was expecting a hug that Chloe found herself obliged to give.

"Oh…okay. Hi," Chloe managed awkwardly, as she hugged Kyra back and found herself engulfed in the whiff of floral perfume.

Kyra laughed. "You forgot the Hollington Hello? What's this shaking hands stuff? I want some sugar, girl."

Chloe tried to glance around the other guests having lunch in the faculty dining room and was relieved to see that no one was paying attention to this dramatic greeting. Not at all used to this from someone she hadn't seen in ten years, Chloe nonetheless gave in and followed Kyra's lead. Even as she would have withdrawn after they touched cheek to cheek and air-kissed, Chloe found Kyra's hello more suited to a favorite girlfriend or a beloved relative. They had not really been friends as undergraduates and certainly hadn't moved in the same circles.

With a gentle push Kyra directed Chloe to the empty chair opposite her at the large square table. Chloe settled herself in the comfortable high-back chair and, in the thirty seconds it took Kyra to take her own seat again, she closely observed the other woman.

Kyra was dressed in an eye-catching broad floral-print black-and-red silk blouse, worn with a black skirt. She wore black two-inch heels, probably in the hope that they would add height to her petite frame. She managed to look professional, feminine and cheerful. Her hair was worn straight to chin level and was parted off center so that it curved gently to frame her pretty face. As if on cue Kyra was making her own observations of Chloe.

"Your hair used to be short."

Chloe sat back and spread her napkin over her lap.

"Actually, I wore it mostly cornrowed. It was easier to take care of and cost less than going to the beauty parlor every two weeks. I stopped wearing the cornrows when I got my first job. I wanted to look—"

"More mainstream." Kyra nodded, knowingly. She eyed Chloe thoughtfully. "Is it all yours or a weave?"

"Mine," Chloe said with a small, satisfied smile. "Every strand."

"I know what you're thinking." Kyra sighed, settling back in her chair that seemed to swallow her small frame. She crossed her legs. "We're still putting ourselves through hoops to be taken seriously in business. I can tell you I would not be PR director if I appeared Afrocentric. Hollington has a different message to send out about its students."

"So did I. For myself," Chloe said.

"I hear you. So…when I was told that the Alumni Association had asked you to organize the homecoming this fall, I said Chloe who?" Kyra remarked, chuckling at her own humor. "It took a while before I could recall you. Then I remembered you and I were tortured together in that African dance class with that professor who was eighty if she was a day!"

Kyra broke out in a merry giggle, making it impossible for Chloe to take offense. To her Kyra's observation was proof that she'd done a good job of staying under the radar as an undergraduate. Chloe knew she had good reasons to be cautious, but Kyra didn't need to know what they were.

Anyway, she remembered Kyra from the aforementioned dance class but only because Kyra had been terrible at the ritual movements that called for a looseness of limbs and gyration of hips and butt. Instead, Kyra treated the class lightly, becoming the loveable uncoordinated participant who broke into laughter at her own mistakes and was accused of not having any natural rhythm. Crossing her legs and straightening the hem of her summer linen dress, Chloe also recalled that at first she'd thought Kyra was silly. But she'd come to admire that, rather than take a two-point elective class too seriously, Kyra had set about simply having fun and probably enjoying herself more than anyone. *And* she passed the class.

"It was either that dance class or the history of textiles," Chloe contributed to the memory.

"Right!" Kyra nodded, rolling her eyes. "I figured with the dancing maybe I'd get into my African roots. Forget that!" she said with a dismissive wave of her hand, giggling again.

Having been presented with the single-paged menu for the day, both Chloe and Kyra selected the grilled salmon with julienne carrots and saffron rice.

Chloe's assumption of a straightforward business meeting with Kyra had to be revisited as her former Hollington College classmate proceeded to treat her like a long-lost friend, gossiping about other classmates, school scandals and changes in college policies.

"I was also surprised to hear from you," Chloe said. "I didn't know you'd been hired by Hollington. How long have you been here?"

Kyra sighed as their moment of levity faded away. "Six years. I was just another assistant before they made me PR director. Let me tell you, it feels so strange to be back here and not have to worry about term papers and grades. As an administrator I have a whole 'nother perspective," she said wryly. "Remember how much we held the faculty and staff with suspicion? They were all, 'the other.' Now I'm one of them."

Chloe remembered no such thing—only how grateful she was to have been chosen to attend Hollington on a full scholarship. She hadn't treated any of those four years lightly.

"That's fine. You can see and appreciate both sides."

"That's true, but it's an interesting balancing act. I totally empathize with the students, having survived myself as one here at Hollington. But I also understand the responsibility from the college point of view. And there are other memories." Kyra shrugged.

Chloe watched Kyra, the girlish giggling replaced by an articulate but animated and attractive young woman.

"So, what is it you do, exactly?"

"I advocate for the college. I look for ways, and people, to keep up our reputation and profile as a contender in the higher academic community, especially for African-American students. I work to get us good press and try to find high schools with the caliber of student who'd be a good fit for Hollington."

Their lunch was served, and both women busied themselves with enjoying it. Finally, after more light conversation and as they were finishing, Kyra sat back in her chair. Her expression became thoughtful, her voice quiet.

"Remember Terrence Franklin?"

Chloe considered a moment. "I think so. Hot athlete, right? Very popular. I think he's a pro football player."

"Was," Kyra corrected. "He got cut after his last serious injury. Messed up his knee. The boy is out of the game," she ended flippantly.

"Oh," Chloe said. She wasn't a football fan, herself.

"Anyway, Hollington would like to have him come back to the college. We want to offer Terrence the position of head coach or even athletic director. It's my job to try and sign him up. It's not going to be easy," she said, frowning slightly.

"Why not?"

"Oh…lots of reasons. Money and title and benefits. Let's face it. Being a coach at a college is a huge step down from being watched by zillions of fans on Monday Night Football. Terrence and I…we have a history."

"Oh," Chloe said again. She didn't know anything about that, either.

"Yeah…" She paused. "We were engaged when we were students. So, it could get complicated."

"Maybe not. Who knows? Terrence may be looking for something stable and comfortable now that his pro career is over."

Kyra quickly revived herself and smiled brightly. "Not your problem. And that's not why I wanted to meet with you today. I wanted to talk about the homecoming. You do realize it's also the tenth anniversary of our graduation in 1999?"

"Yes, I know," Chloe said, absently watching their plates being removed. She declined the dessert menu. "That's one of the reasons why I agreed to take it on. You know, I own and manage an event planning business. I've been thinking a lot about October."

"Well, I hope you haven't just been thinking about it. It's already July, and homecoming is on the calendar for the second weekend of October. That's three months."

Chloe smiled confidently. "I'm on it. The weekend schedule is pretty much set. The invitations went out in June."

"I saw it. Fabulous! You used the school colors very well. The invitation looked classy but fun. I like that the Hollington Lion mascot is silhouetted on the front, with a crown tilted at an angle on his head. He looks large and in charge." She laughed and said, "The varsity guys will appreciate that."

"We're already starting to get registration RSVPs. I think it's up to about two hundred."

"Good. Now, what do you have in mind for Friday night?"

"Well, I thought there should be a private cocktail party for the elite alumni who are big contributors to the college. You know…the president can tell them how important and wonderful they are. I've invited the trustees."

"Make sure you have Lucius Gray on the list. He's an alumni and a very successful attorney in Atlanta. Also Beverly Clark. Her mother and a cousin graduated Hollington."

"I'm glad you mentioned Beverly. You know she was homecoming queen in 1998, the fall before we graduated, and I want her to ride in the parade float on Sunday again as homecoming queen. I'm having trouble reaching her. She hasn't returned any of my e-mails or phone calls."

Kyra pursed her lips. "Don't worry about it. I'll talk to Beverly. She and I were best friends in college. We were in the same sorority." Kyra glanced briefly at her. "What sorority were you in?"

Chloe was not about to admit to the embarrassment and rejection she'd experienced when she hadn't been asked to pledge by any of the sororities. With her limited resources, cheap clothes and troubled background, it was probably just as well. The less anyone knew about her the better.

"Oh, I didn't bother," Chloe said, trying to appear a

little indifferent. "I didn't have time. I worked several part-time jobs. I was on scholarship so I had to keep up good grades." She chuckled lightly, to cover that encroaching reminder that she didn't fit in and never really belonged.

"Oh, but you were valedictorian at graduation, right? So it all paid off."

"Yes. It all paid off," Chloe reflected quietly.

Kyra signed for their lunch, and they left the small elegantly appointed room and headed back to her office. It was in one of the newer administration buildings along the south side of the college quad. On their walk back Kyra pointed out to Chloe other changes to the campus. Chloe admitted that since graduating she'd only been back on campus a few times. Kyra talked about the new stadium and science building with state-of-the-art labs and equipment. There was also restoration taking place on one of the original buildings, designed in the style of Stanford White.

As Kyra accepted messages from her assistant and walked into her office, she went back to the subject of the first night of homecoming weekend.

"Okay, so I know about the Friday reception with President Morrow. What about everybody else that night?"

"A meet and greet in the library gallery followed by Night Owl chats. I'm setting up rooms for many of the special interest clubs or groups so people can easily find classmates who had similar interests. Like, one for the sports jocks, one for the humanities. You know, art and creative writing students, music majors. And one for gays and lesbians—"

"Whoa. I don't know about that last one. Just acknowledging them didn't fly with the trustees last year," Kyra warned.

"Well, I'll have to remind them and the president that a very well-known gay journalist who graduated from Hollington with top honors and has a flourishing career gives to the college. He's going to be at the Friday night party. We can't leave him out or make him invisible." Kyra continued to look skeptical and raised her brows. "Don't worry. It'll happen," Chloe said confidently.

"If you say so. Now," Kyra said, getting comfortable in her desk chair, scooting closer to the desk and staring at Chloe with an almost-childlike excitement, "what about the big dance on Saturday after the game? Have you found a place for that yet?"

"I'm considering several—"

"Don't need to. Book Bollito."

Chloe felt an odd little flutter in her chest at the mention of one of the hottest clubs in Atlanta. Housed in what appeared to be an industrial box that was formerly a manufacturing warehouse, the club had opened to rave reviews just a few years earlier.

"I know you've been there. Everybody within a hundred miles of Atlanta has come in for dinner and dancing. It's a huge club space, but you don't get that feeling. There are five full floors and each floor has its own kind of decor and music. The concept is brilliant, but that's Kevin for you. He always comes up with the big ideas. You have to talk with him and get him to agree to use Bollito for the Saturday night dance. It's perfect."

Chloe was glad that Kyra had so much to say about Kevin Stayton's club in downtown Atlanta. It gave her enough time to gather her wits and come up with a response. Of course Bollito was a great choice of venues. She didn't object to that. She was having an adolescentlike moment at the thought of dealing with Kevin. And it wasn't like they'd known each other as students. But their few encounters together had been profound. Simple and as brief as the moments had been, Chloe realized that she had lived with the memories of those moments for ten years.

"Like I was about to say, it's on the list—"

"No, no, no, no…" Kyra said repeatedly, shaking her head and dismissing Chloe's explanations. "That was not a suggestion, Chloe. You *have* to book Bollito. Think about what it's going to be like to have it listed on the program. Think about the press. Bollito is way hot right now. It's impossible to book it for private functions, but Kevin is one of us. A ninety-niner!"

Chloe found herself laughing at Kyra's enthusiasm and logic. The truth of the matter was, Bollito would be perfect. But Bollito was not the problem.

"If it makes you feel better, I'm working on a proposal to send to Kevin."

"You need to *talk* to Kevin. I can't imagine him saying no. He better not." Kyra brightened suddenly. "You know what? I'm going to call him right now and set it up."

Despite Kyra's small size it was clear to Chloe that Hollington had chosen well in making her the director of PR. She had exactly what the job needed. Not taking no for an answer but with charm and good humor.

"Hi. This is Kyra Dixon. I'm PR director for Hollington College."

Chloe stared down at her hands, feigning indifference but listening to every word of the one-way conversation.

"Is Kevin available?…Oh…Will he be back soon?… You're not sure."

Suddenly, Chloe reached over the desk and, to Kyra's obvious surprise, took the phone out of her hand.

"Hi. I'm sorry to interrupt. I'm Chloe Jackson, president of RSVP. I'm an event planner here in Atlanta. Perhaps I should be asking about Mr. Stayton, although I appreciate Ms. Dixon making the call. I understand he's not in, but I'm hoping he'll spare me some time this afternoon. Tell him—" she glanced at Kyra "—tell Kevin that I have a business proposition for him. It's about our homecoming weekend in October. We graduated from Hollington the same year…Yes, yes, that is kind of funny, isn't it?"

Chloe looked at Kyra and found her rolling her eyes. She had to grin.

"I'm hoping that Kevin can see me this afternoon… Yes, I know how busy he is. The man practically supports the economy of Atlanta all by himself. But, this is important, and I know Kevin would want to be in on the discussions. Why don't I come over in say…" She looked at her watch. "About an hour?…No, I won't stay long. This is just a getting-back-in-touch meeting. Yes, I really appreciate your assistance."

Sensing that the call was about to end, Kyra snatched back the phone.

"Now, don't let Kevin yell at you because you messed with his schedule this afternoon." She smiled and laughed into her phone. Winking at Chloe she gave her a thumbs-up.

"This is so kind of you. Ms. Jackson will be over within the hour. Bye."

"Well, that wasn't very businesslike," Chloe mused. "I probably should have asked to stop by tomorrow, give myself more time to prepare."

"Girl, you don't need any more time. You need to get over to Kevin's office, tell him we want to use his club for a party and send him a contract. And tell him if he's going to be difficult he'll have to deal with me!"

Chloe decided that however Kevin Stayton managed his multimillion-dollar enterprise, Stayton Investments, he certainly didn't stand on ceremony. Upon arriving at Kevin's office his assistant, Peg, didn't hesitate to show her directly into his office and leave her on her own. Unasked, Peg had returned five minutes later with a bottle of chilled mineral water, a cut Baccarat crystal glass and a linen cocktail napkin on a glass tray. Chloe's eyebrows had shot up in surprise and appreciation. The offering showed a lot of class.

Kevin's offices turned out to be a full floor with several rooms and a comfortable, if small, reception area. It was above Flavor, the first restaurant he'd opened in Atlanta. It was the business that had put him on the map, built his customer base and garnered regional reviews. Chloe was surprised by how modest, but attractive, professional and efficient the office was. It wasn't at all what she'd expected from someone with Kevin's level of success.

Left alone Chloe remained standing, pacing and

looking around. The office was comfortable with a good modern desk and chair. Against an adjacent wall was a leather love seat, a glass-and-chrome coffee table and two more side chairs to create a more informal area to receive guests. Just above the back of the love seat was a gallery of framed photographs, most taken of Kevin with, Chloe could see, entertainment royalty. She recognized Alicia Keys, Jesse Jackson, Adam Sandler, Scarlett Johansson, Jada Pinkett Smith and Will Smith.

The office was neat and orderly; "a place for everything, and everything in its place" went through her mind. There were contracts, delivery receipts and inventory lists on his desk. There was a window-ledge-high bookcase behind Kevin's chair organized with business magazines. At the base, strangely out of place, was a pair of soft leather loafers. A number of fancy glass and silver awards sat on his desk. With irreverence two were being used as paperweights. That made Chloe grin, and she attempted to relax. But she was ever mindful of the last time she and Kevin Stayton had seen one another. Without conscious thought her fingers touched her lips and she briefly enjoyed a memory that held steadfast and refused to go away.

The door suddenly opened, making Chloe start, and a man stood in the doorway clearly surprised at her presence. It was Kevin Stayton, dressed in running shorts, a sleeveless athletic tank top, a bandanna tied around his forehead and perspiration wet and shiny on his handsome face.

Dressed as he was it was easy to see Kevin was in superb shape. He hadn't let his body go to fat as often happened in post-college years. If anything Kevin was even more handsome than the image that had been stored ten years in her memory bank. She started to speak, but Kevin turned in the doorway and called out.

"Peg? I don't recall a meeting this…"

"You didn't have one planned," Chloe said, having recaptured her poise and confidence. "I'm sorry if I caught you—"

"Undressed?" Kevin said with an unexpected show of humor.

"Unprepared. I understood you were expecting me."

"You're right. I probably forgot. Sorry for showing up hot and sweaty and in need of something cold to drink."

Chloe blinked at him. He sounded more amused than annoyed by her appearance. And she reacted instinctively to his comment. She reached for the bottled water on the tray, opened it and held it out.

Kevin, whose gaze had barely left her face since he entered the room, glanced briefly at the water before accepting it. He took a swig that emptied half the contents. As Chloe watched, fascinated, the water rushed down his throat as was evident by his swallowing muscles. He let out a short satisfied sigh of repletion and ran his forearm along his chin to wipe the sweat away.

"Thanks."

He turned in the open door to speak to someone waiting in the reception area—someone Chloe could not see.

"That's it, CB. I'm cool. I'll catch you later."

Kevin turned back to Chloe, his gaze again openly studying her.

"I'm Chloe Jackson," she announced, holding out her slender hand to him. It was a little disconcerting to have Kevin stare so blatantly at her. Immediately, however, she could tell her name meant nothing to him. He took the hand but rather than shake it, he simply held it.

"Hello, Chloe Jackson."

"Kyra Dixon and I called earlier and spoke to your assistant who arranged for me to stop by. Kyra and I had lunch together. I assumed your assistant would have told you… I can see now this is not a good time."

Kevin let her hand go, indicated a chair she was to sit in and closed his office door.

"I decided to go for a run. Not her fault I'm meeting you like this. Kind of funky." He flapped his elbows up and down and grinned broadly.

"I'm not offended," Chloe said carefully.

Kevin took his seat. He pulled off the sweat-soaked bandanna and tossed it on his desk.

"So what's this about Kyra?"

Briefly, Chloe outlined the lunch meeting with Kyra, the discussion about homecoming and the tentative plans for each day of the weekend. All the time she was talking she wasn't sure if Kevin was actually paying attention, and he continued to stare. But she'd found her balance and decided she wasn't going to feel intimidated, or giddy, just because she was sitting opposite Kevin Stayton, once the object of her daydreams and affections.

"I'm planning a dance party on Saturday night of homecoming. I think it will be a great way to bring the weekend to an end, before everybody heads home on Sunday after service and brunch. So…"

"So Kyra sent you to persuade me to use one of my clubs."

Suddenly Chloe didn't like the slight derision she heard in Kevin's voice, as if the idea was laughable.

"Not exactly," she said clearly. "I'm in charge of the planning and arrangements for the weekend. In case you don't remember it's also the tenth anniversary for the class of ninety-nine."

"I got the invitation," he said and nodded.

"Kyra and I are on the same page about how to celebrate the occasion. I'm the one who will persuade you to let us book one of your clubs. Bollito, to be exact."

Kevin arched a brow and a sardonic smile lifted a corner of his mouth. "You aim high."

"Why not? You don't get what you don't ask for."

"Or demand," Kevin added, a glint in his eyes as he squared off with her.

"I never demand," Chloe said calmly. "I don't have to. I can give you not only sound business reasons why using Bollito for a homecoming party makes sense, but I can tell you why personally you'll even enjoy it."

Kevin sat back in his chair, lifted his sneaker-shod feet onto the edge of the desk and crossed them at the ankles. "I doubt that. The thought of overaged former coeds let loose on my best club doesn't work for me. But, you have my undivided attention. Go."

Chloe arched a brow herself. It was actually something she'd taught herself to do, recognizing that the simple gesture implied everything from surprise, to skepticism, to contempt. At the moment Chloe used it to show Kevin that she was going to beat him at his own game. She knew how to negotiate a deal.

"To begin with, we're expecting seven, maybe eight hundred graduates from our class, plus spouses and dates. Of course homecoming events will be open in general to all Hollington students, but the anniversary celebration on Saturday night is just for our class. I think it's safe to say you were very popular on campus…" Again his eyebrows rose, although his expression remained otherwise impassive. "The party is an amazing opportunity to see folks you haven't seen in ten years. It will be a big reunion.

"As to the business part. Really, Kevin, I think you know them better than I do. First of all I plan on charging an admission to the party. I'll have a way built in to make sure that only those from the class of ninety-nine will attend. Second, your club serves alcohol. You get a bunch of overaged former coeds, as you call them, together who haven't seen each other in years, it's a chance to talk and spend money on liquor."

Chloe had the satisfaction of seeing the interest grow in Kevin's appraising gaze.

"You can throw in a selection of finger foods to serve butler-style. And nothing cheap. Provide the kind of foods we like. Make them delicious and well prepared and easy to manage with a drink in hand and the attendees will be raving long after the weekend. They'll be talking not only about Bollito but what a great job Kevin Stayton did. Third, provide good music. You know we love to dance. Bollito has five dance floors. They'll be put to good use. Give everyone a chance to shake their booty."

He was smiling slightly now. With his elbows on his chair arms and his hands clasped together, he considered her over his knuckles.

"Fourth, we could set a time limit for the party, if

you still want to open it to the public late in the evening. Maybe nine to midnight or eight to eleven. You decide."

She stopped for a moment to let what she'd said sink in. Slowly, Kevin lifted his feet back to the floor. He turned his chair into the desk and leaned across the top to face her.

Chloe was taken with the maturity she now saw in Kevin's face. During their last year at Hollington he'd been tall and thin but toned. He'd been smart and popular but never allowed his social life to take over his grades. He had a future planned, and he stayed on point. But Kevin was also known to be a serial dater, never without a girlfriend or two his entire four years of college. She counted it as astonishing that Kevin had once confused her for one of his girlfriends.

His face was a little bit long with a high forehead and a square chin. It had filled out just a bit, grown more expressive. His phase beard—just a dusting of facial hair—added an inordinate amount of masculine appeal to his brown skin, shadowy…and sexy.

Chloe remembered Kevin as being a fun-loving guy. He laughed easily and had been open, cocky and full of himself but not in an obnoxious way. Everybody liked Kevin Stayton. What was not to like?

But she could also detect that there was more caution now behind the direct gaze. It was assessing. Thoughtful. A kind of "show me" aura. Well, he was a highly successful businessman. Listening to all the facts before making a decision was part of his responsibility.

Kevin considered her for another few seconds before sitting back. He began to gently swivel his chair from side to side.

"Okay, I like the plan. There are a couple of things I want stipulated, but…"

"You'll do it? We can use Bollito?"

He grinned. "I'm sure you didn't come in here expecting me to say no."

"Of course not," she hastened to say. "But I did expect more of an argument."

"I try not to argue about anything. Too exhausting and generally doesn't accomplish much."

She agreed, and nodded silently to show it.

"I'll want a contract, of course."

"Naturally."

"But all in all I'm confident this can work out to everyone's satisfaction."

"And pleasure. I want this to be a fun evening for everyone. Memorable."

"Hearing you talk sounds like it will be. Okay, let's see if we can knock out the contract terms. Let me get Peg—"

"Thank you for seeing me on such short notice, Kevin, but I have to go."

"Just like that? This shouldn't take long. I'm willing to bet you've considered everything," Kevin told her with a smile.

She smiled graciously. "I have other appointments."

He pursed his lips and stood as well. "Busy lady. So when do I see you again?"

"At your convenience."

"Dinner tonight."

Chloe's gaze targeted him abruptly. "What?"

"Dinner," Kevin repeated, ignoring the surprised expression on her face. "At Bollito, if you like. I'll show you around. You can see what you're getting."

"No. But thank you," Chloe finally managed. "I do want to see the club but maybe another time. With dinner, if you insist."

"It's part of sealing the deal. How about breakfast tomorrow morning? Or lunch. Or dinner. That's twenty-four hours. At some point you'll have to stop and eat."

Chloe moistened her lips and gave Kevin her best "let's keep this business" look. He shrugged as if to say that he couldn't be blamed for trying.

He gave in with a slight shrug. Bending over a desk calendar he ran his finger down a list of time slots for the next day. "I can see you at nine-thirty or eleven tomorrow morning."

"Eleven. My office," Chloe decided. She reached into her bag and took out a small silver case. Extracting a business card she handed it to Kevin.

Kevin was staring at her, hard and skeptical. "How did you get into the event planning business?"

Chloe smiled, not offended by his need to know. "I started out taking over the details of parties in my dorm. It spread beyond that to helping people I worked with. After graduation I spent almost five years in New York working for the wedding planner at the Plaza. What began as an internship turned into a career. I'm good at it," she added. He arched a brow.

"Chloe Jackson," Kevin murmured, almost to himself as he stood beside her at his office door. "The name does sound familiar. Class of 1999?"

"Yes."

He narrowed his gaze on her. "Did we know each other?"

Chloe gave him what she hoped was a mysterious smile, one that didn't give away any of what she was feeling or remembering.

"In a way," she said, walking past him and out of the office.

Chapter 2

After Chloe left, Kevin leaned out his office door to speak with Peg. "Call Kyra Dixon at Hollington for me."

He didn't wait for his assistant's response but returned to his office. He walked behind his desk and peered out the window, scanning up and down the street. He caught sight of Chloe as she crossed the street to a parking lot and handed over her ticket to the attendant. While she waited for her car, Kevin took his time studying her from a distance.

She was tall and slender and stylish but in an understated way. As if she didn't want to be noticed too much, or distract from the business at hand. She had a softly curved body. No part of her rolled, or bounced, or jiggled or swished. She walked with grace, and everything about her said "lady."

It wasn't a term he used often for women he knew,

Kevin considered dryly, which was too bad. Because he always remembered his Nana Mame telling him to honor his own self-worth, not to settle for less than he wanted or less than he deserved. Kevin always knew his grandmother's sage advice to him had been in part to remind him that he could be much more than his own father. A self-absorbed man whose ego and libido made him irresponsible, selfish and a ne'er-do-well. He'd deserted his wife, two daughters and baby son when Kevin was barely three years old. He hadn't seen the man more than a dozen times since.

There was a part of him that always wondered, every time his attention was drawn to any woman, what would Nana Mame think of her? But his beloved grandmother had passed away in April, leaving Kevin with an even stronger determination that he would not disappoint her. He would not let her or his mother's expectations of him go unjustified.

He took a deep breath as his thoughts shifted back to the lovely lady waiting for her car. Chloe also didn't fall under the glamorous, hot, booty call or babe headings. As a matter of fact, he would say that her feminine mannerisms seemed cultivated and displayed almost like a defense.

Her shoulder-length hair was combed slightly off center and fell in soft, very loose curls. She wore no makeup that he could tell but he decided that, except for maybe lip gloss or blush, Chloe Jackson didn't need any. That made her look younger than he knew her to be. And no other women he knew would chance wearing light-colored linen at the height of a Georgia summer when the humidity promoted wrinkles, distortion and stains. Chloe was absolutely eye-catching in her dress, managing to look fresh, pulled together and in charge. If she intended her simple attire not to draw attention to herself, she failed.

She suddenly pulled out a pair of oversize sunglasses that only added to her allure. Why was she hiding? She waited patiently for her car to be brought to her, taking a quick moment to consult her PDA before dropping it back into her purse. When the car pulled up next to her, she smiled demurely at the attendant, passed him a tip and sat behind the steering wheel, swinging her long shapely legs in. The action caused her dress to hike up her thighs, and she took the time to pull it straight before closing her car door. Then she was driving out of the lot, and away.

"Chloe Jackson," Kevin murmured again under his breath, as if saying her name out loud might conjure up some memory. If she graduated in his class he was sure the details would come to him sooner or later.

One thing he knew for certain. She was not a former girlfriend. No way would he have forgotten her. He was already wondering how he ever could have missed her on campus.

The phone rang on his desk, and he picked it up on the first ring.

"Kyra, hey. It's Kevin Stayton. Yeah, it's been a long time. Pretty good, and yourself? Good. Before I forget, congratulations on your appointment at Hollington. Yeah, I want to hear all about it sometime. Chloe Jackson was here. Just left." He chuckled. "No, I can't say that I remember her but, yeah, she got what she wanted. I didn't put up much of a fight. Her plan was good. We're getting together tomorrow to work out the details of the contract. Listen, I have a favor to ask." He sat down in his chair again. "Tell me everything you know about Chloe. Who did she run with in school?"

Kevin sat back to listen, draining the rest of the mineral water Chloe had given him.

Chloe read the initialed clauses again and, finding no fault with the language, added hers next to the KS for Kevin Stayton. She signed and dated the contract at the bottom and gathered all the copies.

"That was easy," Kevin said, sitting casually opposite Chloe at the table in her small meeting room.

"Yes, it did go well," she sighed, finally offering a smile that indicated her satisfaction. Still she glanced at him with a bit of lingering hesitation. "Are you sure you're okay with the club being used until 2:00 a.m.?"

"Hey. It was you who convinced me that the folks would want to party hearty till all hours. I really do want everyone to have a good time. These are *our* classmates," Kevin added dramatically.

Chloe chuckled quietly. "Thanks. I'll take the agreement over to the college later and have everything signed in the finance department. I should be able to get you your set tomorrow. Is that okay?"

Kevin pursed his lips and shrugged. "No rush. I understand you need to move forward with other arrangements, so don't wait until I have my copy in hand. I trust you to honor what we've agreed to."

Chloe glanced at him. "That's big of you."

"No, just smart. Neither of us wants to get bogged

down in technicalities at this point. If I need to pull off the kid gloves later, I will."

Chloe put the contracts inside a Lucite binder and stood up. "That wasn't a threat, was it?" she asked with an expression of feigned shock.

Kevin stood as well. "No, ma'am. But business is business. Even with old college classmates."

Chloe nodded. "Fair enough. I don't plan on disappointing you."

Kevin, whose expression had been one of mild amusement throughout their discussion, an indication that he was enjoying sparring with her, now studied her silently for a moment in calm appraisal.

"No. I don't believe you will."

Chloe realized that with their business taken care of, the discussion, their meeting, was over. She neatly organized her papers, trying to avoid looking directly at him as he silently studied her. But from the moment he'd arrived at her office he'd managed to disrupt the routine, the flow of efficiency, the very air, with his presence and friendly demeanor. He'd always been good at being the center of attention. She realized she was no less susceptible to his charm. And if she'd never lost her head when she was a young, naive coed, it certainly wasn't going to happen now.

It began with the dropped-open-jaw staring of Lynette, the receptionist, when Kevin breezed through the double glass doors of RSVP two hours ago. Chloe had detected the stir when she'd glanced out her office at the excitement he was creating. Then her assistant, Franco, could not contain himself from rhapsodizing over one of Kevin's cafés, a small unpretentious place called What It Is. Kevin, to his credit, had accepted the greetings with brief smiling patience, but had cut it short by announcing he was there to see her.

Chloe had to admit she'd liked that.

He was dressed comfortably in a pair of stylish Dolce & Gabbana taupe-colored slacks, worn with a black short-sleeved shirt that made him look cool and composed. And, she noticed that he was wearing those same soft leather loafers that had been discarded by his desk the day before when he'd gone out running. He still sported that unshaved, but intriguingly handsome, face from the day before as well, clearly a personal style.

"So," Kevin said now, rubbing his hands together as he regarded her. "Are we cool?"

"I think so," Chloe said and nodded. "I'm really grateful that you've agreed to this, Kevin."

"Well, you can show your gratitude by having lunch with me."

"Lunch?" Chloe asked blankly. The very idea created a flutter in her stomach. "Well… I… No, I don't think so. I have work to do."

He tilted his head and did not give the appearance of a man who'd been turned down. "You do eat, don't you? I can see not much, but still…"

Chloe sighed, trying not to smile or be persuaded by his potent charm. "Yes, but not with clients."

"Aah, but you see, I'm not a client. I'm a former classmate. We studied together. Rooted for the Hollington Lions together. I'm sure we even broke bread together," he ended on a hopeful note.

She grinned at him. "Not."

He laughed.

Chloe was about to present another excuse when Kevin suddenly turned to the door, opened it and looked out. "Good, you're here."

"What's going on?" Chloe asked, suspicious.

"I had a feeling you were going to say no, so I've brought lunch to you. Now, you're not going to make a fool out of me and kick me out, or sit and watch me eat alone, are you?"

"Kevin, I really think—"

"Chloe, don't think. This is only lunch, not another contract negotiation. Now, would you like to eat here, or shall we go sit in the courtyard atrium?"

Chloe looked at him, trying to discern his game plan, trying to stop second-guessing herself. Trying to control a sudden inordinate, if cautious, pleasure that he was being so charmingly persistent. So far Kevin had given her no reason to hold him suspect, and perhaps it would be unfair to use the tabloid gossip and paparazzi exposure against him as well. Chloe had to admit, the idea of an informal surprise picnic lunch had won her over.

"Where do you want this?"

Chloe's gaze shifted from Kevin's questioning expression to a tall broad Black man with a shaved head who now appeared over his shoulder.

"CB." Kevin inclined his head to indicate the man. "Ms. Chloe Jackson."

"Ms. Jackson," CB acknowledged formally with a slight bow.

He carried a heavy canvassed tote bag with rawhide fittings and handles that was neatly packed, the top opening covered with a cloth napkin.

Kevin wasn't giving in. He silently raised his brows and continued to wait for her answer.

"The atrium," Chloe said finally.

Kevin smiled, not triumphantly but with real pleasure.

Chloe had never considered sitting in the atrium of her downtown Atlanta office building before, let alone having lunch at one of the two-dozen bistro tables that dotted the flagstone deck. Even in the height of summer the area was cool and pleasant, placed among a man-made forest of trees that also provided shade. In the three years since she'd started her event and party planning business, RSVP, her time, attention and money had all gone into promoting and marketing her business, hiring talented and reliable staff. Cultivating new customers and making the right kinds of contacts. She wasn't about to admit to Kevin that she usually combined lunch with business meetings. It saved time, the relaxed setting more conducive to people signing a contract with her. But that was hardly the case now with Kevin. Chloe was avoiding accepting the fact that she was enjoying herself.

They had just begun eating when Kevin's cell phone chimed with a popular musical ring tone. He answered and was several sentences into his conversation when he happened to look at her. He correctly read her aloof expression.

"Listen, I'd love to catch up, but I can't talk with you right now… I'm having lunch with a friend." He suddenly chuckled. "No, you don't know who it is and I'm not talking. Later." He hung up but made no further reference to the call. He set his cell on silent after that.

She occasionally glanced around the atrium, and there were couples and groups of workers, shoppers and people just enjoying a lovely place to sit and relax. It was surprisingly quiet and each table was afforded reasonable privacy for conversation. Chloe knew that she would use the space more often in the future, even if she ate alone.

At one point she spotted a woman who was clearly out of place in the setting. Of average height, she was thin, poorly dressed in jeans and layered in sweaters. They were far too heavy for the summer heat and too oversize for her frame, as if the clothes were hand-me-downs. The woman was standing near one of the porticos of the atrium, pacing. She wasn't bothering anyone, although she did draw curious glances with her odd appearance. Chloe herself would have given her only a passing glance, but the woman at times seemed to be staring at her.

Kevin finished his glass of iced tea, deliberately slurping the remains through the ice at the bottom. The sounds distracted Chloe back to her lunch companion. She shook her head but smiled at Kevin's obvious attempts to get her attention.

He put his glass down and wiped his hands with one of the cloth napkins that were packed with their lunch. The delicious meal consisted of chicken salad, warm sliced sourdough bread, a container of chilled watermelon chunks and the tea, all made at Kevin's restaurant, Flavor.

"Thank you for providing such a wonderful lunch. It was thoughtful, and everything was perfect."

"I'm glad you liked it," he said graciously. "Am I forgiven for tricking you into joining me?"

Chloe stirred her straw in her drink. "I have a feeling you wouldn't have taken no for an answer. I hope I didn't seem so disagreeable about it," she murmured.

"Not at all. I understand that you like to keep the demarcation line clear between business and friendship. But it's not like we're strangers, right? This is our tenth anniversary."

Chloe couldn't help but laugh at his unique twist on the circumstances of their relationship.

Simultaneously they began to wrap up the remains of lunch and repack the tote bag, working smoothly together. Lunchtime was over, and the atrium was now more than half-empty. Even the curious woman had gone.

"So, who else are you recruiting to help with the October weekend, besides me and Kyra?" Kevin asked.

"Well, I'd love to have Beverly Clark ride in Sunday's parade as the homecoming queen again, but she seems reluctant."

"I know Beverly. She's a lovely lady. But the last few years have been kind of rough on her."

"Yes, so Kyra hinted. Anyway, Kyra said that she and Beverly were best friends, so maybe she can persuade Beverly to change her mind."

"Do you remember Micah Ross?"

"Oh, yes. Micah and I were friendly in school. I was always running to him with my computer problems.

And I got to hear some of his romantic woes. Poor Micah. He was so shy."

Suddenly, CB appeared again and silently removed the tote bag that held their lunch.

"Anything else?" he asked Kevin politely.

"I'll just be a few more minutes," Kevin said.

CB nodded but smiled silently to Chloe before walking away carrying the bag. Chloe's curiosity got the better of her.

"Is CB your…driver?" she guessed.

Kevin grinned but shook his head. Chloe was also aware of a light frown that momentarily passed between his brows.

"No, not my driver. CB is…I guess you can say he's my assistant. We started out together in my first business. He showed up one day looking for work, and he was willing to do anything and help anywhere. His biggest talent is that he's reliable, honest and discreet. He's helped me out of some, shall we say, difficult situations."

"I bet," Chloe said dryly.

"I know what you're thinking," Kevin said smoothly. "But you'd be surprised at the kind of troubles that seem to find you when you have a business and you've gained some success. It's not always pretty or fun."

"Well, what kind of trouble?" she persisted.

Kevin hesitated. "The kind where tempers flare, voices are raised and sometimes people get arrested."

"You're serious?"

He lifted a corner of his mouth in a caustic smile. "Very. You know, as hard as it is to believe, there are some folks who just don't like me."

Chloe grinned. "I can't imagine why not. Is CB some sort of bodyguard?" Chloe asked.

"Sometimes he's that, too."

Kevin was suddenly so serious that Chloe felt regret at assuming that he had somehow brought it all on himself.

"I'm sorry."

"Don't worry about it," he said quietly.

He turned to begin walking, very slowly, back to the entrance of the building. Chloe fell into step next to him. She felt somewhat awkward being next to Kevin, because it felt almost like they could be a couple. Chloe glanced up at Kevin's profile, and her breath caught in her throat. They seemed to share a natural stride and pacing in their walk. Even more of a surprise, against all reason and common sense, she felt…safe.

"You were asking about Micah Ross. How come?" she said, to get past the sudden silence between them.

"We've been in touch over the years. He's a good guy. Did you know he's a hotshot record producer in L.A.? Has his own label."

"I do know that. Although we were friends at Hollington I lost touch with him in the last several years."

"I think we should get in touch with him. He represents some of the hottest talent on the charts today. Maybe we can get him to loan us a singer or a group."

"You mean for homecoming?"

"That's right. I thought we could have someone appear at Saturday's party. What do you think?"

Chloe's eyes brightened. "Kevin, that's such a great idea."

"That's all I need to hear. I'll get in touch—"

There was a sudden flash of light. And then another. Chloe blinked and glanced around, momentarily confused. But Kevin reacted more instinctively, immediately finding the source and identifying it. Chloe quickly realized they had just been photographed.

Her first thought was one of confusion. Why would anyone be taking a photograph of her?

Kevin firmly grabbed her arm and pulled her out of the line of vision of the photographer, placing himself between them. He then put his free hand up in front of the lens.

"Hey! Back off. What do you think you're doing?" he asked, his voice annoyed and hard.

"Come on, man. I've been trying to get a decent shot since last Friday night at the club. Don't play hard to get on me now," the young man said with a broad smile, even as he took several steps back from the tone of Kevin's voice and still shot two more frames.

"I'm not at the club," Kevin announced clearly. "This is private time. I don't appreciate that you've been following me. And you don't have the young lady's permission to take her picture."

The young man seemed unfazed. "This is a public place. You're both fair game. New arm candy? Never seen her before."

Chloe, more rattled than she realized by the intrusion, let Kevin handle the situation. She had no idea how she would. Kevin made sure that the photographer never got another chance to take a clear picture of her. But Chloe knew that people were staring, stopping to watch the encounter. There was no place for her to hide, except behind Kevin who still had hold of her arm. Almost as if he knew she would leave if he didn't.

Then, she saw a now familiar figure returning to the scene. With a slow confident walk, CB approached, assessing the situation. The photographer, having gotten what he came for, turned to leave, only to find himself nearly colliding with Kevin's assistant. Another quiet discussion ensued.

"Let's go," Kevin said.

With a protective arm around her waist he purposefully steered her away from the atrium where people were once again going about their business.

"What's CB going to do? What's going to happen?"

Kevin looked at her with an amused grin. "Don't worry. CB is not going to touch him. I can trust him to handle the situation calmly."

"But…"

"Chloe, I'm sorry," Kevin said once they were inside the building near the bank of elevators.

His apology got her attention, and Chloe stood looking closely at him. She felt some of her tension drain. He looked sincere and contrite. And, in a strange way, Kevin seemed almost helpless, as if what had happened *was* entirely his fault, and not at all what he wanted to have happen.

"Why was he taking our picture?"

Kevin faced her and put his hands in his trouser pockets. "You don't read the local gossip rags, do you? Or the Atlanta magazines? I'm kind of a regular in their pages. For whatever reason everything Kevin Stayton has become fair game. I'm at one of the clubs, I get photographed with friends and it ends up in print. I show up at an opening, or a sporting event, the photographers are there. It's annoying, but it also brings in business."

"You mean, our picture is going to be used?"

He frowned. "You sound unhappy about it."

Chloe glanced down at her summer sandals and moistened her lips. She shook her head. "I'll be honest. It makes me uncomfortable."

"Why?" he asked, mystified.

"Because people will presume that they know something about me that they don't."

He was silent for a long moment, and when Chloe looked up again she found Kevin studying her with frowning consideration.

"Maybe I'm going overboard, but..."

He reached out and gently stroked her bare arm with his fingers. A curious warmth and reassurance spread throughout her.

"Look, let me see what I can do. I know some people. Maybe I can get the picture killed."

Chloe silently nodded.

"It'll be okay, I promise." He glanced briefly over his shoulder at CB. The photographer was gone, and CB stood waiting for him. "I have to go, and you'll want to get back to work."

When he looked at her now Chloe thought his gaze was warm, his expression relaxed after their encounter of a moment ago.

"This was fun, Chloe Jackson. Thank you for joining me. Let's do it again sometime."

Then, before Chloe realized what he was up to, and obviously intending that she not have time to think about it, Kevin took hold of both her arms, leaned for-

ward and brushed his lips against her cheek. He stepped
back, raising his hand in farewell as he turned away.

Chloe watched him for several seconds before she
called out.

"Kevin?"

He turned back to regard her.

"Thanks. I enjoyed it, too."

"'Scuse me for bothering you, but Tiffany Warren
just arrived. She's looking for you."

Kevin glanced up from the pages of a book spread
open in front of him. His brows furrowed slightly.

"Is she alone?"

"She arrived with two other women."

"Did you tell her I'm busy at the moment?"

"Yes, Frank told me. Since when don't you have time
for me, Kevin? I'm very hurt that you'd put me off."

Kevin quickly stood and nodded his maître d' away.
In the same motion he closed the book he'd been pe-
rusing. He smoothly turned his attention to the beautiful young woman waiting and gave her one of his most
charming, most warm smiles.

"Hey, Tiff. It's been a while." Kevin embraced her
warmly, but lightly, ending it quickly as he touched his
cheek to hers.

Tiffany Warren looked only amused that her efforts
to have him kiss her had been cleverly thwarted. Still,
Kevin did let his gaze openly take in and appreciate the
perfect heart-shaped face with its flawless complexion
and expertly applied makeup. Her hair was a lush fall of
looping curls but, although coiffed to appear easy and
carefree, Kevin knew from firsthand close-up and per-

sonal experience that the hair was expensive and not all hers. He certainly didn't hold that against Tiffany. He knew well that she had other attributes to recommend her to any able-bodied man.

"Since you weren't going to call me, I came to the mountain," she said in a soft feminine purr.

"You look fabulous, as always," Kevin remarked, completely ignoring her comment. "Frank was doing what he's suppose to be doing. I pay the man a lot of money to run interference. Sit down."

Tiffany cast a sloe-eyed look at Kevin as she gracefully slid her curvaceous five-foot-five frame into the banquette. Her emerald green, spaghetti-strap dress was tasteful and perfect for a night out in Atlanta. Kevin took the seat opposite and swiftly noted that everything that had first drawn him to Tiffany was still evident: the exquisite taste in clothing, the feminine mannerisms, seductive glances and soft pouting of her well-shaped mouth. And she had a body that, behind closed doors, had demonstrated a creative, willing and passionate proficiency at sex.

"Why don't you have your friends join us?" Kevin asked, already knowing the answer.

"No. I want you all to myself," she said.

"I'm sorry I can only give you a few minutes. Had I known you were coming..."

"You probably wouldn't have been here when I arrived," Tiffany said, cushioning her observation with a sweet smile.

Kevin signaled one of his waiters and ordered Tiffany a champagne cocktail and a round of drinks for her friends. He was waiting for the hormone kick-in that he was still receptive to her charms. Nothing happened.

"I've moved on," Kevin said with a slight shrug. "What brings you here?"

"Girl's night out. This is still one of the best restaurants in the city. My girlfriends had never been before. I told them I know the owner."

"You're always welcome. I'll let the chef know what you like," he offered politely.

She nodded, watching his face. "So you're still angry with me, right?"

Kevin stayed calm, carefully studying her. "Let's just say I'm disappointed by what happened."

"But nothing happened."

"Not for lack of trying on your part. I thought I was clear that I didn't want any kids yet. When it happens, I want to be in on it and not have my fatherhood orchestrated. I don't like surprises. When you told me you might be pregnant…"

She nervously brushed a lock of hair behind her ear. "You know I wouldn't trap you. I'd never do anything like that," Tiffany defended herself, indignant.

"'It was an accident' wouldn't have worked for me," he said quietly.

She sniffed, taking a dainty sip of her drink when it was set before her. "Then you're probably thrilled that it was a false alarm."

"For your sake as well as mine," Kevin said meaningfully.

She sighed. "Did I ruin everything between us?"

Kevin made a vague gesture with his hand. "That little episode didn't help. Maybe we would have run out of steam anyway." He looked at her, his gaze momentarily heated with memories. "Hooking up with you was awesome, Tiff. But I'm not sure how much of a relationship we really had beyond going to bed together."

Even though there was a hint of a blush under her high-yellow skin, Tiffany smiled slowly at him. It was the kind of smile Kevin recalled used to make him want to drag her off somewhere alone.

"Well, at least it was a start."

Kevin laughed lightly. He reached across the table and took her hand, kissing the back of it. "Yeah, it was a good one. It just didn't have any place to go."

Finally, Tiffany noticed the album-like book, in white cloth binding with navy blue lettering. She began absently leafing through the pages.

"What are you reading? Hollington Class of 1999. It's a yearbook?"

Kevin smoothly took the book and slid it out of her reach to a corner of the table. "That's right."

Her sophisticated poise slipped for a moment as she made a moue of her lips and arched a brow. "I was a sophomore in high school."

If Kevin ever needed proof of the wisdom of breaking it off with her, she'd just provided it. If he wanted to salvage things between him and Tiffany, he knew he could do it right now with the right words. He left well enough alone.

"I'm sort of involved with plans for homecoming weekend in October."

"Ugh. I have to tell you it sounds boring. I can't think of a single person I graduated with I'd want to see again."

"That's too bad," Kevin said with sympathy.

Thanks to a call from Kyra Dixon he could think of several.

Chapter 3

For the fourth or fifth time Chloe pulled the now much-thumbed-through copy of *Luster* magazine from her tote bag. It had already been opened and folded back to an article that she'd hoped would not appear. Now, she found herself staring at the color image that dominated the page. It was a photo taken of her and Kevin Stayton the day they'd had lunch together two weeks earlier. The caption read "Who's That Girl?" while the brief one-hundred-word article talked about the latest Kevin sighting and the most recent happenings at his club. Only at the very bottom of the piece was she identified as Chloe Jackson, owner and director of RSVP, "…the new, much sought after, event planning operation in Atlanta."

Her initial reaction was one of confusion. On the one hand the article implied a more than passing acquaintance between her and Kevin that seemed very premature. On the other hand, Chloe was thrilled at the prominent mention of her company. She knew immediately the marketing value, even as she wished it had been separated from Kevin's own high-profile businesses. But…beggars can't be choosers. Publicity was publicity. Not twenty-four hours after the issue of *Luster* had hit the newsstands, she was getting calls into the RSVP office requesting her services.

The day before, when her assistant, Franco, had brought in his copy and thrust it under her nose to read Chloe had, at first, been shocked at seeing her face in the middle of the page. But after she'd gotten over the first rush of surprise, she'd read the piece and looked more carefully at the photo. She fully noticed the fact that she was smiling, and she looked relaxed… and happy. The second thing was that Kevin was looking directly at her, not posing for the camera and not even aware of it just then. It was harder to interpret his expression, but Chloe didn't think it out of line to say he appeared happy as well.

She grinned. Not bad. Not bad at all!

Letting her gaze travel back and forth between them, Chloe allowed herself a momentary flight of fancy; they could be an actual couple, except for the reality check of her past that warned her she was probably not Kevin's type.

But each time she pulled out the article, like now, she had the same reaction…the photograph was a lovely one. Of course she'd heard from Kyra with her teasing innuendos about her and Kevin together. She'd gotten a call from Terrence Franklin. As it turned out there was a two-page spread about his visit to Atlanta as well. She knew that he was being courted for a position at Hollington.

Chloe could still feel the humiliation course through her over the memory of the one time she'd worked up the nerve to talk to a high-profile classmate. She'd seen Terrence after a college game one Saturday and, crossing paths with him as he'd headed to the lockers, congratulated him on a resounding win against the visiting team. He'd completely ignored her as he strode by, a dirty and sweaty giant with his helmet under his arm.

And now, out of the blue, and ten years later, he was calling to comment on a magazine photograph.

"I owe you an apology."

Chloe, startled, looked up to find Kevin smiling down at her, apologetic. His brown features were shadowed by the tree under which she was sitting, but his white teeth were a brilliant flash in his face. Given the sway of her thoughts recently, Chloe felt pretty guilty herself as she only stared at him. He was dressed in a pair of clean, pressed jeans, the leather loafers and a pale yellow oxford shirt with the sleeves rolled up. Her gaze came back to his face.

"What? Why?"

Kevin pointed to the magazine in her hand. Then he sat next to her on the low retaining wall outside the main administrative building on the quad. It was Friday afternoon, and the campus was nearly deserted. He took the magazine out of her hand and stared at it himself for a long moment.

"I tried to stop it from getting printed. I offered the photographer fair money for it."

"You did?" she asked in disbelief.

"I knew you weren't happy about having your picture taken, so I..."

"That was nice of you."

"Know what? It's a great picture, Chloe. I like it."

Hearing Kevin's admission allowed Chloe to agree as well. It *was* a great picture of the two of them together, and she was not about to let him know that. So she stared at him, feeling uncertain and confused under his open gaze.

"The couple of the hour! Everyone is talking about that picture. You two sure know how to create buzz."

Chloe and Kevin stood up to face Kyra as she exited the building and approached. She waved cheerfully.

"It wasn't planned," Kevin said with a wry grin for Chloe.

"Whatever. You do look great together. Is something going on I should know about?" Kyra winked broadly at her.

Chloe opened her mouth to deny Kyra's question but never got the chance. Even Kevin didn't have time to respond, one way or the other.

Kyra turned to him, and they embraced and kissed each other on the cheek as Chloe watched. Then Kyra took the magazine and shook her head at the image.

"Girl, you can't pay for this kind of PR. You know what you need to do now? Call the magazine, and see if they'll do a story about the homecoming weekend. You know Tamara Hodges, don't you? She's one of us, and she writes for the magazine. Play up the fact that Kevin's a big contributor. I hope you don't mind," Kyra said quickly in an aside to Kevin before rushing on. "See if you can work in that Beverly Turner will be back as homecoming queen…"

"Shouldn't you be doing that?" Kevin asked Kyra.

"No, she's right," Chloe said quickly. "I'm in charge of homecoming. Actually, I've already made contact with *Luster*."

Kyra looked pleased. Kevin looked impressed.

"I did remember that Tamara wanted to be a journalist," Chloe said. "Now she's a writer at *Luster*. She called me right after the latest issue came out."

"Did you know her in school?" Kyra asked.

Chloe hesitated. She looked at Kevin, but he was also waiting for her answer. She didn't know Tamara all that well in school, but she'd certainly heard a lot about Tamara from Micah Ross. Chloe had the feeling that Kevin had also been privy to a lot more than he would say at the moment.

"English class," Chloe admitted, which was the truth. "I also worked with her junior year on the school paper."

"What did she say when she called you?" Kevin asked.

Chloe shrugged. Her mind was busy censoring some of that conversation. To say she'd been surprised to hear from Tamara would have been an understatement. Micah had been the common ground between them, not English or creative writing, although she doubted that even Tamara knew that.

Now, Chloe suddenly realized that Kevin, silently, was sending a signal to her, and she totally understood his message. *Whatever* they both knew was not for general knowledge. Chloe smiled at Kyra.

"Oh, just chatty stuff. She told me that I look great. She said she didn't realize that Kevin and I…"

Chloe stopped. To repeat what Tamara had surmised about the picture of her and Kevin would be to submit to gossip and hearsay. The most popular man on campus and the coed most likely to succeed hooking up? She wasn't going to go there, because it wasn't true.

"…Ah…knew each other. She was surprised to hear about my company, RSVP, and said she might call on me with business in the future. And then she suggested doing an article for the September issue about homecoming."

Kyra squealed.

"OHMYGOD! Chloe, that's fabulous! Girl, you get a big hug for that."

Kyra wasted no time in grabbing Chloe and enfolding her in a tight embrace that forced Chloe to bend down to accommodate their height difference.

"Can I get one, too?" Kevin asked with a teasing smile.

"Oh, come on. You don't…" Chloe began, but then found herself encircled by his arms as well.

Of course there was a difference.

Instantly she had another recall from the past. Instantly she felt a warmth surge through her, and she inhaled the fresh masculine essence that was Kevin. She felt the sinewy strength in his arms and the spread of his large hands on her back and waist. She felt the flatness of his abdomen and his hips. In just that brief moment. Not given a choice, Chloe returned the embrace as impersonally as she could. But she wasn't indifferent.

Could he sense that?

"Good girl," Kevin whispered in her ear.

Chloe knew at once there was a double meaning, and she got them both.

The warmth was replaced by a titillating tension as he covertly but lightly kissed her cheek. Then he stood back, releasing her.

"Kevin! Hiiiii."

The three of them turned at the loud shout-out to Kevin. Walking toward them was a young attractive woman, her very short hair dyed blond. Tight black jeans hugged her long legs and rounded butt, and a baby-doll-type top showed off cleavage and a lithe, playfully sexy body.

Kevin excused himself and walked to meet the woman halfway. She dramatically threw up her arms in the air and boldly pressed her hips and chest against Kevin as she greeted him, slowly wrapping her arms around his neck.

Chloe caught Kyra's reaction, a silent expression that basically said, "Oh, please." But Chloe realized that she was hardly amused by the little reunion, and she covered her response as she fumbled with her summer shoulder bag. She knew instinctively that theirs had not been a casual relationship.

Kyra watched the encounter for a few more seconds and shrugged. "A fling thing. At least a one-night stand," she whispered dismissively.

"Why are you telling me this?"

"Look, I don't want you to get the wrong impression about him. Kevin is eligible and popular. He likes women, but he does have standards. She is *not* what he'd take home to meet his mama."

Chloe glanced up in time to realize that Kevin was, from a distance, introducing her and Kyra to the blonde.

"Hiiiii," the woman sang out again, waving.

Kyra and Chloe waved back, and then Kevin was saying goodbye and lightly jogging back to them.

"Sorry 'bout that."

"Who was that?" Kyra asked with mock teasing.

"A moment out of my past. Right where it belongs," he admitted with a guiltless chuckle. "Where were we?"

"Catching up on reunion business," Kyra said. "And that reminds me, how did it go with Terrence?"

"I'm going to meet with him now. He's flying back to New York later. I told him he'd be a fool not to look at the offer seriously, but I get the feeling he's playing hardball. Like, he wants someone begging him. Know what I mean?"

Chloe noticed that Kyra didn't look directly at her or Kevin as she silently nodded. If anything she looked taken aback.

"Is it money?" Chloe asked, not sure of Kevin's meaning.

"No, I'm almost sure it's not about the money. I think there's another stumbling block," Kyra said, and then forced a cheerful smile to her face. "What about you, Chloe? Did we have a meeting planned I forgot about?"

"No, we're good. I just met with a committee from the alumni office to go over the thousand and one little details that we have to get done for October. I'm told it always gets crowded, but I want to make sure that our tenth anniversary is headlined. So I asked for a special tent just for the class of 1999 on the Square, or in front of the band shell stage. Things like that. Right now I'm on my way over to check out President Morrow's house. He's invited us to make use of it in October."

"Then you don't need me, and I'm late for my own meeting."

Chloe squinted at the sky. "I think it's going to rain, so I better hurry."

"I'll talk to both of you later?" Kyra asked. But typically she didn't wait for a response, hurrying away with her confident bouncy stride.

Chloe faced Kevin, once again alone with him.

"Well...I know you have to rush off, too. Good luck with Terrence. I'll talk with you..."

"When you're finished. Wait for me."

"Wait for you? Why?"

"Because I thought we could hang out a little, long as we're here." Kevin chuckled silently. "You sure don't make it easy. Are you always this tough on the men in your life?"

What men in her life?

Chloe stared at him. Was she being hard on him? Did he just say he wanted to see her again?

"Look, it's not going to take you long to look at President Morrow's house. I've been there. And I doubt that I'll need more than thirty minutes to convince Terry to snap out of it and get serious about working at Hollington. Meet me back here. Unless you have serious plans for later."

Like Kyra, Kevin didn't give her a chance to respond. He was already walking away to the other side of the campus to meet with Terrence Franklin, most likely at the main building, which had a spacious and comfortable reception and lounge area. Chloe stood watching his retreat for a long thoughtful moment, as she'd so often done when they were undergraduates. Always admiring, from afar, the man with so much presence, personality, charm and potential that had labeled him early on as future master of his universe.

She began to wonder just how long her meeting with Walter Morrow was going to take. Chloe also wouldn't allow herself to think that Kevin might actually be serious—that he wanted her to wait for him and had done all but extract an actual promise.

She hurried.

Kevin frowned as he checked the time again. He cursed quietly under his breath. He'd been with Terrence for more than an hour.

To his left he heard the distinct rumble of thunder, and the sky had turned a smoke-gray, the clouds low on the horizon, bellowing like dirty sheets in the wind.

Walking just past the library, Kevin briefly reviewed his meeting with Terrence, even as he walked briskly. They'd known each other as undergrads and lived in the same frat house off campus. Terrence was a jock, an overgrown Herculean talent who, on Saturday afternoons throughout the school year, literally mowed down the opposition. For doing so Terrence basked, for three of his four years, in the glory of winning for the Hollington Lions as their awesome and unstoppable running back.

Kevin had assumed that Terrence's reluctance to openly deal with the offer from Hollington to be the head coach was nothing more than a reluctance to face, once and for all, that his pro ball career was dead and buried. He'd not been asked to do play-by-play commentary for any of the networks, or to be assistant coach or trainer for any national team. There were other options but not a lot. What Kevin found out, instead, was that the source of Terrence's soul-searching and second-guessing was…a woman. Kyra Dixon, to be exact.

While the information had stunned him, Kevin was more surprised that, after all these years, the big guy still had unresolved feelings for his petite classmate. He couldn't recall if, even recently, Kyra had ever indicated that she and Terrence used to have a thing going on. Or, what had happened to it. But even listening to Terrence hint and make veiled references to, but never actually say it out loud, some sort of failed affair had made Kevin squirm. Not because he didn't care about his friend and his obvious confused state of mind but because it was too clear a reminder of the trail of emotional debris he himself had been responsible for. Obviously Kyra had left quite an impression on Terrence's psyche—and his heart.

"Man, I don't want to know the details, and I can't help you with that," Kevin had joked, eliciting an understanding chuckle from Terrence. "Sure I had my fair share of lovely young things, but it's not like I ever really thought about what I wanted for real. Now if you're asking me about getting a good deal from the college, I can advise you what to hold out for. To be frank, you could have them by the short hairs. Your name hooked up with Hollington could bring in a lot of sponsors, financial support and maybe even a deal with a local affiliate to broadcast the Hollington games. You control a lot of capital, my man. But first, you *got* to take care of this business between you and Kyra. She's a cool lady. She's sweet. Don't hurt her if you can help it. And do what you gotta do."

Kevin only remembered that Terrence was ambivalent, feeling a little guilty about his past and a little scared about the future. It was a powerful enough combination to stymie his ability to make a decision—at least for now. And, Kevin had to admit, nothing he'd ever faced himself. Thinking about it, however, rather than feel lucky he suddenly felt empty.

Kevin sighed deeply, trying to shake off the heavy pall that had accompanied his time with Terrence. What he really wanted, and it came to him strongly during their meeting, was to finish and see if he could get back with Chloe.

The irony was not lost on him. In fact he'd never been with Chloe in the first place. The four years leading up to, and including, senior year, had been totally devoid of any knowledge or awareness of her, as far as he could remember. So here he was, ten years on, trying to figure out how she'd managed in just about a month, what had not happened in four years. Get his attention.

For one thing, Kevin knew for certain he'd finally grown up. It had taken a woman he'd thought about becoming engaged to, an ugly accusation and a DNA test to provide a serious reality check. So...what was so different about Chloe Jackson? Unlike almost every woman he'd ever met or been interested in...Chloe Jackson, for all the world, just didn't seem that into him.

How could that happen?

As soon as Kevin shook hands with Terrence, leaving him at the building lobby, his thoughts turned to Chloe.

He was already late, and he was pretty sure she was not the kind of woman to hang around waiting for any man.

The thunder rolled again. He was worried that the rain would start before he could find her. Suddenly, Kevin realized this was important to him—urgent, almost. He began a light jog, cutting across the quad to shorten the distance.

It had taken him several days and a copy of the 1999 yearbook to piece together who Chloe Jackson was. And still there was almost nothing to go on, which made his quest, as he now saw it, even more exciting.

Who in the world was Chloe Jackson?

The more he'd seen her and spoken with her, the more Kevin had a sense of something between them, here at Hollington, when they were students. Not an affair or a seduction…he knew he would have remembered that. No lab buddy thing, or mentoring, or friend of a friend of a friend. No hanger-on at the frat parties or groupie for the football team. Chloe had so stayed under the radar that she might almost not have existed, except for that vague feeling that they'd somehow met before. But he couldn't nail it down. That is, until he'd hit on the idea of looking through the yearbook.

Unable to locate his copy Kyra, who confessed that she remembered even less about Chloe, had sent him one by express mail. It had been enlightening, if frustrating.

Kevin felt the warm wind picking up. A few fat drops splatted on the paved walkways and tree leaves overhead. A quick scan around him showed no sign of Chloe, and she would have been so easy to spot. She was dressed in a khaki-colored pencil skirt and a black

V-neck jersey top with three-quarter length sleeves. She'd also worn black ankle-tie espadrilles. Her hair had been pulled back into a ponytail and twisted into a casual knot. The style made Chloe look even younger than she normally did with her hair down, more vulnerable.

Kevin stopped near a corner under the shelter of a tree. With summer lightning another possibility he knew he couldn't stay there for long. Since graduating he'd only been back to the campus maybe a half-dozen times. He was not given to being sentimental about anything or anyone, except for his grandmother and what she'd taught him. Of course there was also his mother, who had maintained her own pride and integrity even under fire from a difficult marriage, and worthless husband and father. But, for whatever reasons, Kevin suddenly felt a connection here at Hollington that seemed tangible solely because of its connection as well to Chloe Jackson. He was still trying to understand why.

It was starting to rain for real. He looked at the time and sighed in annoyance, sure now that Chloe had left. And then he glanced up and there she was. Pressed back and huddled against a door with a very small inset. It was a side exit only from one of the buildings. She was, in essence, trapped there.

"Chloe!"

He watched her look quickly around, trying to find the source of the voice.

"*Here!* I'm over here!"

She spotted him. Relief and what Kevin imagined was surprise passed over her features. Chloe smiled at him, lifted her shoulders in a helpless shrug and rolled her eyes toward the sky. He laughed.

But he knew the rain could continue this way for twenty minutes before stopping. Or not. He tried to figure out how to get them together. Kevin calculated that he was perhaps fifty yards from a small classroom building behind him. Chloe was about ten feet farther away. The building was locked now, but its entrance was beneath an arched cement portico. It was deep enough to shelter them both with room to spare.

Kevin got her attention and pointed to the building.

"Make a run for it," he shouted.

"No." She shook her head. "I'll get soaked."

Kevin abruptly stepped out into the open and was immediately pelted with rain. He spread his arms, laughing at the shocked expression on her face.

"Kevin!" Chloe admonished.

"I'm drowning here. Come on! I'll wait for you."

As Kevin felt the water run down his face, drip from his chin and eyelashes, plaster his shirt to his chest and arms, Chloe seemed to take a deep breath, clutch her purse to her chest and dash out into the rain toward him. She made a small surprised yelp as she got wet.

He stood and just watched her. She ran all out, knees pumping despite the slim skirt. All slim long legs, fearless and graceful. She stumbled once, her wet feet slipping on the inner soles of her sandals. As she drew near to him Kevin held out his hand to her as he began to move toward the other building. Chloe stretched to reach for it. He grabbed hers firmly, pulling her along with him. Together they sprinted the last few dozen yards to the building.

They arrived breathless and panting and started to

laugh. Kevin wasn't sure why or what was so funny. He just knew that it felt good.

"I'm probably going to catch a chill," Chloe muttered good-naturedly, using her hands to wipe her face and smooth back her hair.

"Hey. I could catch one, too, you know. I could die," he groused.

"Serves you right. Making me wait in the rain for *you*."

He looked at her, knowing that her argument was feeble and teasing. "I waited in the rain for you."

Chloe looked caught off guard but then recovered with a sweet smile. "That's true. But I'm worth it."

Kevin doubled over in laughter at her audacity. At her humor and how fresh she looked, wet all over.

"That was *cold*." He chuckled. "But that's okay. My mama raised me good, and I did the right thing."

He tried to look affronted and waited for a sharp retort from her. When she remained silent Kevin turned to her. Chloe had pulled herself more or less to rights, impressing him even more with her lack of complaint and fussing about her clothing.

"I guess it's my fault that your hair got wet."

"It's not a problem."

"Aah. Better hair through chemistry," he cracked.

She chuckled silently. "At least it's *my* hair."

"I stand corrected." His humor faded as he considered her. "I was only teasing you. I'm glad I waited, Chloe. I wanted to."

Now, she was once again the centered reserved woman, all poised and professional, except for the contradictory brightness of her gaze.

"I'm…glad, too."

Her voice was a whisper, as if she wasn't sure she should make such a confession. There was no way for her to know that, as far as he was concerned, it was an admission of her trust and, he hoped, more than a degree of like.

The rain didn't look like it was going to let up, and for a moment Kevin stood next to Chloe, silently watching the visible vale of water wash over the landscape. Not even thinking, he put his arm around her shoulder, briskly rubbing his hand up and down her arm. The motion forced her closer to his side, until her shoulder was pressed into his chest.

"Are you cold?" Kevin asked quietly.

She sighed, shaking her head. "No, I'm fine." She inhaled deeply. "It smells like grass and leaves, doesn't it?"

Kevin didn't answer. He didn't think it was required.

"I've always loved that smell about Hollington. I've always loved Hollington," she said with a silent chuckle.

"Did you? Why?" Kevin asked, keeping his arm around her but no longer stroking her arm. He was enjoying the way she was leaning against him. Trusting and open.

She shrugged. "I'd never seen a place like this. Where I came from…well, it was different. Hollington was like visiting some foreign country. The campus, the buildings, were so old and beautiful. The minute I got here I was happy to be here."

"Well, I have to tell you, to me I only saw four years of lectures, papers, final exams and terrible cafeteria food."

Chloe laughed.

"I'm exaggerating, naturally. I liked Hollington. And I was glad to come here and get away from... Anyway, I can't complain. I don't think my memories are like yours, but I can tell you I'm glad to be back and involved with homecoming."

"Are you? I'm glad, Kevin. Because you've been so helpful."

Kevin shifted slightly, so that he could see her face. "You don't understand. I'm glad because I got to meet you. Really, for the first time."

She looked out at the rain.

"You're probably confusing me with someone else from your past."

"I know it's long and sordid," Kevin admitted dryly, "but there's no confusion. You're like a breath of fresh air. To be honest, I'm a little glad we never crossed paths when I was young and stupid."

Chloe looked up into his face. "Who said we never crossed paths?"

Kevin, suddenly uncertain, frowned. "Did we?"

"It's not important anymore. This is like starting over, isn't it? For me, too."

He dared to pull her a little closer. She didn't resist. "That's good." He took a deep breath, took another chance. "I got a hold of a copy of our yearbook recently."

A small smile curved her mouth. "It's been years since I've looked at mine."

"Well, I had a specific reason," Kevin said. Chloe tilted her face up to him, waiting for an explanation.

"I was looking to find out more about you," he said honestly.

"Why would you do that?" she asked, looking down at the ground.

There was no denying that she sounded suspicious.

"Because I'm interested. And to be honest, at first I felt like a fool for not remembering you."

"Don't feel that way, Kevin. I deliberately stayed in the shadows. I felt so different from everyone else that I didn't want people to know about me."

"What's so different about you? Are you an alien life-form? A voodoo goddess? Were you raised by wolves in the wild?"

Chloe shook her head, but he was glad when she laughed at his outrageous suggestions.

"I've had challenges to overcome. Let's just leave it at that."

"Okay," he conceded, recognizing the wisdom of not pushing her.

"So, what did you find out?" she asked quietly.

Kevin inhaled. Suddenly he could smell exactly what she'd tried to describe to him. He inhaled again. He let his hand slip down to her waist. She put up no resistance.

"Damned little. There's not a single decent photograph of you in the whole book!"

"I worked at it," she said flippantly.

"One of these days you'll have to tell me why. As a matter of fact the one good picture wasn't all that good. It was graduation day, and you were giving a speech." He glanced at her face, and she met his gaze. "You were valedictorian. In the picture there's a shadow right across your face because of that cap thing."

Suddenly, Kevin conjured up a real memory from that day. It was behind the liberal arts building on the field where concerts had been performed, and craft fairs had been displayed, and rallies had been held and they had graduated, ten years earlier. He was startled by how clearly one detail in particular was now coming back to him.

"Then I looked up your name on the page of achievements and awards. You volunteered at a shelter in Atlanta."

She didn't respond.

"And I read that you had, like, this private tutoring service for other students that you operated out of the student lounge."

She said nothing.

"How'd you get away with that? I'm surprised President Morrow never asked for a cut of your earnings."

He won a small shy smile from her.

"And I know you were on full scholarship, and given some money by some women's group or other." Kevin stopped suddenly and turned her to face him. "Chloe, you are amazing."

"Doesn't mean a thing to anyone but me. I did it for *me*. I wanted to make sure I could have a different kind of life than…than just being a foster kid. That's what I wanted, Kevin. The key to my own life."

"If RSVP is any example to go by, you've succeeded. And I remember your foster parents. Seemed like really nice people."

"Yes," she whispered. "They were very good to me. I was lucky."

"How are they?"

"Mr. Fields passed away about four years ago. I'm still in touch with Mrs. Fields, now and then. She moved to Memphis to be near her grandchildren."

Kevin studied her expression. A thousand questions were forming in his head. There were some serious omissions and holes in her story. Did she have any birth family, any siblings? Was there or had there ever been a significant other? What did she remember about him from when they were students? That question evoked in Kevin a string of uncomfortable memories that he preferred she not know about. More to the point right now, what did she think of him?

"Chloe…" Kevin began.

Then he couldn't seem to find the right words. He raised his other hand, wanting to touch her face, stroke her cheek. There was the uncomfortable realization that she had been far more focused and disciplined than he'd been. She'd had to be.

"Chloe, we're more alike than you know."

"Did you make me run in the rain and get wet just to tell me that?"

It was a real question, but he didn't detect any rancor or annoyance.

"The truth? Yes. But there's more. What I know absolutely right now is that I find you incredibly attractive. I like what I see, a lot," Kevin confessed, his voice deep, quiet and sincere.

"Do you? You know what's really strange about coming back to Hollington and getting involved with the homecoming and our reunion? I wasn't a friend of yours or Kyra's or Terrence's or Beverly's back then. Now, I'm getting to know all of you. You were all the 'in' crowd."

"Does that mean you wish things were like they used to be, or you're happy that everything has changed?"

She seemed to be staring out into space. The rain was finally letting up. He noticed an almost imperceptible change in her body, her shoulder resting against him. Kevin repositioned his hand on her waist.

"Chloe?" he prompted.

She nodded. "I'm glad. It's all been…very good."

He took a deep breath. "There is one thing I do remember from that day we graduated. I was on the band shell field, looking for someone when I saw this tall, slender coed standing in front of me in her cap and gown. I snuck up and grabbed her from behind because, at the time, I thought she was someone else. I caught her off guard. I didn't say anything, didn't even identify myself, but I kissed her. Like this."

With that Kevin lowered his head and pressed his lips to Chloe's. There was a slight stiffening in her body, but she made no attempt to evade his embrace. Kevin sensed it was almost as if Chloe didn't believe that he'd actually do it.

But he had been remembering just this, in detail, for the past several days. And once he'd pieced together the moment in that afternoon, so many years ago, Kevin knew he wanted a repeat. Not at all because of what he recalled of Chloe back then, which was nothing at all, but because of what he'd come to know of her in the past month. The yearbook memory, and her own admissions, had only confirmed his instinctive response to her. He'd had an "aha" moment.

He began to move his mouth, manipulating her lips gently, until Chloe responded to him. He detected a slight tremor in her breathing. He blindly felt for her handbag, pulled it from her grasp and dropped it at their feet. His arms went around her, loosely holding her against him. Not too close, because he feared that she was still skittish enough to push him away. A part of him was surprised and pleased by Chloe's surrender to the moment, to the two of them together, if only because he also read in their innocent foreplay her lack of experience.

Kevin began to kiss her in a way meant to incite excitement, passion and desire. He wanted her to take him, and his kiss, seriously. He let his tongue breach the warm cavern of her mouth, applying more pressure so that his tongue could tease and play with hers. And he was slow and gentle. He thought he heard a soft moan. He thought he felt her fingertips touch his jaw and chin. Kevin released her mouth but only long enough to turn his head in the other direction and find his place again against her lips. He made a point of not letting Chloe feel the evidence of his sudden erection that had taken even him by surprise. Kevin would have enjoyed pulling her hips tighter to him and rocking himself against her so she understood he was hard because of her.

Too soon.

One thing at a time.

He forced himself to ease up, to slowly stop. He laid his cheek against the side of her head, her face pressed into his throat. He could feel the warmth of her hurried breath against his skin. Even that was exciting. He held her still and felt Chloe's body relax into him. He stroked her back.

"I knew I'd made a mistake that day," Kevin murmured. "I said I was sorry after I kissed you, but I'm not sure I was. I thought you'd haul off and slug me good. But you didn't." He turned his head so that he could see her eyes. "I'm still not sorry, but here's your chance again to punch me out."

He waited as she seemed to give her options serious thought. The fact that Chloe did nothing right away gave Kevin hope. Watching the interplay of emotions across her expressive face said everything else. Unconsciously he brushed the back of his hand down Chloe's cheek. She leaned into the caress.

"I knew there was a mistake, too, Kevin. But it never entered my mind to be mad at you."

Chapter 4

Every fiber in her body had anticipated that he'd try to kiss her.

Chloe had waited because it was exactly what she wanted Kevin to do. If was as if she sensed this was the only time, the golden opportunity, she would ever know Kevin as she'd always dreamed of. It was worth every moment of that wait just for the euphoria of that moment in which she felt cherished and desired.

They stood in each other's arms, with Kevin looking every bit as bemused and surprised as she was by what had just happened between them. Thankfully, he did not say anything smart or funny or suggestive. He kept quiet, as she had, and just let the moment sink in.

After a moment he put his hand out from beneath their covering.

"It's stopped raining," he murmured.

"Yes."

"Why don't we go somewhere?"

Her stomach roiled. "What…do you have in mind?"

He'd looked at her long and considering, as if weighing his options. Then he grinned. "How do you feel about pizza?"

Simple. Safe. It was so right for the moment.

"Yes, that sounds great."

"Good. Let's head over toward the stadium. I know a place."

Kevin placed his hand on the back of her waist and steered them toward their destination. Fortunately, by using one or two shortcuts between buildings and across a grassy lawn, they arrived quickly at a campus hangout.

"Wait," Chloe said as they were about to enter. Bending over she untied and removed her soaked espadrilles.

"Okay. I'll go along."

Kevin also removed his soaked leather loafers. The minute they walked into the place Kevin was hailed and greeted by the middle-aged manager. Chloe observed that the pizza parlor was half-filled with students at least ten years younger than themselves.

She took a booth Kevin directed her to and watched the exuberant hello between the men. A conversation took place, during which Kevin handed over their shoes in exchange for a small stack of paper towels. Soon he was walking back to her. He surprised her by bending on one knee and spreading towels on the floor under their table. Then he took a few more and, lifting her feet one at a time, dried them off and wiped them dry and free of pebbles and dirt.

"That's Caesar. Great guy. Can't believe he's still here."

She was too speechless by Kevin's gentlemanly act to say anything but was secretly delighted at the extra attention. Finally she murmured a thank-you.

"We'll probably be okay. But if you hear that I came down with tetanus because I cut my feet on something deadly, it's going to be on your head."

She chuckled.

By the time they'd both cleaned up and settled into the booth Caesar had arrived carrying a big tray with a piping hot cheese pizza, a beer for Kevin and a paper cup with cappuccino for Chloe. It was frothy and rich.

Kevin regaled her with tales of the nights spent at a table there, trying to study or finish a paper. Despite his very rich social life, he had no intentions of flunking out of school. He learned to force isolation on himself to make sure he didn't.

"Nana Mame told me, 'Boy, don't even think about coming back home if you don't get your degree.' Since I didn't have an ounce of self-discipline when I got here—" she laughed at that "—I had to figure out a plan to get my butt in gear and do the work. I can't tell you how much pepperoni pizza I ate in four years."

"I'm surprised you haven't gotten as big as Terrence Franklin."

"Jogging," Kevin said. "Saved my life. Got a lot of thinking done by myself. Kept my stress under wraps. Solved problems, made decisions…"

"Stayed fit," she added without thinking.

Kevin smiled at her. "Thanks for the compliment."

For a few moments they just ate in quiet enjoyment,

finally dry, warm and content. At least that's how Chloe felt. And with that comfort came bold curiosity.

"I have to ask you something. What did you mean when you said we're alike?" she asked him.

Kevin chewed thoughtfully, sipped from his beer and looked at her for a long moment. "You grew up in foster care, yet you ended up valedictorian, went on to form your own business and have made a life for yourself."

Chloe wasn't sure what she expected Kevin was going to say, but she was surprised by his astute observations. And he was very much on point. Rather than feel exposed, she was relieved that he was sensitive enough to understand what made her run.

He finally pushed his paper plate aside and leaned toward her, his arms crossed on the table. "You had a plan to overcome the past. Well, that's how I felt. I have a mother and father, but he's not a do-right kind of man. I don't want to be like him. I saw what he did to my sisters, to my mom and me. I also wasn't going to be like some of the guys I grew up with, having kids with different girls and just walking away from the responsibility. My Nana Mame and my mama weren't having it. 'Don't bring me no more kids to raise.'"

Chloe couldn't help it and laughed hysterically at Kevin's imitation of a Black woman's high and sassy, don't-make-me-hurt-you tone.

"Nana Mame used to tell me I was a special baby. She said they got it wrong with my father but they're making up for it with me. There was *no way* I was going to disappoint my family—or myself."

Chloe had watched Kevin as he spoke and was moved by how open and honest he was being with her.

It made her feel good that he trusted her with his personal history. It made her feel like maybe he did understand what her abandonment had done to her.

"Did your grandmother see you graduate?"

"She sure did. That was a big thing for me, that she could watch me get my degree. She died last spring."

"I'm so sorry."

He shrugged. "I was lucky. She was there for some important times of my life."

When they'd finished Caesar cleared away the table and returned their shoes, miraculously dried if a little stiff. He'd placed them next to the oven.

It was dark when they left, the air clear and dry after the quick storm. It was a lovely night, and Chloe had the warm sensation that all was right in her world. At least, in that moment. She'd just spent some of the most fun few hours of her life in the company of Kevin Stayton, the man of her dreams.

They began heading back to the parking lot where she'd left her car earlier in the afternoon.

Suddenly, Kevin stopped and turned to stare at her.

"Wait a minute."

She frowned. "What?"

"Now I remember," Kevin said in a voice of astonishment.

He stared at her with deep concentration, either looking for something, or recognizing something in her. He pointed a finger at her.

"It was you." He stepped closer. "Like, freshman year. No. Maybe sophomore. March or something like that. It was cold and raining real hard."

Chloe could only stare back, realizing that Kevin was

about to key into another of her sacredly held memories, and the very foundation of their relationship at Hollington.

All she could do was shake her head at him, feigning bewilderment. Maybe he wouldn't piece it together. Maybe he would leave it alone.

"I was driving back to my frat house after a really bad date in Atlanta." His gaze wandered as he struggled with details. "And then, I passed someone on the road, slogging through the rain. They had a coat over their head for cover, for all the good that did. I kept going. I was mad and pissed off at this…this girl who…"

Kevin stopped, clearly not interested in revisiting the incident or the girl. He squinted at her.

"Then I felt like a dog. It was going to be a long, wet walk back to the campus."

"Why did you think it was a student from Hollington?" Chloe asked.

Kevin shrugged. "There's nothing much on that road. The campus was only another mile or so away. But that's how I knew I had to go back. Walking in the rain wasn't going to be fun. But that made me even madder 'cause I couldn't just leave somebody out on the road like that.

"I drove back and turned around and pulled up next to this person. They didn't even look to see who'd stopped."

"What did you do?"

"Opened the window, said it was raining and asked if I could give them a lift. It was a girl. She said she was going back to campus. I said, so was I and to get in. So, she did. Got my front seat all wet, but…"

He tilted his head and stood with his hands on his hips as the pieces fit into the jigsaw puzzle of his memory.

"It was you. I know it was you."

Chloe grimaced, staring at his chest.

"I asked you, what were you doing on the road like that in the rain? You said, 'bad date.' What do you remember?"

She made a vague gesture with her shoulders. She'd never told anyone about that night and the date who'd put her out of his car because she'd refused to put out for him. She saw no reason to make a confession now. It was still humiliating and hurtful.

"I thanked you for stopping, but I didn't say much of anything else. I felt tongue-tied because I knew right away who you were. I hoped you wouldn't tell anyone you'd found me walking home on the road."

"I don't think I ever did. Probably forgot about it by the next morning. What else happened?"

"You drove me back to my dorm."

Kevin waited. "That's it?"

No.

He saw that she was cold and shaking and stopped at a gas station to get her coffee. He'd taken a sweatshirt from his car trunk and given it to her to put on. He'd not only driven her all the way to her dorm but watched until she'd gotten inside the building. She'd gone out for the evening with a young man who'd quickly turned out to be a frog and gotten safely back home that night with someone else who was a prince. That one-night encounter with Kevin had formed the basis of a fantasy and faith that had afterward sustained her for years.

"That's it," Chloe said. "I'm surprised you remembered any of that night."

"I never would have if I hadn't gotten to know you now. You know we just had a date, right?"

Chloe frowned at him playfully. "Oh, really? I don't recall you asking me."

"The thing is, if I'd asked you would have turned me down. Don't think I've forgotten when I had to trick you into lunch a few weeks ago. At this rate it'll be fall before we even have a glass of wine together."

"I just figured out a way around you always saying no. I don't ask, I just do it." He grinned broadly.

"That's very arrogant of you."

"Listen, I'm a take-charge kind of guy. Do you object?"

"I appreciate your resourcefulness."

"Are you mad at me?"

"A month ago, maybe I would have been. I don't know. But I had a really good time today. Rain and all."

"Me, too. Thanks for being such a good sport about the weather."

She looked around as they approached the visitor's lot. "Where's the mysterious and silent CB?"

"The man does get time off, you know. I didn't need him today. I think I'm safe with you, all by myself."

Chloe smiled silently at him.

You're much too sure of yourself, Kevin Stayton.

They reached the lot, and Chloe pointed out her car. As she stood unlocking it, Kevin leaned against the hood, staring at her over the top of the open door.

"When am I going to see you again?"

She gave him a skeptical grin. "You mean, another date? Are you asking this time?"

"Don't want to push my luck but I'm going to ruin my reputation if I can't do better than a picnic lunch and pizza." He stepped around the open door to stand in front of her, boldly placing his hands on her narrow waist. "I want the real thing next time. I pick you up, we go out, we enjoy ourselves and then…"

"And then?" she challenged him.

"We'll see what develops."

With that Kevin kissed her again. This time Chloe was ready. She'd learned quickly how he liked to kiss, and she wanted a repeat as if to make sure it had been real the first time. It was. The way he held her, kissed her with tenderness and sexy expertise, had the power to create havoc in her head and tension in her body. Chloe adapted herself to his lead. He was direct and sure. But, as before, Kevin didn't rush or move too suddenly. He built the excitement with the erotic control of his tongue. He had a way of thrusting it slowly into her mouth that was as effective as it was evocative of another intimate action.

Kevin slipped his hands around her back, and Chloe willingly pressed herself to his chest. She felt so protected and safe there, like nothing was going to get between them. She could feel his heartbeat and the toned columns of his thighs.

She didn't want him to stop. And that scared her. This time she was the one to step back, draw her bottom lip between her teeth and hope he couldn't tell how deeply he affected her.

"Will you?" he asked.

Chloe nodded.

"Friday night?"

"Okay," she whispered, finally looking into his face. It was dark and hard to see his features. But his lips were still moist from their kiss. His dark eyes sparkled through the reflection of a nearby lamppost. "Okay," she repeated, giving in.

Only she knew this was a fulfillment of a lifetime of dreams.

It had been two weeks since that rainy campus day with Kevin and their Friday night date. Chloe was still basking in the warm memory of it. Kevin had warned her in advance that formal attire would not be required.

"Think good music and wine. But not at one of my places."

That had intrigued her.

He'd actually taken her to the Phillips Arena for a concert with Sweet Honey and The Rock. True to his intentions and her wishful thinking it had been a genuine date complete with appropriate amorous good-night kiss, a little titillating petting, but he hadn't pushed for more. All during that night Chloe had tried to second-guess Kevin's actions, wondering if he'd found her wanting. That is, until about six in the morning when he called to complain. "I didn't get to sleep at all last night."

Sweet words for her on a Saturday morning.

Since then had been nearly daily calls, but most of their getting together had turned out to be over home-coming arrangements, as Kevin willingly became more involved and more hands-on. Sometimes after work they'd end up at his wine bar, CORK, and just enjoy conversation and rather open and earnest conversations about everything from their families to their years at Hollington. And as much as she was coming to trust Kevin, Chloe still did not give a full reveal about her background.

So, on Monday morning two weeks later, the furthest thing from Chloe's thoughts was the woman waiting again when she left the parking lot and headed toward the entrance of her office building. There she was, same time, same place. Finding the woman loitering a few times might have been a coincidence, but she now knew otherwise. Against all her fervent hopes that she was mistaken, Chloe had to accept the horrific truth that the down-on-her-luck woman who had claimed a corner of the street where she worked was her mother.

Her fervent desire to deny her worst fears and make it go away was no longer possible. Lost forever in this skinny, ill-dressed, middle-aged woman…neglected and worn down…was another woman to whom life had not been kind. And Chloe remembered her own bewilderment and helpless desperation that this person whom she depended on to keep her sheltered and safe didn't and couldn't.

Mother.

The very word caught in Chloe's throat, like an insult, or blasphemy, a bad joke. It evoked such contradictory feelings and emotions that, after first seeing the woman, the very day that Kevin had persuaded her to join him for an alfresco lunch in the atrium, she had returned to her office and refused any calls for the next several hours. Until she could catch her breath, regain her balance and stabilize her senses.

"Ain't you gonna say hello to me? I'm your mama, girl. You sure did grow up pretty. I used to be pretty."

There it is, Chloe thought, a heavy feeling pressing in the middle of her chest. Confirmation. Truth. Only for a second did she consider ignoring the flat, street voice, as if by doing so her mother would disappear. But she'd known from their first encounter that the vagaries of her life were rarely so simple. This had to be dealt with. She had to find closure to her past. She had no idea how.

Chloe slowed her steps facing the woman and, by doing so, acknowledging her. She still didn't want to believe that this was her mother, but there were remembered mannerisms, the pitch of her voice and the way her face changed when she smiled that struck a nerve. Painful details were falling into place.

"What do you want from me?" Chloe asked, her voice even and mildly curious.

"Haven't seen my baby girl in so long. State took you away from me, like I don't know how to raise my own chile," she sniffed. "I got paroled two months ago."

Chloe's stomach roiled violently and felt like her body heat was draining right out of her. She'd long ago, still a child, been told her mother had to go away. It had never been made clear where.

"Then I seen you in the newspapers. You real smart. Got you a degree and even got your own business. I see you going in there to work." She laughed.

There was an unmistakable pride in her revelation.

"I told my parole officer that you my little girl. He

don't believe me. But you know, right? Baby, I'm your mama."

Chloe was rooted to the ground. She was fascinated. She was horrified. She was even disappointed. For several years after she'd been placed in foster care she'd prayed for her mother to come and get her. Slowly that desire had faded in the face of the loving care the Fields had given her, well beyond their legal obligation of her eighteenth birthday. They had sent her care packages, letters and even an occasional small check to help her get by when she'd been accepted to Hollington, an elite college normally beyond the reach of someone with her background. Chloe had not seen nor heard from, or about, her mother in twenty-three years. The statute of limitations had run out long ago on her caring. Whatever relationship birth had given them was not enough to repair the past and give them back time.

Chloe shook her head. "I'm sorry that things have been tough for you. But, it's too late. I don't know you anymore, and you don't know me…Billie."

She whispered the name as it suddenly came back to her. She hadn't spoken it in years.

Billie. Wilhelmina. Wilhelmina…Burns.

"You used to call me Mommy. Not Billie. I don't mean to cause no trouble. Can't you help me out? I need a little help to get back on my feet."

Chloe stared at her. She realized that she was never going to be able to appeal to her mother to accept responsibility for what had happened to them both. And now, there was nothing between them and nothing that she wanted from her, *ever*.

Chloe sighed, resigned to what she needed to do. "Let me take you for breakfast. We can talk."

They were seated at a local café, mostly empty now that the morning rush hour was over. Still, Chloe was well aware of the glances and stares directed at them. They were an odd couple; Billie was dressed in stained and wrinkled clothing too big for her rail-thin frame, and Chloe was in her sleeveless Eileen Fisher shift with a matching cardigan tied around her shoulder.

She let Billie order anything she wanted: grits and eggs and biscuits and sausages. And then a second order of pancakes swimming in syrup and more sausage. She drank only orange juice, needed lots of paper napkins for spills and generally had the table manners of a child.

Chloe ordered a bowl of fresh fruit and cream and then never ate it, too concerned that it might not stay down. Mostly, she sat and listened to Billie talk, much of which was rambling and inarticulate. And Billie kept calling her "my baby." Chloe was too dispirited and shell-shocked to do much more than sit silently and stare.

A new concern suddenly twisted her stomach further with tension and distress. What if Kevin found out about Billie? Would the sins and shortcomings of her mother be visited on her and taint her life forever?

"I need the bathroom," Billie announced, staring down at the debris of breakfast that littered the table.

"In the back," Chloe pointed out.

As Billie pushed away from the table Chloe's purse, positioned near her elbow, tilted over and fell to the floor. Its contents spilled out but did not scatter.

"I'm sorry," Billie whined, bending over to retrieve the items.

Embarrassed by the disturbance they were causing, Chloe quickly picked up her purse and began haphazardly tossing her things back in.

"I'll take care of it. You go on," she said to Billie.

By the time her mother had returned, their meal had been paid for. Chloe stood up.

"I can't stay any longer. I have to get back to work."

"I know you gotta do what you gotta do," Billie said and nodded.

"Let's go outside. I have something for you."

The promise of a treat did the trick, and they left the café. Chloe reached inside her bag and pulled out a number of bills folded over. She held the money out to Billie, who didn't hesitate to accept. She immediately stood counting the money.

"Thank you, baby. This is good looking out for your mama."

"You have to stop coming here," Chloe said quietly but firmly. "I can't help you. I can't give you any more money. I know you've had some bad breaks, and I hope things get better for you. I mean that. But I want you to leave me alone."

With that Chloe turned and rushed across the street.

"Bye, baby!" she heard behind her but did not turn around.

Chloe did not enter her building but kept walking right by the entrance. Her cell phone rang, and it was Lynette wondering where she was. She put on a harried voice. Everything was fine, but she was running late. Not to worry. She continued walking, agitated and confused, for nearly a half mile before she got tired and turned back. Billie was nowhere in sight. But Chloe wasn't sure her mother was really gone.

By that Friday Chloe was beginning to relax again. Four new clients came in to sign on for her company's services, all spurred by the recent article in *Luster* and word of mouth. Tamara Hodges called and requested an interview for her magazine, but Chloe convinced her that Beverly Turner would be a better subject. She admitted that she was still trying to get Beverly to agree to reprise her part as homecoming queen in the Sunday parade during homecoming.

"I don't suppose you know if Micah Ross will be here in October?" Tamara asked.

And Chloe totally understood why she was the one Tamara asked. But she was just as relieved she could answer truthfully that she had no idea.

She made it to the end of the week. No more from Billie. She was looking forward to another date with Kevin. It was starting to feel like a long-awaited reward for being patient and having dodged a bullet.

Kevin helped her into his comfortable luxury car, a Nissan 350Z Roadster. He'd asked if she was okay and then closed the door to come around to the driver's side. In the meantime she glowed in the realization that it appeared, for real, that she and Kevin were now dating. Not a colleague or coworker or professional contact get-together for drinks, but a *date.* As in, nice cocktail dress, panty hose and heels, hair swept up with decorative hairpins, perfume and drop earrings, a cute little evening bag big enough for lipstick and an emergency fifty-dollar bill…in the unfortunate possibility that Kevin might still turn into Mr. Hyde in the middle of the evening and she had to get home alone.

She'd added one more small item, her heart racing all the while thinking how sad and foolish she was behaving. So girly. But her poise and decorum had taken a hit recently, and all bets were off.

Or, maybe she was just responding to the part of her that wanted the past to stop rearing its ugly head and leave her be. She was going to actually live her fantasy with Kevin. Chloe had a fatalistic sense that she might not get another chance.

"Wow," he'd murmured under his breath when he'd picked her up from her home in Grove Park.

His admiration gave a much-needed boost to her confidence. Kevin's attentiveness, even something as simple as holding her hand every chance he got, worked to settle her nerves.

She had no idea what he'd planned for the night and didn't ask. Sooner than she realized he was pulling into a private parking lot, and a valet appeared to get the doors. She realized that they'd arrived at his most popular club, Bollito. He led her inside through a private door where they were met by CB who politely greeted her, nodded silently to Kevin and then quietly began walking away. She realized that CB expected them to follow. Kevin stood back so she could walk in front of him.

"Since you want to hold the Saturday night reunion dance and party here, I wanted to show you what you're getting," Kevin said and smiled at her. "You've never been here before. I would have known."

He escorted her through a corridor that bypassed

the public areas and opened onto a viewing gallery that allowed them to see all five floors of the club. He explained what kind of music each floor represented, how each was accessed, how many people the floors could hold. Eating was not allowed in the dance area, but there were cocktail tables where people could leave drinks and personal things while on the dance floor.

"No one knows I'm here tonight except CB. He's taken care of everything so we can have an uninterrupted dinner."

But they were just about to enter a small private salon when the maître d' spotted them and called out.

Kevin muttered an oath under his breath but then recovered.

"This won't take long. Let me introduce you…"

She held back.

"Go ahead. They want to talk with you."

He would have none of it. He grabbed her hand, wouldn't let go and she lost the tug of war when she tried to pull free.

"Bob. Cassidy. Good to see you again." He kissed the gorgeous willowy blonde on the cheek, and shook hands with her equally handsome husband.

"How's it going, Kev? Hey, we don't have reservations. Can you help us out? Didn't want to draw any attention. You know how it is."

"Don't worry about it. You know I'll always have a table for you." He signaled behind the couple to the maître d' who nodded his understanding and went off to arrange the table. "Let me introduce you to Chloe Jackson."

Chloe smiled graciously at the couple and murmured

hello. Then she recognized Cassidy Daley. She was the sharp and popular hostess of a morning program on one of the local TV stations. What she really enjoyed was the effortless way that Kevin chatted her up to Cassidy and Bob, making her sound far more accomplished than she was. He didn't make it about himself.

Their private dining room was cozy and romantic. The invisible sound system allowed for soft music that was far more romantic than the hip swinging music played elsewhere in the club. As a matter of fact, as the evening wore on Chloe realized she couldn't even hear what was happening beyond their salon.

To her surprise CB was their waiter, quiet and efficient, well trained. Chloe teasingly asked if he had a twin brother. CB showed he appreciated her humor with a small genuine smile just for her but otherwise didn't respond.

Kevin was gracious and gallant, confidently making sure that their selections were prepared and presented to his satisfaction. He'd chosen one of her favorite merlot wines for dinner. Their conversation was light and amusing and a good give-and-take between them that seemed so easy and natural. And they laughed a lot. He was complimentary about her appearance, her couture dress. She was no less so with Kevin. He did a business suit justice, appearing always at ease and relaxed... and in charge.

The sudden reappearance of Billie Burns began to seem an apparition to Chloe. After her second glass of wine she was sure she'd overreacted and didn't have anything to worry about at all. And she was especially relieved that she held no bitterness for a woman whose life had fallen into ruins long before Chloe had been taken away and rescued by the state.

She momentarily squeezed her eyes closed, as if to banish the image of Billie with her malnourished and unkempt presence, old before her time.

There but for the grace of God…

All in all there was not a single part of the evening that Chloe could find fault in. Perhaps, only, that it would have to end.

It was a little after midnight when she and Kevin left, slipping out the same way they'd come in. And then Kevin decided he had to have ice cream for dessert. She laughed when he began to drive like a crazy man, all over Atlanta, looking for any place that was still serving at one in the morning. They were unsuccessful and Chloe, feeling for him, promised she'd treat for ice cream another time.

They drove out of downtown Atlanta and headed… Chloe hadn't really been paying attention. Did it matter? Leaning back against the headrest she felt dreamy. She was tired and sated and silently reflecting that, as dates go, the evening with Kevin had been unexpected, fun, noisy, sweet and had given her enough memories to almost make up for her longing.

It was a moment before Chloe realized that they were stopped, the car idling, Kevin sitting motionless next to her.

"Kevin? What's wrong?"

Kevin sighed deeply, reached out for her hand and held it. "Nothing's wrong. I'm thinking. I should take you home."

His thumb rubbed slowly on the back of her hand.

He turned to gaze at her, and she felt the air they were breathing change. She knew when her heartbeat changed, her anticipation suddenly sharpened and the tension between them seemed a living tangible thing.

Kevin put the car in neutral and leaned over her. She let her eyes drift shut as his mouth teased across hers, sending a wave of delight that she felt in her breasts, in her stomach and in her now warm heated sex. It was delicious. She was already imagining more.

Kevin played and pulled at her lips, knowing exactly what he was doing. He gave her just enough to make her yearn for more. He kissed her fully, deeply, his mouth rocking across hers. Chloe felt his fingertips trail down her throat to just above the valley between her breasts. Her breathing was shallow and rapid. He ended the kiss but stayed to rub his cheek against hers.

"Chloe, I don't want you to go."

"What are my options?" she asked softly, her breathing still a little labored.

"Come home with me."

It wasn't a question. It wasn't a demand. It was a clear statement of what he wanted. Which, as luck or providence would have it, seemed like a very good idea.

So, this is what it's like being at a crossroads, she thought to herself. It was now or maybe never. How many second chances would she be given?

"Okay," she said, her voice barely above a whisper.

Kevin lightly kissed her again before shifting gears and continuing to drive.

Driving into Kevin's exclusive gated community went right over her head. She could neither see nor appreciate the beautiful design and layout of the development, apparent even in the dark. They approached a two-story house of contemporary Tudor design with a detached multiple-car garage adjacent to it. Not a word was spoken as Kevin parked the car and then led the way inside, disarming the alarm system next to the door.

Chloe stood nervous and uncertain experiencing, once again, her adolescent insecurities. Even in the dark she knew the house was grand. She was momentarily overtaken with a strong feeling once again, like when she was growing up, of not belonging. Kevin was setting the alarm again, turning on a light to illuminate a hallway and the staircase at the end. He reached for her hand, and Chloe placed hers trustingly in his. But then they stood, in the dark, facing one another.

"Would you like something to drink?" Kevin asked.

"I'm fine."

"Are you having second thoughts? Maybe it's too soon. I'd understand, Chloe."

She squeezed his hand. "No, you wouldn't. And… it feels right."

She allowed herself to be led through the darkened house, up a stairwell and into a bedroom. She was glad that he didn't turn on the light. There was a night-light on the baseboard just inside the room and another visible from a master bath and dressing room. They were enough.

Chloe made the first obvious move. She stepped out of her heels and put her purse on a nearby bureau. Kevin shrugged out of his jacket, pulled off his tie and began unbuttoning his shirt. She hesitated, a little uncertain, and then stepped forward to take over the chore of removing his shirt. It was apparently the right move, as

Kevin cupped her chin and kissed her for it. He eased out of his own shoes, opened his trousers and pulled down the zipper.

Chloe turned her back. It would have been too easy and obvious to look and see the evidence of his erection. She wanted to be surprised. She wanted to feel it first. She opened the dress zipper under her arm. The thin spaghetti straps slipped from her shoulder, and she felt Kevin's hands slip around her. In one quiet motion he pushed the dress down her slender body as he also stepped close behind her. He was still wearing his shorts, but there was no mistaking the stiff length of him that pressed against her lower back. She kicked the dress aside, with nothing else on but her bikini panties.

Her head fell back against Kevin's chest as he held her and nuzzled her shoulder and neck and ear with his lips. His hands gently rode up her torso and cupped her breasts, simultaneously kneading them and rubbing a fingertip across the nipples.

Chloe was not so much a neophyte that she didn't know what would happen or hadn't anticipated what Kevin would do. But what he was making her feel was so far beyond any previous experience that she now knew she'd been cheated in the past. Shortchanged of passion and desire and satisfaction by young men who didn't know what they were doing. Or hadn't cared if it was good for her.

She couldn't find her voice. She wanted to say Kevin's name. She wanted to utter something that would express her surprise and sheer joy of discovery of what it was supposed to feel like between a man and a woman.

"Get on the bed," Kevin said urgently behind her.

"Kevin…wait. I have something."

"I've got one."

They talked over each other. When they again stood facing one another each held out an open palm. Each held a wrapped condom. And then they tried to see each other's face. Chloe guessed it was fair to say that neither had expected the other to consider protection.

Kevin took hers from her hand. "We'll save yours for later." He put them both on the nightstand.

Kevin put one strong arm around her and, bracing one knee on the bed, came forward lowering them both to the surface. He was on top of her. He was kissing her, the effect making Chloe feel dizzy and disoriented, almost panting with a need for something to happen. An easing of the powerful ache she felt. A release of this hot tension in her stomach and between her legs. She was ready and instinctively wanted to position her body to lie on her back. But he had other plans.

He shifted to his side, holding her and still kissing her. But one hand was free to stroke her, her breasts and stomach.

"Kevin," she moaned, pleading.

"Not yet," he whispered.

His hand glided along her thigh, down and then up again between them. His cupped over her mound. Chloe's breathing became agitated in her awareness of what he was going to do. He soothed her with his voice, crooning and whispering and coaxing and gentle. He reassured her with kisses.

"Just relax, Chloe. Relax. I know what I'm doing."

Kevin began to move his fingers against the sensitive lower lips. She was wet, and it was easy for him to control the pressure, the stroke and caress, circling and rubbing and letting her response tell him what else to do. Immediately she responded, caught off guard by the exquisite sensation, the delicious feelings that spiraled through her body but centered exactly where his fingers explored. Quickly her pelvis developed a rhythm, rocking and rotating against his fingers, following the movement that created the best feeling for her.

"Oh…oh, my God," she moaned breathlessly, her breathing erratic and deep and panting.

"That's it. Go with it," he encouraged, his lips against her ear.

She clutched at his arm, holding on as if otherwise she would fall into some invisible abyss.

"Kevin…ah…aah…"

Chloe realized the tension was tightening in her body, and with it came the sudden wrenching contractions and a deeply physical euphoria that she'd never felt before. She felt shattered, floating, mindless, limp.

"Let it happen. Let it happen."

She couldn't move, and she felt no need to. Kevin stroked her a moment longer and removed his hand with a final caress.

"First time?"

She was too embarrassed to admit it but in any case only had the strength to nod to acknowledge the explosive orgasm.

He kissed a shoulder and leaned over her to find one of the wrapped condoms.

"There's more where that came from," he boasted.

Chloe lay in a dreamy state just beginning to come to her senses. She marveled over what her body had been capable of. What Kevin had done to her. For her. The bed shifted and rocked, and finally Kevin came back to poise over her. She stretched up a hand to stroke his hard bare chest. To caress his cheek. He turned a kiss into her palm. She felt like a beached whale waiting to be washed out to sea. Then Kevin took her hand and placed it around his penis, neatly and safely sheathed in a condom.

"We're good to go," he murmured.

He stretched out atop her body with a sensuous, undulating pressure, starting to make love to her.

It was not lost on Chloe that not only did Kevin believe in being prepared with protection, he'd obviously never had to worry about opportunities to use it. But there was also no evidence, no mention of other women in his life, almost from the moment they'd met in July.

Kevin did not allow her to completely recover from the first earth-shattering climax he coaxed her to. She was still feeling a sweet throbbing ache between her legs when he positioned himself, careful not to put his full weight on her slender frame. With blind precision he slowly entered her.

There was very little resistance, and what there was she felt as a titillating stroking inside her. She was still so sensitive that her back arched reflexively, and she tilted her hips upward to make the passage for him easy. Her knees pulled back, and she wrapped her legs around the base of his buttocks. She began to pant again, her insides already twisting with that painful delight of stimulated tissue and nerves. Kevin grunted softly, thrusting slowly but deeply until they both found the rhythm to move together.

Chloe's hand caressed his shoulders, feeling the muscles work and flex under her fingers. She rubbed his neck, held the sides of his face and reached up to kiss him tenderly. He hungrily kissed her back while his hips danced against her.

Then Kevin found her hands, threaded their fingers together and held them down on either side of her head. With only their hips and thighs and pelvis and stomachs working, it was easy to concentrate on the center of the storm. Chloe knew when Kevin finally broke over the edge. He strained into her groin, undulating his hips. She was almost there. And he quietly released a hand to wiggle between them, found the spot he was searching for that let loose the rush of pleasure once more from within her. The deep throbbing left her heart racing.

She awakened fairly early the next morning and found herself alone in Kevin's bed. She knew by the deep silence all around her that she was alone in the house. Immediately Chloe knew he'd gone jogging. She languished in the bed that was filled with the subtle scents of them both. And she didn't feel at all as if she was in a strange place…a strange bed.

When she finally did get out of bed Chloe realized she had nothing to put on. There was just her cocktail dress from the night before. She didn't even have a bra since the dress didn't require one. Glancing around Kevin's dressing room she noticed a short pile of sweatshirts and athletic tank tops. She selected one shirt, and upon lifting it found that it was a Hollington shirt in the school colors, navy blue and white. It was well worn, the fabric soft and the colors faded. Chloe pulled it on over her head.

Sometime during the night, somewhere in Kevin's bed, she'd lost most of the hairpins from the upswept style. Not finding a comb, Chloe simply used her fingers and hand to shake her hair out, letting it fall around her face. She rolled up the sleeves of the shirt, but the hem caught her a little above mid thigh.

Despite the urge and curiosity she didn't want to explore Kevin's home without his knowledge. But she made her way to the first floor in her bare feet and found the kitchen. It was easy enough to put on coffee to drip and to locate several pieces of fresh fruit. There was an ample supply of bottled water in the refrigerator and several containers of leftover food. From one of his restaurants? Food he'd cooked for himself? Or had someone cooked for him?

That Saturday morning was not a pretty day. Not as lovely and clear as the night before had been. Already the Georgia air was humid and still. She had a suspicion that Kevin normally didn't use the formal entrance for getting into his own house but probably preferred the more convenient and not so visible side door through which he'd led her the night before. So Chloe went out that way, discovering a smaller area and flagstone path leading to the garage where there was a home gym in a back room of the garage. Outside the door on a cement garden bench is where she sat to remember making love, smile secretly to herself, make daydreams and wait for him.

Less than ten minutes later Kevin suddenly appeared, coming to a flat stop outside the gate. His breathing was only slightly labored. The bandanna tied around his forehead was soaked, and the visible parts of his body glistened and ran with perspiration. He came through the gate, pushed it shut behind him and used the tail of his tank top to wipe his face. Then he opened his eyes and spotted her. He hesitated in his steps but slowly reached her on the bench. Without a word Chloe retrieved the chilled bottle of water she'd set on the ground next to the bench. She popped the cap and handed it to him. Silently, Kevin accepted the water, placing it to his lips and in four or five quick gulps emptied it. He sighed in repletion, just as he had the first day they met in his office. He stretched out long legs and crossed them at the ankles. He swung an arm behind Chloe's head, draping it around her shoulders, his large hand dangling. After a moment he cupped her shoulder and squeezed it.

"You're some sight for a weary man, Chloe Jackson. I'm glad you stayed…"

Chapter 5

"Welcome back, and good morning to those of you just joining us for this segment of the show—what we call 'What's New in Atlanta'..."

Chloe sat still and poised, a sedate smile fixed to her face. She'd been told not to look directly into the camera but to keep her gaze on Cassidy Daley, the host of the program and the one who would be interviewing her. But Chloe was sure she probably looked unnatural and certainly not relaxed. The two-minute piece, meant to tell the viewing audience all about RSVP, was going to be a disaster.

"It's so nice to see you, Chloe." Cassidy smiled in her cheery TV persona.

"Thanks so much for having me," Chloe got out.

"Now, I have to confess I'd never heard of your company, which is an event planning service in Atlanta,

until Kevin Stayton introduced us a few weeks ago."
Cassidy spoke directly to the camera. "Now who doesn't
know Kevin and his amazingly successful string of popular restaurants and clubs in and around Atlanta. I just
happened to be dining one evening at Bollito and ran
into Kevin himself and Chloe Jackson. So, how do you
two know each other?"

Chloe sighed inwardly. So here it was. Not a real interview to promote her business but a veiled attempt to
find out about her and Kevin together at Bollito. But
she also remembered the seriousness with which Kevin
had advised her of the incredible publicity she would
get because of Cassidy's appeal and huge audience. But
she'd expressed her doubts to Kevin.

"Kevin, frankly I'm suspicious of her motives. I can't
tell you how many press releases I've sent out hoping
that I'd at least get a mention for my business."

"I understand, Chloe, but that's not how things work.
Sorry to say, but it's about who you know. Look, if being
with me makes Cassidy curious enough to have you on
the show, then you have to make sure she stays focused
on RSVP. Figure out how to work it."

It was good advice and of course Kevin was right,
but Chloe bristled at what she felt was essentially a dog
and pony presentation.

"Kevin offered to help with some of the planning
for the October homecoming weekend at Hollington
College. We both graduated from Hollington, and I've
been chosen by the college to organize all the events.
That's what I do, as you pointed out."

"That's right," Cassidy jumped in, smiling brightly
at the camera. "Chloe operates a fairly new business in

downtown Atlanta, actually it's been around about three years, called RSVP." She turned to Chloe. "You know I got excited about having you on the show when Kevin, who's a dear friend, mentioned the fantastic things you do. I also found out that several people around the studio had good things to say about your service..." She quickly consulted her notes. "There was a bridesmaids' luncheon at the historic Herndon House, and a sleepover children's birthday party at the zoo! Doesn't that sound like fun?

"All of you out there in the Atlanta area with special events coming up should check out Chloe's Web site. That information will be up on the screen in a minute, along with a phone number and e-mail. When I first met you with Kevin Stayton at his fabulous club, was it for business or pleasure?" Cassidy asked boldly, her smile in place.

The question threw Chloe for a moment, making her stomach churn as she quickly fashioned a response.

"Business," Chloe said and smiled back. "I recently signed a contract with Kevin to use Bollito in October. I'd never been there before. It's a perfect party place for homecoming weekend."

"Makes me want to be there. Chloe Jackson, owner and president of RSVP. Keep both in mind, folks, for your next anniversary or birthday celebration." She shook hands with Chloe. "Chloe, thanks for being our guest on 'What's New in Atlanta.' We'd love to have you back in October to tell us all about Hollington College's homecoming."

"Thank you. I'd love to."

"Coming up next..."

Chloe let out her breath and stood passive as she was disconnected from her mike. Cassidy graciously thanked her again and said goodbye before she turned her attention to the next part of the show after their commercial break.

Chloe was gratified when, as she left the set of Cassidy's *Rise and Shine* show, she was asked to leave some of her business cards. She was also congratulated for being a great interviewee. Chloe was out of the studio in barely ten minutes. It was another few minutes before she finally released the tension from her body, which she'd dealt with ever since getting the call from the local affiliate that she was being invited to appear on the show.

She walked to the station's parking lot and got into the driver's seat of her car. Immediately her cell phone rang.

"Chloe, you were great! I know you heard everybody in the office screaming when you came on!"

"Thanks, Lynette. What's going on?"

"Well, everybody ran over to that electronics store in the lobby because they have all those flat screen…"

Chloe sighed and chuckled. "Lynette, I'm talking about business. Is there anything I need to know or do? Should I come back to the office?"

"No, we're good. You looked beautiful! See, I told you that Stella McCartney was the right dress for the camera," Lynette raced right on, ignoring Chloe's officious focus.

"Okay. Sounds like you and Franco have things under control. I think I'm going to head over to the company that's making the floats for the homecoming parade. They're falling behind, and we only have two months to finish. Also, I'm expecting a call back from Beverly Turner. Well, Turner *Clark*. I keep forgetting she was married. Anyway, if she calls, transfer it to my cell. I really need to talk with her as soon as possible."

"Will do."

"Then I'm going to…"

"Ah, Chloe. There is something else. You know that woman who's been hanging around the building? Franco thinks she's homeless and is looking for handouts. You've seen her, right?"

Chloe's stomach went right back to churning. The tension was making her feel almost ill.

"What about her?"

"She was here this morning. And she asked for you by name. I didn't think it would do any good to lie and say I don't know who she's talking about. I mean, she's been standing out there in front of the atrium since July. She finally left, but I thought I'd better let you know. Maybe the next time I should call the police."

Chloe closed her eyes. "No, please don't do that," she said. "She's not…dangerous, I don't think. She's homeless. She needs help."

"But, how come she knows who you are? That was spooky when she used your name. I hope she's not a stalker. You've been in that magazine and then on TV this morning. You don't know what she might do."

I think I do, Chloe said to herself.

"I wouldn't worry about it, Lynette, but I appreciate you letting me know about her. I'll see everyone later, but call if anything important comes up."

Chloe sat with the cell phone cradled in her hand and

stared blankly out the windshield. She suddenly had the uneasy feeling that life was getting very complicated. But, more specifically, all of her hard work and determination to make something of herself, to overcome a grim childhood without any prospects could still come to nothing. Was she foolish to believe she was out of the woods and home free? That her life was really her own and nothing more could hurt her, because she wouldn't let it?

Her head fell back against the headrest, and she closed her eyes, wearily. Her business was thriving, but was it due to her own diligence or Kevin's innocent intervention? She was getting the kind of press that her business needed but which she didn't personally want. She had reinvented herself and created the life she'd always wanted, except for the untimely reappearance of a mother she no longer felt was her mother. And against all odds she and Kevin had actually come together, formed a relationship on their own. For all intents and purposes he was her boyfriend, her significant other, her lover. The very fact that it was happening still sometimes left Chloe breathless and in disbelief. She had the joy and luxury of evoking some of the recent time they'd spent together, out and about…or behind closed doors…that had been so memorable. Or…was she just another conquest for Kevin? Was she being used to further hone his skills as a ladies' man?

How was she going to separate fact from fiction or dumb luck from genuine opportunities? Could she know for sure her friends or lover? But Chloe also was starting to sense that, in a very real way, she had to be careful what she wished for. What *was* it going to take to make her happy?

Her cell phone rang again. It was Kevin.

"I watched you this morning. You did a fantastic job."

"Thank you. I can't tell you how nervous I was."

"It didn't show. As a matter of fact you looked pretty cool, and on point. *Never* let them see you sweat." He chortled quietly. "And you did a great job of shutting down Cassidy when she tried to get too personal. I know she was only doing her job, but I don't want our personal life used to boost her ratings."

Our personal life.

Chloe smiled. She *so* needed to hear that.

"She did invite me back. I think I want to pick someone else to return and represent homecoming. If I ever hear back from Beverly she would be perfect."

"I think Micah Ross would be better," Kevin added.

"Really? He is coming?"

"I don't know yet. But I'm going to find out. I promised you I'd get in touch with him, and I will. So where are you now?"

"Oh…" She glanced around the quiet safety of the interior of her car. It seemed to be the only place for the moment where she could feel totally alone. "I'm just leaving the studio to head over to Hollington. I have another checklist of things to do. The ground manager is complaining that the tents I want to set up on the Square will damage the grass. I may have to fight."

Kevin chuckled. "Go get 'em, Chloe. I'm betting on you."

She sighed. "I don't want to fight anybody."

"I know. You also said you don't make demands. I liked that. Listen, anything I can do to help?"

She could think of a few. Starting with having him make love to her again. Like he had that first time, when all he'd used was the gentleness of his voice and his clever fingers.

She shifted and squirmed in her seat. "I'm okay, but thanks for asking."

"Okay. Here's another question. When do I get to see you again?"

Now Chloe smiled, for real and with relief. Kevin had just said what she needed to hear, in that wonderful deep rumble of his voice that seemed to ripple down her spine. That's what he'd asked the first night she'd stayed with him. Actually, it had been the next night, after the day when she really knew she should go home, and he didn't want her to. She'd offered no resistance to speak of when Kevin had used his own unique method of persuasion...

It was the morning after the magical night of the two condoms. It turned out that was all they had between them, despite a rather desperate search on Kevin's part through medicine cabinets and dresser drawers.

"Chloe? Did you hear me?"

"I'm thinking." Chloe sighed, her recollections fading, feeling much better and more peaceful in the afterglow of them. "I don't know, Kevin. I have an event to oversee tonight. I can't say when I'll be finished."

"Tonight doesn't work for me, either. I promised a friend to help out with something. How about tomorrow night?"

She laughed. "Don't you have a club or two to run?

Don't you have groupies who would kill for a chance just to see you? Get a hug?"

"Don't go there," he threatened.

She wasn't worried. She heard the smile in his tone.

"I'd really love to but I have to keep my options open. The homecoming details are starting to come together and, unfortunately, there are problems cropping up here, there and everywhere. I've been spending as much time at the campus as I have at my office."

"Okay, breakfast. Look, you gotta give me something to look forward to."

"You sure do know how to say the right things," she murmured.

"Maybe. But I don't say them to just anyone."

Chloe stayed back at the very edge of the crowds, slowly pacing from one side of the large white space to the other. Behind a discreet screen the catering service was preparing another tray of finger foods to be served among the attendees of the gallery opening at Art and Soul, a new artists' space. On the other side of the screen an open bar had been set up where wine, beer, water and club sodas were being served. The lights were up full, which was better to see the artwork that hung on all the walls. Near the center of the space the artist himself, Hans Dexter, a teddy bear of a man with wild hair in serious need of a cut and a beard also out of control, held court. Unlike his fashionably dressed guests, which included collectors, he looked decidedly shabby but artistic and therefore cool. And just to make sure people were clear on his creative eccentricities, he was wearing a pair of dilapidated sandals that Chloe was convinced he'd owned since he was an undergrad at Brown.

After a moment she realized that there was someone in the room she recognized. Tamara Hodges. The attractive writer seemed to know many of the folks there—or she gave the impression that she did. She was a writer and a reporter, after all. It was obvious that with her friendly, open demeanor, her charm and ability to make people feel special, she was on the clock covering the opening for *Luster.* Catching her gaze at one point, Tamara waved a greeting to her.

"Shall we go ahead and open the champagne?"

She turned to the bartender. "No, wait a little longer. The artist wants to say a few words first. We'll save the champagne until he finishes."

The noise level made it nearly impossible to hold a reasonable conversation. Not a single note could be heard from a trio of young musicians playing a flute, an oboe and a harp. But they played with such concentration and earnestness that it didn't matter that none of the guests were paying any attention. They seemed to be playing for themselves.

The commissioned photographers were snapping the most beautiful, the most bizarre, the most entertaining of the guests and, of course, everyone tried to position himself or herself right next to the artist, because the picture was sure to make the social pages of the *Atlanta Journal-Constitution* on Sunday.

"What do you think of the work?"

Chloe grinned as she turned to Tamara, who stood next to her with her recorder and notebook. Chloe eyed them skeptically.

"Is this off the record?"

"Of course." Tamara dropped her equipment into her oversize purse.

"Not much. But I'm not being paid for my opinion. I didn't know you were going to be here."

"I hadn't planned on coming. I get so many invitations to these openings that after a while they all blur together. How are you? How's business?"

"Pretty good. To be honest, word of mouth has been so great that I don't think I can handle any new clients for a while."

Tamara wrinkled her nose and grinned. "I'm glad to hear that. You know, I was thinking about how many of us from our class went on to such success. What are the odds that so many students from one graduating class would do the college proud?"

Chloe let her gaze study Tamara, wondering where this was leading. "You have anyone particular in mind?"

Tamara shrugged, seemingly indifferent. "Well, of course there's Kevin. Stayton Investments is on the Atlanta Fortune 100 list, and he started that charity last year to help mentor young boys without fathers or other strong male role models in their lives. And Terrence Franklin. I know his career ended too soon, but I bet he's a shoo-in in a few years for the hall of fame. And then there's yourself and Kyra." Tamara looked down at the floor. "And Micah Ross."

Chloe knew she'd have to be blind not to notice the confusion and even underlying pain in Tamara's hazel eyes. She shook her head. "I don't know if he's coming or not."

"To be honest, I was out in L.A. this summer and… Micah and I saw each other."

"Really?" Chloe said, genuinely surprised and unable to hide it.

"I'm writing a series on up and coming Black talent in the music business. I arranged to interview a few who are signed on with Micah's label. It's hard to believe that he went from being a computer genius to a big-time music producer."

"Did you interview Micah, too?"

"Actually no." Tamara laughed nervously, her high-yellow skin betraying her blush. "I thought I'd get to interview him as well, but…it never happened. I got…a little off track. He never did say if he was coming in October."

"It's easy enough to find out. I could check to see if his RSVP to the reunion invitation was received."

Tamara shook her head, her smile clearly forced, and her eyes overly bright. "No, don't bother. If he comes, he comes."

So it's not over. After all these years.

Of course Chloe recognized that the very same thing could be said of her and her feelings about Kevin. The chances had been slim and none that they would ever get together in her lifetime. And yet, they had. Not only had her feelings for Kevin not changed since the days of her young crush but she knew they'd grown considerably deeply. But the realization had not brought her comfort so much as high anxiety. Was the thing going on between them really too good to be true?

"You know, I haven't spoken with Micah or e-mailed in a long while. My fault," Chloe confessed. "My last year in New York before deciding to return to Atlanta was very stressful. I was distracted. I dropped the ball. We lost touch."

"I know he considered you his best friend. I'm sorry he never considered me one," Tamara said.

Her despair was hardly concealed, and Chloe felt for her. But she had no chance to respond, to reassure Tamara that time heals a lot of wounds and ill feelings. What a hypocrite that would make her, she thought, as she considered her reaction to the return of Billie Burns in her own life.

There was a commotion at the door, a flurry of movement and a wild snapping of digital flash cameras.

"I better get into this," Tamara said, having pulled herself together. "Might be something I can use in the magazine."

With that she disappeared into the crowd. But Chloe quickly found out the reason for the sudden buzz. Standing in his own royal arena was Kevin. He politely greeted people he knew, allowed himself to be hugged and kissed, posed and photographed with them, as he inched his way into the room. The artist, Hans, bellowed out his own greeting and, dramatically throwing up his arms, burst through the crowd to wrap his arms around a startled but amused Kevin.

Chloe stood back and watched.

He was enjoying himself, she realized.

He liked being the center of attention, the golden boy, baby of the family…crown prince.

And then Chloe realized that he wasn't alone. As much as Kevin tried to accommodate everyone's pull on his attention, he was just as caring and solicitous of the young woman who was with him.

Chloe stood stone still, feeling as if the very life was running out of her. His companion couldn't have been more than eighteen or nineteen years old. She had amazing red hair and translucent flawless skin. Contradictory to her flaming hair she wore a deep red slash of lipstick on her mouth. She was tall and willowy, pretty but sullen. A model, Chloe guessed. And she held on to Kevin's hand as if her life depended on it. He made sure that the girl wasn't jostled or pushed aside. Everyone made room for the great man, the artist himself, who gave the young woman an equally exuberant hello.

Kevin's gaze began to roam the crowd. Eventually it settled on her. Chloe expected him to look stunned. Shamefaced. Embarrassed. Compromised. But instead Kevin's eyes seem to light up, and he smiled a smile that had become very familiar to her. She wasn't expecting him to be so open. Confused, she turned away busying herself with the details of seeing that twenty bottles of champagne were opened and poured.

"So this is why you couldn't see me tonight."

The caressing tone of his voice did not fail to leave its mark on her nerve endings. She took a deep breath and forced her face into an expression of calm surprise.

"At least I'm really working, as I said. What's your excuse?"

His brows shot up, and then he looked puzzled as he stared into her eyes, trying to interpret her words, her mood.

"Ouch," he murmured.

"Daddy wants you to come over."

They both turned at the girlish voice, and Chloe found the young redhead looking into Kevin's face. Close up she could see the girl was younger than she'd first imagined.

Kevin instantly gave his attention to the girl and smiled at her. He put his arm around her shoulder. "Okay, I'm coming. But I want you to meet someone first. This is a friend of mine, Chloe Jackson," he said to the girl.

"Hi," the girl said, not much interested. And then she blinked and regarded Chloe closer. "I saw you on TV. Kevin told me to watch. You looked great."

"Thank you. That's so sweet of you to say," Chloe said, completely caught off guard by the guileless comment.

Kevin stared into Chloe's eyes once more. "And this is Elizabeth, Hans's daughter. He asked me to escort her to the opening."

Kevin sat in his car for fifteen minutes with the motor running trying to decide if this was a good idea. Should he just show up on Chloe's doorstep demanding an explanation, or let it go? He wasn't even sure why, except for the very cool reception she'd given him at the gallery opening for Hans Dexter.

He'd known she was in charge of the reception for the show and thought to surprise her with his appearance. But that had been before Hans had commanded him to escort his daughter, and only child with his fourth wife, to his opening. If Chloe had been surprised that wasn't what came across in her dark eyes. It was…frankly, Kevin had no idea what to make of it.

He took a deep breath and gazed out toward Chloe's house, a lovely contemporary ranch-style house on a half-acre lot, well spaced from the other homes around her. There was a light on under the entrance eave, and one in an upstairs room. Another, not in the front of the house but in a room along the side. He could see no movement inside, and he felt awkward just sitting and waiting, as if expecting Chloe to walk past a window or open the door and find him there. But what if someone, a neighbor, thought he was casing the house, or was a stalker? What if someone called the police, in this exclusive little community, not recognizing his car or with any knowledge of what he was doing outside their neighbor's house? Silently watching with his motor running.

Kevin wanted answers. But really, he also wanted assurance that he hadn't done anything to upset Chloe, to hurt her. He'd figured out long ago that there was a vulnerability about her. It was exactly why he'd quickly come to feel so protective toward her. She was fearless in a lot of ways. But she could be hurt.

Impatiently Kevin shifted into drive and then slowly drove away. It was too soon for confrontation and indignation. Too soon to climb mountains made out of molehills. And maybe it was still too soon to know what he was really feeling for Chloe. But it was something.

Chapter 6

"Is it okay if I drop you off here?" Kevin asked, rolling to a stop and double parking.

"It's fine," Chloe said, preparing to climb out of his car.

"You sure?"

"I know how to cross the street by myself, and the building's right there." Her hand was on the door, but she turned to smile at him. "Thank you for lunch."

"My pleasure. Again, I'm sorry that we could never pull it off for breakfast a few days ago."

"Well, business is business. I understand. I'm sure you weren't expecting to open up so early for the mayor so he could have a private breakfast meeting at What It Is."

"No, I wasn't. But I did him the kind of favor that will have a payback down the road. I'm glad you could work it out so you could meet me for lunch."

He twisted in his seat and leaned to her. Chloe met him halfway, and they exchanged a quick teasing kiss. It reminded Kevin of what was good about being with her. The comfort and ease of being together. The total lack of female histrionics and drama. No pouting or attitude. As he tasted the soft giving of her mouth he also concluded that maybe he'd misunderstood the unexpected aloofness he'd felt with Chloe the week before at the gallery opening.

He stroked her cheek. "Chloe…"

She laughed lightly. "I know. When are you going to see me again."

He nodded.

"You're going to get bored with me."

He arched a brow. "Lots of things could happen, I give you that. Boredom is not on the list. Tonight?"

"I can't. I'm meeting with the volunteers for homecoming. I have to give everyone assignments and work out schedules and times. Some of the school officials will be there, so this is important."

"Anything I can do to help?"

She opened the door and put one leg out. "Yes. Get in touch with Micah!"

Kevin cringed, his expression contorting to indicate that he had forgotten his promise.

"I'm on it," he said.

Chloe smiled as she stepped back and closed the car door. She waved at him as she stepped in front of his Nissan 350Z to cross the street, jaywalking against traffic.

Kevin's cell phone buzzed and he answered, his attention briefly draw away from Chloe.

"Yeah? Hi, CB. I just dropped Chloe off and I'm on my way back. Yes, I still want to hold a staff meeting—" he looked at the dashboard clock "—set it up for two-thirty. Anything else?"

As he listened Kevin looked over his shoulder to the other side of the street to see if Chloe was still in sight. He expected to find her close to the entrance of her building, or just going through the revolving doors. But when he caught sight of her distinctive tiny polka-dot black-and-white skirt, and the crisp white sleeveless blouse she was wearing, she suddenly stood talking with someone.

"Uh-huh," he murmured so that CB knew he was listening.

But he was suddenly distracted and frowned at the scene unfolding near a row of potted *Ficus benjamina* trees that decorated the edge of the atrium. It was the appearance of the woman, her mannerisms and, even more important, Chloe's body language and expression that said there was more going on here than chitchat. In the upscale business area of downtown Atlanta the woman stood out as someone who had definitely seen hard times. She was very much out of place here.

What were they talking about?

The more Kevin stared, it came to him that he was pretty sure he'd seen this same woman before. Weeks and weeks ago, in that very spot. He didn't recall if Chloe and the woman had had an exchange, but he had the suspicion that the encounter he was watching was not the first time.

If the woman was just a habitual beggar he could understand if Chloe was moved to help out whenever she saw her, and he wouldn't have been the least surprised. What Kevin knew of her background showed that, for years, even as an undergraduate, Chloe had a sensitivity and commitment to help people less fortunate than herself, especially women and young girls. But something else was going on here.

"Ah...CB...look, this doesn't sound urgent. Let me get back to you."

Kevin put down the cell, his gaze still directed to the scenario across the street. He released his seat belt, having decided to see for himself what was going on, and to make sure that Chloe was all right.

She was shaking her head, holding up her hand as if to ward the woman off, make her stay back. The woman, for her part, didn't seem threatening, at least not physically. But she certainly appeared in need of help and was pleading a case for herself, given her gestures and expression and the wringing of her bony hands.

Just as Kevin was about to step out of the car Chloe opened her purse, took out money and thrust it into the open palms of the woman. The woman grinned her thanks profusely, as also indicated by her nodding head. Chloe then hurried to the building in a little run and pushed through the revolving door. Behind her the woman was still calling out her thanks. She counted her bounty while slowly walking away.

Kevin sat back and closed his door. And he continued to sit, watching the woman until she'd disappeared a few blocks away into the crowds. He picked up his cell and punched in Chloe's office number. But he hung up on the first ring. Suddenly, he didn't think it was necessarily a good idea to let her know he'd watched her and what had happened. Suddenly, Kevin sensed that it might be far more complicated than he had the information to understand.

"This box is done," Kevin said, lifting a cardboard file box and moving it to a table with other, similar boxes.

Each was filled with neatly alphabetized registration packets. They consisted of bright neon nine-by-twelve Lucite envelopes, that themselves contained copies of the homecoming schedule, program, instructions like guest house assignment, parking vouchers, tickets and passes. Everything the returning Hollington students needed for a successful reunion weekend at their alma mater.

Kevin put the box down and turned to watch Chloe. She hadn't even responded to his comment, and he knew she was deeply distracted. But frowning, he was unsure as to whether her concentration was all about the work at hand, or if there was something else on her mind. Usually happy to banter and spar verbally with him, and not giving much quarter, she had been unusually quiet since they'd arrived at the alumni offices, which was agreed to be used as a staging area for stuffing envelopes.

But even the afternoon before, when he'd called her at her office to confirm the meeting, Chloe had not really been present. Even teasing and baiting her had not gotten a rise out of her.

Something was wrong. Something was troubling her.

Is it me? Kevin had asked himself a dozen times. Were the homecoming details and a full-time job becoming overwhelming? Or did Chloe's pensive withdrawal have anything to do with that woman he'd seen her with outside her office? He was willing to bet it was the latter. If for no other reason than that he'd covertly sat and watched the two women meet and talk two additional times.

By then Kevin was worried and concerned.

Who was this woman, and what was her hold over Chloe?

"I could use something to drink. I think I'll check out the vending machines downstairs," he said to Chloe. "Can I get you something?"

She didn't answer, didn't even appear to have heard him.

Frowning, Kevin approached and gently touched her shoulder. Chloe started, her gaze wide on his face.

"What?"

"I was asking if you want something to drink. I'm going to the first floor."

She shook her head, "No, thanks. I'm fine."

Kevin wanted to argue otherwise but instead left her in the room with her other two volunteers from the committee while he went in search of the machines. But actually, he didn't do that right away, either. He waited until he reached the first floor and continued out the entrance and began strolling the narrow pathway that wound, in part, around the building. He took out his cell phone and keyed in a number.

"It's Kevin…I'm fine, CB…I'm still on the campus with Chloe…Yeah, I know I should be at the party tonight, but I wanted to hang around a bit…No, I haven't asked her, yet. She's smart, CB," he said dryly. "She'll get suspicious and want to know why I'm asking. I have a feeling she doesn't like asking for help. She's used to taking care of herself. Let's face it, she's done pretty good…I'll check in with you later tonight. I want to make sure Chloe gets home okay… Yeah, I will."

Kevin slipped the phone back into his pocket, more frustrated than ever. He was hoping that CB would have some news for him. Maybe it was too soon. It was only three days ago that he'd asked CB to come with him on his second surveillance of Chloe and the stranger. There was no guarantee that they'd actually see anything but, sure enough, the scenario that Kevin had witnessed by accident was being played out again. He and CB watched silently from his Nissan 350Z, parked discreetly a half block away.

He had not told CB anything about the meetings, but had only said that he wanted to show his assistant something. They'd had to wait about twenty minutes before Chloe appeared, wearily to Kevin's way of thinking, to approach the building and lower her gaze to the ground when she realized the woman was waiting for her, again.

"I want you to just watch," Kevin had said quietly to his assistant.

The scene was repeated as before. Except this time there was less of an argument from Chloe, more resignation. There was distinct distress in her fine features and the furrowing of her brow. But now Kevin could also detect anger and frustration.

The exchange lasted less than a minute. Chloe hurried into the building, and the woman wandered away.

Kevin sighed deeply and settled back against his seat.

"Well, what do you think?"

"She's being squeezed," CB said smoothly. "The lady is being hit up for money."

"Okay, I think I get that. Any idea why?"

"Blackmail, most likely. Why else? Secrets. Bad news. Information. Lies. Take your pick."

Kevin tapped his fingers in agitation against his steering wheel, and scowled helplessly out his windshield.

"You don't like what's happening to her, do you?"

Kevin was slow in responding. Thoughtful. He shook his head. "No, I don't think I do."

"The lady mean something to you?"

Again he took his time answering. He nodded. "Yeah. I think she does."

CB sat silent for a moment.

"She sure ain't like the others, don't mind me saying so."

Kevin chortled. "You noticed."

"I get paid to notice things, remember? Want me to check out the other one? Try to find out what she's up to?"

"If you can, I'll owe you big time."

"Don't worry about it. We're cool."

"I don't want Chloe to know, CB. Maybe I'm way off base."

"No problem. I'll be careful."

Kevin, still deep in thought, reentered the building. He was about to start up the stairs when he remembered his reason for stepping away. He went to the vending machine and perused the choices. He got something for everyone and then headed back. Kevin distributed the drinks to the appreciative thanks of the volunteers. He sat next to Chloe and gently took a pile of papers out of her hands and folders from her lap. He replaced the papers with a bottle of apple juice.

Chloe looked at him blankly, and then her gaze filled with warmth and a look that he'd grown to feel was reserved just for him. Her hair was pulled back in an unglamorous ponytail, and she wore no makeup. And she looked about eighteen years old. The exact way she would have looked, Kevin noted, when they were in school. Incomprehensible to himself, he was very glad he hadn't met Chloe then.

She smiled. "Thank you. I could use something to drink."

"Despite your comment to the contrary when I asked you ten minutes ago."

"Oh," Chloe murmured wryly. "Was I completely zoned out?"

"Totally. Want to call it a night?"

"No. We don't have that many nights left. If we can get the registration packets done tonight, I can move on to writing up a list of signs I need and give it to the print shop tomorrow. We need individual ID badges, and special ones for the children with cell-phone numbers printed as well, in case they get separated from parents. You know it's going to happen. Plus…"

"You're tired," he interrupted calmly. But had an ulterior motive in hinting at a work stoppage for the night.

"So's everybody else. And you've been really fantastic about helping me, Kevin. This is so way and above what you were asked to do."

"I did it for you. You can count on me, Chloe. But

don't think I'm not going to spend the capital I've earned."

She almost blushed. "Really? Want to give me a hint?"

"Absolutely not."

Then Chloe seemed to become completely aware of where they were and that they were not alone. She still gave him one more personal look.

"Thank you," she mimed again, silently.

Kevin leaned a little closer. "You can show me how much, later."

Chloe stepped into the stall and under the spray of water. She let it soothe her and cleanse away the cloak of worry that she couldn't seem to shake and that was becoming more and more oppressive. She braced her hands against the tiled wall, and the water hit her shoulders, massaging the tension and running it off down her spine, and over her buttocks.

She had begun sleeping badly, waking up in the night with images of Billie haunting her, with the fear of discovery making her almost nauseous, and the deep concern that everything she'd worked so hard for would be taken away. But the worst was imagining Kevin's reaction, his rejection, once he knew who she really was. She had come from the streets, didn't have a father and had never even known him. The name Jackson was his only legacy to her, but even Billie had admitted she couldn't remember what man had gotten her pregnant with Chloe when she was seventeen years old. Even her name, Chloe, had been a by-product taken from a pair of designer sunglasses Billie had somehow acquired. Chloe had been stamped in gold on an inside arm.

I'm completely made up. Not real. I don't belong anywhere, or to anyone.

That was the mantra that she'd been living with for weeks, ever since her mother had miraculously found her and succeeded in insinuating herself back into her life.

"Oh, God." Chloe moaned, letting the water spray her face.

What am I going to do?

"Chloe? You okay?"

She sighed. Then inhaled. "Yes, I'm fine."

After another moment the shower curtain slowly pushed back. She instinctively crossed her arms over her chest and glanced over her shoulder. Kevin stepped in stark naked behind her, his long, lean body filling the stall and crowding them together.

"Kevin! What are you doing?"

"Whatever I can to conserve natural resources."

"There's not enough room for both of us."

Moving her aside he got under the spray, turning around completely to get wet. Chloe let Kevin turn her around so that her back was to him.

"Let me," he said.

He found the sponge, soaped it good and began methodically, and with gentle thoroughness, to wash her body. Chloe let him do with her what he wanted. For that moment she wanted to give over all responsibility and just submit. She so needed someone to take care of her. For the moment. Until she could pull herself together and think straight again.

Kevin silently began on her back, from her nape down to her thighs, with an even circular motion. He made her lift her arms out and soaped each. Her sides, around to her neck and throat. Breasts and stomach. Pelvis. She stood with her eyes closed, feeling the pumping of her own heart in the trapped heat of the shower. Letting the telltale tendrils of desire pulse through her veins, swelling all her erogenous zones with languid desire.

Then, Chloe was aware that Kevin no longer used the sponge but his hands. His very large, capable, expert, sensitive hands. This time her moan was not from despair but from the depth of feelings of another kind. The carnal and physical kind. He pulled her back against his chest, and she felt his full and powerful erection against her buttocks and lower back. His hands were gently, erotically kneading her firm breasts. Her head fell back against his shoulder, and her arms reached behind to hold his hips. Just to hold him. Chloe gasped when one of his hands snaked down her body and eased between her legs. She whispered his name and didn't have the strength to disguise her need, desperation or pain.

"I'll make it better," he whispered hoarsely. He began to kiss and nuzzle her neck.

Even in the foggy state of her mind Chloe took Kevin's words to mean much more than their passion of the moment. Maybe because she so wanted to believe he really could make it better.

He turned off the water.

Water trickled down her face. It wasn't from the shower heat but air mixing with their body heat to create a steam bath. They were panting. Sweating. She almost couldn't breathe in the confined space.

Kevin pivoted her around into his arms and, holding her close, kissed her with a deep, hungry passion that disoriented her. She felt like she was going to fall.

He put his hands under her buttocks and lifted her off her feet. Chloe put her arms tight around Kevin's neck and held on. She wrapped her legs around his hips. Somehow he managed to step out of the shower stall with her in his arms. He got the door open, and their wet bodies were hit with a brutal wave of cold air from the open room.

"Kevin…hurry," Chloe urged.

They reached her bed, and together they fell onto it, Kevin on top. Their mouths were locked, and she didn't want to let go. She felt Kevin stretch and reach for the condom packet. She sighed into his mouth with relief. He was prepared. He was ready, too.

They were a tangle of limbs, twisting and rolling on the coverlet, hands stroking and caressing and clutching each other. Kevin finally succeeded in applying protection—and not a moment too soon.

They had dispatched with foreplay. There was no time for finesse. They were synchronized in joining their bodies and beginning the movements that would bring them both release and satisfaction. Yes, it was temporary. It would get them through the night. It was all either needed for now.

Kevin sat in the car alone, waiting. The engine was off, and so were his headlights. Anyone walking through the lot could easily have missed seeing him in the driver's seat, so he had the advantage. He didn't dare move his gaze from the building and its one entrance, through which an interesting parade of people continued to pass, or to loiter outside, smoking, shooting the breeze, laughing, even pretty openly paying for and passing out what could accurately be controlled substances.

He read the address on the paper CB had given him several hours earlier and compared it to the number on the building he was staked out across from. He had not driven his Nissan 350Z, which would have been an obvious contradiction in this neighborhood. Instead Kevin had borrowed CB's car, a modest Saturn SUV, unpretentious and easily ignored. A regular vehicle for errands and supplies.

It had taken almost a week to covertly gather the information, but CB had ascertained that the woman in question who routinely managed to collect money from Chloe lived here. It was a shelter for women in transition. They had either gone through rehab, graduated from a shelter or recently been released from jail as parolees. CB had learned that the woman, a Wilhelmina Burns, forty-eight years old, was on parole. She had served time for grand theft, possession and sale of stolen merchandise, forgery and passing bad checks. But her whole life had been a saga of bad choices in order to survive—dealing drugs, aiding and abetting. Hers had been an ugly, hard, dysfunctional existence.

But the most stunning revelation had been that, upon sentencing for her first conviction, Wilhelmina's child, a little girl of seven or eight, had been taken from her and made a ward of the state. The little girl had quickly passed into the Atlanta foster care system. Placed with a family, her records had been sealed.

Without any further details it had not been a stretch for Kevin to figure out that the little girl had been Chloe.

Kevin, staring at the changing group of characters in front of the building, suddenly sat straight and peered steady at one woman in particular. It was *her*. Wilhelmina Burns. He'd seen her better in daylight, but that didn't stop him from searching for anything in the woman's stature or face that he had also seen in Chloe. Something that would mark one as being connected to the other. The nose and shape of the face. Incredibly the same. It was enough.

Having found what he was looking for Kevin felt no need to stay longer. He didn't like being a voyeur. And now that he'd found out what he wanted he wasn't sure what he should do with the information. For a brief time two weeks ago, when he'd first decided to investigate, it was only with the purest of motives. He was concerned that Chloe was either being threatened or could be physically hurt. He wanted to protect her. Or save her.

But what, exactly, did he think he could do?

Satisfied that he'd pieced the puzzle together, Kevin started the engine, turned on the lights and drove slowly out of the lot. He didn't even glance in the direction of the building or the people standing around in front. At best this world held a bare tenuous connection to Chloe. Largely on her own she'd risen above her past.

More than ever Kevin was grateful for the pushing and prodding and unconditional love of the first ladies in his life: his mother, grandmother and older sisters. Together they had circled the wagons around him and encouraged, even demanded, he be a better person and have a more fulfilling life than his own father.

Kevin recognized how lucky he'd been. But his accomplishments didn't hold a candle to what Chloe had managed just by believing in herself.

Chloe put the secondhand suitcase into the trunk of her Acura RL car and slammed it shut. Then she quickly got into the driver's seat. Immediately she started the engine.

She wasn't alone, and it felt strange and unnatural. Having someone else share the space, the drive and her time felt very much felt like an invasion of privacy. This was the very first time she'd ever had a passenger, and that had been by design. She studied her mother, who was in the next seat. Billie, in a kind of childish awe, ran her hands over the smooth leather armrest, played with the sun visor overhead and boldly searched through the storage compartment between their seats.

"Please put your seat belt on," Chloe instructed her.

"This your car? It's so nice," Billie crooned, delighted with this new experience. "My baby got her own car!"

Chloe didn't answer, instead pulling into traffic when Billie had done as asked. It was late Friday afternoon, and she knew she was going to hit rush hour traffic. She'd always set her work schedule to avoid this, using her drive to and from her office as a period of needed time for silence and meditation. Then, the driving was easy and automatic and enjoyable. It had actually become nicer since getting involved with homecoming planning because many nights, by the time she was headed home, there was almost no traffic at all. Now that she and Kevin seemed to be an item, as her assistant Lynette liked to tease, many of the rules had changed and she had been forced, willing, to accommodate the time they spent together. On those nights she stayed with him or, just as often, he stayed with her.

This weekend she was doing neither.

Next to her Billie entertained herself with the changing scene outside her window, pointing out things that caught her attention and commenting or asking questions. But she quickly became bored with that and wanted to listen to music. She couldn't decide if she wanted the air-conditioning on or if she felt better with the windows open. And for the third time since Chloe had picked up Billie at her shelter, Billie wanted to know where they were going.

"Well, first we're going shopping," Chloe reminded her. "I think you need clothing that fits better than what you're wearing. We'll get whatever you need."

Billie nodded but frowned. "What else?"

"Then I thought we'd stop and get something to eat."

"I want to go to Captain D's restaurant," she demanded.

Chloe sighed. "Okay. If that's what you want," she agreed patiently.

"Then what we gonna do?"

"After we have some dinner we're going to my house. You're staying with me for the weekend, so we can get you ready for Monday. Do you remember what we're doing on Monday?"

"I forget."

"I found you a nice room all by yourself in a group home for women."

Billie shook her head vigorously. "No! I don't want to stay in no group house. They take your stuff."

"You said that's what people did at the shelter. I think the group home will be safer."

"No group home! They take your stuff."

Creeping along in traffic and boxed in by cars on every side, Chloe began to feel almost claustrophobic. Despite the comfortable coolness from the air-conditioning she opened her window and turned her face to inhale the exhaust-filled air.

"Look, we'll do this, okay? We'll just go and take a look at the home. And if you really don't want to stay there then we'll think of something else."

"Okay." Billie nodded, agreeable. "Then what else?"

"Your parole officer told you to find some work. Life would be a lot easier if you had a job and could make your own money."

Billie made a face. "Work?"

"I know it's a new concept," Chloe murmured sarcastically, speaking before she could think. "You wouldn't have to stay at the shelter or have anybody tell you what to do. Wouldn't you like that?"

Billie was silent for a few minutes, and Chloe hoped that the logic might actually sink in and make sense.

"I don't know. Working is hard. I'd have to take care of myself."

"Yes, I know. That's the idea," Chloe said.

She was discouraged by Billie's silence. Billie actually became sullen. But Chloe was grateful that the rest of the drive didn't require conversation. She could, for a little while, bury herself in her own thoughts. The uppermost of which was the fear that someone would find out about Billie and their relationship. It would get to the press, she'd become exposed and business would suffer. She'd lose customers and respect. She'd lose Kevin.

But did she really have him?

Chloe pressed her hand against her stomach, trying to calm the fluttering and churning and not become overwhelmed by the very thought. She'd been in love with him since she was just eighteen. Foolish, perhaps, but there it was. That happenstance, circumstance or that the gods had seen fit to grant her wish and bring them together had surpassed everything. That Kevin himself, as a man, was so much more in reality and not just in her dreams left her breathless but afraid. Because despite everything to the contrary, Chloe was still waiting with bated breath for the other shoe to drop.

Kevin had called the previous Tuesday morning and suggested they visit Centennial Olympic Park on Saturday, hang out for the day and maybe head to Little Five for music and dinner later on. She'd lied and told him she'd love nothing more but was a little behind on a project and needed to squirrel herself away. In that case, Kevin had replied he'd do the best he could to survive without her. She could not tell him that she had prior plans involving her mother.

Finally Chloe took the exit that led to the local mall. She decided they would shop a little bit first and then eat. She had to be firm and cunning with her mother in order not to walk away with clothing for Billie that was cheap, unattractive or inappropriate.

It was almost ten when they finally left the mall.

Billie fell asleep in the car. Chloe guessed that she was used to sleeping whenever she wanted and then staying up late into the night…or early morning.

Her cell phone rang. It was Kevin.

"Hey. How's it going?"

"Oh…okay," Chloe improvised, feeling guilty, and talking quietly to avoid waking Billie.

"Getting any work done?"

"Not tonight. I'm only now heading for home."

"Have you eaten? Can I bring you a doggy bag from the restaurant?"

She smiled. "That's sweet, but don't bother. I ate something quick a few hours ago. I just want to get some sleep."

"Alone?"

"Yes, Kevin. You know, we're not attached at the hip."

"Well, the hip connection is not exactly the place I had in mind."

"You're disgusting," she said and laughed.

"I don't know if I like the idea of not seeing you."

"Don't expect me to believe you were ever celibate and a homebody. I've seen the publicity pictures of you and every gorgeous woman in Atlanta. I've been there when your cell phone was burning up with incoming calls from old lovers. I don't want to be added to the list. It's too easy to be dropped and forgotten."

She thought maybe she'd gone too far with her teasing when he didn't answer right away. But Chloe knew she was only half teasing. It had begun to dawn on her that Kevin could get tired of her. He might throw her over. Much better to let him believe she could just walk away, too.

"I've been to the circus, Chloe. I'm no longer attracted to flash and magic and colored lights. I want the real deal, and I'm not going to settle for less."

"I thought we were talking about the weekend, just a few days," she murmured quietly.

"No. That's what *you're* talking about. *I* have something else in mind."

Of course, he didn't say what. But her speculations made the rest of the drive back to Grove Park pleasant, and dreamy and hopeful. And she couldn't wait for the weekend to be over.

Chloe had thought long and hard over where Billie was going to sleep for three nights. It seemed a bigger problem even than what she was going to do with her during the day. She finally decided on the home office on the first floor. There was a leather love seat sleeper and a bathroom right off the room. It would give Billie privacy and the run of the first floor. She would be near the kitchen, and she could help herself to whatever she wanted from the refrigerator. Better yet was the flat-screen TV. Her limited attention span made it the ideal entertainment and babysitter.

She gave Billie an abridged tour of the house, keeping to the main floor. Chloe didn't think she could get into much trouble down there. Her master suite and the two guest rooms were on the upper floor, and Chloe had already closed off the end of the hallway, making it far too much trouble to try and get into the rooms. Her room, at the top of the stairs, allowed her to see and hear noise from below or on the stairs. And her room could be locked.

It was after one in the morning when she finally said good night, exhausted and unable to stay awake any longer. It was clear that Billie was not going to go to bed and to sleep before she did. As she climbed the stairs to her room Chloe had a sudden vivid memory of the last time Kevin had stayed over, of their lovemaking and falling asleep in each other's arms. Of waking up to hugs and kisses and whispered endearments and languishing in bed. For a moment she wished she'd told Kevin her plans.

No.

Out of the question.

Chapter 7

"Micah. How you doing, man? It's Kevin Stayton."

"Kevin Stayton," the rich voice repeated lazily on the other end of the line. "Not *the* Kevin Stayton? The only Kevin Stayton I know was a resident heartthrob in college, but grew up to become one hell of a businessman."

Kevin's laughter boomed in response. "Yeah, you got it right."

"Ah…which part? The resident heartthrob or the astute businessman?"

"I only cop to the second. I'm getting too old to play the ladies' man."

"I doubt that. I read the glossy magazines. You get a lot of play. What's up? Haven't heard from you in a long time. Everything all right?"

"Yeah, everything's good. No complaints. How about yourself?"

"I'm making myself and a lot of talented Black singers obscene amounts of money. Five will probably get Grammy nods. I have one under contract for a TV series."

"Yeah, yeah, I assume all that. I'm talking about you? Seen any action?"

"By that I assume you mean arm candy? L.A. is, as they say, target-rich territory, but the women out here don't do it for me. And to be honest, it's been a rough summer, know what I mean? I just want to lay low and out of sight for a while."

"Sounds like something or someone's got you on the run, Micah. You're usually much too cool for that."

"I don't know, man. Maybe I'm tired. Maybe I need a break from all this. Who knows?"

"Well, the break we can do. One of the reasons I'm calling is to see if you're coming to the Hollington homecoming next month. And don't tell me you didn't get the invite, 'cause Chloe Jackson said you were on the list."

"I got it," Micah said with almost indifference. "Hadn't planned on going, Kevin. Not sure if it's my thing. Once I left Atlanta, I *left*. You can't go home again."

"Nobody's asking for all that, man. We just want to see you for a few days. Play catch-up. Drink beer and wine. Sing corny school songs."

Kevin could almost see Micah giving it careful consideration, as was his way. He never jumped into anything he wasn't sure he could get out of. Most of the time.

"Gee. Sounds like fun."

Kevin frowned. The voice was now perfectly flat. Micah was a fairly private man, even given the very high-profile entertainment line he was successful in. But he was rarely cynical, and that's exactly what Kevin picked up on. And even given that in school Micah had been known for being a brilliant but shy and geeky computer nerd, he had grown into a very cool guy.

"Hey! What's up with that? Where's your school spirit?"

"I left it behind when I graduated in 1999."

"Look, I'm going to be there. Remember Beverly Turner, homecoming queen? She's going to reprise her role at the parade. Terrence Franklin will be there. You know he's been offered the head coaching spot? Kyra Dixon, Tamara Hodges…"

"Did I hear you say Chloe Jackson? How's she doing? You know I *so* owe her a call. We were good friends back in the day."

"Chloe is…she's one heck of a lady. You know she's planning the whole reunion thing. Really knows what she's doing and has great ideas."

"Ooh. I hear admiration. And something else. What's going on, Kevin? The last time you got this excited about a woman she had thirty-six-triple-C cups."

Kevin laughed sheepishly. "Naw, man. I don't play that anymore. Like I said, I'm over it. I'm looking for something more, know what I mean? I didn't even remember Chloe from school, but we met back in July and…it's been pretty special. I like her. I like her a lot."

"Wow. And I don't even take confession on Saturdays. So, you finally met Chloe. I wish I was the fly on the wall when that happened."

"What do you mean by that?"

"Umm. I don't think I'll tell you. But I will say this, so listen up. Chloe *is* very special. She's smart, and she works hard and she doesn't play games, either…and I would bet she's still vulnerable. She's tough, but I know she can be hurt. I don't want to see her hurt, Kevin. I like you a lot but I will kick your—"

"Where the hell is that coming from? What makes you think I'd hurt her? Is there something I don't know? I always thought you two were just good friends."

"We are. I consider her my very dear friend. She's there for you when you need it. She doesn't ask a lot of questions, or preach, or say I told you so when you mess up. And she doesn't judge people. That's a talent unto itself. She had it real hard growing up. In fact, it sucked."

"I know," Kevin acknowledged quietly. "She's actually told me a little about it." He decided not to reveal how much. He knew about her mother purely by accident. He didn't believe that it was the kind of thing that Chloe would want anyone to know, even Micah.

"So, you two dating, or what?"

"Well, as a matter of fact, yes. For a couple of months now, and…and it's getting intense."

"Intense like you think you love her, or intense that she's wearing you out?"

Kevin laughed again. "You know, I almost forgot that for someone who used to be kind of shy you don't pull any punches."

"I expect my friends to be just as honest with me. So which is it?"

"Micah, being with her is great. You can actually talk to her about things. She makes me laugh. She's not coy, thank God. And she has no problems with sending me home if I get on her nerves or she has something else to do. She's not a clinger."

"So, you love her."

Kevin sighed. "I don't know. I don't think I've ever been in love before. In *lust?* Yeah, a lot of times. It just feels different. I miss her when we're not together. But…I'm careful. I nearly got burned real good a couple of years ago."

"Really? How?"

Kevin sighed. "You know. Got blown away by this woman. She was all that, but I should have looked deeper."

"Beyond the big cups and the perfect hair."

"You got it. Before I know it she's pregnant and claiming the kid's mine. Well, it might have been, but I got suspicious. I insisted on a paternity test. Man, I started getting all kinds of threats from her family. But I won the case. Ever since then I look before I leap."

"What about Chloe?"

"She takes care of herself. We take care of it. I can really relax. Do I sound pitiful?"

"No. You sound like a man who might be in love. I'd like to know when you figure it out. As long as you don't mess with her."

"I hear you," Kevin murmured, amused and surprised.

"What else can I help you with besides sage romantic advice?"

"Need a favor. On Saturday night of the homecoming there's going to be a tenth anniversary dance party at Bollito, my downtown Atlanta club. Chloe arranged it."

"Did I also mention that she's persuasive?"

"I got that," Kevin said dryly. "Now I know you have this hot new singer named Justice Kane. Any chance you could get him to perform that night? Thirty minutes would make the folks very happy. An hour would bring down the house."

"Yeah, I can do that."

"I didn't think you'd be so easy."

"I'm not agreeing for you. This is for Chloe. You said she's in charge of the planning, right?"

"However you want to do it as long as it happens. Thanks, man. We both owe you."

"Glad I can help out. I've been thinking about the invitation…tell you what. I might want to come after all."

"That would be great. I won't say anything yet if you don't want me to."

"You might not be able to keep that promise. The thing is, Kevin, if you can guarantee that Tamara Hodges will be there, then I'll come."

For the moment Kevin could not begin to guess why, of all their classmates, Tamara would be the deal breaker on his attending.

Everyone has secrets.

"Tamara Hodges?"

"That's right."

"Okay. I'll see what I can do."

When Kevin finished the call with Micah he immediately felt restless and lonely. His office was in an area of the restaurant that was not accessible to the public. Anyone wanting to see him had to be announced and escorted back. That's what CB was for. As he recalled his conversation with Micah he wondered if he should have been so frank about that paternity suit four years ago. He'd still been young, cocky and stupid and it had scared him good. But only a handful of his friends or even his family knew the details. The woman involved had tried to make a public case for herself and to embarrass Kevin. The commotion faded quickly when he was proven not to be her baby's daddy.

It was quiet, and he could hear no activity from the lounge or restaurant. He thought briefly of going out to the table that was always reserved for him, whether or not he was with a guest, and being served a light dinner. But he wasn't into eating alone tonight. And he wasn't up to going to one or two of the clubs to check out the action. Not for cruising purposes but to see how business was doing. It then suddenly occurred to Kevin that, since he and Chloe had become friends and lovers, he hadn't given any thought to looking for another woman.

Which brought him back to Micah's question. How serious was he about Chloe?

Kevin noticed the file folder on his desk marked "Homecoming." For want of anything better to do he opened it up and began leafing through the accumulation of information. There was the invitation to the weekend and a letter from the alumni director, stating that valedictorian Chloe Jackson was planning the event. He frowned. How had he missed reading that the first time? Before he'd actually met Chloe.

There was the program, several hundred of which he'd helped her and her committee stuff into plastic envelopes, along with coded maps of the campus and all the buildings, and a schedule of daily events and where they were to be held.

There was a photocopy of the yearbook page of Chloe delivering her speech, and the more recent one he'd torn from *Luster* magazine that had been shot without their knowledge. Kevin examined the photo, again taken with how natural they seemed with each other. The picture had managed to capture something in their faces as they smiled at each other that seemed so right.

And, unbeknownst to Chloe, he'd also managed to get a copy of a photograph that had been snapped at Hans Dexter's gallery opening. Although some of the pictures had actually been of guests, he'd asked for copies solely because of Chloe's image in the background, standing quiet, watchful and, as usual, in some simple but fashionable dress or ensemble that showed good taste and personal style. So, it was ironic that at the bottom of the pile lay CB's handwritten notes about Chloe's natural mother, Wilhelmina Burns. Just a few days ago CB had reported that he had not seen the woman either at Chloe's workplace or the shelter recently.

He abruptly closed the folder and left his hand flat on the top, as if to keep it closed.

Nothing had been resolved, as far as he knew. Chloe might still be giving her mother money, out of guilt, to keep her quiet, to help her out. Who knew? But he was still worried about her.

And right now, he really missed her.

For just a moment Kevin actually thought of overriding her pleas for the need to get some work done at home. A smile played around his mouth. Maybe he should surprise her. Have the kitchen put together a nice boxed dinner with a bottle of wine. They both liked merlot. Better still, champagne. Chloe liked carrot cake. He'd make sure a couple of fat slices were included.

Then he smiled at the recollection of her accusing him of trying to get her fat. No chance of that. She was disciplined and careful, and her lithe, nicely proportioned body showed the results. He closed his eyes, and there was a very vivid and explicit recall of the last time they were together and made love. He suddenly sprang forward in his chair and cleared his throat.

"Better not go there," he muttered. It was probably not a good idea to let that scene play out in his mind, he thought.

His phone rang, and Kevin snatched it up, hoping that it was Chloe, giving in and calling him to her.

"Hey. I knew you'd…"

"Kevin, is that you? It's Sharon."

"Well, hello. This is a nice surprise." Kevin smiled.

He recognized the voice of his oldest sister. Then he immediately became alert. It was late. Her voice seemed…

"What's going on? Everything okay? How's Mom?"

"We're all fine. Mom said I should call you. Daddy died a few hours ago. He had a stroke."

Chloe closed the door to the laundry room and headed down the hall. She was greeted and accompanied by the bass and high-volume background music, dialogue and special effects of whatever program Billie was watching on the flat screen. As she passed the door to her office, where she'd installed Billie, Chloe closed it. It helped, somewhat, in drowning out the noise but not enough to make it go away.

She'd avoided looking in to see if Billie was okay, as she did on Friday night and most of Saturday. But by Saturday afternoon there was no point. Billie seemed perfectly content never to leave the room, insisting on even eating her meals there and playing the TV practically 24/7. The good news was that Chloe didn't have to do a thing to try and keep her entertained, and she always knew exactly where Billie was. Her time was free to actually get the work done that she'd used as an excuse not to see Kevin that weekend. The bad news was Chloe herself wasn't sure she could last another day with the constant background of noise. It felt like being trapped forever in a movie theater with some over-amplified movie on a repeating loop. And someone constantly going back and forth to the bathroom or concession stand—her kitchen.

Chloe went into that very room and saw that it was still fairly clean and organized. That morning she'd had to run her dishwasher just for glasses alone. She'd gotten up to find spilled orange juice on the counter, two different opened boxes of cookies and a broken plate. While Billie slept, as she had until nearly two in the afternoon, Chloe had sat alone drinking coffee at the center island counting the remaining hours until Monday morning, and beginning to seriously doubt the outcome of her mission.

Now she realized that the answering machine on the counter indicated messages from missed calls. Given the thumping sounds from her office Chloe wasn't a bit surprised she hadn't heard the phone. One call was from Kevin, the night before.

"Chloe. It's me. Listen, I'm not calling to interrupt you or your plans or anything but…I wanted to let you know that…ah…something's come up back home. I'm flying out early tomorrow morning. My sister called to let me know…my…my father passed away. So…I gotta go take care of whatever I can. You know."

There was an audible sigh on the message that made her ache with sympathy. She could well imagine Kevin, see his expression, know exactly how he was sitting as he made the call and left her the message.

"I was hoping to talk to you before I leave. I tried your cell phone. I needed to…well…anyway." He cleared his throat. "We'll talk when I get back. I'm not sure when, yet."

And then was the part that Chloe felt deep in her heart, separate from the sad news because it was just for her.

"I miss you. Bye."

It wasn't just the words. She felt breathless at the depth of emotion that came through so clearly in just three words. *I miss you.*

Chloe sighed in frustration because she'd missed both of his calls. She hadn't used her cell in two days and knew the battery probably needed recharging since it hadn't rung. She resisted the urge to replay the message again. At the same time, Chloe knew what he must be going through.

With nothing else much to do Chloe continued to review her punch list for the October weekend. There was now a definite shape and form to the weekend. She could mentally walk, day by day through all the planned activities, check to see if enough time had been given to the start and finish of events, and time in between to allow the attendees to go from one to the other. It was far too early to start tracking the weather forecast, but Chloe also came up with workable contingent plans in case it rained for the Saturday tailgate party, or the Sunday brunch on the lawn of the Square.

She was thrilled when she got the call from Kyra and then one from Beverly Turner Clark herself, confirming that Beverly would ride on a float in the Sunday parade.

"I'm so glad to hear that, Beverly," Chloe told her, relieved.

"I got tired of Kyra fussing at me," Beverly had said with caustic humor. "She's so persistent."

"I know what you mean. You know you really don't have to do anything but sit and wave. You can choose your own gown to wear, and I know it will be fabulous, I'm sure something of your own design. There's not a thing you have to worry about. Just come and be queenly." Chloe grinned.

"Well, I haven't felt very queenly in years. It's been rough. I've had some rough times."

"I understand," Chloe murmured.

She only knew some of the tragic details of what had happened to Beverly, one of the most beautiful and popular girls on campus. She was tall and statuesque, and from one of Atlanta's prominent Black families. But she had not used that as leverage for special privileges and favors on campus. Beverly had fit in.

Not like me, Chloe said to herself.

"If you have any questions or concerns you know

you can call me. I'll do whatever I can to make this easy and fun. That's the important thing. I want you to have a good time."

"Kyra said you've been great to work with. She said Chloe don't play. She asks you to do something you better do it, or she'll want to know the reason why."

"She makes me sound like a witch."

"I'd say she admires you. You know, I remember you were valedictorian when we all graduated. But I'm sorry we never knew each other on campus. Maybe we can make up for it from now on. I know you have a business here, so I guess you're planning on staying in Atlanta."

"Seems so. But who knows what could happen down the road. Things change. Things happen."

"Yes." Beverly sighed. "And don't I know it first-hand."

When her phone rang just after noon on Sunday morning there was only one person Chloe really wanted to hear from.

"Hello," she answered.

"It's Kevin."

"Oh, Kevin. I got your message. I'm so sorry."

"I appreciate that."

"I'm glad you called. Are you okay?"

She hated that she couldn't think of anything more original to say. She was afraid that he wouldn't hear that she genuinely felt and understood what he was going through. Chloe knew it was probably a number of things.

"Very tired. I just got home from the airport from Philly."

"Is there anything I can do?"

"Glad you asked. I know you had your time all scheduled to get some work done. Uninterrupted. How's it going?"

Chloe was relieved that she could be totally honest with him. "It's been very productive. I settled a lot of details for October and finally heard from Beverly. She'll be our homecoming queen. But you never finished…"

"I really want to see you. I need…"

"You don't have to explain. I'll be there. I'm on my way right now."

But Chloe held the phone even after the call ended, trying to think how she was going to pull this off. What was she going to do about Billie?

She went to the room that Billie was using and quietly dared to peek in. Billie was buried under the sheets, not even her head visible. She was curled in a fetal position, asleep. The room was pretty much a cluttered mess and, for now, Chloe didn't care. It had been remarkably easy to handle Billie given her short range of interests. There was evidence that she'd explored all of the first floor and had even gotten into the backyard. But she was confident that Billie had not even gone up to the second floor. In any case Chloe believed she would have seen or heard her since hers was the first room on the second level.

Would it be okay to leave Billie alone?

She looked at the time. Almost one. It would take her at least twenty minutes to a half hour to get to Kevin's house. If she stayed an hour or two she could be back by four. Five, at the latest.

But what would Billie think or do if she got up and didn't find her?

But Chloe knew it wasn't as if Billie sought her out or expected Chloe to keep her company. She seemed only to want to eat, watch TV and sleep. The day before, Saturday, there had been almost no contact between them at all. No conversation. Like strangers simply occupying the same space.

We *are* strangers, Chloe considered bluntly.

Although she continued to consider the realm of possibilities, Chloe already knew she was leaving. She had to go to Kevin.

She wore a pair of olive drab capri pants and a pale yellow button-down fitted linen blouse. Her hair was loose and down, and she didn't even take the time to comb or style it. She roughly tousled the locks with her hands, slipped on a pair of ballet flats, grabbed her purse and keys and left.

She couldn't wait to see Kevin again. They'd only been apart four days, but the time and distance had added perspective and insight about their relationship. There had been a loss during that time, and it changed some of the emotions they might be feeling. For her part, Chloe realized that she was concerned and anxious but happy they would see each other again. It wasn't until he'd been forced away that she fully realized how much a part of her existence Kevin had become. And when privately confronted with what her feelings meant, love was the word she had in her head.

After her futile attempts to communicate with Billie over the past few days Chloe had wished desperately that he had been available to talk to. Not about Billie but about anything else. He would have made her laugh. And, like now, she might have figured out how they could be together for a little while, without blowing her cover about her houseguest.

Chloe parked her car in the garage space next to Kevin's car. With easy familiarity she entered the little side gate and entered the house.

"Kevin? It's Chloe," she shouted out, always careful not to take liberties by just walking about unannounced.

There was no answer, and the house was very quiet. But she found a lightweight jacket and an overnight leather tote bag inside the door, where he'd apparently left them.

Chloe quietly climbed the stairs to Kevin's room and saw his clothing discarded on a chair, his shoes on the bathroom floor.

He'd gone running.

Chloe opened the French doors to the balcony off Kevin's master bedroom. Below was a deck off the living room that was twice as large. Both overlooked a man-made lake bordered on the far bank by an even row of trees. It was a beautiful setting early in the morning and late at night.

She positioned the two lounge chairs and the table on the balcony, got fresh towels and set them aside. Made other preparations in the room that would make him comfortable, and then went downstairs to wait. She was just turning from the refrigerator when the door opened and Kevin appeared. Sweaty, a little short-winded, and with a strong scent of masculine energy and body heat.

He saw her right away, and she was already smiling and walking to meet him. He seemed taller to her, if that was possible. The shadow of hair on his face seemed stark against his skin, and he seemed almost dangerous. She held out the bottled water, and Kevin accepted it. But he was staring at her hard with hunger, relief and something else in his eyes. It held her mesmerized.

Kevin put the bottle down on the counter and reached for her. Chloe willingly went into his arms, and he crushed her to him. His running clothes were soaked through. And everywhere else she touched the skin was warm and damp. When he kissed her it wasn't desperate or hard but a kind of careful tenderness in which he relayed his feelings.

I'm so glad you're here.

Not a word was spoken, but their embrace and kiss pretty much said everything. For a long moment all Kevin did was hold her, his hands holding and working and kneading her body. She could feel the emotions of the last twenty-four hours in the heat of his breath on her neck and cheek.

"I'm glad you're back," she whispered, breaking the silence.

In response, Kevin grabbed his water in one hand, took hers in the other and led the way up to his room. She'd left the balcony doors open, and there was a gentle breeze rolling in that was cooling. Kevin headed out and stood drinking the water. He inhaled a deep breath, let his head fall back and closed his eyes, as if clearing his senses.

"Will you mind if I just get in the bed for a little bit?"

Chloe stroked his back. "Whatever you want, Kevin. Come on. Back inside."

As he returned to the room he was already peeling off the wet shirt and pushing off his running shorts. His thighs and butt and the muscles bordering his spine were taut and toned and defined, flexing with his every move. He grabbed one of the towels she'd left out and quickly rubbed himself dry. Dropping it on the floor he collapsed in the bed, sprawling on his back. She watched as he lay there and he released his tension. He looked at her through the narrow slits of his eyes. Under his gaze Chloe silently undressed and joined him naked in the bed. Kevin held up an arm to welcome her, and she positioned herself with her body along the length of his side, her hand on his chest.

He kissed her forehead, covered her hand with his own and, with a final exhale, was instantly asleep.

Chloe lay still and awake. She, too, felt herself relaxing, only then realizing how much tension she was holding in from the last few days. She quickly put Billie out of her mind. She was here with Kevin, where she really wanted to be. She closed her eyes but didn't sleep. She just enjoyed lying like this with him.

In twenty minutes Kevin moved, coming awake. What started as a stretch of his long limbs turned into something else as he carefully rolled his body toward her, his penis stretching and stiffening. He pulled her properly into his arms. Chloe tilted her head back and let him find her mouth. She was almost on her back, and his knee settled between her legs, pushing them apart.

"Kevin," she whispered in understanding, in solidarity. Her nipples were stiff little peaks.

But he didn't forget, and she waited patiently while he readied himself. She boldly stroked his length and momentarily distracted him but got the desired effect. He was stiff and hard when he turned back to her.

The minute Chloe felt the tip of him searching to

enter her she became limp with desire, panting in anticipation of him being completely inside her. Their lovemaking was sweet and slow, the pleasure drawn out and their release held back for as long as either could bear. She loved it when she came first, because she stayed sensitive long enough to ride out Kevin's climax with equal pleasure. Then they cuddled for a little while longer.

Chloe showered and dressed first and went back to the kitchen while Kevin did the same. When she returned he was back on the balcony sitting in a chair, resting with his hands locked behind his head, staring out over the grounds.

"Here," she said, handing him a dish of ice cream.

Kevin looked stunned and then chuckled at the surprise, taking the dish filled with rum raisin.

"Nice idea. Thanks."

Chloe sat in the other chair with another dish. They began eating and enjoying the cool treat.

"Would you believe I can't remember ever having ice cream when I was little. Not until I went to live with the Fields."

Kevin glanced at her with an odd expression, but she didn't mind sharing this one memory with him. It was a good one.

"If I got upset about something, wasn't feeling well or was just feeling sad and quiet, they gave me a dish of ice cream. It was like a magic potion or something. Give me ice cream and life was good."

"I didn't know you were so easy to please," he commented.

She shook her head. "I'm not. But back then I had nothing, so it didn't take much."

Kevin was staring at her for so long that she frowned at him, wondering what was going on in his head. She finished her ice cream and put the dish on the table. She reached out and caressed his thigh.

"Are you okay?"

Kevin sighed and sat back in his chair, also having wolfed down the ice cream.

"Yeah, I'm okay. My father had a stroke. It was sudden and massive, but no one knew for more than a day."

"Oh, Kevin," she murmured in horror and sympathy.

"When my sister Sharon called with the news, my immediate reaction was, I'm not going. The man is nothing to me. I hadn't seen him in maybe ten years, never heard from him. Why bother?"

"Why did you change your mind?"

Kevin closed his eyes, his brows furrowed. "'Cause if I didn't it was going to haunt me. I was going to be angry every time I thought about the man. I didn't want to live the rest of my life that way. I wanted it done. Over." He looked at her calmly. "I went to say goodbye."

"Did it help?"

"Yeah. I think so. Right now I'm still tired, but I'm glad I went for the service. He's being buried today. I didn't want to stay for that."

"Still, it must have been hard for you."

Kevin chortled, stretching out his legs and suddenly yawning.

"Probably the same for you and your mother."

Chloe froze. Her body went on the alert, and the lethargy of love and comfort she was basking in vanished instantly. She felt like the nerves and wires of her brains had just shorted out, and she was cold.

"What did you say? What about my mother?"

Kevin seemed to collapse, dropping his head with his chin on his chest.

"What about my mother?" She raised her voice. "What do you know about her?"

"Chloe…"

She stood up. She could tell by the tone of his voice, the careful enunciation of her name. She expected him to tell her to calm down next.

Anger welled up in her. And it was equally as strong as a fear of exposure and the pain of disappointment.

"How did you find out about her? Oh, my God. Have you been following me? Spying on me?"

He stood up. "Not on purpose. Not deliberately, Chloe. It was a coincidence that I saw you and this woman together one day. She looked rough, and I was concerned about you…"

"What did you do?" she asked tightly, stepping back from his attempt to touch her.

"Listen to me! I was worried about you. You're in the public eye. I know you hate that, but it comes with the territory. You're successful, you've been seen in the press. People recognize you. I thought maybe the woman was tapping into your sympathy and wanted a handout."

She stared at him, unable to show any understanding or forgiveness for the fact that he'd peeled back the scab on a wound that refused to heal.

"Why didn't you just ask me? Why did you sneak around getting into my business?"

"I'm pretty sure you wouldn't have been honest with me. Yes, I know the woman is your birth mother. In fact Chloe, I know more about her than you can imagine. Why? Because I wanted to make sure she wasn't capable of doing you bodily harm. I was trying to protect you."

She whirled on him and, judging by the stunned and apologetic expression on Kevin's face, knew he was witnessing the full range of what she'd endured her whole life. It couldn't be a pretty sight, but she was helpless to control it, and she was so angry that he had to see her this way. It was over. Everything was ruined, and it was Kevin's fault for peering into her locked box of secrets.

"You can't protect me. No one has ever been able to do that. I have no family. My background is a mystery. I'm nobody. And no matter how hard I work I'll *never* overcome that, Kevin. People will always throw it up to me.

"That's why I kept to myself in college. I didn't want anyone to know that…that I was practically homeless. I didn't belong anywhere!"

Chloe was in a fit of anguish. She couldn't seem to stop the flow of words. They flew out of her mouth all by themselves. Thoughts tumbling one on top of another. She swung away from him trying to hold herself together.

She wasn't going to cry.

She wasn't going to cry.

Kevin was right behind her. He took hold of her upper arms, holding firmly. She jerked away.

"Chloe, stop. This is not about you. You're fantastic! You're beautiful and strong! You're not responsible for your mother or what she is. That's why I went to my father's funeral. His life was sad, but it wasn't my fault!"

She turned and rushed back into the room, headed out the door and hurried to the staircase. He was right behind her. She ran down.

"It's not the same, Kevin. You had other people to nurture you and love you. I was alone."

"Right, and you survived a bad start. Like me and my father, there's nothing you can do for your mother."

"I have to try!" she screamed. "You don't understand. I have to."

She shut out anything else Kevin was saying. Chloe didn't know what she would do if he tried to comfort her again, to touch her. She was afraid she was going to lose it altogether. She found her purse and her keys and headed for the door.

"Don't run away. Talk to me, dammit!"

Chloe, as he knew her, was gone. She had reverted to the young girl who felt it was her against the world. It was going to take her a while to get beyond that defense again. And she had to do it alone.

She got into her car and backed out so fast from the garage that she nearly hit a car driving by behind her. The driver blew his horn, and she hit her brakes with a screech. She heard Kevin calling her. Chloe continued backing up, shifted into Drive and shot off down the street, demons from her past hot on her trail.

Chapter 8

"You want me?"

Kevin sighed wearily and glanced up at CB, who stood quiet and stalwart, as usual.

"Yeah. Have you heard or seen anything?"

"'Bout Ms. Chloe? That woman's not coming around no more to bother her. I drove by her house the other night, just to make sure. She seems okay. Keeping to herself. The only place she goes is to work or to the college. She's there most nights late. Want me to keep watching?"

"No, I don't think so. I just wanted to make sure she was safe."

"You two broke up?" CB asked.

Kevin smiled ruefully. "Looks like it."

"Too bad. If you want my opinion you belong together."

"Thanks. I feel the same way."

"What you gonna do about it?"

"Nothing for now. She needs some space. But I'll think of something."

"Good." CB nodded and left.

Kevin smiled to himself after CB had gone. A man of few words, but every one of them counted.

For a moment he was distracted from his main concern to his recurring curiosity about his self-appointed "assistant." He'd never pried into CB's background. It was enough to have learned that he was fiercely loyal, completely dependable, and Kevin trusted the man with his life. He'd never known if it was gratitude on CB's part because Kevin had found a job for him when it was clear that he had no obvious skills or talents. But CB, with his own quiet ways and hard work, showed he had talents that were invaluable and had served Kevin well since they'd met.

The most significant had been the attack he'd suffered, cornered on a deserted street on the wrong side of Atlanta, one night as he'd left Flavor for home…

Unusual for the time, he'd been alone, having decided he wasn't up to dealing with any of a half-dozen women who would easily have submitted to his request that they join him for the night.

So when the black SUV behind him suddenly sped alongside and then sharply cut him off, nearly causing a collision, Kevin knew something serious was going on. He glanced around for an escape. There was none.

Three men moved so fast from the other vehicle that he'd had no chance to capture a clear image of any of them. No request to open the door. They used a metal pipe to smash through his driver's-side window, reaching in and opening the door.

The odds were definitely against him, but Kevin had decided that whatever the outcome he wasn't going down like a chump. It was *on!*

Fists blocking and punching, he stayed on his feet and tried to keep the three men in front of him. But they had the pipe, and they were using it. He blocked the first blow with his hand and felt the bones in his wrist give way. He took a hard punch to the head and chest.

Then he saw another set of headlights drive up on the scene and thought it was over. More armed men to finish the job. In that moment Kevin was truly scared.

What the hell was going on?

Why me?

He was on his knees. He couldn't hold out much longer.

Thank God he didn't have to.

He heard CB's voice. He was alone, but he approached the scene of three men bending over him fearlessly. He started swinging. He was bigger than any of the others, and he was relentless, putting his body and bulk behind each hit. Kevin remembered that he'd fallen to the ground panting in relief, clutching his throbbing wrist and tasting the blood that ran from his mouth.

Then he heard a pop—a gunshot. And then the smashing of glass, cursing, shouts.

"Get in the car! Get in the car! *Move!*"

Doors slammed, and the SUV sped off down the street quickly disappearing around a corner.

"You're okay, man. Come on. Get up," CB urged, not even out of breath, and as calm as ever.

"CB. Man, am I glad to see you. Did…did you recognize any of those guys?" He was on his feet, being helped to CB's car.

"Couldn't see their faces. I bet it's all about that girl that said you're her baby's daddy. You told me she and her family said they're going to get even. Good thing I was right behind you. I wondered about that car following you."

Kevin sighed deeply, with relief and pain, once he was in the front seat of CB's car.

"You probably saved my life. Why'd you come after me?"

CB started the car, calmly turned it around and headed to a local hospital that they both knew was about three miles away.

"You left your cell phone at the maître d's desk. I knew you'd be ticked off if you didn't have it until tomorrow night…"

Kevin could calmly recall the whole incident now, because it had had a good ending. But he really had no idea how to deal with Chloe and her stubborn, if understandable, defensiveness and pride. One thing he did know. Just like that awful night on that deserted street, he wasn't going down without a fight. Chloe meant that much to him.

The office door opened, and Peg stepped in holding several sheets of paper.

"Sorry to bother you. You got a minute?"

"Sure. What's up?"

"Where did this contract come from?" She handed it to him.

Kevin glanced at it quickly and handed it back.

"That's for the second Saturday in October. I'm letting Hollington College book Bollito for a dance party for their reunion."

"There's a problem, Kevin. You can't. There's another contract."

"What contract? For Bollito?"

"Yes. Don't you remember you agreed to a corporate party that night. They're expecting a turnout of about six hundred people."

"I don't recall any of this," Kevin said, frowning. He snatched the two contracts back and began reading carefully. "How did this happen?"

"Well, to be honest, you spoke with the CEO of the company, agreed to the plan and turned it over to me to draw up the contract. So you never really had anything more to do with it. But you never told me about your deal with the college. That second contract is not from us but from them. I'm only just seeing it now. Bollito is double booked, and both events are less than a month away."

Kevin read every detail of both contracts. When he was done he cursed quietly under his breath. Then he nodded to Peg.

"Thanks, Peg. This is not your fault."

"But what do you want me to do? Somebody's got to be notified."

"You don't have to do anything. I'll take care of it."

Chloe twirled the lock of hair around her finger over and over again. She stared at the list in front of her, but it was all a blur. She'd canceled her afternoon appointment for the simple reason that she didn't have it in her to fake interest and patience for someone else's social event. And she was tired. It was a bone-deep, joint-sore, headachy exhaustion. She hadn't been able to sleep more than four hours a night for almost a week.

She stared at her desk phone, as she was also wont to do with the one at home, as if the Devil himself was going to spring through it and confront her. She didn't want to touch it, and every time it rang there was a possibility that Kevin was going to be on the end of the line. She couldn't talk to him.

And it wasn't as if she didn't want to. Chloe didn't have a clue what she could say to Kevin after that out of control display at his house. What a terrible thing to put him through after he'd just lost his father.

What in the world would he say to her? I'm sorry your mother's a lunatic, but I can't see you anymore? I don't think we're right for each other? I have my image and business reputation to think of? The range of possibilities was too awful to consider, and she just couldn't face rejection right now.

What Chloe could do, and what she'd done several times a day behind the closed door of her office, was to play back the voice-mail messages that had filled her machine with Kevin's onslaught attempts to reach her. He was calm, reasonable and persistent. Then the calls had deteriorated to pleas and begging…and worry. By then she was ashamed of her pouty attitude, but there seemed to be no turning back.

Billie Burns was still an issue but in another previously unimagined way.

Chloe lamented to herself that there was still no adequate way to describe how stunned, how speechless and betrayed she'd felt when she'd returned home after storming away from Kevin. The house was strangely quiet when she'd walked in. The TV had been off when she'd left, and Billie was still asleep. But the quiet then was different. She immediately became suspicious when she didn't hear the TV. She walked right to the room Billie was using and looked in. Her stomach sank. Billie was not there.

Chloe walked through the house calling out the name but by now wasn't expecting to get an answer. She found the front door unlocked and the door ajar. Billie was gone.

With that confirmed Chloe began a methodical walk-through again of the house. She started on the upper floor. Although the barricade at the end of the hallway closing off the two guest rooms seemed to be in place, it was clear that it had been moved, with little attempt to put it back. Chloe shoved it aside and walked into both rooms. The comforters had been pulled off and thrown aside, and the sheets and pillowcases on the beds in both rooms had been removed and taken. In the bathroom soap and even toilet paper were gone.

With real reluctance Chloe went into her bedroom. The closets and all her bureau drawers had been opened and gone through, but it was hard to tell if any of her clothing were missing. None of it would have fit Billie, but Chloe didn't worry about possible missing clothes or shoes. She hurried to find her jewelry box that she kept, not on the dresser top but inside the armoire. She lost all strength to feel anything when she saw that Billie had, apparently, methodically and with obvious knowledge, taken all the good pieces and left just the costume jewelry.

Numb and her spirit broken, Chloe returned to the first level. To her astonishment it looked as if Billie had thoughts to actually remove the flat screen TV. Cables and wires had been pulled out but the attempt abandoned probably when Billie realized she had no way to get it out of the house, let alone transport her booty safely.

There was no point in continuing to look at anything else, Chloe decided. She would eventually discover that Billie had managed to leave with ease because she was carrying small things. Nothing too heavy or too large. She had no idea how Billie might have gotten out of the community undetected, but she had. She made the decision not to report the thefts to the police but called at once for all the locks to be changed, and to have an alarm system installed on the first floor windows and doors.

No good deed goes unpunished, Chloe thought, dispirited. Billie had made a clean getaway and left her, once again, dealing with the aftermath.

It had been the second most terrible day of her life.

"Chloe, Kevin Stayton called again. He said it's really important. Something to do with Bollito and the reunion."

Chloe's stomach churned. She knew she should take the call, but she was still suspicious and cautious enough that she wouldn't put it past Kevin to use homecoming as an excuse to get her to respond. Well, he might win that point. But not right now.

"Lynette, I have an appointment across town in twenty minutes."

"But Chloe, the man has been trying to reach you for two days. This is not like you. And I thought you two liked each other."

"I've been busy," Chloe said, not too convincingly.

"You've been in a daze." Lynette sighed. "He's going to call again. What should I tell him?"

I don't know. *I don't know!*

She realized that she was unfairly putting her staff in a difficult position. They shouldn't have to run interference for her to this extent. They didn't have to know that Kevin's calls weren't really about business.

Chloe picked up her purse and her sunglasses from her desk. She looked at Lynette's concerned expression and gave in.

"Okay. Okay. I promise, I *swear,* I'll deal with it when I get back. If Kevin calls again tell him I've had a lot on my plate recently. I *will* get back to him about whatever the problem is."

Lynette nodded silently, still not convinced, but returned to her desk.

Chloe was reaching the end of her rope, and she knew it. When she'd gotten a call the day before from Attorney Lucius Gray, it was like the final nail in the coffin. Mr. Gray had been quick to reassure her that she was not in any trouble. He wanted to talk with her about Billie Burns, her mother.

"Can't you just tell me over the phone?" she'd asked, not willing to get any closer again to Billie than a phone call.

"I'd rather not. When you hear what I have to say

you'll agree that the matter is personal and you'll want the information confidential. It won't take long. My office is on Peachtree, southwest. There's parking available. Can you make it tomorrow…"

Feeling like she was on a death march, Chloe left to keep her appointment. With each passing mile of her drive her tension increased. Her anxiety grew to monster proportions. And suddenly, she wished that Kevin could be with her as she tried to prepare herself for the worst. And then she denied the wish. She'd have to deal with this on her own, as she'd always done.

Lucius Gray's office was a professional and upscale complex of offices in one of the newer business highrises. The reception area was spacious and comfortable, with a discreetly partitioned-off space where visitors could get coffee, tea or bottled water. There was a small wall-mounted flat screen stationed to CNN, which was headquartered in Atlanta.

Chloe gave her name and rather than have her take a seat, as she'd expected, she was told that someone would be right out to get her. She hadn't expected it to be Lucius Gray himself.

When he appeared Chloe found herself shaking hands with a tall, well-built man not any older than herself. She'd thought Lucius would be a more mature man. Although his skin was a medium-brown he had hazel eyes that were startling in his face; a nice-looking man. He was impeccably dressed in a perfectly fitted suit and he'd deigned to wear the jacket when he introduced himself, rather than appear more casual without one. This small factor indicated to Chloe that he was serious and adhered to a certain protocol.

As he escorted her to his office Lucius thanked her for coming in and apologized for being so mysterious about Billie Burns.

"I don't think you were mysterious at all," Chloe said caustically. "Once you told me this is about her, I knew it couldn't be good news."

He smiled but frowned slightly at her comment. He led the way into his office, a large light-filled space with its own conference corner, an oval table that comfortably sat four people. Instead of sitting behind his desk, Lucius suggested the more comfortable seating arrangement on the opposite wall. It consisted of a love-seat sofa with coffee table and adjacent side chairs. Chloe chose to sit on the sofa, and Lucius took the chair next to her after retrieving a folder from his desk and closing the door.

"I got the invitation," he began.

Chloe, distracted and nervous, stared blankly at him. "What invitation?"

He smiled pleasantly. It transformed his face, softening his expression. "For the reunion. Class of 1999."

Chloe raised her brows. "We graduated together?"

"We did, but we obviously didn't know each other. I do, however, remember that you were valedictorian. You've changed," he observed with a gleam of admiration in his gaze.

"I guess I should thank you. Nobody remembers me," Chloe said without rancor.

"That must have been what you wanted," Lucius said bluntly. "There was certainly enough opportunity to be involved, pledge, get pinned, stand out, make out."

She smiled. He was right. But none of that was really her thing.

"Just a few more weeks until homecoming. How's the response been?"

"Amazing. For the reunion we have about four hundred attending. For the homecoming overall it's close to a thousand."

"And you were in charge of it all?"

"How do you know that?"

"After I got the invitation I called the alumni office and asked. They turned me over to Kyra Dixon."

Chloe relaxed. She'd half expected Lucius to mention Kevin's name. She was glad that he didn't.

"And that more or less brings us to the issue of Billie Burns," he began, instantly serious again.

"Where is she?" Chloe asked, overcome with curiosity.

"In jail."

She stared at the attorney. She saw not sympathy but another look that felt like he understood and he supported her and how the news might affect her.

"In jail. So how did you connect me to her?"

"Well, it's a little convoluted. And it was just by accident that I even came across the case. But let me backtrack a little.

"There was an arrest warrant out for her for violating the terms of her parole. She'd moved out of the shelter she'd been placed in and never notified anyone where she was going. She neglected to report in as she was ordered to."

My fault! Chloe was horrified to learn.

"When she was finally picked up it was not because of the warrant but for trying to sell credit card numbers and information to a fence. She and the fence were caught together. He'd been under surveillance for months. Billie just happened to be meeting with him when the authorities decided to shut him down. The credit card numbers were registered to you," he said, staring at her.

Chloe closed her eyes and lowered her head. She felt embarrassed and humiliated.

"They also found jewelry and knew they couldn't be hers, but the police weren't sure they'd ever find the real owners. Now, did you ever hear from the police?"

"Not yet. But I have received calls from the credit card issuers about my account. I was told only that the accounts had been compromised. That's the term they used. They were closing those accounts and issuing me new cards."

He nodded. "Okay. That's the information I have. Once there was a name to go with the card numbers the decision was made to contact you and see if you could identify any pieces."

"But I still don't understand how you got involved in this? Are you Billie's court-appointed attorney?"

"No. I'm not a criminal attorney. The thing is, Ms. Jackson…"

"Chloe, please. We're old classmates, remember?"

Lucius gave her that wonderful smile again, apparently pleased with her comment.

"Fair enough. Your name is familiar to a lot of people in Atlanta. They remember you from a recent magazine article, earlier this summer, and your TV interview… and a lot of local folks graduated from Hollington. Atlanta is a small universe. Some folks have asked me about you. I said I didn't know you personally, but I could certainly find out.

"I also learned that you and Kevin Stayton have been dating. You've been seen together around town. But I decided not to get Kevin involved in this. I don't know him either, but I've been to a number of his establishments. This matter of Billie Burns…I decided I wanted to try and keep it out of the papers, if you get my meaning."

Chloe averted her gaze, horrified that she felt on the verge of tears. She swallowed the lump away in her throat and gave Lucius what she hoped was a smile of sincere gratitude.

"I appreciate that, Lucius."

"As I said during our phone conversation, Chloe, this is very personal stuff. I don't think it will serve any purpose for it to become public domain. It still could, but I want to see what we can do to prevent that from happening."

"What's going to happen to her?"

He sighed. "Well, it's not pretty. She has quite a history. Unfortunately your mother seems to have spent nearly all her adult life institutionalized, in jail." He sat forward, his expression puzzled. "She told authorities that you were taking care of her. That she was living with you and that everything she has of yours you gave to her. Can you explain, or is she being delusional on top of everything else?"

Her chin quivered with the memory of what she'd gone through with Billie, of how much her mother's indifference had hurt and disappointed her. Of how Kevin had cared enough to want to protect her…of how she had hurled only accusations at him.

Tears fell finally. She discreetly tried to wipe them away.

"Most of that is true, I'm afraid. Somehow Billie managed to find me early in the summer. She kept showing up at my office downtown. I was afraid she'd make a scene so I…gave her money. And…"

"You kept giving her money, and she kept expecting it," Lucius concluded.

Chloe nodded. Lucius reached behind to the edge of his desk and faced her again, holding a box of tissues. She gave him a watery smile and took several to blow her nose.

"Pretty much. I don't think my staff ever guessed why I was doing it, but they knew that I was giving her money and wanted me to stop. I couldn't."

"I can imagine. You felt some responsibility for her, even though she'd chosen her own path to follow."

Her look thanked him again for his understanding. He used the phone extension on the coffee table to call out to his secretary. Lucius asked her to please bring in some hot tea.

"I wanted her to leave me alone, Lucius. I was terrified that someone would figure out that this…this bag lady was my mother. And someone did. Kevin Stayton. I was so angry that he'd found out I lashed out at him. I broke it off between us."

Her voice warbled again. Lucius listened without comment.

"Billie started accusing me of trying to get rid of her. She hinted that she could cause me big trouble. She was going to tell everybody that she was my mother and I was making her live in a shelter."

The tea tray arrived. Lucius took it and waved his secretary away. He poured her a cup, pushing it across the coffee table in front of her. Which was a good thing since she knew her hands might shake and the cup would drop.

"So I came up with a plan. I met with some city agencies and found out how I could get Billie into a group home. It would be better than a shelter. And I even found a supermarket willing to hire her on a trial basis, to bag groceries. I took her shopping to buy decent clothes. I…" Her voice broke again, and she stopped to take a sip of the tea before continuing. "I had her stay with me at my house for a weekend. But the minute I left her alone to take care of something important, I came back to find she'd gone, and she'd taken things from my house."

"Jewelry?"

"That's right. Lucius, the jewelry isn't that important. I just couldn't believe that she could actually do that to me. After all I tried to do to help her."

Her confession seemed to make him sad. He slowly shook his head.

"I'm so sorry, Chloe. Unfortunately, any parole officer, or judge, or mental health expert, or social worker or correction officer will tell you, what people like your mother do is *not* about you or what you are to them. It's all about what *they* want. In some ways I guess it's like dealing with a small child who doesn't know any better. Me, me, me. I, I, I.

"Okay, here's what's going to happen. Billie is going

back to jail for a long time. She will appear in court again on the more recent charges. She was caught with a significant amount of stolen property with a street value in the thousands. That's not going to go away. Now, do you want to press charges?"

"No."

"Fine. What would you like to have happen? What will help you?"

Chloe stared off across the room. She thought of all those years as a child when she'd prayed for her mother to come and get her. To remember her birthday or Christmas with a card or gift. All those years she waited to be told she mattered. After a while she'd stopped. Whatever her life was going to be was up to her. She stopped depending on anyone to help her, save her, love her.

Until she'd finally met and connected to Kevin. She couldn't believe she was finally being rewarded, being *blessed,* to be with someone so strong and so gentle.

And she'd ruined it. The fault for that could not be laid on her mother. Chloe knew she'd let her own insecurities destroy her one chance at happiness.

"I never want to see her again, Lucius. I don't want any more connection to her. It was so foolish of me to think I could make a difference."

He poured more tea. "I wouldn't say foolish. You were very hopeful of a different outcome to what sounds like a sad story. And you were very brave to try."

Kevin had waited long enough. Chloe wasn't going to call back. He didn't know if it was intentional or if something had happened. He only knew this Mexican standoff could not continue. He'd waited at Bollito long enough, hoping to bring her up to date with what was happening concerning the contracts. But he was now headed over to his main office at Flavor.

CB had complained that he was becoming hard to live with. Peg had been avoiding him. He had not been as outgoing with some of his top customers, squirreling himself away in his office, night after night, to brood. Going for runs at off hours when he couldn't sleep, alone through quiet neighborhoods and dense parks and city streets with traffic flashing by.

Kevin had given up the guilt he'd felt for snooping around the issue of Billie Burns. And he wasn't going to apologize for it, either. He'd had only one goal in mind. To protect Chloe. But now he was angry that she'd shut him out. He was angry that she'd put him through this, worrying about her, missing her, still wanting to be with her, so much.

He and Chloe were headed for a showdown.

Kevin was just pulling into the parking lot when his cell phone rang. He gave the car over to the valet and answered the call as he headed inside.

"It's Kevin."

"What's this about a problem with the contract? We both went over the details carefully."

His stomach tightened hearing her voice. It was the first time they'd been on the phone together in more than a week.

"Hello, Chloe. It's nice to hear from you," Kevin said sarcastically.

"I'm sorry I didn't call back sooner. I've been busy."

"So have I, and your time is not more valuable than

mine," he shot back. "This is business, and you owed me the courtesy of a prompt call back. I've been trying to reach you for two days."

"Don't you dare yell at me! What's the problem with the contract? Aren't you being paid enough money?"

Kevin's jaw muscles tightened.

"You want to know what's happening, you be in my office in the next hour!" He snapped the flip phone closed and exhaled.

There. Take that!

Already he was feeling better.

Once in his office, Kevin prepared. He had no illusions that the face-off was going to be easy, but he was not about to let Chloe off the hook or let her get away any longer with ignoring him. He'd been patient long enough.

CB knocked quietly on the door and opened it just enough to speak.

"She's pulling into the parking lot right now. Warning. She's loaded for bear."

Kevin chuckled silently at the image CB had drawn. "Thanks. Once she comes in, my office is off-limits, and I don't want to be interrupted no matter what you hear, got that?"

"If you say so. Anything else I can do?"

"Stand by, CB. In case it's worse than I think."

Kevin sat behind his desk and took up a comfortable position. He lounged back in the chair with his feet propped on the edge of the desk. He pretended deep concentration on an inventory list when he heard the minor commotion outside the door. He detected Chloe's voice. It was firm and no nonsense. Good. CB's was quiet, polite and helpful. Kevin heard CB tell her to go right in.

Game on!

She quite literally burst through the door.

"Why are you doing this? What's going on, Kevin?"

He took his own time in drawing his attention away from the paper, as if the contents were far more important then she was. That was hardly the case. He began to smile as he looked up at her, and the smile quickly faded when he gazed into her face.

She'd lost weight.

There were faint circles under her eyes, and her eyes indicated she hadn't been getting enough sleep. She was dressed as carefully as ever, but she wore not a single piece of jewelry and she seemed, somehow, underdressed and plain. And the look that made her eyes overly bright was not anger but anguish and distress.

She was complaining, in full confrontation mode, but he really didn't hear much of what Chloe was saying, he was so shocked and concerned about her appearance. No one would have necessarily noticed the small differences, but to Kevin they stood out in sharp contrast to when he'd last seen her.

He slowly came to his feet.

"Chloe…are you all right?"

"Of course I'm all right. I just want to know about the club. I can't believe you'd do this to me three weeks before homecoming. What conflict are you talking about, or are you just making it up to get back at me?"

His jaw tightened, and then he relaxed. He had to remember that something else was going on, and he seriously doubted it had to do with his call to her about Bollito.

"If I wanted to get back at you there are a lot of easier ways I could have done it. I think you know that. I'm not that much of a jerk. I care too much about you to take advantage."

He deliberately kept his gaze on her face, and his voice modulated low. He had to be nonthreatening, but more than that, he had to be the one in control. It was painfully clear that she was not. She faltered.

"I don't know if I believe you."

"Fine. You'll have to figure that one out for yourself."

Again she looked taken aback by his cool responses. She was not going to get a rise out of him.

She raised her chin defiantly. "I want to know about Bollito. Do we have it for homecoming or not?"

"It was double booked, I'm afraid. I neglected to ask my assistant about its availability when you approached me about using it for the dance party."

"So…so…"

"So, the club had been booked a full month earlier for a corporate event the same night."

She blinked. She opened her mouth to speak and stammered. Chloe closed her eyes and rubbed her temple, confused.

"What does that mean? Someone else is getting to use it? What about homecoming and the reunion? What about…me?"

"Chloe, I've taken care of it."

It was beginning to make him uncomfortable and angry to see what she was going through, what she must have been going through. He wasn't sure she'd heard him.

"What am I going to do?"

He frowned. "Did you hear me? I said it's taken care of."

"How? *How?* It's too late to find another place."

Kevin stepped around his desk and reached out to take her arm.

"Chloe..." She pulled away. "You're not listening to me."

"It's too late."

He firmly grabbed her arms and pulled her around to face him. "Look at me. I bought out the other contract, the first one that I didn't know about. I've directed the company event organizers to another facility. They're just as happy. You still have Bollito. You won't be disappointing our classmates, understand?"

Her eyes seemed glazed over, her chin began to quiver. And it was then that it finally sunk in for Kevin that she'd reached her limit. She was nearly on the verge of collapse, and it had begun the first time Billie Burns, Chloe's natural mother, had tried to bogart her way into her life.

"Christ," Kevin muttered angrily under his breath. He released her arms and framed her face with his hands. She grabbed his wrists, holding on, not trying to pull away again. "Everything's going to be okay. You're going to be fine."

"No. It's never going to be okay. I tried to help her. I prayed so hard to find the strength to forgive her. And she only wanted to use me."

Tears began to spill unchecked down her face.

Kevin's heart ached at the baring of her soul.

"She's not going to hurt you anymore. I'm not going to let anyone hurt you *ever* again."

One more time she found the strength to pull away, whirling on him in all her fury and helplessness.

"Well, you did! You spied on me. You wouldn't stop until you'd found out my dirty little secret. You don't do that to people you say you care about."

"You do if you love them. You do whatever you can. I love you."

Chloe clamped her hands over her ears, squeezed her eyes shut and shook her head furiously. The clamp holding her hair in an upswept ponytail came loose and flew across the room. Her hair fell across her face, and her shoulders began to shake as the floodgates of months of stress finally shook their way open.

Kevin murmured her name again and took her into his arms, holding on to her as tightly as he could. She fought him. But Kevin was smart enough to know he wasn't the target. He wasn't the issue. It was the soul of an eight-year-old little girl who had been discarded and left alone in the world to find her own way. And the one person who should have taken care of her hadn't.

Chloe sobbed and twisted and he grabbed her arms, and she cried so hard her legs gave way and she began to slip to the floor. Kevin held on, controlling the descent as they both ended up on the carpeted floor of his office. This was *not* what he'd expected to happen when she'd walked into his office, full of spit and vinegar. But they were safe here to ride out the crisis. CB would know if he was needed, but he wasn't going to be. Kevin knew what he had to do.

For the moment, he had to hold her to him and let her cry and rage and get it out. They couldn't move forward until she did. He kept whispering to her, soothing her, stroking her hair from her face, kissing the tears from her cheeks, holding her forehead into his shoulder... absorbing every sob and quake and tremor. Reminding her, over and over again, that he loved her.

It took a long time before Chloe was just lying in his arms with her breathing even and steady. The crying had ended, and for a while Kevin wondered if she'd actually fallen asleep. And then, Chloe's arms came up to circle his neck, and she rolled onto her back. She undulated against him.

"Kevin. Make love to me."

He drew back to look into her exhausted face. "Here? Right now?"

She was already trying to pull up the hem of her dress, heaving her derriere to bunch the fabric around her waist. Wiggling her panties down her hips as far as she could. She was nodding, beginning to breathe rapidly.

"Yes. Here."

Kevin didn't need any persuading. The roll of her hips and pelvis against him was doing the job of getting him aroused, as was the two-week abstinence away from her. He opened his trousers and managed to kick out of them and his shorts. He got her panties off and tossed them aside.

He groaned and stopped. "Dammit," he muttered. "Chloe, wait."

"No, it doesn't matter," she whined. "It's okay. I don't mind."

"Are you sure?"

"Oh, Kevin," she whispered, gazing into his eyes, and caressing his jaw. "Are *you* sure?"

"Yes. I've wanted to tell you that for weeks." He was starting to rock against her, waiting for the signal that would let him go the distance.

She sighed, closed her eyes and drew her knees back so that he fell into place between her legs. The rest, after that, was easy.

"Love me," Chloe said softly.

It was the easiest thing she'd ever asked of him.

Chapter 9

"Excuse me." Chloe signaled one of the homecoming volunteers, identified by the white T-shirt with the initials HC stenciled in the center of the chest, and beckoned the young man to her. "I don't want these people standing in this heat trying to register. This can go a lot faster if you set up another table and get two more of you to sit and help out, okay?"

"Sure, no problem, Ms. Jackson." He nodded and jogged away to do her bidding.

Chloe walked slowly along the registration area, making note of every little detail, and making notes as to what looked like a problem, what wasn't needed anymore and other changes to make the process smoother for all. Registration had been scheduled to last until five o'clock, but the remaining lines meant it would have to be extended at least another hour, the result of CPT and so many of the alumni arriving late, some with cranky and tired children in tow.

She searched for and found the volunteer she'd put in charge of registration for the weekend and pulled her aside.

"I'm going to let today's registration go until six-thirty and then we'll close it off. Everyone will want to freshen up before they head out for dinner or other gatherings tonight. Oh, and we'll definitely stop at noon tomorrow. If people aren't here by the start of the tail-gate party, they're not planning on being here."

"I hear you." The young woman laughed and went to make changes on the signage.

As she walked away to see if there was any action at the "Be True To Your School" vendor market, her cell phone rang.

"Yes, it's Chloe," she answered breezily, walking briskly to navigate the crowds of returning alumni who were meandering and strolling the grounds of their alma mater. Laughing and reminiscing and excited about being back.

"How are you holding up?"

She smiled broadly, waving to a faculty member she recognized in passing.

"Listen, it's only the first day. It will probably get harder as the day goes on. I'm good."

"Are you sure? Anything I can do to help?"

"No. It's not like you're sitting at home with nothing to do until the reception tonight. How did you make out with your redirected corporate event?"

"Well, the good news is that they really wanted to use one of the clubs, so they were perfectly happy with my suggestion to use KISS KISS as a stand-in for Bollito. That's the first club I opened in Atlanta."

"I'm so glad. I really felt bad that you might have faced a financial loss so that I could still get Bollito for tomorrow night."

"Did you? How bad?"

She chuckled. "Are you asking for some sort of bribe or payoff?"

"Sometimes that's how business gets done."

"I have a feeling this has nothing to do with business. What would you like?"

"Come home with me tonight."

"It sounds lovely, but I have to be back here by eight in the morning. I'm in charge, remember?"

"You're in charge so you can delegate responsibility to others. I won't make you late. Don't forget I'm coming for the tailgate party."

"That's really nice of you," Chloe said quietly.

She slowed down as the tented vendors' fair came into view. She stopped to sit on a bench and finish her conversation with Kevin.

"I know you can't stay for everything, but you've been so good about changing around your work schedule today."

"Chloe, I had a great time at Hollington. I think the homecoming weekend is a fun idea, but what I'm doing I do for you. As long as you're clear on that."

"I am. Thanks."

"Where shall I meet you?"

She looked at the time and gasped. "Oh! I didn't realize how late it's getting, and I still have to change.

I should be arriving at CORK in a half hour. I'll park my car first and then meet you inside. Is that okay?"

"You got it. Love you."

He'd already clicked off. But Chloe continued to smile as she dropped her phone into the pocket of her skirt.

"Love you, too."

She rushed over to the stalls and tables where school merchandise and independents with permits from the college were selling anything and everything that had to do with Hollington College. It was mostly the usual fare of baseball caps, scarves, buttons and mugs, but there were some really cute and creative things as well. Miniature put-together models of the historic main Hollington College building, the roaring lion mascot stenciled in frosting on cookies, a white handkerchief with the college logo repeated around the edge decoratively. And Chloe's favorite, wine commissioned and bottled especially for the weekend, with a clever graphic label for *Hollington Chardonnay* and *Hollington Zinfandel*.

The faculty member acting as manager for the fair waved as she approached.

"Don't worry. I've taken care of everything."

"Thanks, Professor Seymour."

"You said you only needed sixty-five bags, but I put together five extra, just in case. I know from experience that there's always someone you forget to include."

"That's so nice of you." Chloe smiled graciously at the older gentleman, retired and emeritus in economics. "Have they been sent over to the restaurant?"

"This afternoon. I grabbed a couple of these able-bodied young men, and everything was delivered a few hours ago. It's all waiting for you when you get there."

She looked at the time again. "I've got to go. Thanks for everything," she shouted as she made a run for Kyra's office in the building behind the fair setup. There, she was going to change for the president's reception she'd arranged to acknowledge and honor notable alumni who were also big donors to the college.

When Chloe drove into the parking lot of CORK the first person she saw was Kevin, watching and waiting for her. She knew that ever since that dramatic meltdown in his office that he'd kept an eye on her, still worried after all the stress she'd been under the whole summer. Chloe knew herself well enough to know that his worry was no longer warranted, but she wasn't ready to tell Kevin—yet. She was so enjoying his treating her like Dresden china.

He waved as she drove past and found a nearby spot for her car. They had discussed earlier the need for decorum and maintaining a proper image and proper distance between them. That meant no holding hands or blowing kisses, or kisses or anything else that was far too personal at such an open and public event. But Chloe also loved the little game they played to see how often they could break their own rules.

"Good evening, Kevin," she said cheerfully, as she approached him.

He looked handsome and cool in a dark summer suit and an eye-catching but tasteful tie. And she hoped she looked equally as fetching in her navy blue Donna Karan sheath dress with its off-the-shoulder neckline and short neckline slit just above her breasts. She was wearing a single strand of Mikimoto pearls, one of the few pieces of good jewelry that Billie Burns had not taken probably because she didn't recognize the value. Simple pearl studs adorned her ears and faux pearls made up the headband she wore that held her loosened hair back from her face.

"Good to see you, Chloe. Everything going to plan?"

"So far, so good." She smiled as they turned to enter the modern all-glass entrance of CORK, Kevin's wine bar.

Chloe separated from Kevin long enough to check on the arrival of the goodie bags for the attendees. Chloe also thanked the CORK employee Kevin assigned to help out with the President's Reception.

"You can begin setting up the table with the goodie bags as soon as the last person on the guest list has arrived. I'll help you make sure that each guest gets one on their way out. Thanks."

And then Kevin, with an urgent look on his face, pointed her toward the maître d's podium, now moved out of sight for the night. Chloe followed him behind the column only to have Kevin turn so he could take her in his arms.

"Kevin," Chloe protested. Not that it did any good.

He kissed her. It was brief but pretty deep and was filled with promise. But he took his time ending it. At which point Chloe nervously looked around in dread that they might have been spotted.

He cleared his throat and straightened the knot of his tie. "Okay. Now I'm ready."

She giggled as they moved away from the entrance. Kevin led the way to one of the private VIP lounges of the wine bar. The room was subtly lit, with an aura of a contemporary, well-appointed private club. There were fresh lavender cuttings arranged in giant glass vases around the room.

Inside Chloe smoothly moved away from Kevin and proceeded to say hello to President Walter Morrow. He gave her a paternal hug and kiss on both cheeks and told her how lovely she looked. Chloe quickly scanned the group to see who and how many guests had arrived. One hundred invitations had gone out. Eighty-two alumni had responded that they would be attending, but she knew from registration that only sixty were likely to show up. Kyra was one of the first to arrive.

Chloe just stood and listened to the exuberant PR director exclaim over the setting for the reception. More people arrived, most of whom she didn't know but who were from a number of different graduating classes, spanning some twenty-five years.

Terrence Franklin came in quietly, but if he hoped to go unnoticed he underestimated his own notoriety. Terrence was quickly surrounded by the men in the room, who could quote stats and plays from Terrence's career. It was obvious to Chloe that he was reveling in the attention. Every now and then her and Kevin's gazes would meet and hold for a nanosecond. Just long enough for her to be assured of his feelings, and hopefully he could see she felt the same way.

Tamara Hodges arrived when the room was already beginning to get a bit noisy and full. She smiled wanly at Chloe but made no attempt to come over and say hello, preferring, it would seem, to stay near the door. Several times during the evening Chloe watched her go in search of the ladies' room. Chloe was concerned that perhaps Tamara wasn't feeling well, but there was never an opportunity to seek her out and find out for sure.

Through the crowds Chloe caught a glimpse of Beverly, towering above even many of the men in attendance, and was pleased to see Lucius Gray. They greeted one another as if it was the first time, and Chloe was grateful that he was gracious and friendly toward her. But he couldn't stay. A divorced father, he was having his young daughter with him for the weekend. But he promised he would be at the dance party the following night, if only for a few hours early.

Chloe heard her name called and, literally across a crowded room, saw Micah Ross. He saluted her and blew a kiss. But someone was tapping a spoon against the side of a glass for attention, and she knew there was no time to say hello to the one person she'd truly hoped would be attending.

Chloe waved back, mimed a telephone call and moved to take up her position off to the side of President Morrow. The plan called for him to welcome everyone to another homecoming weekend, especially the class of 1999 for whom it was their tenth anniversary. He then mentioned how important alumni were to the life of the college and its continuing growth and development. Much of what the school accomplished could not be done without their generosity. Chloe checked her notes to make sure that President Morrow would then finish his opening and encourage everyone to enjoy themselves. She was not prepared for Kevin to quietly take the hand mike after whispering some quiet words to the president.

"Good evening, everyone. Welcome to Hollington's annual homecoming weekend, and the tenth Anniversary of the class of ninety-nine."

Chloe frowned at Kevin, because he was usurping what the president was to have closed with. He winked covertly at her and went on.

"I'm Kevin Stayton…"

That was as far as he got before the room erupted into shouts and applause. Even Kevin seemed caught off guard by the response. He quickly put up his hand to quiet the group down and regain control.

"Thanks for that, but the reason why I muscled the mike from President Morrow is to make sure that everyone is made aware of who is responsible for the important and complex job of organizing this weekend."

Chloe's stomach roiled as her eyes pleaded with Kevin not to do this to her. He ignored her and continued with his introduction.

"As it turned out the best person possible was selected. And she's one of our class of ninety-nine, y'all!"

There was enthusiastic applause until Kevin again signaled for quiet.

"Typical of her, and some of you will remember this from our undergraduate years, she doesn't like drawing attention to herself. She works quietly behind the scenes but she gets the job done, as all of you will experience during the course of this weekend. Ladies and gentlemen, Chloe Jackson!"

Chloe didn't move. She stared down at her feet hoping the whistling and applause would quickly die down. And then someone took her hand and pulled her forward to be recognized. It was Kyra, using her small hands to encourage the audience to keep up the applause.

Chloe half raised her hand in a shy salute and quickly stepped back behind the president.

Kevin gave the mike over to the president who followed the program as she intended.

There was no time for Chloe to really enjoy the socializing with her fellow classmates, all of whom greeted her like a long-lost friend, and who all seemed inclined to engage her in lengthy conversation. But she couldn't, promising to try and catch up with everyone at some point over the next two days.

The reception was set to end by eight. Chloe took up a position at the private room entrance, to thank everyone for coming, collect a mess of business cards and make sure everyone got a goodie bag. Each contained a Hollington scarf and one of the two bottles of specialty wines. Everyone seemed surprised, touched and impressed. They all left with happy smiles.

The president thanked her for a sophisticated and happening setting for the reception.

"Now, I got to tell you my nose was bent out of joint when you said you didn't think the president's house on campus was quite the place for tonight's reception. Chloe, I have to admit you were absolutely right. I shudder to think where I would have put Terrence Franklin, let alone sixty-five of your classmates. So I thank you for saving me from myself."

With that President Morrow kissed her cheek and left to go home.

Chloe had to be the last one to leave. She wanted to make sure that CORK was being left in good condition, and that the private room had been checked for any lost or forgotten items. She knew Kevin was going to reopen the room for the late evening customers, but she stayed focused on finishing the job she'd started.

The lights were being dimmed. The room was now empty of Hollington alumni and stripped of their voices and laughter and camaraderie. It was only as she finished one last look around that Chloe realized that she was tired. It had been a long day already, and the weekend was just getting started. She walked back to the front of the wine bar where the general public was now arriving for the evening. She left, heading toward the parking lot. Kevin was waiting. They were alone, and he didn't hesitate to put his arm around her and hug her to his side.

"An impressive turnout, don't you think?"

"You put me on the spot, Kevin Stayton."

"Sorry. You deserved the attention. They needed to know who was responsible, Chloe. Know what? You're definitely in the right business. I don't think anyone else could have pulled off an event on the scale of this weekend."

"Right. I bet you say that to all the girls."

He kissed her cheek. "Only the one I'm in love with."

They finally remembered where they were. Her car was in one place, and his was in another. They faced each other.

"We're okay," Chloe said to him.

"You bet your sweet bippy we're okay."

She laughed. "No, I'm serious. I'm talking about that little meeting we had in your office two weeks ago. You know. And we used the floor..."

He put his arms around her and brought their hips together. "Hmm. It's engraved on my mind. It was every bit of a risk worth taking."

She smiled at him. "My place or yours?"

"Yours. It's closer."

Chapter 10

Kevin hadn't realized how difficult it was going to be.

He had to oversee the details of having what seemed like a thousand and one of his former classmates and friends at his club Bollito and have a good time himself. Although it looked like the club was packed to the rafters he'd kept very tight control over the number of people allowed in, ever mindful of the city's fire codes. He wanted everyone to have a good time, but he also needed to make sure they were safe.

Early on Kevin realized that he had to give up on the idea of just being a guest. At least twice an hour he was reached on his walkie-talkie to confer, often at length, over one issue or another.

He found himself moving back and forth between floors, trying to sneak in a few minutes with old friends and classmates who just wanted some of his time. It had turned out to be a daylong effort, starting at noon with the pre-game tailgate party, which had been strategically set up around the new stadium just north of the Hollington campus.

Everything that had happened since very early that morning was all starting to blur together. After he and Chloe had spent excellent quality time to unwind at her place the night before, and despite his expectations to the contrary, she had sent him home. He'd barely seen her since.

But Chloe had always been near for critical moments to his plans.

She'd confessed that she was not a football fan, and as much as she loved Hollington and was moved with school spirit in all other ways, she couldn't sit for two or three hours to watch a ball being carried up and down a field. But he'd been successful in telling her she *had* to be available during halftime because the president was going to be there, as well as Terrence Franklin, Hollington's closest thing to a national treasure.

As requested, Chloe had returned to the stadium. She'd been escorted down to the sidelines where mikes and cameras recording the game were set up. When he saw her Kevin had broken into a broad grin, not because she'd arrived—he knew she would—but because she looked so amazingly fresh and lovely. For the tailgate party and the game she'd worn navy blue chinos and a white turtleneck sweater. Unlike the traditional blue and white game windbreaker with the Hollington Lion on the back, she was wearing one in an orange-red color. It made her stand out and easily identified by her volunteers or college officials looking for her. As per their agreement, Kevin waved her forward but didn't greet her with a kiss, even a chaste one, as he'd really wanted.

He stood behind President Morrow, with Chloe next to him, as Morrow welcomed the crowds, congratulating them on their school spirit. And he thanked the Lions for the halftime score of eighteen to seven against their opponents, the Greenville Rangers.

Then Chloe was urged forward, as always, against her will.

"Is everybody having fun yet?"

The stadium crowds erupted into yells and screams that they were.

"We're just getting started, and there's so much more to come. Just a reminder that there are several places where you can leave your order forms for official homecoming and class photographs. And there will be someone at the brunch on Sunday to collect them as you're getting ready to leave the campus.

"Be safe, respect school property and don't forget we need your contributions to the alumni association. Remember that Hollington is educating our kids for tomorrow."

There was another outburst of response from the crowds, and even President Morrow seemed very pleased that she remembered to put in a plug for fundraising.

Then Kevin stepped forward to talk into the mike. This time he didn't bother to introduce himself.

"One more thing before we get out of the way and let the performance begin, I think you all need to know who was the moving force behind this weekend."

Kevin felt Chloe pulling on the tail of his coat, trying to stop him from mentioning her name.

"She doesn't think she deserves any recognition but how about a Hollington shout-out for *Chloe Jackson!*"

It wasn't Kevin but one of the grounds crew who actually got behind Chloe and gave her one gentle push forward. Her image was immediately enlarged and displayed on the screens erected at both ends of the field. She didn't take the mike again but merely pivoted to wave at the crowds who applauded her, as the night before. She smiled and quickly stepped back.

She'd playfully punched him in the arm. "I'll never forgive you if you do that again, Kevin…"

Kevin made the decision, at seventy-thirty, to open the doors to Bollito because of the number of alumni pressed together outside the club all the way back to the parking lot. By eight-thirty the place was jumping. But it was a testimony to the design of Bollito and the attention to detail that gave the impression of comfortable spaciousness. The setting of the sound systems insured that all guests could enjoy and dance to the music and hear themselves think.

Each of the five floors of the club had different kinds of music being performed. The interior of the club had been thoughtfully and meticulously considered and laid out for maximum use and impact. The color theme was black and white. Black leather sofas along with acrylic tables hugged the walls on the main dance floor. Similar sofas and tables, side chairs, ottomans and lush drapery for the VIP areas outfitted the upper floors near the balconies, allowing guests to overlook the action on all floors. The floors were made of frosted plate glass from beneath which monochromatic lights for accent flickered and flashed.

In every nook and cranny allowable there were thirty-something Hollington alumni. The place was buzzing with conversation, boisterous greetings, laughter and even sudden outbursts of old school songs! And everyone danced, waves of people on every floor swaying and rockin' and rollin' and grinding to the beat.

Kevin stood to the side of the first-floor entrance watching the activity and monitoring his security for any potential problems. But there were none. His former classmates had come to have fun, not to carry on as they might have ten years earlier when they thought they were invincible.

"Need me for anything?"

"Have you seen Chloe?" Kevin asked CB, even as he kept his gaze trained on the crowd in the lower level main performance and dance area, in hopes of spotting her.

"I last saw her on her cell phone maybe fifteen minutes ago."

Guests were already in place, anticipating the arrival of up and coming R & B singer Justice Kane. Micah Ross had come through for him and Chloe, arranging for Justice to appear. It was one of the highlights of the night. Kevin had insisted on Micah making the introductions. His appearance was another surprise for the guests, most of whom were not on the guest list the night before for the President's Reception. And Kevin had gone a step further. Knowing the condition for Micah's cooperation in the evening's program was that he guarantee Tamara Hodges's attendance, Kevin glanced around and found that CB had seated Tamara near the performance stage. She was exquisitely dressed in a strapless dress with a chic drop waist and ostrich feather skirt in black. Her hair was loose and full of waves created by twists.

Someone called his name, and he glanced up to find Kyra Dixon looking down from the balcony of the dance floor above. Behind Kyra was standing a man whom Kevin didn't immediately recognize. Kyra had her hair done up in lustrous curls, and she was wearing a gold, curve-fitting strapless dress, and leather stiletto pumps with ankle straps. The girl was hot!

But glancing around once again Kevin located Terrence, who was a standout in a three-button suit with a blue vest underneath, and matching fedora tilted dangerously to the side. Diamond stud earrings sparkled from both earlobes.

Everything and everyone was in place. Except for Chloe.

Justice Kane began his performance and commanded the attention of everyone in the club.

Anxious when she wasn't there for the start of Justice Kane's appearance, Kevin called Chloe's cell phone and was directed to voice mail. This had been the response each time he'd tried to reach her.

"Chloe, this is important. I need you on the stage at ten o'clock. Call me back."

Instinctively CB again appeared at his side. Kevin clamped his hand down on his shoulder.

"Okay, we go into special forces Plan B. I'll cover the upper two floors. You do the rest. We *have* to be back here in fifteen minutes."

"I hear you."

"Okay, let's do it."

"Is she going to be okay? Do I need to get her to a hospital?"

Chloe, standing outside the club, leaned against the side of the building, one finger in her ear so that she could better hear and understand the information on the other end. She caught the admiring open stares of any number of men walking by, who appreciated her lithe figure sexily attired in a Ralph Lauren drop-shoulder dress in pomegranate red with a wide V-neck and cap sleeves. She never noticed. She'd been following the progress on the case of one of the weekend guests who'd apparently suffered a mild allergic reaction to peanuts she'd ingested at some point either during the tailgate party or in the first half of the game earlier in the day.

Chloe had gotten the call as she and Kevin were leaving the stadium and the halftime performance had gotten under way.

"Kevin, I have to take care of this. I have to see to it that someone gets medical attention."

"Call me if you need me. If all else falls I'll see you at the club?"

"Yes, I'll be there."

"I want the first and last dance," he'd shouted after her, making her laugh.

"Well, I'm glad to hear that. Make sure there's someone to stay with her. I'll check in with her myself in the morning. But call me whenever you need to if things get worse, okay?"

Chloe sighed deeply as she ended the call. She absently rubbed her ear. It was tender and sore from the constant use of her phone and the pressure of it pinching her earring.

The unseemly growling in her stomach reminded her that she'd not had anything to eat since having a cold and overcooked hamburger thrust into her hand at some point during the tailgate party. She had only taken a bite or two. Kevin, passing her as she rushed off to find out why they were two tents short for the lawn brunch on Sunday, had given her his half-finished soda to take with her. It had been that kind of day.

She'd wisely brought a change of clothes for the dance party with her that morning. The plan had been to meet Kevin at Bollito where she would have access to his office there and could change. Chloe smiled at that memory. She realized that Kevin's generous offer had an ulterior motive. That they might finally have a little time together before heading back into the field of action.

But it hadn't worked out that way. She'd ended up having to change in the ladies' room at the campus library just before the building was closing and then dashing like mad to get downtown.

Chloe knew she would have welcomed a tryst with him. She would have loved to let herself go and let Kevin hold and kiss her and take care of everything. A little love in the afternoon would have gone a long way toward easing her tension. They were already in the homestretch of the weekend, and there had been no serious mishaps.

And then her cell phone rang again.

"Hello…I'm at Bollito for the dance party. What's

up…Well, yes, I have the key for the office. Can't this wait until the morning?"

She glanced at her watch. It was almost nine-thirty. She was missing Justice Kane's performance. She hadn't seen Kevin since the midafternoon, and she knew he'd been trying to call her.

"Look, that was not the plan, and I can't drive back over to the campus to help you. I can meet you in the morning before brunch…"

By the time Chloe finished that call it was nine forty-five. Kevin had said something about an announcement after the performance. She rushed back inside and into the exuberant response to the singing of the Black recording star. Someone grabbed her hand.

Chloe turned and found Kevin behind her.

"Kevin." She sighed in relief.

"Thank God I found you," he said, his voice strained. "Why didn't you call me back?"

"Kevin, there was so much going on. I'm sorry. I was being pulled in all directions, and…"

"Okay, doesn't matter," he said, giving her a strained smile. "I found you and I'm not letting you go. Come on, Justice is on his last song. We need to get to the stage."

"Why do I need to be there?" she asked, nonetheless following as he attempted to get them through the press of people and down the stairs. "You're not going to introduce me again, are you?"

"I think everyone knows who you are by now."

Suddenly, Chloe realized that someone was pulling on her other hand. Looking over her shoulder she saw Beverly Turner. Chloe began to feel like a piñata that was about to be pulled apart.

"I've got to talk to you," Beverly said urgently.

"But, Kevin wants me…"

"I *really* need to talk to you. It's about tomorrow."

Chloe saw the distress in Beverly's beautiful eyes. It was stark fear. She turned back to Kevin, who'd had to stop when she did. She released his hand and the crowd closed in between them.

"Chloe!" he shouted.

"I'm coming. I'll be right there," Chloe shouted as he disappeared in the crowd. Then she began to retrace her way back up the stairs and to Beverly.

Beverly had moved away from the stairs and stood near the quiet corridor that led to the restrooms. There was no traffic for the moment.

She stood gnawing on her lower lip and shifted back and forth from one black-heeled foot to the other. She was a gorgeous towering Amazon, tastefully dressed in a black sheath dress that was sheer across the shoulders. Chloe detected uncertainty and insecurity.

Beverly grabbed her hand as soon as they were together.

"Are you all right? What's wrong?"

"Chloe, I'm so sorry to do this, but I can't be in the parade tomorrow."

Chloe stared at her, openmouthed. Even as she tried to get her mind around what she was just told, there was a roar of screaming and whistles as she sensed that Justice Kane had just ended his last song and left the stage.

"Wha— What did you say. You're not…"

"I can't. I know I said I'd do it, and I really hate to put you on the spot like this, but I can't."

"But why, Beverly? I mean, you don't even have to

do anything. You ride on the float and smile and wave. You don't have to *say* anything."

"I know that but…I'm afraid I'm going to fall apart. I'll embarrass myself. I can't do it," Beverly said, her voice trembling.

Chloe's head began to swim. What was she going to do?

She heard someone talking from the stage. It was Micah. Something about Justice Kane's future with the Red Ross label in L.A., Micah's company. His words faded as Chloe stared at Beverly, trying to formulate a response that wouldn't scare the obviously skittish woman.

"Maybe you could think about it overnight? You can call me in the morning. But please don't say no right now."

Beverly shook her head.

The voice had changed downstairs. It was Kevin at the mike now. Chloe gasped. She was supposed to be with him downstairs. Her gaze went to the stairwell and then back to Beverly.

Suddenly, out of nowhere, a man grabbed Beverly's arm and forcibly pulled her away. Again Chloe gasped, staring at his effrontery, not sure who he was. She was about to intercede, or call someone for help, when someone spoke behind her.

"Ms. Chloe."

She whirled around. "CB…"

"You gotta come downstairs. Right now."

"I know. I told Kevin I would but…"

"Sorry. He really needs you."

With that CB swept Chloe up into his powerful arms

and marched off, smoothly and purposefully, to head down the stairs. Heads turned as he descended, people breaking out into murmurs and giggles, and parting the way for them.

Chloe was too stunned to say anything. Kevin was still talking. She could catch only a word or two.

"…Classmate…amazing person…captured my heart…my life…"

It didn't make any sense to her. But then CB, unceremoniously, set her on her feet, turned and headed back up the stairs, having done his job. Chloe stood bewildered, realizing that everyone was staring at her, even Kevin. But it was hard to read his expression. At first she thought it was disappointment, almost sadness. And then a light began to appear again. He held out his hand to her.

Very conscious of being watched, and of an undercurrent of anticipation, she walked forward. She gave Kevin what she hoped was a stern look of caution, trying to remind him of where they were, who was around them and the agreement to keep their relationship off the table. But all he did was smile at her. And there was so much love in his eyes that Chloe faltered and averted his gaze.

Everyone was going to see!

"You had me worried," Kevin whispered as he pulled her to his side. "I thought you'd skipped out on me."

In a much louder and more normal voice as he used the mike Kevin addressed the crowds. "And, here she is!"

She was speechless when everyone cheered wildly. She looked around, only recognizing a few folks. Tamara, still looking mostly uncomfortable and unlike her usual friendly self, Kyra and Terrence. Micah, standing right opposite her with his arms crossed over his chest and a Cheshire cat grin on his face.

"Kevin, what's going on?" she hissed in an aside, but snickering next to her indicated that others heard the question.

"I am delighted, thrilled, relieved and proud to introduce Chloe Jackson to everyone."

The reaction was so over the top that Chloe winced and grimaced.

"…As my future wife."

Chloe, programmed for Kevin's habit and way of introducing her unexpectedly, before a room filled with mostly strangers, was prepared. She took the mike and waited until everyone had quieted down.

"I know you're sick of hearing my name by now. I apologize for Kevin being such a bore about it…"

Someone laughed out loud. More laughter followed. She was momentarily confused and thrown by the tittering as she talked.

"I appreciate Kevin's…his…eh…"

Chloe stopped and blinked. The laughter grew. Her stomach churned. Confused, she turned to Kevin and found him regarding her patiently, smiling. Her mind shifted gears suddenly, from what she thought he was going to say to what he actually had. Her eyes widened.

"Did you…what did you say?"

She'd forgotten all about the mike in her hands, the audience and the laughter now, which only grew because, apparently, they were in on the secret.

Kevin took the mike back, put his arm around her waist and pulled her close.

"I said, Chloe Jackson, will you marry me?"

The crowd went wild. Chloe couldn't take her gaze from Kevin's face, from the heart-stopping tenderness in his smile to the look of hope and love in his eyes.

A chant began on one side of the stage. It picked up on the other, and suddenly began a wave around the room.

"Chlo-*e,* Chlo-*e,* Chlo-*e*..."

"Say yeessssss!" a woman yelled. Everyone laughed.

Chloe turned to Kevin, her vision blurred with tears.

"Yes," she choked, almost inaudibly.

It was only meant that Kevin hear her. He had, and the relief and joy spread over his face.

"Yes, I will," she said a little louder, nodding.

"Ke-*vin,* Ke-*vin,* Ke-*vin!*"

Chloe reached for the mike and spoke clearly into it. "Yes, I'll marry you, Kevin Stayton."

The room erupted into wild cheers and whistling and applause.

Kevin kissed her in a way that made up for all their control over the last few days. They had become an unexpected sideshow for homecoming weekend. As Chloe had wanted from the beginning, a weekend that would be remembered above all others. She'd finally met the love of her life, and he in turn, had publicly declared his love for her.

It had all come to pass.

Life *was* good.

* * * * *

TEACH ME TONIGHT
Jacquelin Thomas

To my wonderful husband…just because…

Chapter 1

"The wedding ring is the outward and visible sign of an inward and spiritual bond that unites two loyal hearts in endless love."

Tamara Hodges smiled through tears as she relieved her sister Callie of the enormous wedding bouquet she had insisted on carrying down the aisle.

"It is a seal of the vows Bryant and Callie have made to one another."

She wiped her eyes with a lace handkerchief as she witnessed the exchange of rings between her baby sister and new brother-in-law, wishing them love and happiness for the rest of their lives.

Tamara's thoughts traveled to the one person she kept hidden in her heart—the one man she could never forget. The one person with whom she dreamed of sharing that type of love.

The pastor's words drew her attention back to the ceremony.

"You may now kiss your bride."

Tamara stole a quick peek at her mother, who was seated in the front row, fighting back tears.

Three hundred guests erupted in applause as Mr. and Mrs. Bryant Charles Madison were introduced. The music began, prompting the newlyweds to lead the recessional from the sanctuary.

As Bryant's best man escorted her down the aisle, Tamara could feel her ex-stepfather's heated glare as she strolled past him, her head held up high. She refused to let him put a damper on her blissful mood.

Outside the sanctuary, Tamara and Callie embraced.

"Congratulations," she whispered as she gazed into a pair of hazel-green eyes that mirrored her own. "I'm so happy for you, Callie."

Tamara embraced Bryant next. "I guess we're stuck with you now."

"Yeah," he replied, giving his new wife a sidelong glance. "Because I'm not going anywhere. I love this girl."

"Good," Tamara said with a smile. "That's what I want to hear."

Wedding guests filed out of the church, each one pausing to congratulate the bride and groom.

Tamara's mother walked up and said, "The ceremony was beautiful, wasn't it?"

She nodded. "Yeah, it was."

When Lucas, her ex-stepfather entered into the church foyer, Tamara uttered, "We should go back into the sanctuary. It's time for pictures."

Her mother agreed.

Just being in that man's presence stirred up shadows and fears that made her uncomfortable. Tamara did not want to mar Callie's wedding day, so she decided to stay as far away from Lucas as possible.

After the traditional wedding-party photos, a limo whisked them to the Four Seasons Hotel Atlanta for the reception. Callie and Bryant were in a separate stretch limo, which followed close behind.

Her mother suggested that the photographer shoot some pictures on the grand staircase at the hotel, saying that the brass railing would serve as the perfect backdrop. She had even arranged to have the large floral centerpiece at the foot of the staircase coordinate with the wedding colors and flowers. Whatever Jillian Hodges-Devane wanted she got.

Tamara made small talk with the other members of the bridal party during the ride over to the midtown hotel.

The ballroom where the reception was held consisted of a wall of mirrors on one end highlighted by large crystal chandeliers and large picture windows at the other. Tamara had been in the same room a week ago, covering an event for *Luster* magazine.

She enjoyed writing for the magazine but had dreams of starting her own publication one day.

The wedding party waited in line outside as they waited to be announced. The best man again escorted Tamara into the ballroom. After the wedding party, Mr. and Mrs. Bryant Charles Madison made their grand entrance.

While waiters navigated about the room carrying

trays of hors d'oeuvres, Tamara mingled, pausing to speak to relatives and friends of her family. She felt the sensation that someone was watching her and turned; meeting her ex-stepfather's dark and insolent gaze, she straightened herself with dignity.

He smirked, gave a slight nod and then turned his attention back to his daughter, Callie.

Tamara's eyes bounced around the room, looking for her mother.

"How are you holding up, Mama?" she asked when she found her seated at one of the family tables. Tamara sat down in the empty chair beside her.

"I'm exhausted," Jillian responded. "Your sister looks lovely, doesn't she?"

Tamara agreed. "And very happy. I guess all the whining, fussing and craziness she put us through over the past year has been worth it. I'm so glad that girl is married."

"Seeing Callie and Bryant like this—it was definitely worth it," her mother responded. "One day we'll be doing this for you. Hopefully, it will happen while I'm still young enough to enjoy the wedding."

Tamara drew an invisible pattern on the tablecloth. "Don't hold your breath, Mama. I'd actually have to have a man in my life in order to get married."

"So there's no one special? You haven't met anyone?"

"Mama, have you considered that I might be one of those women who are destined to remain single?"

"Bite your tongue," Jillian stated. "Don't even put that thought in your head. A beautiful woman like you won't have a problem finding a husband. You only have to open your heart and allow him entry."

Tamara caught her mother looking at her ex-stepfather. "Mama…"

"Can you believe he had the nerve to bring that woman here? She is what—barely legal? Lucas Devane always had an eye for young girls." Rancor sharpened Jillian's voice.

"To be honest with you, I don't really care enough about him to even wonder," Tamara retorted.

Her mother leaned over and embraced her. "I love you, Tammy. I hope you know that."

"Mama, I know you do. I love you, too," Tamara assured her. "We all went through a bad time, but thank God that it's over now. Oh, could you please just call me Tamara?" Her eyes traveled back over to the table where Lucas sat with his girlfriend. "I'm not Tammy anymore, so please don't call me that."

Lucas's eyes met hers, and his lips turned into a cynical smile. Tamara's eyes never wavered as she stared him down until he had the good sense to drop his gaze.

"I hate him," her mother uttered. A sudden thin chill hung on the edge of her words.

"I don't have any feelings toward him at all," Tamara stated. "Lucas could drop dead right here in the middle of the room and it wouldn't phase me at all." She turned her attention back to Callie and Bryant, her thoughts roaming once more to the one and only love of her life.

Micah Ross.

He was definitely the one who got away, Tamara decided. She had allowed her fears and insecurities of her youth to keep her from opening up completely and trusting, which caused Tamara to push him away. Micah had always been nothing less than a good friend

to her and her math tutor, but because of her inability
to trust combined with a group of immature boys who
had nothing better to do other than playing pranks, she
treated him cruelly the night of their graduation from
Hollington College.

She pushed away from the table and helped herself
to the caramelized Vidalia onion tart with goat cheese,
lobster and chive risotto fritters and miniature crab cake
hors d'oeuvres.

Jillian rose to her feet and followed her daughter. "I
was thinking… Isn't Bryant's best man single? I heard
that he's the vice president of Atlanta Bank and Trust."

"Not interested, Mama," Tamara said in a low voice.
"Now just drop it."

She released a short sigh of relief when her mother
became distracted by relatives. This would give Tamara
a break from her constant matchmaking.

Twenty minutes later, everyone was seated. They
dined on a duo entrée of tenderloin of beef and salmon,
roasted potatoes, asparagus and béarnaise sauce while
the band, which was personally selected by Jillian,
played softly in the background.

"Mama was right about the menu," Callie whispered
to her. "This was the perfect choice."

Tamara agreed. She sliced off a piece of the tender
salmon and stuck it into her mouth, remembering the argument between her mother and sister over the food for
the reception. They ended up not talking for two days.

Callie won the fight between them over the wedding cake. Her mother, a true Southern lady, wanted
the butter pecan cake with a fresh peach filling while

her sister insisted on the Tahitian vanilla butter cake, Tahitian vanilla custard and fresh berries.

Tamara left the reception shortly after her sister's departure and headed home. After she changed out of the bridesmaid gown, Tamara settled down on the chaise in her bedroom to write in her journal.

August 22
My sister married her high-school sweetheart today. It was a beautiful wedding, making it hard not to wonder if I'll ever have one of my own. I have not been able to have a relationship any longer than six or seven months. As I get older, I find that I'm able to detect the lies much quicker.

If I am to be completely honest, then I must admit that part of the reason I haven't found my Mr. Right is because I treated him horribly when we were in college.

Right before graduation, I overheard some boys saying that Micah was planning on having sex with me and that he was going to play the "you're the love of my life" card because that's what it would take to get me into bed.

I don't know why I believed them, but graduation night, when he told me that he loved me, I told him that I would never date a man like him and basically that he wasn't good enough for me. It wasn't until much later that I realized Micah didn't say those things—the guys had been joking around and knew that I was listening to the conversation.

I want to explain but Micah never returned

my phone calls, and the next thing I knew he had moved to Los Angeles.

Our ten-year college reunion and homecoming is coming up in October, but I'm not sure if Micah will be coming. I hope that he will be in attendance.... I want to try and talk to him one more time.

He is a famous record mogul now, but I don't care about that. I just want a chance to apologize to Micah. The tabloids have him romantically involved with that model Sunni, so it is not as if he is available anyway. The truth is that I really miss his friendship.

I miss him.

Los Angeles, California

Micah Ross stepped out of the sleek black limo in the midst of a sea of hungry media photographers and reporters. He focused his attention on the door of the Wilshire Grand Hotel several yards away while assisting his date out of the car.

He hated all the attention on him, but Micah knew that it was an integral part of his business. He was the man who had turned a tiny music store into million-dollar record label Ross Red. His first two records sold a combined 1.5 million copies before the mainstream music industry knew he existed. Now his $500 million empire included music, clothes, real estate, a product line of computers and communications.

A musician himself, Micah believed that one could only go so far in the music business—something he tried to drill into all of his artists. He pushed to get them to understand that they needed to acquire the necessary skills and education to have other options because one never knew what was going to go up and what would go down.

"Over here, Mr. Ross," a photographer shouted.

Micah glanced in his direction and pasted on a smile. His mouth tightened as Sunni, a supermodel, wrapped her arms around him as cameras flashed all around them.

"Micah, please smile," she whispered. "At least try to look like you're enjoying my company."

He chuckled. "Sunni, you know that I always enjoy hanging out with you."

"Then smile. Just remember that you're the man they all want to be. You are one of the most influential and wealthiest men in the world, Micah. Baby, you should flaunt it."

All Micah wanted to do was get inside the hotel. He hated walking the red carpet and avoided it whenever he could. Of course, in his business one needed the media to be successful.

Grinning, Sunni posed for more photos along the red carpet. She loved the spotlight so much so that it was rumored she called or texted photographers her itinerary from time to time.

Once inside, they were still under the microscope as members of the media scoured the Pacific Ballroom in search of the Hollywood elite and other VIPs attending the charity benefit for the Sickle Cell Disease Association.

Micah sat at a table surrounded by people from his

artists and repertoire (A&R), publicity and product development departments.

They dined on a three-course meal: baby leaf lettuce
with marinated artichoke hearts and wedged Roma to-
matoes and Dijon vinaigrette, breast of Mediterranean
chicken served with sautéed artichokes, goat cheese
mashed potatoes and herbed Italian vegetables, mas-
carpone caramel cake for dessert.

One of the groups from his label walked on stage
to perform.

"Eden sounds great tonight," Sunni stated as she
sliced off a piece of chicken and stuck it into his mouth.

Micah wiped his mouth with the edge of his napkin.
"Yeah, she does," he agreed, silently wishing that he
could've stayed home tonight.

He stood up and smiled politely when his generous
donation was acknowledged along with a long thun-
dering applause.

Sunni reached over and took his hand. "I still can't
believe how shy you are when it comes to stuff like this.
Honey, you are one of the good guys," she stated. "You
should be walking around here with your head up high."

He gave her a narrowed glinting glance. "You know
how I feel about being in the public eye, Sunni. I don't
like being under a microscope."

"You're the CEO of a huge conglomerate, Micah,"
she responded, rising finely arched eyebrows. "You'd
better get used to this because it's not going to go away."

Sunni took a sip of her hot tea.

Thirty minutes later, they left the ballroom. He had
put in an appearance so as far as Micah was concerned,

his work was done. He had a long day ahead of him and wanted to get some rest.

Micah escorted Sunni out of the hotel.

The driver brought their limo around, promptly stepped out and walked around to open the door.

"Micah, why don't we go back to your place?" she suggested with a seductive sparkle in her eye. "I'm not ready for the evening to end." She wound her arms inside his jacket and around his back.

Micah gave her a polite smile and resisted the urge to pull away. He knew Sunni wanted the media to photograph them in an embrace. She enjoyed being featured in gossip magazines and felt it enhanced her career.

"Sunni, it's late and I have a busy day tomorrow. I don't have any plans this weekend—maybe we can do something then."

"I'd love it. I haven't seen much of you lately."

He kissed her gently on the cheek. "We'll do something special then."

Sunni pulled him closer to her. "C'mere, I want a real kiss."

"I don't put on shows for the media," Micah stated. *"You know that."*

He ushered Sunni quickly into the car as paparazzi appeared out of nowhere, snapping pictures of them.

"How long have the two of you been dating, Micah?" someone shouted.

"Are you and Sunni thinking about marriage?" another yelled. "C'mon, give us the scoop."

Micah held up his hands in mock resignation. "I'm afraid there's nothing to tell. Have a good evening, everyone." He got into the car and the driver closed the door in haste.

"What *are* we doing?" Sunni asked when the car pulled away from the curb, merging with the traffic.

Micah did not want to have this conversation. He and Sunni had been spending time together for the past four or five months. She was stunning and he enjoyed her company, but Micah knew she had an agenda. She wanted a husband.

A rich husband.

It was not that he was opposed to marriage because he didn't want to marry. He wasn't in love with Sunni, which is why he hadn't taken their platonic relationship to the next level.

Sunni ran a French-manicured finger along his thigh. "Micah, you know how I feel about you. We are so good together. Why can't you see that? You need a woman like me as your wife."

He gave her an indulgent smile. "That's why we're such good friends."

"Micah, tell me, who did this to you?" Sunni asked.

Surprised by her question, he questioned, "Did what?"

"Hurt you," she responded. "Who broke your heart? That's the only reason I can think of that will explain why you keep this huge wall between us."

Micah did not respond.

"Well, whoever she is, she really did a number on you." Sunni ran a finger down his cheek. "I am a very patient woman, Micah. One day you'll see that I'm not here to cause you pain. If you give me the chance, I'd make you a very happy man."

He smiled. "I'm glad to have you in my life, Sunni. You are a very dear friend to me."

"There's that *friend* word again," she said with a mock sigh.

Micah laughed.

The limo slowed to a stop in front of her building.

"Will you give me a call tomorrow?" Sunni asked before stepping out of the car. "I know you talked about us getting together this weekend, but maybe we can meet for dinner. You still have to eat, you know?"

He nodded. "That's fine."

Micah stepped out of the car and walked Sunni to the door of her home. He kissed her cheek before saying good-night.

"It would've been," Sunni responded with a wink. "But it's your loss, honey. I would've rocked your world."

Micah chuckled. "I'm sure you would have."

She gave him a hug and then sauntered into the building, pausing briefly to speak to the man at the security desk.

Micah returned to the waiting limo.

Sunni was a nice girl and he enjoyed her companionship, but Micah had not fully opened his heart to another person since college. He didn't relish the thought of going home to an empty bed but cared too much to use Sunni in that way. Micah knew he would never give her what she was looking for.

One heartbreak was more than enough for him.

Tamara entered Sylvia's Restaurant looking for her Pi Beta Gamma soror, Kyra Dixon. She was running late for their lunch date due to a traffic accident on Washington Street S.W. near Memorial Drive.

Kyra was already seated at a table when Tamara entered the restaurant. She waved to get her attention.

"I'm so sorry I'm late," Tamara stated as she sat down in the chair across from her friend. "Have you ordered yet?"

"Not yet."

A waiter arrived minutes later prepared to take their orders.

"So how was your sister's wedding?" Kyra inquired after he left.

"Beautiful," Tamara responded with a smile. "My sister looked so happy and in love. It was very romantic."

"I guess the pressure's on for you to get married, huh?"

Tamara laughed. "Can you believe that my mother started in on me as soon as the service ended? We're standing there posing for pictures and she's asking me why I didn't bring a date to the wedding. She asked me if there was anyone serious in my life."

Kyra chuckled. "What did you tell her?"

"The truth," Tamara stated. "That I don't have a man and right now I'm not looking for one." She changed the subject and said, "Homecoming is a couple months away. Time moved by fast."

"Are you planning to attend the cocktail party on Friday?"

Tamara nodded. "I'll be there. Chloe wants me to cover the event for *Luster* magazine. I'm also thinking about doing a story on the fact that the alumni got together and agreed to donate money to restore the original administration building and use it as staff offices instead of tearing it down."

"Sounds good," Kyra said. "The school needs all the free press we can get."

The waiter returned, carrying a tray of food, which he set down on the table. Tamara blessed the food.

She sampled her gumbo while Kyra cut into her chicken.

"I'm actually looking forward to homecoming this year," Tamara announced. She didn't add that it was because Micah might be attending.

"It's going to be nice." Kyra stuck a forkful of macaroni into her mouth. "I can't wait. It's always good to see old friends."

Tamara agreed.

They continued making small talk as they finished off their meal.

"I need to get back to work," Tamara murmured, checking her watch when they were done eating.

"I can't believe how disciplined you are," Kyra declared. "If I worked at home, I think I'd be doing everything else around the house instead of focusing on my job."

An easy smile played at the corners of her mouth. "I like getting paid."

"As if you need the money," Kyra retorted with a chuckle. "Tamara, who are you trying to kid?"

"My mother has money," she corrected, pushing away from the table. "I don't."

After paying the check, she and Kyra rose up and walked out of the restaurant.

They paused at her car to hug.

"It was so good to see you," Tamara told her. "We should get together more often"

Kyra agreed. "We need to do this again real soon, soror."

"Sounds like a plan," Tamara responded. "Talk to you later."

Tamara got into her car and drove the two miles to her home in midtown.

The telephone rang as soon as she walked through the front door of her apartment.

"Hello," Tamara uttered.

"Hey, this is Samantha."

Tamara broke into a smile when she heard her editor's voice. They had recently discussed her becoming the features writer for the entertainment section.

"How would you like to interview Justice Kane?" Samantha asked. "You would have to fly out to Los Angeles for his album release party."

"I'd love it," she responded. Justice Kane was a performer signed to Micah's record company, Ross Red. If she did a great job on the story, this would better her chances in getting the position.

Tamara was sure that he would be attending the party so she considered this a sign. She would finally get that chance to mend her friendship with Micah. She knew that he never married and had read about his relationship with the model.

I had my chance and I blew it.

Micah hadn't only been her tutor but he'd been her friend—her best friend. They had spent a lot of time together. She and Micah used to attend the college football and basketball games together; there were times they went to the movies, clubs and even attended church together. Micah would even join Tamara on her visits to see her grandmother.

"This has to be a sign," she whispered.

Tamara knew that wanting to see Micah again had so much more to do with the fact that she was still in love with him. She had tried for years to get Micah out of her system, but to no avail—he still owned her heart.

She winced at the memory of how cruel she had been to Micah and desperately wanted the chance to explain why she had been so fearful of getting involved with him.

She prayed that once they sat down and talked he would understand and find it in his heart to forgive her.

Chapter 2

Tamara wanted to share her good news with someone, so she called Kyra later that evening. "Hey, girl…you won't believe where I'm going this weekend," she said when her friend answered the phone.

"Where?" Kyra questioned.

"Los Angeles," she announced. "I'm covering Justice Kane's album release party. *Luster* magazine wants me to do a story on him. Can you believe it?"

"That's great," Kyra responded with excitement. "Tamara, this is the kind of story you've been wanting to do for a long time. Hey, isn't Justice Kane with Micah's record company?"

"That's why I'm so excited," Tamara told Kyra. "I'm hoping to reconnect with him. I really miss our friendship."

"We used to have some good times back in the day. I

used to try and get you to party with us, but you wanted to stay home and read. The only time we could get you out was when Micah asked you. Why didn't you two ever get together?" Kyra inquired. "I know you had feelings for him back then."

"Micah was my tutor and my friend," Tamara stated. "That's really all it was. I had too many issues for anything more."

"So you didn't have any feelings for him?"

"I didn't say that," Tamara answered. "Kyra, I was crazy about Micah, but the timing was all off and things just never worked out. You know how it goes."

"I always felt that something was bothering you," Kyra said. "It was just a feeling though because you were always walking around with a smile and you seemed really happy...still, I felt there was something."

Tamara considered Kyra one of her best friends, and they were close, spent time together often, but there were things from her past that she never shared with anyone—including her soror.

She had never told Kyra what happened between her and Micah on graduation night and decided against mentioning it now. Deep down, she didn't want anyone to know just how gullible she'd been back then.

"So what about now?"

"Kyra, he's seeing someone," Tamara responded. "His relationship with Sunni has been plastered all over the tabloids and *People* magazine." She tried to sound as neutral as possible.

"Tamara, you know that you can't believe everything you read in the tabloids. Micah says that he and that model are nothing but friends. At least that's what he told Kevin."

Kyra's words delighted Tamara. She silently prayed that her friend was right because the thought of Micah being involved in a serious relationship with another woman bothered her to the core.

"Whatever their relationship, I hope she doesn't trip if Micah and I grab a few minutes to sit down and talk when I get to Los Angeles," Tamara said.

"Tell him that I said hello when you see Micah," Kyra responded. "I'm so proud of that boy. He came from the Greenwood projects, and look at him now. He left us back here in Atlanta and really made a success of his life. Now all he needs is the right woman to share it with."

Tamara had to hide her inner feelings as a sense of inadequacy swept over her. She thought about Kyra's words and wondered if after all this time had passed if she had anything to offer Micah.

Like everyone else, Tamara had her own share of past pain and trauma but she had worked past the betrayal of trust, discovered her wholeness, the experience shaping her in a way that no other has.

She learned early on that along with happiness, life brought pain. Her grandmother had taught Tamara that in order to heal, she had to forgive and that forgiveness is essential as a means of personal transformation.

Tamara still had seeds of unforgiveness rooted in her. She desired forgiveness, but until she could forgive she would never be completely free.

She and Kyra stayed on the phone for almost an hour,

talking about their college days and the upcoming Pi Beta Gamma fund-raiser.

After promising to get together soon, Tamara ended the call, then stood up and walked over to the window to stare out at the beautiful Atlanta skyline.

"I miss you so much, Micah," she whispered.

Amused, Micah hung up the telephone, but not before Samantha, the editor of *Luster* magazine, thanked him for the fifth or sixth time during their conversation.

He took a deep breath and tried to relax now that the initial part of his plan had succeeded.

He and Tamara would finally come face-to-face again after ten years. Micah wasn't sure how he would feel about seeing her again, so he decided that this meeting would have to happen in a place he could control. It would give him the upper hand.

Micah called and arranged to have Tamara attend the party at the Vanguard Club in Beverly Hills. However, she would have to deal with him first before he allowed her access to Justice Kane.

He wanted a glimpse of the woman Tamara had become, but he also wanted to settle an old score.

His heart bore a permanent scar seared by her rejection. The fact that Micah still harbored deep feelings for Tamara only fueled his anger more. He struggled with loving her and knowing that she thought he wasn't good enough for her.

A few days ago, he typed in her name while online out of curiosity and found a photo of her on *Luster* magazine's Web site. That's when he came up with the idea for the interview and a way to get back at her.

Tamara looked much younger than her thirty-two years and from the looks of it, wore her shoulder-length hair natural and without chemicals, the warm brown color complimenting her light chocolate complexion and hazel-green eyes.

She's still beautiful, he thought to himself.

Micah forced himself to remember the way she had treated him. A computer science major in college, he was the quiet, shy geek who tutored Tamara in math during her freshman year—their friendship birthed out of the tutoring sessions.

He had always thought Tamara was sweet, caring and felt extremely comfortable around her. Micah had even believed that she thought of him as more than a tutor. During their time in college, Micah never once saw signs of Tamara being a snob or elitist—she had always been down-to-earth.

His mouth tightened as he thought about graduation night—the night that Micah made the mistake of confessing his feelings for her. He had even planned to propose marriage; however, he never got that far.

Tamara rejected Micah, telling him directly that she would never date anyone like him. She didn't need him to tutor her anymore. She had landed a job with the *Atlanta Daily Journal* so she had no more use for him.

It was then that Micah realized he did not know her as well as he had initially thought. He never knew she held even the tiniest interest in writing. Micah knew that she kept a journal, but to him that did not necessarily mean she wanted to be a writer.

It had come as a complete surprise when Tamara announced she was going to work as an entry-level journalist with the newspaper. Her degree was in business and not journalism.

If they had been as close as Micah thought they were, why would she keep her love for writing a secret? What else had she been keeping from him?

Micah Ross was *fine*.

Tamara laid a back issue of *Ebony* with Micah gracing the cover down on the chair beside her.

She kept that issue on her coffee table since its release two years ago.

Micah pretty much looked as he did back in college except that he no longer wore those black-framed glasses that Tamara used to think were so sexy on him.

His skin was the color of dark chocolate, smooth and free of facial hair. Those dark brown eyes of his were so intense that she believed they could pierce through stone.

Her heart raced at the prospect of seeing him again.

"I've got to talk to you," she whispered to his likeness on the magazine. "Micah, I feel bad about the things I said to you on graduation night. I really hope you'll give me a chance to apologize and explain why I reacted that way."

I never should have listened to those other boys. I realize that now.

The telephone rang.

Tamara checked the caller ID before answering. "Hello, Mama."

"Sweetie, are you busy right now?"

"No, what's up?"

"I'm here at Lexington's Restaurant. Since it's right

down the street from your neighborhood, why don't you come have dinner with me?"

"Give me ten minutes," Tamara told her. "I'll be there."

"See you then," Jillian stated.

Tamara went into her bathroom to freshen up. She looked down at her jeans and decided on impulse to change clothes. Her mother would be dressed up—Jillian was always dressed in designer suits and expensive shoes.

I've never seen my mother in a pair of jeans or a sweat suit, she thought with amusement. Dressing down for Jillian meant a pair of khakis or linen pants.

Tamara changed into a black linen sundress, silver sandals and accessories. She knew that her mother would approve, as the dress was a gift from her.

She arrived at the restaurant fifteen minutes later.

Her mother was already seated. Tamara almost turned around and left when she realized that her mother was not alone.

I should have known she was up to something.

Jillian didn't care much for Lexington's but came here because she knew that Tamara was less likely to refuse her since it was only a couple blocks away from her apartment.

"Hello, Mama." The greeting was forced at best.

Tamara was furious with her mother for hijacking her into a blind date.

"Dear, I want you to meet Anthony. His mother and I went to high school together. He just moved to Atlanta, and I thought you two should meet. Anthony, this is my daughter Tamara."

She plastered on a smile. "It's nice to meet you, Anthony."

Tamara sent her mother a sharp look as she took a seat.

"So, Anthony, what brings you to Atlanta?" she asked.

"I'll be working at Fitzgerald & Johnson Industries as lead counsel," he said. "Your mother tells me that you write for *Luster* magazine."

"I do," she confirmed.

Tamara was struggling to keep her temper in check. Why couldn't Jillian just mind her own business? She didn't need her mother's help in getting a man.

She managed to enjoy herself while they ate. Anthony had a wonderful sense of humor, and he could hold an intelligent conversation on several subjects. He was definitely an improvement over the last one her mother had tried to set Tamara up with.

Anthony asked for her number.

Feeling pressured, Tamara gave it to him. If she hadn't, her mother would have given it to him anyway.

Jillian excused herself to go to the ladies' room.

She was about to follow her, but Anthony stopped her.

"Tamara, look, it's no pressure. Let's just get through this dinner to appease our mothers."

She gave him the first genuine smile of the evening. "You have one of those interfering mothers, too?"

Anthony nodded. "I'm in a relationship, but she doesn't think Rochelle is the woman for me. I know what I want and that is Rochelle. However, I hope that the three of us can get together sometime. Maybe we can all become friends."

"I'd like that, Anthony."

He paid the bill, then told Jillian that he had to leave.

"Tamara, I know that you're upset," she said when Anthony walked out of the restaurant. "But I saw the way you two were interacting." She broke into a smile. "Admit it. Don't you like him just a little bit?"

"Yeah, I do," Tamara responded. "Actually I like him a lot. In fact, I think he's the man for me, Mama." She gazed into her mother's hazel-green eyes and said, "Anthony has a girlfriend. We're going to have a threesome when I get back from Los Angeles."

"WHAT?"

She burst into laughter at the look of horror on her mother's face.

Jillian gasped and couldn't seem to catch her breath. Tamara reached over and took her hand. "Mama, I'm kidding."

Her mother patted her face with the napkin. "I can't believe you'd say something like that."

"It's what you deserved," Tamara countered. "Mama, please stop trying to set me up on blind dates. Don't you think I'm capable of finding my own man?"

Jillian's lips puckered in silence.

Tamara chuckled. "Good point. I haven't done a great job in that department, either."

"I just want to see you happily married with a family."

"Then let it happen naturally, Mama."

Jillian gave a stiff nod. "Now what is this about you going to Los Angeles?"

She told her mother about the assignment and seeing Micah again.

"It sounds promising," Jillian stated. "I can't wait to hear all about the trip."

Tamara pushed away from the table and rose to her feet. "There you go again. Mama, I'll see you later."

Jillian followed her out of the restaurant.

"Mama, why don't you look for a man for you?" Tamara suggested. "You should try to find someone to spend the rest of your life with instead of trying to shape my future."

A shadow of sadness colored Jillian's expression. "I don't think I can ever trust another man. Not after…" Her voice died.

Tamara hugged her mother. "I had a great time tonight but you are forbidden to arrange any more blind dates. You're making me feel insecure."

Jillian placed a hand to her face. "Oh, nooo…"

"I'm kidding, Mama," Tamara uttered with a laugh. "I need to get home and pack."

"I love you."

"I love you, too, Mama."

Before she headed home, Tamara waited for Jillian to get into her car and leave the restaurant parking lot.

Tamara rehearsed exactly what she would say repeatedly in her head for the rest of the evening and again the next morning as she prepared to leave for the airport.

Tamara flew first class from Atlanta to Los Angeles, both anxious and excited about seeing Micah again.

She hoped that he would be the one picking her up at the airport so that he could clear the air before meeting his performer. It would help the interview along if there was no tension between them.

Maybe I'm making too much of this. Micah's not the type of man who would hold a grudge.

To quell her nervousness, Tamara documented her thoughts.

August 28th
At this very moment, I am on a plane en route to Los Angeles to interview one of Micah's performers. I have mixed feelings about this little reunion because of what happened before we graduated college. Hopefully, Micah will put the past behind us and give me a chance to explain.

I have never forgotten that look of absolute hurt in his eyes. I have never been filled with such guilt as I experienced then. I'm not really sure an apology is enough to undo the hurt.

What if I've overanalyzed that moment? What if what I thought was hurt was actually something else?

I guess this is why Micah and I need to have a conversation. I miss him and deeply wish to repair our friendship.

I just hope that it isn't too late to make amends.

Most girls had considered Micah a nerd back in the day—but not Tamara.

Sexy Chocolate.

That's what she used to call Micah behind his back. He stood six-three, and even with glasses, the man looked good.

She remembered how the basketball coach wanted Micah to play for the school but he refused. Instead, he preferred to focus on his academics and his dedication paid off.

Micah utilized his talent and dual degrees in business and computer science to build his empire, Ross Red. She was proud of him and his accomplishments and hoped for the chance to tell him so.

Things ended so abruptly that night. Tamara didn't know if they could ever truly mend the rift in their relationship, but she was willing to try. Micah's friendship meant the world to her.

She settled back against her seat and closed her eyes. A thread of apprehension snaked through her body when the pilot announced they would be landing in twenty minutes.

I can do this.

Tamara repeated this over and over in her mind, trying to convince herself. Not that it was working. She was extremely nervous at the thought of seeing Micah again.

She assumed that he would be the one meeting her plane, and once they got over the awkward moments, they could talk and Tamara could tell him everything.

Thirty-five minutes later, she stepped off the plane and made her way through the Los Angeles International Airport. Tamara was disappointed when she didn't see Micah at the gate.

Maybe he was waiting for her in the baggage-claim area.

Instead, she found a man in a dark suit holding up

a sign with her name on it. She walked up to him and identified herself. "Hi, I'm Tamara Hodges."

"I hope you had a comfortable flight," he said. "If you give me your ticket, I'll retrieve your luggage for you, Ms. Hodges."

"Thanks," she murmured. "It's red. There are two bags. One large and a medium."

Tamara stood near the exit doors as she waited for her driver to bring her luggage.

He navigated to Tamara and led her outside to the car.

According to her itinerary, she was booked at the Four Seasons Hotel Los Angeles. While en route, Tamara checked her voice mail and returned two missed phone calls. She had hoped to find a message from Micah but it was to no avail.

He was a busy man—she knew that, but Tamara really thought that since he had given the interview his blessing he was ready to reconnect with her.

Now she wasn't so sure.

Micah positioned himself in the lobby area of the hotel where a suite had been reserved for Tamara. He wanted to catch a glimpse of the woman who had broken his heart.

He checked his watch.

She should be arriving at any moment.

He sensed her presence before she actually walked through the doors and up to the lobby.

Tamara was still slender with curves in all the right places, Micah noted as he watched her check into the hotel.

He raised his newspaper to shield his face when she turned to glance around the lobby.

The way she kept looking around, Micah wondered if she was looking for him.

Probably, but it didn't matter.

Micah determined that Tamara would not see him until he was ready for a face-to-face with her. The way his heart was racing and his eyes caressing her body— it was still too soon. He needed more time to rein in his emotions.

From outward appearances, Tamara looked fragile but Micah knew that she possessed a quiet strength—a quality that had drawn him to her all those years ago.

He watched as Tamara strolled over to the elevators and waited. Her eyes traveled the luxury surroundings once more before stepping inside.

Micah waited until the doors closed before rising to his feet and taking his leave.

His cell phone rang.

It was his secretary, Bette, informing him that his guest had arrived safely and was at the hotel. She also reminded him of his meeting with the art director that was scheduled in an hour.

"Thank you, Bette. I'm on my way back to the office now." Micah got up, strode through the glass revolving doors and handed the valet his ticket.

The love of his life was here in Los Angeles, and he was still avoiding her. He had a wall erected around his heart, but Tamara—was a trigger for him, which is why Micah purposed not to see her until he was in control of his emotions.

Micah stood outside, waiting for his car to arrive.

The valet attendant pulled the car in front of him and got out. Micah tipped him and strode around to the driver side.

He experienced a strange sensation, which caused the hair on the back of his neck to stand up.

Micah turned around.

Tamara was standing inside the lobby, looking at him through the glass wall, her expression one of complete shock.

His emotions unsettled, Micah pretended he did not recognize her, stepped into his car and quickly drove away. It had been a mistake coming here, he decided.

Micah knew that he and Tamara would come face-to-face, and when they did it would be on his terms. Micah vowed to make her pay for the pain she caused him all those years ago.

He had done nothing but try to be a good friend to Tamara, but the way she turned on him graduation night proved that their relationship had been one-sided in reality. Micah tried to forget about her over the years, but his heart would not let him.

As much as I want to hate Tamara, I can't. I am still in love with a woman who believes I'll never be good enough for her.

In his college days, Micah had been more of a geek and was not the kind of boy most girls usually went for, but his job as a tutor placed him in a circle of people he wouldn't otherwise hang with. Out of those relationships, friendships formed.

He thought Tamara was different from any other girl he had ever known. She was on the quiet side, kept to herself most of the time when she wasn't with her sorority sisters. On the weekends, she liked visiting her grandmother—he would go with her from time to time.

Micah had been there to comfort Tamara when the woman died. He didn't remember exactly the moment he fell in love with her, but when he landed the job with a software company in Chicago and was due to leave the week following graduation, Micah didn't want to leave Tamara without letting her know how he felt.

That was indubitably the biggest mistake of his life because she crushed him with her rejection. Tamara had tried to contact him a few days later, but Micah was hurt and preparing to relocate to Chicago.

Chapter 3

Tamara rushed out of the hotel but failed to get there in time to catch Micah.

She thought for a moment that he had seen her, too. Apparently, he hadn't or didn't recognize her. Tamara had come back downstairs to visit the gift shop but seeing Micah distracted her from her purpose.

Disappointed, Tamara returned to her suite, settled down on the sofa and pulled out her cell phone.

She sat in the chair for a moment, her thin fingers tensed in her lap to calm her nerves. Tamara inhaled and exhaled slowly, opened her phone and dialed. "Hello, this is Tamara Hodges. Do you have a contact number for Micah Ross please? I'm here to do a story on Justice Kane, and I really need to speak with him."

"I'm sorry but Mr. Ross is out of the office."

Tamara doubted they would give out his mobile number so she didn't bother asking for it. Instead, she inquired, "Would you take down my number and ask him to call me please?"

"What is the number?"

She gave the secretary her cell-phone number and the one to the hotel.

"I'll give him the message as soon as he returns, Ms. Hodges."

"Thank you." Tamara stirred uneasily in the chair, her uncertainty increasing by the minute. She didn't want to consider that Micah still held a grudge where she was concerned or that he didn't want to talk to her.

Tamara strolled out onto one of the two balconies to enjoy the panoramic views of the Hollywood Hills and downtown Los Angeles. She stayed out there for the next fifteen minutes just basking in the late summer sun. It was a clear day with no smog in sight.

She navigated back into the sitting area, which was furnished with two armchairs and a sofa set around a glass-top coffee table, a writing desk, plasma TV and entertainment system.

The bedroom, decorated in a soothing neutral color with muted gold accents, offered a high-back armchair and side table, a second plasma television and large walk-in closet with dark wood furnishings and a comfortable looking king-size bed.

While she waited for Micah's call, Tamara unpacked her suitcase and her laptop to keep busy.

When Tamara put away all of her clothes, she sat down at the desk and opened up the computer to work on an article she needed to finish before the week was out.

Tamara stole a peek at the clock.

Thirty minutes had passed.

She considered making another call to Micah but silently reasoned her way out of calling. The man was busy, and she didn't want to become a pest. Tamara could not escape the feeling that maybe he was avoiding her.

"Please call me, Micah," she whispered in the empty room. "I really want to talk to you."

Tamara had hoped they could have dinner together later this evening, so she made another call to his office.

She received the same response as before.

Tamara replaced the receiver in the cradle. "Micah..." she whispered.

Two hours passed and still no word from Micah. Tamara ordered room service because she didn't feel like eating alone in the hotel restaurant.

Micah was apparently too busy to speak with her; he was working or maybe he had a date with Sunni. Hope sprang up in Tamara as she considered that she and Micah would both be attending the release party, so at some point they would have to talk.

Samantha called her shortly after eight.

"I just spoke with Micah Ross, and we came up with another idea," she stated. "What do you think about the idea of going on tour with Justice Kane? At least for the West Coast cities anyway. You'll be traveling with the artist on the tour bus and writing about the behind-the-scenes action you observe firsthand for our readers. Write the story as if the readers are there with you."

"This sounds like a great idea," Tamara said. "Samantha, I'm all for it. I'm glad I overpacked for this trip."

"Great. You'll e-mail the series of articles as you finish them."

"You said Micah Ross is fine with this?" she asked. Tamara was surprised, considering that she hadn't been able to catch up to him. Why didn't he call her directly? She wondered.

"It was actually his idea," Samantha responded. "This article will let us know if you're ready to become a feature writer for the magazine. This is your shot, Tamara."

"I realize that. I won't let you down, Samantha."

"I know that. Enjoy yourself, Tamara, and e-mail those articles as soon as you finish them."

Tamara broke into a smile. Even though she hadn't heard a word from Micah, it seemed as if he were trying to keep her around for a little longer; however, she wished that he had called her directly to discuss his thoughts.

Another thought struck her. Maybe he was deliberately avoiding her.

"I called Micah's office earlier but haven't been able to speak to him directly," Tamara stated. "I'm assuming we'll touch base sometime tomorrow."

"Oh, he did tell me that he's going to be in meetings all day tomorrow but said that he'll see you at the release party."

Tamara hid her disappointment. Micah's schedule was so tight that she wondered if she would have the chance to apologize. The party just was not the place to bring up the past.

She and her editor discussed one of her other projects before ending their conversation.

A commercial flashed across the television. A thread of jealousy snaked down her spine as she watched a smiling Sunni saunter across the screen wearing the newest bra from Victoria's Secret.

What does Micah see in her? Tamara wondered. She's tall, thin and beautiful, but is she truly in love with him? How does Micah feel about her? Did he love her, too?

She couldn't tell from the many photographs she had seen of the two of them.

Micah rarely made eye contact with the media. They considered him aloof and even a bit eccentric.

Tamara knew that Micah wasn't aloof—just shy and had always been uncomfortable in the spotlight. She wondered if any of the reporters knew that he could sing and that he played the piano, drums and sax. He also loved computers and could write software programs. Even though he studied business and computer science in school, Micah's first love had always been music.

She was pretty sure that those same reporters also didn't know how much he loved reading, his tastes varying from Shakespeare to James Patterson. Micah rarely granted personal interviews, instead focusing on his A-list of performers and pushing their careers forward. He was an astute executive and knew the music industry inside and out.

While the media and other industry professionals considered him a man of mystery, they held him in high regard.

"How could I have been so stupid and so insensitive?" she whispered. "How could I ever have thought he was like…" Tamara shook her head and rose to her feet.

She opened the floor-to-ceiling curtains and stared out the window over the city of Los Angeles. It was so beautiful at night. Tamara loved California and often came to visit her family living in Oceanside, a coastal town near San Diego.

She could not fully enjoy the night air, the shining stars and the moon because Micah dominated her thoughts.

Tamara spent the rest of her evening editing and revising her article about a woman who had overcome breast cancer and was now inspiring others.

An hour passed and still no word from Micah.

Then another.

When the clock struck eleven, Tamara gave up and decided to go to bed. She was still on East Coast time and feeling weary.

Tamara vowed she would not leave Los Angeles until she and Micah had a chance to sit down and talk.

Micah eyed the telephone, still warring within himself whether or not to call Tamara.

She was probably in bed by now he thought and mentally let himself off the hook.

Old feelings that he thought were long buried had resurfaced after seeing her today, and he had not been able to get her off his mind.

Along with those feelings came another emotion—resentment. He hungered to make Tamara pay for the way she used him back then. Micah believed that the only reason Tamara was reaching out to him now was the interview he had arranged.

He wondered what would happen if she didn't deliver the interview as promised and if it would hurt her career.

Micah's lips curled upward at the thought.

Tamara needed this interview to take place if she ever wanted to be considered for something other than writing fluff on debutante balls, charity events and flower shows.

His stomach growled, reminding him that he had missed lunch. It was after eight and he didn't like to eat heavy when it was late so he made himself a salad and heated up a piece of leftover grilled salmon.

Sunni called Micah, wanting to know if she could come over to spend the evening with him. She had been trying to seduce him for months now. He wasn't about to let her into his bed because Micah didn't have any idea what it would eventually cost him to get her out.

"Not tonight. Sunni, I've got a lot of work to catch up on," Micah told her. "I need to stay focused."

"Micah, you've been a real party pooper lately. You used to have time for me."

"Sunni, I have a business to run. You know that."

"You have very capable people working for you, too," she retorted.

"I'll give you a call later," he stated.

Micah knew that she was not happy with his response, but the truth was that he really did not feel like having company tonight. He wanted to spend the rest of his evening deciding exactly what to do about Tamara Hodges.

* * *

Tamara called and left another message for Micah after she ate her breakfast. His secretary told her that he was in a meeting and would not be returning calls until later in the day. She did not expect any other response.

She was sure that Micah was avoiding her. If he were not, Tamara was positive that she would have heard from him by now. This was not her first trip to Los Angeles, so Tamara decided against leaving the hotel for sightseeing or shopping. Instead, she spent her day in the hotel room working on another project until it was time to dress for the party.

Tamara's nerves had been on edge all day long. She even took an instant dislike to everything she packed for the trip and now wished she had gone shopping earlier.

After her shower, Tamara changed into a black Tadashi dress with a sheer top, sleeves and shutter pleating from bodice to the hem.

"This is so not me," she mumbled as she stared at her reflection in the floor-length mirror. The dress hugged her body lovingly, but Tamara wasn't comfortable when it came to showing off her curves.

Next, she slipped on a Proenza Schouler georgette dress that she'd snagged on sale for two hundred seventy-two dollars at Sak's Fifth Avenue department store the day before she left Atlanta.

The black-and-white print, dramatically gathered shift draped at the back with a floating train. The dress looked great with the opaque black stockings and Christian Louboutin open-toe patent-leather pumps.

"Not bad," she whispered. "But I just don't think it's right for this event." Tamara decided she would save this dress for the Hollington College homecoming weekend. She would wear it to the reception.

So what am I wearing tonight?

The new pumps were already torturing her feet, so Tamara practically kicked them off.

"I'm working tonight so I need to be comfortable," Tamara said as she pulled out another dress. She changed again, this time into a Vera Wang silk halter dress in a vivid emerald-green color.

Tamara put on a pair of silver and emerald jeweled thong sandals with straps that wrapped around her ankles. She added an emerald ring, white gold and emerald bangles with matching earrings to complete her look.

She undid her twists and fingered through her hair, combing through the waves. Tamara applied her makeup with a light hand and surveyed the results. Satisfied, she walked out of the bathroom.

How will Micah respond when he sees me again? She wondered. Will he be happy to see me?

Tamara was looking forward to seeing him again after all these years but didn't know how she would handle seeing him with another woman.

Micah, his secretary, the event planner and the owner of the club walked from room to room, making sure that everything was exactly the way it should be. He was very hands-on and always liked to do a final walkthrough before any of his events.

"Where will our sponsors be seated?" Micah asked the event coordinator.

"Over here," she responded, pointing to the right

of where they were standing on the stage. "Just as you requested."

He awarded her a smile. "Thank you."

She glanced down at her watch and excused herself to make sure all the staff was in place for the event.

Micah felt that familiar sensation. He felt Tamara's presence before he actually saw her.

He turned around to find her walking toward him.

Their eyes met, and Tamara broke into a beautiful smile. "Micah, it's so good to see you. It's been a long time," she murmured.

"Ten years," he responded. Micah couldn't believe that she was standing in front of him acting as if she had not ripped his heart out.

"Can you believe it?" Tamara asked as if trying to lull him into a conversation. "We've been out of school for *ten* years."

Although she was trying to hide it, Micah could tell that Tamara was very nervous. He heard it in her voice. She wanted to be all warm and fuzzy, but it was not gonna happen. Micah knew that it was only because she wanted this story on Justice Kane.

His heart thudded once and then settled back to its natural rhythm. She was even more gorgeous than Micah remembered.

"Tamara, you haven't changed at all," Micah stated. It was not meant to be a compliment.

"You're so sweet for saying that, but I do own a couple of mirrors and they don't lie."

Their eyes locked as their breathing seemed to come in unison.

A tall leggy woman wearing a curve hugging, one-shoulder beaded mini dress with stellar results approached them, breaking the tiny thread that drew them like a drug.

Ignoring Tamara completely, she slipped an arm around Micah and said, "I've been looking for you, darling. Are you ready to sit down?"

Tamara was not about to just disappear into the woodwork. She held out her hand and introduced herself, saying, "Hi, I'm Tamara Hodges. I'm here to do a story on Justice Kane."

The woman eyed her from head to toe, a smirk on her flawless face. "I'm sure you know that I'm Sunni. It's nice to meet you."

Tamara didn't acknowledge one way or another. Instead, she glanced over at Micah as if waiting for him to say something, but it was Sunni who broke the silence.

"What magazine do you write for?" she asked.

"Luster," Tamara responded.

"I was featured on their cover a couple months ago." Sunni ran her fingers through her long spiral curls. "They couldn't keep that issue in print."

Tamara pasted on a polite smile. "I remember."

There was no point in telling the deluded woman that the issue did not sell out because of her face on the cover—it was because it was a special fashion issue.

Slipping her arm through Micah's, Sunni said, "Make sure you get lots of photos of me and Micah."

Tamara glanced over at him, noting the amused glint in his eyes. He was enjoying this while Sunni was getting on her last nerve. Tamara took great delight in reminding her, "The story is on Justice, his life and music."

Her cell phone rang.

"If you two will excuse me...I need to take this call." Tamara walked away, leaving him alone with Sunni.

She stole a peek over her shoulder. Micah was gazing down lovingly at Sunni. Even from where she was standing, Tamara could see that he cared deeply for her.

She felt the edges of jealousy pulling at her. Kyra didn't know what she was talking about—Micah and Sunni were definitely involved from the way they were acting.

Tamara, get yourself together, she silently chided herself. *Why are you acting like this? You have no right to be jealous or possessive.*

She stole another look over her shoulder and found Micah standing there watching her. There was something in his expression that indicated he wasn't all that happy to see her again.

Tamara was even more determined to talk to Micah so that she could straighten things out between them. She was going to have to pry him out of Sunni's viselike grip. The woman wanted to make sure that she knew they were a couple. Tamara did note that while he was very attentive to Sunni, he had never been a man who openly displayed affection but she could sense an intimacy between them.

She was so caught up in her musings that she did not notice that they had walked up behind her.

"Tamara," he prompted, touching her arm lightly.

"Huh?" Embarrassed, she glanced up to find him and Sunni watching her.

"I'm sorry, were you saying something to me?"

His brown eyes met her hazel-green ones, probing

to her very soul. "Tamara, I asked if you wanted something to drink."

"A glass of white wine please."

Micah signaled a waiter and placed their orders.

They stood for a moment in uncomfortable silence until Sunni stated, "I see someone I need to speak to, honey, but I won't be long. Please excuse me."

"I'm glad we have a few minutes alone," Tamara began as she tried to force her confused emotions into order. "I would like to sit down with you and talk, Micah. There's a lot I have to tell you."

"So talk," he responded, his expression a mask of stone.

Taken aback by the coolness of his tone, Tamara quickly noted that Micah was no longer the same man she knew all those years ago. He had changed.

"Micah, this is supposed to be a party," she reminded him with a nervous chuckle. "I don't want to do this here, but I do want to talk about this another time— maybe tomorrow if you're not busy."

He did not respond immediately.

Their drinks arrived.

He handed her the glass of wine.

"Thank you," she said and took a sip. "Mmm…this is good."

Again Tamara's words were met with silence.

She released a short sigh of frustration. "Micah, will you please talk to me?"

"Tamara, what are we supposed to be talking about? You really haven't said anything."

She took a deep breath and adjusted her smile. It was clear that Micah wasn't going to make this easy for her. "Okay… Well, let's talk about Justice. First off, I really want to thank you for allowing me to go on tour with him. This opportunity is going to guarantee my position as the feature writer for the entertainment section of *Luster* magazine and take my career to the next level for sure. This is my trial run so I really can't mess this up. Micah, I've got some great ideas about this story and I—"

"Actually, I'm glad you brought that up," Micah stated. "I've changed my mind. After further consideration, I've decided that the interview may not be a good idea for my artist. As you know, Justice Kane has come a long way from being that thug from the ATL, and I'm just not sure it makes good business sense to bring his past back up. You *were* planning to write from the hometown bad boy gone good angle, weren't you?"

Tamara finished her glass of wine in one swallow. "You can't be serious about killing the article, Micah. Justice *has* come a long way from the person he used to be—why not write about his journey to the man he is now? His story would inspire others, don't you think?"

His hard gaze met hers. "I've never been more serious in my life."

Chapter 4

I've never been more serious in my life.

She had said those very same words to him ten years ago. In fact, they were the last words she had spoken to him on graduation night. Right after she told Micah that she would never date someone like him.

Tamara still remembered the hurt expression on his face. When he asked her if she was serious, she had replied that she'd never been more serious in her life.

Granted, she had treated him badly a long time ago, but now he was messing with her career.

A wave of hot fury washed over Tamara. "Micah, I don't know what's going on with you. I came to Los Angeles under the impression that you were fine with me interviewing Justice."

His expression was a mask of stone. "As I've said, I changed my mind."

Tamara held her temper in check when Micah's secretary joined them briefly to let him know that Justice Kane had arrived.

"Would you mind telling me why?" she demanded when Bette left to complete the next item on her to-do list. "Micah, why are you acting this way?"

Micah frowned as if he were irritated by her question. "After further consideration, I just don't think this is the right direction we should go in right now. If you will excuse me, I need to check on some things backstage," he told her, his tone cold and exact. "Enjoy your evening, Ms. Hodges."

He stood up and walked off without waiting for her response.

Tamara chewed on her bottom lip and tried to control her anger. She knew that she had treated Micah badly in college but the man she knew and loved would never set out to destroy her career just to prove a point.

Or would he?

One thing was for sure, she did not intend to just give up.

Tamara caught the eye of Bette, the secretary, and got up to speak with her. "Is there any way I can go backstage? I'd like to get some comments from Justice."

"That's fine, Ms. Hodges," she responded. "Your press pass will allow you entry."

Tamara walked through the double doors with purpose. Micah was in the hallway talking to one of the band members.

He stepped into her path, showing no signs of relenting. "Tamara, what are you doing back here? I thought I'd made myself clear that there will be no interview."

"Micah, I get it," Tamara said, cutting him off. She kept all expression from her voice as she talked. "Okay...I get it. I hurt you. Look, I didn't want to do this here, which is why I have been calling you and even tonight—I tried getting you to commit to a time when we could talk."

Keeping her voice low, she continued. "Micah, I'm sorry for the way that I treated you in college. I really am, but when I heard those boys talking about how you were planning to sleep with me graduation night—I was so hurt."

Tamara paused a moment before adding, "Back then, I was going through a lot of stuff, and I couldn't believe that you had been planning something like that."

"I never said anything like that. I would think that you would've known me better than that, but I guess you don't."

"Deep down I knew that you weren't that type of person, but I'd already said some pretty cruel things to you. I didn't know how to come back to you and apologize. I could never take back the words."

"We were all going through something, Tamara. I just wish you had come to me and asked if I'd said whatever you heard instead of believing the rumor."

"I realize that now, Micah. What you don't understand is that something happened to me that had me really messed up for a long time." Tamara took a deep breath and then exhaled slowly. "You know, I actually thought that I would come out here and apologize and that you'd forgive me. I thought that we'd be able to move past the hurt and be professional, Micah."

Her angry gaze met his. "Tell me something. Did

you set all of this in motion to deliberately hurt me?" she asked. "Are you that thirsty for revenge? The difference between you and me is that I never set out to hurt you deliberately. I made a mistake, Micah. But none of that matters, huh?"

Without waiting for a response, Tamara turned and walked away.

She asked the valet to alert her driver that she was ready to leave. While she waited, Tamara struggled to keep her tears at bay.

When her car arrived, she got in and returned to the hotel.

Tamara waited until she was in her hotel suite before breaking down in tears. She had not been prepared to face Micah's wrath. She never considered that those seeds of rejection she planted in him had sprouted into a wall of bitterness.

He actually hates me enough to try and ruin my career.

The thought saddened Tamara as ten long years of regret assailed her. He was no longer the man she knew in college. That much was obvious.

Grief and despair tore at her heart over the loss of a man who was once a very dear friend.

How could she have been so stupid?

She should have realized all along that Micah was still upset with her. It probably would have been a good idea to insist on talking to him before making the trip.

Tamara sighed, then gave a resigned shrug.

She considered calling Samantha, but it was three hours later on the East Coast—well past midnight in Atlanta. Besides, she had no idea how to explain what happened. Tamara ignored the heavy feeling in her stomach and began to pack.

"What happened to that reporter girl?" Sunni asked when she walked backstage to join Micah.

"She's not a reporter girl, Sunni," Micah stated. "But to answer your question, Tamara's probably out front at our table."

Sunni shook her head. "No, she's not. I just left there." She played with her curly tendrils. "Matter of fact, I haven't seen her in a while. I thought that maybe Tamara had come back here to talk to Justice or hang up under you."

His eyes searching around the room, Micah pulled out his cell phone and called his secretary. "Bette, have you seen Tamara?"

"She left about twenty minutes ago, Mr. Ross. Would you like me to contact Ms. Hodges for you?"

"No," Micah stated. "I'll take care of this myself."

"What are you going to do?" Sunni asked after he ended the call.

"I need to leave for a little while, but I'll be back before Justice performs."

A thread of guilt ran down his spine over the way Micah had treated Tamara. It was childish, and he now regretted his actions.

Sunni glared at him. "I can't believe you're going to run out on me like this. You're going after her, aren't you? Micah, is there something going on that I should know about?"

"Look, Sunni, she was an old friend of mine from college and I haven't seen her in almost ten years. We had a misunderstanding," Micah explained. "I need to apologize to her."

It was clear that Sunni was not happy about this sudden turn of events. "I'm sure it can wait until after the party. There is no way that I'm letting you abandon me—the media will be all over something like this. Besides, I doubt Tamara will be going anywhere tonight. She wants you to come running after her."

"Sunni, this is not your call. I won't be gone long."

"Whatever," she muttered; her eyes were stony with anger.

Micah had his driver take him to the Four Seasons Hotel Los Angeles. The car had barely stopped before he was out and rushing into the lobby. He took the elevator up to the sixteenth floor suite and knocked on the door.

Tamara opened the door as if she had been expecting him, but the expression on her face told him otherwise.

"I thought you were room service," she said. "Micah, what are you doing here? I figured after the way you were treating me earlier that you didn't want to be around me. If you came to kick me out, then you don't have to bother. I'm flying home on the first flight to the ATL."

"I'm here because it's my turn to apologize to you. May I please come inside?"

Surprised, Tamara stepped aside to let Micah enter the room and then closed the door. "You should be at the release party. There's no need to worry about me. I'm a big girl." She stood with her hands on her hips, waiting.

"I'm sorry, Tamara. I don't want to ruin your career—that was never really my intent."

"What was your intent then?" Tamara asked, folding her arms across her chest.

A loud knock on the door placed a temporary break in their conversation.

Micah glanced over at her. "Are you expecting someone?" He hoped that Sunni hadn't decided to up and follow him to the hotel.

"It should be my food," she announced. "I ordered room service."

Micah took care of the bill despite her objections.

After the server left, Tamara sat down at a table and removed the lid covering her meal. "Have some," she offered. "I remember how much you used to love French fries."

He smiled. "No thanks."

Micah sat down in a nearby chair.

Tamara's eyes traveled to the clock sitting on the mantel of the fireplace. "Micah, you should probably get back to the club. Justice will be performing soon."

"Look Tamara, I would still like you to do the interview. Eat quickly."

"Are you sure about this?" Tamara wanted to know. "I'm not in the mood to go back and forth with you on this, Micah. I know things ended badly ten years ago and that's one of the reasons I've been trying to reach out to you. I had hoped that we'd talk so that I could try to make things right."

He nodded. "As you said earlier, this is not the time for a talk like that. But yes, I'm sure about the interview. Tamara, I want you to write the article."

She wiped her mouth on the edge of her napkin.

"What about the tour? Will I still be allowed to go along?"

Micah nodded a second time.

When she caught him eying her fries, she said, "Just go on and eat some."

Standing up, Micah chuckled as he crossed the room in long strides. "I was trying hard to resist."

Tamara held out her hand. "Friends?"

"Let's see how tonight goes," Micah responded. He wasn't ready to let down the walls guarding his heart.

"Fair enough," she said quietly. Tamara concentrated on her dinner while Micah made several business calls.

When Tamara finished, she pushed away from the table. "I need to freshen up, and then I'll be ready to leave."

Micah watched her from across the room. Tamara was so beautiful, even more than he remembered. He just wasn't sure that he could trust her ever again. He had no idea the type of woman she had become.

Ten years was a long time ago, but the wound of Tamara's rejection was still fresh, almost as if it had just happened.

Get over it, Micah's heart urged.

Tamara was the only woman he had ever loved, and now she was back in his life. He had one of two choices. Micah could let her walk out of his life a second time or he could move forward and give Tamara a second chance.

Micah's words stung but more than that they filled Tamara with shame.

He had every right to be angry with her because her actions that night were cruel.

Tamara had considered him one of her best friends—
yet she chose to believe a lie without even consulting
him about it. How could she ever hope to make this
up to him?

She brushed her teeth and then touched up her
makeup and hair.

When Tamara walked out of the bathroom, Micah
stood there eying her from head to toe. For a brief moment, his eyes brimmed with tenderness and passion.

"You look beautiful."

"Thank you."

He reached out and pulled her into his arms, sur-
prising her. "We're friends, Tamara. That won't ever
change." Micah paused a moment, then said, "I have to
be honest with you. I haven't gotten over what you said
to me ten years ago, but I never stopped caring about
you. I won't deny that there were days I wished I didn't."

She hugged him back. "Micah, I never meant to hurt
you."

He kissed her cheek. "We'll talk later. Now let's get
going."

They left the suite and took the elevator down to
the lobby.

On the way to the club, Micah told her, "Just so you
know, I'm not trying to avoid a discussion with you. I
know that we need to talk, Tamara."

She nodded and hid her trembling hands in the folds
of her dress. "I just want a chance to explain what was
going on back then."

"We'll do it before you go back to Atlanta," he promised. "There are some things I need to say to you, too."

"I hope you'll let me go first," Tamara stated.

He laughed and shook his head. "Some things never change."

She relaxed as the tension between them evaporated.

Micah and Tamara continued their light banter during the short drive back to the club, making it just minutes before Justice was due to perform.

Micah went backstage while she sat down across from Sunni.

"Oh you're back, I see," she commented drily when Tamara joined her at the table. "Where's Micah?"

"He went to check on Justice."

"You ran out of here in a hurry," Sunni stated. "What happened? Did you have a family emergency? A sick child?"

"No, I didn't," Tamara responded. "And I don't have any children."

Sunni's eyes strayed down to her left hand. "Oh, I just assumed you were married."

"Well, I'm afraid that you assumed wrong," Tamara retorted with a tiny smile.

"How well do you know Micah?" Sunni asked. "He mentioned that you were friends in college, but your friendship could not have been as close as you believed, especially since he never mentioned you to me. You won't believe all of the people coming out of the woodwork claiming some close relationship to Micah. We all know that it's because he's a celebrity."

Tamara held her temper in check. She was not going to let Sunni bait her into an argument. She had no idea what Micah saw in a woman like her.

Micah sat down in the empty chair between her and Sunni. Tamara was glad to have him at the table. Maybe

Sunni would keep her snide comments to herself in his presence.

She turned to face the stage, bobbing her head to the music. Justice was an amazing performer. Tamara made mental notes when he dedicated one of the songs to the memory of his mother and spoke of how much he missed her.

After the performance, Micah led Tamara backstage for a one-on-one interview with Justice.

While she talked with the performer, Micah quietly observed them in the background. Tamara could feel the heat of his gaze on her, causing her heart to hammer foolishly. She managed to finish the interview.

"So what did you think?" Tamara asked him.

"It was an interview," Micah commented. "I'll reserve judgment until I see what you put in print."

They walked outside of the club.

"I need to call a taxi," she stated.

"No," Micah replied. "I'll have my driver take you home. After I drop Sunni off I'll come to your suite unless you'd rather talk sometime tomorrow. However, you'll be leaving to join Justice on tour."

"Tonight's fine."

She rode in the limo with Micah and Sunni.

The woman had no shame, Tamara thought silently. Sunni was draped over him in such a possessive manner that she was tempted to laugh.

Tamara uttered a soft prayer of thanks when the limo pulled in front of her hotel. She didn't care for Sunni at all and couldn't figure out what Micah saw in the woman.

She took the elevator up to the sixteenth floor and into her suite. She surveyed her reflection in the mirror.

Micah returned to the hotel shortly after midnight.

"I wasn't sure I'd be seeing you again tonight." Tamara could not resist adding, "I was sure Sunni would try to keep you with her all night."

The beginning of a smile tipped the corners of his mouth. "I told you that we'd have our talk, Tamara. *I meant it.*"

They sat down on the sofa.

Tamara spoke first. "Micah, I owe you a huge apology for the things I said to you graduation night. I feel like I can't say sorry enough."

His closeness was so male, so bracing that she had to wrench herself from her preoccupation with his handsome face.

"Tamara, I accept your apology," he said in response.

"I was so messed up back then," she explained. "My life was crazy, Micah."

"It is what it is," he stated without emotion. "Tamara, there's really nothing that you can say now that will ever change what happened."

"You're still angry with me over it," she acknowledged. "Micah, I can tell by the way you're treating me. What I need to know is if we can ever get past what happened? I'm willing to try if you are."

A muscle quivered at his jaw. "Things changed between us that night, Tamara. I can't understand why you would believe something a bunch of guys told you. We had been friends since our freshman year at Hollington."

She shriveled a little at Micah's expression. "I know

that, Micah," Tamara responded. "I eventually came to that conclusion but then I found out that it was just a nasty joke. I tried to contact you but you refused my calls."

"You'd have refused my calls if the situation had been reversed, Tamara, but then again, I never would have believed what somebody else told me. After four years, I figured I knew you pretty well."

Tamara agreed. "You're right. I should have known better, but Micah, my head wasn't in the right place. I was so focused on getting out of school and landing a job so that I could take care of myself."

"So you keep saying."

"Micah, back then it was hard for me to trust anybody."

He released a long sigh before saying, "I guess what it comes down to is that none of it really matters anymore."

Micah rose to his feet. "It's late, and you need to get some rest. I'll see you in the morning before you leave."

"I miss you, Micah," Tamara blurted. "I really miss our friendship."

He didn't respond.

Tamara met his gaze. "Will you please say something?"

"I don't know what you want me to say."

"That you miss our friendship as much as I do or that you want us to be friends again." She shrugged. "Something like that, maybe."

Micah drew his lips in thoughtfully. "I'll see you in the morning."

He was still guarded so Tamara didn't press him.

Instead, she walked Micah to the door and said, "I really appreciate this opportunity in spite of what happened between us. I just hope you will consider letting me back into your life."

Micah hugged her and then left the suite, leaving Tamara alone with her thoughts.

"I'm going to find a way to win back your trust," she whispered. "And your heart."

Chapter 5

Tamara was up early the next morning packing for the tour. She was so excited about the tour that she couldn't sleep. She ordered room service and had just enough time to eat a bagel with cream cheese and a couple of strawberries.

Tamara jumped at the sound of a loud knock on her bedroom door.

She walked briskly across the floor expectantly.

"I thought it might be you," she stated when Micah entered the suite. "I remember how punctual you used to be. I guess some things never change."

"And I recall that you were never ready whenever I arrived," he countered, looking around the suite. "Do you have everything packed and ready to go?"

Tamara broke into a smile. "Micah, you'll be proud

of me. I'm *almost* ready. Just need to pack up my computer."

"Some things never change," he said with a chuckle. "Did you sleep okay?"

"Not really," she responded. "But it's because I'm really looking forward to this tour. I'm sure I'll catch a nap at some point while we're on the bus."

Tamara packed her laptop and closed her tote. "Okay. I have everything."

Looking up as she approached, Micah openly studied her. Things were still a little tense between them but they were both attempting to be cordial.

"Did you eat any of your breakfast?" he inquired. "It looks untouched."

"I ate a bagel and some fruit. I don't know if you remember, but I'm not really a breakfast person."

"I remember," he stated. "I used to have to force you down to the dining hall every morning."

Tamara was touched that he remembered. He had warmed to her some since their talk, but Micah was still guarded at times.

They left the suite and took the elevator down to the lobby.

Tamara chewed on her bottom lip.

"Nervous?" Micah asked.

"I am," she confirmed. "I'm the outsider. I don't know how the band members are going to respond to me."

"You don't have to be nervous. Everyone is really down-to-earth. You'll see."

He drove her over to his office building where they were loading up the buses.

Following behind Micah, Tamara entered the first crew bus. She swiveled slowly, her delight growing.

"You'll be traveling on this one," he told her. "You will be sleeping in the executive suite located in the back of the bus—there's a double bed and a full bathroom. You'll also have your own TV and DVD player in the suite. The other TV is in the bunk area."

"Wow," Tamara murmured. "This is really nice, but where is Justice and everybody else sleeping? He should have the suite."

"There are eight bunks for the others. Justice will sleep in the suite on the other bus."

She surveyed her surroundings. The lounge area featured a leather sofa and two overstuffed chairs, a flat-screen LCD TV, DVD player, CD player and a surround sound system. Doors separated the bunk areas from the lounge.

The fully equipped kitchen came with a large fridge, coffeemaker, microwave and toaster.

"You will be able to get on the Internet if you need to," Micah said. "There is a collection of movies and PlayStation games available on board, as well."

"This tour bus is incredible," Tamara commented to Micah.

"I like for my artists to travel in style. You will be going to Seattle, Vancouver, Portland, San Francisco and then back here to Los Angeles. You'll fly out the day after the L.A. concert—I've already arranged for your ticket."

"Are you coming with us?"

Micah shook his head no. "Not on the bus," he responded. "I'll be flying to Seattle tomorrow for the concert."

"Oh, okay. I guess I'll see you then." Tamara had hoped they would be traveling together. She had so many questions for Micah.

She wanted to know what inspired him to start his record company, why he wasn't performing himself and how serious he and Sunni were. She and Micah had ten years to catch up on, but apparently, he was not as curious about her life.

She and Micah embraced before he departed the bus.

"I'll see you tomorrow," he promised.

A couple of band members started up a game of chess while another played his PlayStation. One was sitting across from her in the lounge with his eyes closed, listening to his iPod device. Justice Kane was in the back of the bus talking to the road manager and one of the female background singers. He had decided to ride on this bus for the first leg of the trip.

Justice joined her a few minutes later.

She spent the morning listening to him and making notes as he talked about the effect music had on him and how it essentially saved his life.

"I went to Micah's store one day, and this music came on that really spoke to my spirit and I just started singing."

"Was this a song that you had written?" Tamara asked.

He shook his head no. "It just came to me. I could see the words in my mind. I know you think I'm tripping, but I'm not. I have never been able to remember any of that song since that day. I guess it was just meant for Micah's ears. We started working together after that."

"Is it true that he put up the money for your first album?"

"He sure did. I didn't have nothing but a police record. Micah told me that he would rather invest in my future than have me out there trying to steal the money for a demo. I ain't gon' lie—that's what I was gonna do. After that song, I was determined to get the money for my album by any means necessary, but you know what? It wouldn't have worked out this way."

"So how exactly did music save your life?" she asked him.

"It gave me a dream. Micah told me that God don't give you a vision without giving provision. I believed him."

"I read in *People* that you're very passionate about helping other young men get their lives together. What are you doing outside of the concerts to promote anti-gang activity and speaking in the schools?"

"I sponsor two Pop Warner football teams—one in the ATL and the other one in Los Angeles. I also have a college scholarship fund to send kids to college who may not be straight-A students but have the desire to better their lives. I'm considering building a boarding school for boys somewhere in the Midwest who really want out of the gang life. I want to put them in a safe environment, and the location will have to be kept quiet. I'm still working all that out, you know?"

"This is all very impressive."

He smiled. "Somebody held out a hand to me when I was out there. I have to pay it forward, you know? Do the same thing. Help others because everybody deserves a second chance."

She nodded in agreement.

Tamara made more notes as they discussed his new album.

When they stopped for lunch, Justice returned to his bus to take a nap.

She navigated to her own suite and shut the door to type up her notes.

Tamara liked to write while the story was fresh in her mind. She turned on her iPod handheld, stuck her earphones in and worked.

Three hours passed before she emerged from the suite to get bottled water from the fridge.

One of the background singers approached her.

"So how are you enjoying yourself so far?" she asked. "I'm Marty. I didn't get a chance to introduce myself earlier."

"Marty, it's nice to meet you. I'm Tamara. Things are going well. I love the bus."

"By the end of the week, you may not feel that way," she said with a chuckle.

"How long have you been touring with Justice?"

"About a year now," Marty responded. "He's my cousin. When I lost my job, he offered me this gig. I don't like being away so much from my family but it keeps a roof over our heads."

"How many children do you have?"

"Two. My son is almost five and my daughter is two. They're with my husband. He lost his job six months ago. He's in school trying to finish up his degree so that he'll be able to apply for some management positions."

"Marty, that's wonderful," Tamara stated. "But I'm sure it's hard with him in school and having young children."

"Thank the Lord for my mama. She watches them when I'm on the road and Terry's in class." Marty picked up an apple and bit into it. "Do you have any children?"

"I don't," she responded. "Maybe one day. Hopefully a husband will come before the baby."

"A woman as pretty as you won't have any problems in that department. I saw the way Micah was looking at you. You definitely have his attention."

Tamara smiled. "Micah and I have known each other for over ten years. We were best friends in college, but after graduation we lost touch with each other."

Marty became animated. "So this is the first time you two have seen each other since you graduated?"

She took a sip of water and nodded.

"That's so sweet," Marty murmured. "I love reunions of any kind. It's just something special about a coming together in unity."

"Would you like to watch a movie or something?" Tamara asked. "I have that huge suite to myself. We might as well enjoy it."

"Do you mind if I ask Yuri to join us?" Marty inquired, referring to the other female singer.

"That's fine. The more the merrier," Tamara responded. "Hopefully, the others won't think that we're antisocial."

Marty laughed. "Girl, they'll be thrilled that we're not out there trying to watch some chick flick or Lifetime. Yuri and I usually end up in the suite watching television most of the time."

"Oh, no…did I get you kicked out of the suite?" Tamara questioned. "I could sleep in one of the bunks."

"You don't want that, trust me." Marty took another bite into the apple. "I'ma go get Yuri. We'll be back there in a few minutes."

Tamara enjoyed spending time with the women. Marty and Yuri were very friendly and both possessed a wonderful sense of humor—something they stated was necessary when on the road.

They continued bonding over dinner. She listened in amusement as the women heaped praises on Micah about how thoughtful he was and how blessed Tamara was to have him as a friend.

That evening, she changed into a pair of shorts and a T-shirt for bed. After she pulled down the covers and climbed inside, Tamara pulled out her journal and began writing.

August 30

I can't believe that I'm actually on tour with Justice Kane—at least the West Coast leg of the tour. The crew and band have all been so nice and friendly. They've gone out of their way to make me feel welcomed.

I really thought that Micah and I would have some time to just talk but he's really a busy man. He's flying to Seattle tomorrow for the concert, but I'm sure Sunni will be with him so we may not have the chance to talk then, either.

I don't know how I know this, but that woman

is not as nice as he thinks she is—when he wasn't around, she got in her share of digs but I simply ignored her. I didn't come out here for drama. I am not sure how I should feel about Micah never once mentioning me to her. I guess he must have really hated me.

At times, he seems like the person I used to know but then other times he acts so distant. It's all my fault.

How could I have ever believed those boys? I should have known better—Micah had always been a perfect gentleman. I should have realized that when he professed his love for me it wasn't a ploy to get me into bed.

He had been speaking from the heart, and I rejected him in the cruelest way possible.

The next day Micah took an early morning flight to Seattle.

He wanted to spend some quality time with Tamara before the concert. This was her first trip to Washington state, and he wanted to show her around the city.

Micah wavered between forgiveness and unforgiveness where she was concerned. Although Tamara had given him an explanation for her actions, he wasn't convinced it was for that reason alone. There was more that she wasn't telling him. Until he knew the truth, Micah was not sure that they could ever recapture the closeness they once shared.

Micah arranged to have his overnight bag delivered to his suite after checking in, then headed straight to see Tamara.

"I'm so glad you're here," she told him. "This city is beautiful. At least the little bit I've seen so far."

"While the others are in rehearsal, I thought I'd take you on a tour of the city," Micah announced. He smiled in that old familiar way that used to make her heart turn over.

The sound of her voice did things to Micah. Just seeing her again nearly left him breathless. He sat down to try to hide his state of arousal. Micah tried to wrench himself away from his thoughts of Tamara in various states of undress.

"You don't mind?" she asked, bringing him out of his reverie.

"Not at all. There are some places I'd like to show you."

"That would be great," she responded. "I'm dressed and ready for once." Dressed in a crisp white sleeveless shirt and a pair of walking shorts, Tamara was ready to tour Seattle.

"You might want to change your shoes. Those sandals are nice and fashionable, but I'm not sure they're going to be so comfortable."

Tamara gave him a sidelong glance. "So what should I wear?"

"A pair of tennis shoes," he suggested.

She smiled. "I have those. Give me a minute to change."

Micah laughed.

"I was still ready," she uttered. "This doesn't count."

Tamara glanced down at her feet and said, "They don't go with my outfit. I think I need to change." She glanced up at him. "Don't you utter a word."

They left the suite thirty minutes later.

"Our first stop is going to be the Woodland Park Rose Garden," Micah told her. "I know how much you love roses. They have over two hundred sixty different types of roses." He further explained, "The garden is one of twenty-four All-America Rose Selections Test Gardens in the United States."

"I can't wait to see the different varieties. My mother has been experimenting, trying to come up with a new hybrid tea rose."

"What about you?" Micah asked. "Are you still into gardening?"

Tamara shook her head no. "Not since my grandmother died. I think that I loved it because I enjoyed being with her. Micah, I miss her so much."

She put a hand to her neck. "When I lost the necklace she gave to me…things just haven't been the same. It was really special, and I felt close to her when I had it."

Micah glanced over at her. "Your grandmother is in your heart. You do know that, don't you?" He remembered how upset Tamara had gotten when she realized it was gone. He vowed back then to find one like it because he knew how much that piece of jewelry meant to her.

"Yeah, I know, but it would be nice to have something of hers to keep with me. That necklace always made me feel safe."

As soon as Tamara stepped out of the car, her sensitive nostrils caught the mixed fragrance of exotic roses. "It's so beautiful," she murmured as they entered the park.

"Am I allowed to take pictures?" she asked. "My mother would love to see this."

"You can take as many photographs as possible."

Micah reached over and took her hand, leading her along the winding paths and through soft bright green grass. There were hundreds of explosions of bright colorful blooms everywhere.

Tamara enjoyed the feel of his skin touching hers. It had been a long time since they walked anywhere holding hands like this.

"This reminds me of old times," she confessed, savoring his touch.

Micah smiled but did not respond.

She was touched that he remembered her love for roses and brought her to Woodland Park. Tamara felt like they were reconnecting finally. Maybe now he would let down the wall guarding his heart.

Tamara released his hand to take several digital photos to e-mail to her mother when she got back to the hotel.

"Do people get married out here?" she asked.

Micah nodded before responding, "All the time."

"I can see why. It's so romantic."

"Yeah, it is," Micah agreed, his eyes focused on Tamara's face. "Being surrounded by so much beauty."

Tamara shivered a little from the way Micah was staring at her. She loved him so much, but now was not the time to make that declaration. She did not want to scare Micah away.

They walked through the entire park, stopping every now and then for Tamara to get a closer look or inhale the fragrance of a particular hybrid.

"Micah, you've got to smell it," she stated. "It has a very exotic scent."

He bent down and sniffed. "You're right."

His face was so close to hers. Tamara tried to slow her racing heart as she straightened up her body.

"You okay?" Micah inquired.

She nodded. "I'm fine."

Tamara took more photographs. "My mom is going to love these pictures."

"I'm glad you're having a good time."

"Micah, I am," Tamara confirmed. "Thanks for bringing me here."

Deep down, she was thrilled to have this time alone with Micah. If she were going to win back his friendship, they needed to become reacquainted with each other.

"So where are you taking me now?" Tamara questioned as they headed back down to the car. She was really enjoying herself and prayed that Micah felt the same way.

"To Snoqualmie Falls," Micah answered. "Have you ever heard of it?"

"Yeah," Tamara uttered. "I've heard that the Falls are unbelievable. I can't wait to see it for myself."

They made small talk during the drive. Tamara did not want to push Micah too hard. She knew that he needed a chance to feel comfortable around her.

Micah and Tamara walked along the paths through the two-acre park hand in hand listening to the roar of the whitewater as it tumbled over granite cliffs.

Tamara noticed that there were several secluded picnic areas—perfect surroundings to share a romantic lunch.

They strolled along the tree-lined trail, and then went up to the gazebo inspired observation deck so that Tamara could take pictures of the two hundred seventy foot waterfall.

"We used to always talk about traveling to Africa to see Victoria Falls," she reminded him. "Do you remember that?"

Micah nodded. "We had planned to go to Egypt, too. Remember? We talked about seeing the Pyramids of Giza and the Sphinx. We were going to travel the world."

She chuckled. "We made a lot of plans, didn't we?"

A strange, faintly eager look flashed in his eyes. "Yeah, we did."

"Did you ever go?"

Micah glanced over at her. "Where?"

"To Egypt," Tamara replied. "I read somewhere that you went to Africa. You supplied several schools with computers."

"*Ebony* did a big article on that," he responded. "But to answer your question, I haven't gone to Egypt. In all honestly, I guess I was waiting on you."

"Micah, we should go," Tamara blurted. "Not this year but next summer. What do you think?"

"I don't know that we're ready to take trips together, Tamara. We still have a lot to work through, so let's not get ahead of ourselves. Let's just take this one day at a time," Micah said with quiet emphasis.

"Of course," Tamara murmured. She was thrown

by the coolness in Micah's tone. There was no warmth in his words.

I'll just have to work that much harder to get him to trust me again, Tamara decided. Theirs was a friendship worth saving.

After taking in all that the park offered, Micah and Tamara ventured to The Falls Gift Shop. They paused to check out some of the memorabilia. Tamara purchased a few items for Kyra, her sister and her mother.

Micah hadn't said much since they left the shop, but he warmed up a little by the time they sat down to have lunch. He was more himself then.

They enjoyed burgers and shakes at the Snoqualmie Falls Candy Factory while watching candy being made.

"This is so cool," Tamara whispered. "I haven't had this much fun in a long time."

Her words amused Micah. "You need to get out more."

She gave him a gentle jab with her elbow. "Stop being so mean."

"I'm just saying…"

"I have a life, I'll have you know," Tamara said with a chuckle. "I've learned to enjoy going to dinner alone, going to the movies and I even take in a few NFL and NBA games."

"Okay, then what you need is a man."

"Now you sound like Mama," she uttered. "That woman is always trying to hook me up with somebody. I think her friends are starting to keep their single sons hidden away."

Tamara and Micah laughed.

"My mom was like that before she died. She wanted me to get married and settle down," he said.

"How long has she been gone?" Tamara asked. She had met Micah's mother shortly after he began tutoring her. She was a very religious woman who had little patience for nonsense. A college education was very important to her and she constantly reminded Micah to stay focused.

"Four years now." Micah shook his head regretfully. "She wanted me to find you. My mom always said that you were the one for me."

"My grandmother used to tell me the same thing," Tamara confessed.

For dessert, they shared a bag of caramel corn.

"I can't hang with you," Micah stated. "I haven't eaten this much junk food since college."

Tamara folded her arms across her chest. "Oh, so now I'm bad for your health?"

He laughed. "Sweetheart, I didn't mean it that way."

"You've gotten mean in your old age," Tamara uttered. "We should probably head back to the hotel. I think you need a nap."

Their gazes locked, and both of them could see the attraction mirrored in the other's eyes.

Micah pulled her into his arms. "A nap is the last thing I need right now."

The prolonged anticipation of kissing her had become unbearable. His mouth covered hers hungrily.

Raising his mouth from hers, Micah gazed into her eyes.

Tamara drew his face to hers in a renewed embrace. He kissed her again, lingering, savoring every moment.

"What are we doing?" Micah whispered. He marveled at the soft, satiny texture of her skin. He knew that Tamara would feel as good as she looked. He had seen breathtaking women from all over the world, but the woman standing with him possessed an unrivaled beauty.

Tamara had it all as far as Micah was concerned. She had it all—perfect features, silky flesh, a refined bone structure and a beautiful head of hair.

But could he trust her with his heart?

Tamara's emotions whirled. Blood pounded in her brain, leapt from her heart and made her knees tremble. After fourteen years of knowing him, Micah had finally kissed her—and it had been everything she'd dreamed it would be.

He released her. "I'm sorry. I shouldn't have done that."

"Micah, you don't have to apologize for anything. This is something we both want," she stated, his apology darkening the moment.

"I have always been drawn to you, Tamara," he confessed. "As much as I've tried to fight my feelings, I can't stop thinking of you."

Her face clouded with uneasiness. "Are you complaining? Are you saying that you don't want to want me?"

"No, of course not," Micah replied. "I just want to make sure we're not rushing into anything. Our friendship is still too fragile."

There was a pensive shimmer in the shadow of his eye.

"I'm glad to hear that we still have some form of

friendship. I was worried earlier," she said. "I don't want to keep looking back into the past, Micah. I've done that most of my life. I thought we were starting over."

"We are," he confirmed. "You're right, Tamara. We won't look back." Micah gathered her into his arms and held her snugly. "I have really missed you."

He touched his lips to hers.

Tamara kissed him with a hunger that belied her outward calm. She was shocked by her own eager response. She felt blissfully happy and fully alive.

They didn't linger any longer because they needed to head back to the hotel.

The concert was in less than three hours.

"I told you that you needed a nap," she teased as they got inside of the rental car.

"Actually, I was thinking that you might need to rest up before the concert," Micah retorted. "I know you can't hang like you used to."

"You're the same age as I am," she reminded him, enjoying the easy banter between them. "Besides, if I remember correctly…you were the one who used to get sleepy."

Micah laughed. "That was ten years ago, and back then I was the studious one, not the party animal."

Tamara tried to stifle a yawn, sending him into another round of laughter. She was struggling to keep from falling asleep during the ride back to the hotel, but she wasn't about to tell Micah that as soon as she returned to her suite she was taking a nap.

Her mind was still on Micah when she was alone in her hotel suite. A delicious quiver surged through her veins as Tamara recalled how much she had enjoyed his company.

"We had a nice time," she whispered to herself. "And he kissed me."

Tamara removed her clothes, showered and slipped on a pair of silk shorts with a matching top.

Restless and Micah dominating her thoughts, Tamara attempted to ignore the strange aching in her limbs.

"Micah, you're driving me crazy," she groaned. "I need to get you out of my head."

Tamara had a brief chat with her sister and her mother. As usual, she and Jillian had words over her mother's constant attempts to find a suitable husband for her.

Her mother had called to see when Tamara would be returning home. She wanted to host a dinner party and already had a date selected for her daughter. Only Tamara wasn't having it and told Jillian so.

Jillian also wanted minute-by-minute reports of her relationship with Micah. Tamara recalled when her mother could not stand the thought of her daughter spending time with someone like Micah—a kid from the projects who attended college on an academic scholarship.

On the other hand, Tamara's grandmother adored him. Now that he was a powerful and wealthy executive, Jillian suddenly had a change of heart where Micah was concerned. Her mother was not born into wealth so she was determined to marry well and wanted the same for her daughters.

Tamara loved her mother but wished deep down

that Jillian wasn't so motivated by money. The woman would sell her soul for a million dollars.

Alone in his suite, Micah was enraptured by the vision of Tamara in his mind and was beside himself with want.

He strode into the bathroom and turned the cold water on full blast. After removing his clothes, he stepped beneath the freezing spray of water.

Micah welcomed the cold and painful comfort in an attempt to cool his ardor. However, the water did very little to lessen his desire that Tamara had aroused. He kept thinking of the heated kisses they had shared and how she'd responded to him.

He towel-dried his shivering body ten minutes later.

A still-frustrated Micah walked quietly out of the bathroom and padded barefoot into the living room. He sat down at the desk and called Bette, his secretary, to check in.

Work would keep his mind off his thoughts of Tamara.

He turned on his laptop and responded to the e-mails he deemed priority. Fleeting images of Tamara crept into his head now and again, but Micah forced them away.

An hour later, he was still unable to focus on his work. Micah hoped that Tamara was having just as hard a time keeping her thoughts off him.

Tamara and Micah returned to the Alexis Hotel after Justice's concert at Key Arena. Despite the late hour, Micah wasn't ready for the evening to end. He invited her up to his suite. Tamara did not know it, but Micah had arranged for a private catered late dinner to be delivered to the suite.

"Is this where you usually stay when you're here in Seattle?" she asked, following Micah inside the room.

He nodded. "Why do you ask?"

Tamara sat down on the sofa and crossed her legs. "They seemed to know you at the front desk." She gave him a sidelong glance. "I bet I know why you like this place so much."

"Why?"

"Because of the restaurant," Tamara responded, referring to the Library Bistro & Bookstore Bar. "I took a peek inside when I arrived. I really love those high-back booths and the tall bookcases."

Micah sat down in one of the overstuffed chairs. "I admit that I do enjoy the ambiance. The food's not bad, either."

"I wouldn't know," she replied. "I haven't eaten there yet."

There was a knock on the door of his suite.

Tamara glanced over at Micah. "Are you expecting someone?" She fervently hoped that Sunni hadn't decided to surprise him. Tamara was not one for drama, so she hoped there wasn't going to be any.

She and Micah had not really discussed his relationship with the model because Tamara was hesitant to bring up the subject.

He got up and nodded as he crossed the room.

Micah opened the door to allow the waiter to enter, pushing a cart laden with food. He worked quickly, covering the table with a white tablecloth.

She rose to her feet, moving to stand beside him.

Tamara's smile widened in approval. "Wow. You sure are full of surprises."

"I know how much you like to eat," Micah teased. He gave her body a raking gaze, lazily appraising her.

She elbowed him in the arm as they silently observed the waiter placing their dinner on the table. "So what are we having?" Tamara whispered.

Micah took her by the hand and led her to the table. "For starters, we're having seared scallops with bacon, mushrooms on baby lettuce, seared ahi tuna for our entrée and for dessert, your choice of a lemon or almond pear tart."

Tamara rubbed her hands together. "Sounds delicious."

Micah signed the check and gave the waiter a fifty-dollar tip.

They sat down at the dining table to eat.

He quickly blessed the food before they dived in. Tamara could feel him watching her. "Shouldn't you be concentrating on your food?"

"I can't believe we're here like this," he confessed. Micah's eyes traveled over her face and then slid downward. "Frankly, I never thought I'd see you again. I'm glad I was wrong."

"I'm glad, too. I always believed that we'd see each other again—I just didn't think it would take this long." Tamara wiped her mouth with the edge of her napkin. "It probably wouldn't have if you hadn't stayed out of my life."

"I didn't know what I wanted or how I wanted to

handle it. I needed time, I guess." He stuck a forkful of food into his mouth and chewed slowly.

Tamara took a sip of her ice water. "Micah, if you had returned at least one of my phone calls, we could've gotten all this straightened out a long time ago."

He agreed. "Maybe, but I wasn't ready to talk to you then."

"We've had so much fun today, but I can feel that you're holding back. Micah, I'm not out here to hurt you. You *can* trust me. I want you to know that."

The air around them suddenly seemed electrified.

Tamara picked up the coffee pot and poured a cup for herself.

"We agreed not to look back anymore," she told him. "Didn't we?"

Sipping her coffee, she stared back out the glass patio doors, quietly observing the Seattle nightlife.

Taking her hand in his, Micah nodded. "You're right. I'm sorry."

She looked up into the face that God had lovingly created. Tamara had dreamed of his muscular body brushing against hers, the sensuous feel of his sinewy arms wrapped around her.

He cut into her thoughts. "Is something wrong with your food?"

Tamara felt the heat rise to her cheeks. "Oh, no… everything is fine."

I've got to stop thinking about this man like this. It had been a while since she was intimate with a man and she was human, Tamara reasoned silently.

After they finished eating, she pushed away from the table and stood up. "Dinner was delicious," Tamara murmured. "Now I have to go to my room and put together some notes for the article."

Micah kissed her, sending waves of shock through her body. Tamara had certainly not expected him to do this.

She pulled away slowly. "We also agreed to take whatever this is very slow. I actually do have some work I need to finish, and I need to make sure I'm ready when the crew buses pull out."

All evening, the tantalizing picture Tamara represented distracted Micah. Her lips, slightly parted, were full and generous, turning up at the corners in a perpetual smile. He visually traced the shape of her mouth with his eyes. A smile played across his lips as he recalled what hers felt like against his own.

"You're sure that's what you want to do?" he inquired hoarsely. "You really want to leave?"

"Micah, it's not that I want to leave," Tamara admitted. "I just think that it's the right thing to do."

He watched beneath hooded lids as Tamara drew back to study him. Micah wanted to beg her to stay but resisted the urge. "I guess I'll see you in the morning then."

They embraced.

"Good night," she said with her voice barely above a whisper.

"Let me walk you to your room." A shiver of wanting ran down Micah's spine. He moved toward her, impelled involuntarily by his own passion.

Tamara shook her head. "I'm pretty sure that I can make it across the hall by myself," she told him with a chuckle. "If you walk me over there, I know that I won't be strong enough to make you come back to your own room."

"You're worried you won't be able to resist me?"

She grinned. "Actually, I was thinking that you wouldn't be able to keep your hands off me."

"You're probably right," Micah acknowledged.

"I'll see you in the morning."

When she left, Micah headed to the bathroom.

He was in desperate need of a cold shower. He found himself taking them often since Tamara was back into his life.

Chapter 6

Over breakfast, Micah announced, "I won't be joining you in Vancouver. I have to return to L.A."

"Oh, no," Tamara murmured. "I thought you'd be finishing out the rest of the tour with us." She finished off her cranberry juice.

Had she known that Micah was not coming on the tour, she might not have slept in her own suite last night. Tamara was looking forward to spending more time with him. They shared a connection that not even he could ignore.

She felt a certain sadness that their time together was ending. The buses would be pulling out within the hour. Her feelings for Micah were intensifying, and Tamara couldn't deny the spark of excitement at the prospect of a relationship with the love of her life.

"Micah, are you sure you can't come to Vancouver with us?" she asked when he escorted her to the bus.

"I have some meetings scheduled that I can't postpone. I'll see you in Portland."

He kissed her cheek and gave her a hug. "Get on your bus. You guys need to get out of here."

"See you in Oregon. Oh and just so you know…you owe me a real kiss when you get there." She knew how he felt about showing affection in public. Micah didn't want his relationships exploited over the tabloids and tried to keep as much of his private life private.

He smiled and nodded. "Bye, Tamara."

They were soon on their way, heading out of Seattle.

Tamara spent the first half of the ride in her suite working on her notes. She struggled to stay focused. Micah dominated her thoughts. *I have never wanted a man as much as I want him,* she thought.

When Tamara found that she couldn't concentrate on her work or rein in her emotions where Micah was concerned, she decided to call it a day. She picked up her journal and opened it.

September 1
Today Micah and I had a wonderful time in Seattle looking at all of the many different types of roses in Woodland Park. We had such a great time together that I really wish he were going to be with us for the next leg of the tour. The more I spend time with Micah, the more I find myself thinking about him.

I can't even write about the hot dreams I have

of the two of us together—they will forever be ingrained in the recesses of my mind.

I'm crazy about this man, but I know that he has this wall around his heart. I have to find a way to get him to give me another chance. I know that he has Sunni in his life and I'll respect that. Although I have to admit that I wish she wasn't around.

At least I'll see him in Portland. I think that the more time we spend together the more Micah will begin to trust me.

I'll write more later.

When Tamara arrived in Portland, Oregon, three hours later, she checked into the hotel and went straight to her room.

As soon as she unlocked the door to her suite, her eyes were drawn to the enormous bouquet of roses in vivid hues of pink, yellow, red and white. Tamara bent to inhale a whiff of the sweet fragrance.

She caught sight of the card attached and smiled as she read the note: "I'm really glad we're working on our friendship. I miss you already but I know that I'll be seeing you very soon. Micah."

"I miss you, too," she whispered as she stared at the lonely hotel bed.

When Justice and the band members headed out to Vancouver for rehearsal, Tamara went along with them. The concert was in Vancouver, which was less than twenty minutes away, and with the next concert being in Portland, it was easier to have them stay at one hotel for both nights.

Tamara made notes of her observations and con-

ducted several interviews with the road manager, Marty
and the drummer, Eric, who had been playing for various performers for over twenty years.

After rehearsal, they returned to the hotel so that Justice could get some rest before the concert that night.
She and some of the band members gathered at a nearby
restaurant to have lunch.

Micah called Tamara a few minutes after she arrived to her suite.

"How's it going?" he asked.

"Great," Tamara responded. "Thanks for the roses.
Micah, they're gorgeous."

"I'm sorry I couldn't be there with you for the concert tonight, but I'll be in Portland tomorrow morning."

"I can't wait to see you," she confessed.

"Same here," Micah responded. "I have a meeting
in fifteen minutes so I have to go but wanted to check
in with you."

They hung up.

Tamara strolled over to the bed and sat down on
the edge, clutching a pillow to her. Her eyes traveled
back over to the vivid display of roses. They were really breathtaking and red roses were her favorite, but
there was no romantic meaning behind them—Micah
had made that clear in his note.

She sat there like that for nearly thirty minutes, wondering how to make Micah fall in love with her.

Portland, Oregon

It had been a long night.

After the concert in Vancouver, Tamara went back to

the hotel. Marty and the others invited her to go clubbing with them, but she begged off. Instead, she spent her evening watching television.

Sleep did not come easy for her, mostly because Micah dominated her dreams. Tamara believed it was because of the anticipation of her need for physical intimacy. As much as she tried to ignore the truth, it was there. She wanted Micah to make love to her.

Micah called her again last night, but they did not talk on the phone that long. He only wanted to make sure things were going well with her and Justice Kane.

Tamara woke up several times during the night, and finally at 6:45 a.m., she got up.

She worked on her article until room service delivered her breakfast.

When she finished eating, Tamara showered and put twists into her hair.

Every so often, she would check the clock. Micah's plane was scheduled to land at 10:05 a.m. Tamara was really looking forward to seeing him.

She swung open the door to her suite and into Micah's arms two and a half hours later.

His lips pressed against hers and then gently covered her mouth.

His masterful kiss turned her legs into jelly as tantalizing tremors undulated through Tamara. She never believed it possible to derive so much pleasure from merely kissing a man.

Micah's lips brushed against hers as she spoke. "You're the man who's been dominating my dreams at night. You know that, don't you? I'm glad that you're here, Mr. Ross."

"I'm actually happy to be here, too." After a brief pause, he added, "More than I thought I would be."

"So does that mean you really really missed me?" she asked with a chuckle.

Their eyes met and held.

"More than you can imagine," he told her.

Micah broke their lust-filled trance by saying, "Any idea what you want to see in Portland?"

Tamara nodded. "Rose City Park. It sounds like it's similar to Woodland Park Rose Garden in Seattle."

"It is," he affirmed.

They left the hotel in a rental car.

"You seem to know your way around this place," Tamara stated. "How often do you come here?"

Micah laughed. "A GPS system is a wonderful thing."

When they arrived at Rose City Park, Tamara picked up a brochure for the self-guided tour.

"Micah, according to this pamphlet, there are over six thousand, eight hundred rosebushes that present over five hundred varieties," Tamara stated. "This is Rose City."

He took pictures with her digital camera.

"The next stop is the Royal Rosarian Garden," she announced as they followed the brick path around the garden. "The brochure says that Royal Rosarians are ambassadors of goodwill for the city. They participate in many festivals throughout the Northwest and plant a rose at each site. A rose was planted for each prime minister."

Micah and Tamara completed their tour and ate lunch at a nearby restaurant.

"Where to now?" she questioned when they finished eating.

"The Japanese Gardens aren't too far from here," he told her.

Tamara found the walk uphill from the parking lot to the garden somewhat steep. Micah grabbed her hand and led her up to the top where they saw a set of stairs.

"Okay, I'm working off my lunch today," she murmured with a short laugh.

Five separate gardens made up the Portland Japanese Garden. Tamara snapped pictures of Micah strolling along the pond garden. He took pictures of her with the tea garden as a beautiful backdrop.

A couple nearby offered to photograph them together in the natural garden.

"We look like lovers," Tamara told him when they reviewed the photo on camera.

Micah nodded in agreement.

She gave him a sidelong glance. "Does it bother you?"

"No," he responded. "Because we know the truth."

Tamara stopped walking. "So are you saying that you don't want to be my lover?" She folded her arms across her chest.

Micah laughed. "Sweetheart, I'd be lying if I said that."

She grinned. "Just checking."

He pulled Tamara into his arms, holding her close.

"What's gotten into you?" Tamara asked. "You are not the type of man who is openly affectionate."

Micah gave her a tender look. "You're right, which

is why this should convince you of how much I really care about you, sweetheart."

She cleared her throat, pretending not to be affected by his words.

In a surprise move, Micah covered her lips with his in the middle of the garden.

Tamara put her arms around his neck, giving herself freely to the passion of his kiss.

"Wow…" she murmured as they parted.

He smiled. "Would you like to see the rest of the garden? We still have the stone and the flat gardens to explore."

She nodded.

Tamara and Micah made it back to the hotel shortly after four.

She lay down to take a nap before she had to meet him for dinner. Tonight they were planning to attend the after party and would be out late.

Tamara believed that Micah was beginning to trust her again and it thrilled her. Their friendship was still on the mend, but she sensed that it was also changing. She had strong feelings for him and from that kiss that Micah laid on her earlier she felt conflicted. There were times she was almost positive that he returned her affection, but then other times, Micah acted like there was nothing more between them than friendship.

Perhaps Micah was acting this way because of his relationship with Sunni, Tamara decided and made a mental note to ask him about his relationship with the model. If they were involved, then there was no place in his life for her.

As much as it would break her heart, Tamara knew she would have to move on with her life.

"Would you like to dance?" Micah asked her. They came over with the band and Justice Kane for the concert after party at a local club in downtown Portland.

She nodded. "I love dancing. I just haven't done it in a long time."

Micah eyed her in amazement. "What? Not the party animal herself…"

"Ha-ha…" she muttered, taking him by the hand. "I hope you've learned something other than that two-step you used to do."

Micah pretended to be offended. "I know you're not talking about me. Girl, I was too cool back then."

Tamara stood up, waiting for him to escort her to the dance floor. She walked slowly, her body swaying to the music. "This is my song."

He took her to the middle of the front of the dance floor and began dancing to the music. One song ended and another began while they were still on the dance floor.

Justice Kane tapped Micah on the shoulder. "Hey man, can I dance with the pretty lady?"

Marty sashayed toward them. "Tamara, I'll take Micah off your hands. I *love* this song."

Some of the partygoers stopped dancing to take pictures of Justice.

"This is the part of my life that I'm not feeling," he told Tamara. "The lack of privacy. Sometimes I just want to leave my house and just kick it with my boys or my girl, you know?"

Tamara broke into a smile. "The price of fame, huh."

He nodded. "But you know what? I'ma have to just deal with it. I wouldn't be Justice Kane if it wasn't for these people. I can't forget that."

"It's a nice way of looking at it," Tamara responded. "It shows that you appreciate your fans—that's what will keep them buying your albums. Besides the wonderful songs you sing, anyway."

When the music stopped, Justice escorted her back to the table in the VIP lounge of Avalanche, a hot, hip new club. Micah was talking to the cocktail server when they arrived.

"I just ordered you a glass of white wine," he told Tamara.

She met his gaze and smiled. "Thanks."

They sat down.

"You look like you're having a good time," he stated.

"I am," Tamara confirmed. "I have to share this with you, Micah. I'm not trying to sound corny, but the best times of my life were when I was at Hollington College, with my grandmother and with you."

Micah shook his head in denial.

"It's true," Tamara insisted. "You didn't just teach me math—you taught me how to hope. When you used to tell me about the things you went through growing up, Micah, you were always so optimistic. I wanted that kind of peace. That same kind of hope for the future."

"Each day that we wake up is another chance for to better our lives. We only have to keep our heads to the sky." Micah reached over and took her hand in his. "Tamara, it's been great seeing you again. I feel like I'm getting my best friend back."

"I'm glad you said that," she murmured. "Because I feel the exact same way."

"I know that we're not looking to the past, but Tamara, I hope there's no hidden agenda here." He was not ready to tell her how he really felt about her because he was not a hundred percent sure of her motives. Micah had allowed her entry back into his life but until he knew that Tamara was legit—he would keep his heart protected at all costs.

It wasn't always easy to keep his emotions under control. Micah wanted Tamara in a way that he never wanted another woman. Whenever they were together, he found it difficult to keep his hands and his lips off her. Micah hoped that he wasn't sending her mixed signals but it was too soon to let down his guard.

San Francisco, California

Micah rode with Tamara on the crew bus for the ten-hour drive from Portland to San Francisco.

She was willing to give up the executive suite, but Micah would not hear of it. He insisted on bunking with the crew if he needed to rest.

He knocked on the door before sticking his head inside. "Busy?"

Tamara shook her head no. "What's up?"

"We're about to play spades," Micah announced. "Interested in playing?"

"Sure," Tamara responded. "I haven't played in a while."

"It'll come back to you."

For the next hour, they played as partners, winning all but one round.

They didn't arrive in San Francisco until after three.

"How is the article coming along?" Micah asked.

They checked into the hotel almost an hour ago and were now sitting around the pool.

"I have so much material for my article," she told him. "Micah, I think I'm going to have to break it up and do a series. At least that's the way I'm going to pitch it to my editor."

His BlackBerry handheld started to vibrate.

"I need to take this call," Micah announced, excusing himself. "I'll be back in a few minutes."

When he left, Marty ran over and sat down in the lounge chair he had just vacated. "I know it's not my business, but something's jumping off between you and Micah. Girl, I'm happy for you. Micah Ross is *fine*."

Tamara broke into a grin. "Really, we're just friends, Marty."

She shook her head in denial. "What he and Sunni are—that's friends. When Micah looks at you, it's like a man in love."

Tamara smiled but did not respond. She was not about to say anything about their relationship. If Micah wanted his people to know anything, he would have to be the one to tell them.

Marty rose to her feet when she saw Micah coming in their direction. "I know what I'm talking about." She winked, strolled off in her skimpy-looking bikini and jumped into the Olympic-size pool.

Tamara's cell phone started to ring. She saw that it was Kyra calling and answered it. "Hey, girl. What's up?"

"Nothing," Kyra answered. "I was calling to see how

things are going on your trip. Are you and Micah having a good time?"

"We are," Tamara responded. She gave Kyra a quick rundown of the tour and her time spent with Micah.

They chatted for a few minutes more.

"I just got off the phone with Kyra," Tamara announced. "She told me to tell you hello."

"I haven't seen her in a while," Micah said with a smile. "I saw Chloe once, but the only person I talk to on the regular is Kevin."

"Are you planning to come to homecoming this year?" Tamara asked. "It hasn't been the same without you."

"I've been thinking about it." Micah checked his cell phone one more time before laying it down on the glass table between them. "Justice will be performing so I might show up."

"Micah, I hope you'll come," Tamara commented. "I have really missed you not being in my life. This week has been wonderful but I want our friendship back. When you're in Atlanta, I expect to get a phone call, dinner or something."

"How about you cook me dinner?" he suggested. "Oh yeah...you can't cook."

"See, you don't know anything," Tamara shot back. "I am a pretty good cook. I took cooking classes."

He laughed. "What can you cook?"

"Everything," she stated. "I have an impressive collection of cookbooks."

He was watching her so intently that she asked, "Why are you staring at me like that?"

"You have no idea how badly I want to kiss you."

She felt her skin become flushed and heated. "It wouldn't bother me if you did."

Just then, a photographer snapped a picture of them.

Micah released a sigh of frustration. "Are you ready to go upstairs?" he asked.

She nodded.

"I wish people could get a glimpse of the man that I see," Tamara said in a low voice. They were inside the hotel waiting for the elevator doors to open.

"I know this is a part of the life I choose, but there are some things that I feel should be left private."

"I agree with you," Tamara stated. "I think you need to address this with the media. By not talking, they are left to form their own opinions, but if you put it out there they will know how you feel about it."

Micah seemed to be considering her words. "I haven't thought about it in that way."

"Just think about it."

She and Micah were alone during the ride up to the twelfth floor. He reached for her. "I'll take that kiss now."

Tamara leaned into his embrace.

"There's something I need to ask you," Tamara said, stepping away from him. "What exactly is your relationship with Sunni?"

"We are nothing more than friends. We hang out but we're not a couple—that's just the media's spin on it."

Tamara gave him a look. "Does she know this?"

"Why?" Micah asked. "What did she say to you?"

"She didn't really say anything to me, but it's pretty obvious to me that Sunni's in love with you. I can tell by the way she looks at you."

"Tamara, I've been very honest with her," Micah

stated. "I don't know what else I can do. She knows that we are friends. Now let me ask you something—does my friendship with Sunni bother you?"

"Yeah, it does," Tamara confessed. "I'm not real crazy about the woman."

He laughed. "A lot of women feel the same way about Sunni. I have no idea why."

"Yeah, right," she grunted.

"We haven't really talked about your love life," Micah stated. "What's up with you? Do I have to worry about some man coming to break my nose?"

Tamara shook her head. "For some reason, I can't seem to find a man who isn't interested in anything other than money, social standing and sex. I'm to the point that I need to run complete credit, criminal and health background checks on a person before I go on a date with him. My sister just got married two weeks ago and so you know my mama." She stared up at him. "Why haven't you gotten married? I've always thought of you as the marrying type—a family man."

"I guess Miss Right just hasn't come along."

Tamara grinned. "So are you saying that Sunni isn't the one?"

He chuckled. "I told you already that Sunni and I are just friends although she is convinced that she's the right woman for me."

"I'm not surprised," Tamara uttered. "It's obvious that Sunni truly believes her own press."

Micah had to agree. "She has a good heart though."

"I'm not saying she's not a good person. She just likes herself a lot."

He laughed.

Chapter 7

The crew buses arrived back in Los Angeles a couple of hours ago.

Micah invited Tamara to spend the following week at his house. Neither one of them was looking forward to their time together ending.

"Well, you have your interview," Micah stated.

"Yeah, I do," she responded, sitting on the passenger side of his BMW X5 luxury SUV. "Thank you so much for the opportunity." She chewed on her bottom lip a moment before saying, "Micah, I've been thinking about something—another feature for the magazine. I have a huge favor to ask."

He glanced in her direction. "What is it?"

"I really want to be a feature writer with *Luster* magazine and this article on Justice Kane was my trial run, but if you would allow me to do an exclusive feature on you, that would seal the position for me."

The car was filled with a pregnant silence.

Tamara began to consider that she had crossed some imaginary line until Micah told her, "If you want to interview me, that's fine. Since you're spending this week with me—now would be a good time. I'm taking some time away from work."

"That's actually perfect, Micah. People want a chance to get to know the real you. They want to see you when you're not at the office." She broke into a smile. "Thanks, Micah. I owe you big time for this."

"You don't owe me anything. You know I'm only agreeing to do this because it's you, Tamara."

She could tell that Micah was not totally comfortable with the idea even though he had agreed to do the interview. "I know and believe me, I don't take this lightly. I'll only write what you want in print."

September 5
I think Micah and I are finding our way finally! He agreed to let me interview him for the magazine. This is a big deal for me because he is an extremely private person.

I'm honored that he's allowing me this chance. I hope that while working on the project together, Micah and I can build a stronger foundation for our friendship. This is more important to me than the article.

Samantha is going to be thrilled when I tell her about this. She will probably try to feature Micah on the cover. I wouldn't mind having him grace my coffee table. Micah Ross is fine!

Micah and I have made great strides after all that happened in the past. I'm grateful to have him back in my life. Until we reconnected, I felt like there was a piece of me missing.

With Micah back in my life, I feel complete.

His heart thumping, Micah couldn't deny that Tamara was having a tremendous effect on him, because under normal circumstances, there was no way that he would have agreed to do an exclusive interview with anyone.

It was Micah's policy to avoid the media and public unless it was necessary. He was a very private man and refused to speak on his relationships or his family, but with Tamara, it seemed natural to open up to her. After all, he had known her for fourteen years.

"Just so you know, I won't be discussing Sunni or my family—just the record company and the artists. Tamara, is that understood?"

"Understood," she responded. "I'm really not out to exploit you, Micah. I hope you know that."

Micah really wanted to believe her, and he would unless Tamara showed him otherwise.

She could not seem to take her eyes off him, prompting Micah to ask, "What? Why are you looking at me like that?"

"You…you've changed from that shy little boy to this high-powered executive. I have to admit that I find that incredibly sexy."

"So when I was a geek I was what? Dog meat?"

"Of course not, Micah," Tamara interjected. "I've always thought of you as sexy, but seeing you confident and secure like this is even more sexy."

Micah bit back a smile. Tamara had a wonderful sense of humor although she was more subdued when they were in college. He loved seeing this new side of her. It was like getting to know her all over again.

An undeniable magnetism was building between them, forcing Micah to accept what he already knew. He still loved her. However, as strong as his feelings were for Tamara, Micah still erred on the side of caution. While they had made some progress toward the repairing of their relationship, there were things he still did not know about her.

Micah still had no idea why there seemed to be a shadow of sadness in her expression at times when she was not aware he was watching her. He had seen it many times when they were at Hollington College. She wanted to forget the past, but Tamara seemed haunted by something that happened to her a long time ago.

"What are you thinking about?"

He glanced over at Tamara. "It wasn't anything."

"Liar," she uttered. "Micah, you have always been a thinker. Something's on your mind, so spill it."

"I was thinking about how much I've enjoyed having you around. I'm glad you agreed to staying out here for another week. We still have a lot of catching up to do."

Micah hoped to unlock whatever she had been hiding all these years.

Chapter 8

Old insecurities set in, and Micah began to have second thoughts regarding his invitation. *Why did I invite Tamara to the house?* It might have been better for her to stay at the hotel, but it was too late now.

Tamara was not the type of woman who would be impressed by his wealth—she had grown up in the lap of luxury with the Devane millions. Her ex-stepfather owned Devane Industries along with several other companies.

He knew the answer. It was because Micah wanted some time alone with her—that was the truth of it.

Micah was afraid that he would not be able to get her out of his system. She was becoming too important to him. Deep down, that scared him.

He had opened his heart to Tamara once and she

ripped it apart. Could he trust her this time? Could he allow her to get that close to him?

For Micah, the next week would be very telling as far as he was concerned. Before she left to go back to Atlanta, he would know for sure whether he could trust Tamara with his whole heart again.

He hoped that she wouldn't let him down a second time.

Sunni called him twice during the drive, but he let them go to voice mail. He would have a conversation with her later. If things worked out the way that he wanted with Tamara, he needed to make sure that Sunni understood her place in his life.

Micah had not objected in the past because he enjoyed her companionship, but things were about to change.

"You really have a beautiful house," Tamara complimented as they settled down in his huge family room. "Did you decorate or hire someone to do it for you?"

"I had some help," Micah admitted. "Decorating was your thing—not mine. My feet still hurt from your dragging me through all those model homes, furniture stores, estate sales and swap meets."

Tamara laughed. "We used to talk about the houses we would one day have." Her eyes traveled the room. "You have yours and then some. I have an apartment."

"You still live in midtown?"

She nodded. "The Plantation at Lenox."

"You don't live too far from me," Micah stated. "I have a house in Tuxedo Park."

"I love the homes over there," Tamara responded,

lying back against the plush oversize pillows on his couch. "Micah, do you come to Atlanta often?"

"Actually, I do."

She was surprised. "Then why didn't you ever try to contact me?"

"I didn't know what to say to you," Micah confessed. "Like I told you before, I wasn't ready."

Tamara pulled at the fringe on her shirt as she talked. "I was so messed up back then. I had all this hurt inside of me that eventually turned into anger, and I took it out on you. Micah, if I could do this all over again—"

He shrugged nonchalantly. "There are no do overs in life, Tamara."

Awkwardly, she cleared her throat. "I know, but it doesn't stop me from wanting to erase the life I had and just start over again."

"You keep saying that, but Tamara, I just don't get what was so terrible about your life—I guess I'm missing something because from where I was sitting, your life didn't look bad at all."

"That's because you have no idea what was going on with me," she told Micah. "You don't have a clue."

He inched closer to her. "Sweetheart, I know that we promised not to revisit the past, but before we can really move forward, I think we're going to have to put everything on the table. What haven't you told me?"

Tamara stirred uneasily on the sofa. "We'll talk about that another time. I would rather not ruin our evening with the depressing story of my life. We haven't been together like this in such a long time. I want to just enjoy tonight."

Micah settled back against the couch. "Sure, if that's what you want to do."

"We *will* have that conversation. I promise."

"So besides Kyra, who else do you keep in contact with from school? I remember how you and your sorors used to walk around like you owned Hollington College."

"I've seen Beverly a few times over the years," Tamara responded. "Remember her? She was the homecoming queen our senior year, but we don't really keep in touch. As for my sorors, we did not act like we owned the college," she pointed out. "The Pi Betas were always involved in some type of community service. That's what we were about." She gave him a sidelong glance. "Why didn't you ever pledge?"

"The whole fraternity thing just wasn't me," he responded. "I wanted to stay focused on my studies. My degree was my way out of the ghetto. I didn't need the distraction of a fraternity. I have nothing against them—they just weren't for me."

Throughout the evening, Tamara silently noted Micah's kindness to his staff.

When he showed her his office, the numerous public service awards on the walls impressed her. Now this same man once tutored and befriended her almost fifteen years ago.

"You've done so much for the city of Los Angeles," she murmured. "And Atlanta, too. Why don't you want people to know about it?"

"Because that isn't why I do it, Tamara. I don't want my donations to be about Micah Ross. God has blessed me so that I can be a blessing to others. This is what I really believe. The world doesn't need to know what I do or how I help other people."

"I know how much you value your privacy, Micah. I appreciate you sharing this part of your life with me. I'm so proud of the man you've become." Tamara cracked a smile. "I even liked the man you were before."

"Would you like something to drink?" Micah asked as he rose to his feet. "I have iced tea, soda and bottled water."

"I'll take some tea," Tamara responded. "Thanks."

She was getting irritated with the way Micah ran hot and cold with her. Just when Tamara felt she was making some headway with him, his demeanor would turn cool. She was determined to break through that cement block he called a heart.

"This view is incredible," Tamara told Micah as they sat out on his balcony. "I could sit out here for hours just looking at the stars in the sky and at the city below."

Micah took a sip of his tea. "It's one of the reasons I bought the place."

Tamara rose to her feet and stood near the heavy railing. "Micah, what do you do when you're at home either here or in Atlanta?" she asked. "What is your day like?"

"I read, work out and sometimes I just lock myself in my studio and play the piano."

"Why don't you record your own music? You used to love it when we were in college."

"I like being in the background, Tamara. I've always been that way."

"But you have such a beautiful voice, Micah," she stated. "I think it's a shame to keep all of that talent hidden. This is what I want to write about—the things people would be surprised to know about Micah Ross."

He shrugged. "As far as I'm concerned, I just don't think there's a lot to say about me. Tamara, I don't think the interview should be about me. Why not focus the story on the record label?"

"Because our readers would be more interested in the man behind the company," Tamara responded. "Micah, don't you dare back out on me. You said you would do the interview."

He sighed. "Fine...I'll do it."

Tamara kissed him. "Thank you."

Micah wrapped an arm around her as they watched a movie on television.

She enjoyed being so close to him and drank in the comfort of his nearness.

"This is wonderful," she murmured. "Being together like this brings back some wonderful memories."

Fighting sleep, Tamara stretched and yawned.

"Uh-huh..."

She glanced over at Micah. "Uh-huh *what?*"

"Didn't have your nap today?"

"Micah, you need to quit," Tamara uttered. "I can hang with the best of them. I don't know what you're talking about."

He laughed.

The telephone rang.

"I bet that's Sunni," she stated. "Maybe you should answer it. She wants to be your Mrs. Ross."

"That's never going to happen. I'm going to have a

talk with her tomorrow," Micah announced. "There's no point in prolonging this."

"I thought you said that you two were just friends."

"We are, and I've told her that," he confirmed. "But I want to make sure that Sunni understands where I'm coming from. I know that she has feelings for me, but I've been nothing less than honest with her."

Later, Micah showed Tamara to the guest bedroom. "This is where you'll be sleeping."

"Great."

Tamara pulled the journal out of her purse before settling down in the queen-size bed to finish the entry she started earlier.

I'm spending the night at Micah's house in Beverly Hills. We've had a great time together just talking and getting to know each other all over again. I have missed my best friend terribly, and I'm so happy to have him back in my life.

I also remember how crazy I am about this man. I love him, and I think that he still has feelings for me. Sometimes I catch him staring at me, and it's a certain way that he looks at me—I can't really explain it.

I want to say something but since we are just beginning to reconnect, I am afraid to bring up the subject mainly because I don't want to scare him away.

I was a little disappointed when Micah told me that I'd be staying in one of the guest rooms. I actually thought we would…

We don't want to rush into anything so I guess

I have to just keep my desire under wraps as if it were easy.

It's so hard. I have vivid dreams of Micah and me riding a wave of passion. I want him badly.

I really want this drought to come to an end.

There was a soft knock at the door.

"Come in," she called out as she quickly put her journal back into her purse.

Micah stuck his head inside the room. "I wanted to make sure that you were okay."

Tamara gave him a sexy smile. "To be honest, I'm not sleepy at all. I'm in the mood for another movie. What about you? You think you can stay up long enough to watch one?"

Micah got into bed with her. "I can't believe that you're still talking trash. You'll be the first one to fall asleep."

She laughed. "You're sure I'm not keeping you up, old man?" Tamara asked.

"I got your old man."

Tamara wrapped her arms around him, pulling him closer to her. She could feel his uneven breathing on her cheek, as he held her tightly.

Micah traced his fingertip across her lip causing Tamara's skin to tingle when he touched her. He paused to kiss her, sending currents of desire through her.

She caressed the strong tendons in the back of his neck.

"Make love to me," Tamara whispered between kisses. She was ready to take their relationship to the next level.

"You don't know how badly I've wanted to hear those words come out of your mouth," Micah confessed. "I've wanted you from the moment I saw you again."

"Then what are we waiting for?" she asked. "Ten years is long enough."

He bent his head and captured her lips in a demanding kiss.

Locking her hands behind his neck, Tamara returned his kiss, matching passion for passion.

Her ardor soaring, Tamara eased away from him and began unbuttoning her shirt.

Micah helped her undress. His breath seemed to catch when he glimpsed her in her underwear, the lavender lace bra and matching thong panties.

"You are so beautiful," he told her in a husky voice.

Micah undressed himself and joined her in the bed. His mouth covered hers again hungrily.

Tamara answered his kiss with a desire that belied her outward calm. Moaning, she drew herself closer to him as his hands explored her body. Fire burst through her arms and shoulders before spreading to her lower limbs. Sparks of pleasure shook her body.

Micah reached into the nightstand beside the bed and pulled out a condom before taking her as his own.

Tamara offered him her lips while offering her body, as well.

Their eyes met. Micah kissed her forehead, then returned his attention to her mouth. The kiss was hungry and fierce.

Together, their fulfillment came with an intensity that defied description. Micah and Tamara lay in a tangle, their chests rising and falling rapidly as they fought to recover from their fervid lovemaking.

Micah moved away from her, then asked, "Tamara, are you on the pill?"

"Why?" Tamara wanted to know, clutching at the damp sheets. "Why are you asking?"

"I think the condom broke." He released a short sigh. "I don't want you to worry though. I had an HIV test six months ago and it came back negative."

"I had one done about that time, too," Tamara stated. "I haven't been with anyone in over a year. To answer your question, I am on the pill."

"My last relationship ended six months ago," Micah declared. "Sunni and I aren't sleeping together."

Tamara gave him a sidelong glance. "Really? You two never once had sex?"

Shaking his head, Micah said, "No, because I didn't want to give her false hope."

She was secretly thrilled to hear that. "I don't have any regrets, if that's what you're wondering. I don't want to spend it talking about the past. What we just shared was very special. Micah, I never imagined it would be this wonderful between us so let's just focus on us."

"What exactly did you have in mind?"

Tamara kissed him. "Well, you're going to need another condom for that."

They made love once more before falling asleep, their bodies entwined in a lover's embrace.

Chapter 9

Micah had lain in bed awake long after Tamara had
fallen asleep. He should've known this moment would
come. He should have figured out long before now that
they would have to define their relationship.

Having made love to Tamara, the time was now.

He did not want to hurt her—he knew what heartbreak felt like and didn't relish going through it again.

"What are you thinking about?" she whispered, looking up at him and wearing a sexy grin on her face.

"You," he responded. "I have a confession to make,
Tamara. I had planned to offer you the story on Justice
Kane and then kill it to ruin your career, but deep down
I could never do something like that to you. I couldn't
because I—"

Micah stopped short of confessing his love for her.

He had made love to her with deep emotion but wasn't ready to give voice to those feelings yet.

"I'm really glad to hear you say that," Tamara said. She sat up in bed with her back pressed against a stack of pillows. "I love what I do, and my career means a lot to me. It's all that I have in my life right now."

He sat up beside her. "I admit that it was a childish thought," Micah stated. "I don't know why I ever considered doing something so petty."

"You were hurt," she told him. "And you wanted to hurt me back. Believe it or not, I understand what that feels like, Micah."

"We've come a long way to get to this point. All this time…"

"Wasted," Tamara finished for him. "We wasted ten years because of a simple misunderstanding." She turned in his arms, facing him.

"Putting my heart on the line isn't easy for me," Micah confessed.

"No more talking," Tamara whispered sleepily. "I just want to savor this moment."

She was snoring softly a few minutes later.

Micah woke up shortly after 7:00 a.m. the next morning.

He was still reeling from the amazing night he had spent with Tamara. Life was funny. You never had a clue if happiness was waiting around the corner or if it decided to show up ten years later. From Micah's perspective, she had definitely been worth the wait.

A smile spread across his face as he watched Tamara

sleep. He planted tiny kisses on each cheek, her nose, her chin and her neck in an attempt to wake her up.

She moaned softly.

He placed a kiss on her lips.

Tamara opened her eyes, stretched and yawned. "Good morning."

She sat up in bed, pulling the covers up to hide her breasts.

Micah attempted to pull her down and into his arms, but Tamara moved out of his reach, leaning over to grab her purse.

"I was thinking that we could go on and get the interview out of the way?" she asked, slipping a tape into the recorder. "I know how uncomfortable you are about doing it."

Her words washed over him like a bucket of ice-cold water. Micah stiffened as realization dawned on him.

This had all been a ploy on Tamara's part. Apparently, the only reason she made love to him was because she wanted to interview him—Tamara cared nothing for him. She had taken advantage of him while they were in school, and she was still trying to make a fool of him now.

He had had enough. "I think I've revealed enough of myself to you already," Micah stated. "I can't believe I fell a second time for the same mess!"

Tamara wore a look of confusion. "I don't think I understand."

"Unfortunately, I do," Micah responded without looking at her. "Look, I have some phone calls to make. Bringing you here was a big mistake, so it'll be best if you leave."

"What is going on with you?" Tamara demanded, her voice trembling. "Why do you want me to leave?"

"Because you're no longer welcome in my house."

Speechless, Tamara climbed out of bed, picked up her clothing and rushed into the bathroom. She had no idea why Micah was suddenly so angry with her. Had this been part of his plan for revenge?

Micah had gotten out of bed and slipped on a robe when she walked out of the bathroom. "My driver will take you back to the hotel or where you want to go."

"Micah, what's wrong?" Tamara asked, her voice trembling. "What did I do to upset you this time?"

"I made the mistake of thinking that you were different from any other woman going after what she wants."

She replayed everything that happened in her mind. "Micah, I only thought you would want to get the interview out of the way so that you wouldn't have to dwell on it. You were relaxed and I thought you were comfortable with me. That's the only reason I suggested doing it this morning."

"It doesn't matter because you won't be getting your interview, Tamara." Micah's tone had become chilly.

"That's fine," Tamara said as she fought back tears. She didn't want Micah to see her cry. She would never give him that satisfaction. "It's pretty obvious to me that you're not the man that I thought you were, either. You can't seem to make up your mind whether to love me or punish me. You won't have to worry about me bothering you. *I get it now.*"

Tamara held her turbulent emotions inside until she was safely in the car.

She was confused by Micah's sudden chilly reaction this morning, especially after what they shared last night. Tamara had assumed that they had broken through all the ice surrounding his heart.

What happened between last night and this morning? He had totally misunderstood her attempt to put him at ease. If his intent was to follow through with hurting her, he accomplished what he'd set out to do. Micah's treatment wounded her to the core, but Tamara purposed in her heart to forget the memorable night she shared with him. It wasn't going to be easy, but in time it wouldn't hurt so much.

In time, she would forget.

Tamara booked herself into a hotel near the airport. She kept her outward calm until she reached the confines of her room. She unlocked the door, tossed her luggage to the side and navigated to the shower.

Beneath the running water, Tamara cried out her heartbreak in the shower. When she came out and dried her body and her face, Tamara gazed at her reflection in the mirror. She lifted her chin and felt a surge of determination and sheer willpower.

She could get through this, Tamara decided. She would do what she had been doing all of her life. She would survive.

Chapter 10

Tamara had been back in Atlanta for two days.

Her mother had called her at least three times since her return to check on her and invite her to lunch, which Tamara refused because she knew Jillian was most likely trying to play matchmaker.

She definitely was not interested in meeting another man. Her spirit was still low from Micah's rejection, so it was best that she be alone for now.

The telephone rang. Seeing that it was her mother again, Tamara answered it. "Hello, Mama." They had already spoken for a few minutes not even fifteen minutes ago. Tamara couldn't imagine what she wanted now.

"I'm thinking of making a nice dinner on Sunday," Jillian announced. "I hope you're free."

"Who else did you invite?" Tamara wanted to know. "Mama, I'm not in the mood for your matchmaking."

"I invited your sister and Bryant to join us. I thought it would be nice to have my family surrounding me."

"They haven't been married all that long, Mama. Callie and her husband might want to spend time alone," Tamara responded. "I'll come over, and we can cook a great meal for the two of us. It'll be fun."

"Honey, what's wrong?" her mother asked. "You haven't sounded like yourself since you came home from California. How did things go out there?"

"I got the information I needed for my story on Justice Kane. I'm almost finished with the last piece of the series."

"Did you and Micah get a chance to catch up?"

"We spent a couple days together," Tamara stated without emotion. "He seems to stay busy, but I'm not surprised. Micah has always been extremely focused."

"What was it like seeing him again?" Jillian inquired as casually as she could manage, but she did not have her daughter fooled for one minute.

"It was nice," Tamara answered. "Mama, please quit with all of the questions. This was a business trip. Not a romantic getaway."

"You mean to tell me that you and Micah spent your entire trip talking about business? I can't believe that he is that committed to Sunshine or whatever her name?"

Tamara chewed on her bottom lip to keep from smiling. "Mama…"

"I'm just saying," Jillian countered. "I know how much that boy cared for you when you were in school.

It was pretty clear to me that Micah was in love with you, Tamara."

"Well, he's not anymore," she responded. "Micah has moved on with his life, and I'm doing the same."

Her mother was not about to let her off the hook. That just was not Jillian's style. "Then why do you sound so sad if that's the case? Honestly, dear, you sound as if you've lost your best friend."

She wasn't about to confide in her mother, so she said, "Mama, can we please change the subject? I don't want to talk about Micah anymore."

"Tamara, you know that I'm here if you want to talk about anything. You don't have to keep your feelings all bottled up inside."

"Thanks," she muttered. "Mama, I just have a lot on my mind right now. I have to come up with some ideas to pitch to Samantha tomorrow."

"Are you enjoying your new position at the magazine?"

"I am," Tamara admitted. It was the only thing in her life that gave her joy now.

After promising to have dinner with her mother on Sunday, they ended their conversation. She hung up the phone and stretched out on her sofa, hoping her headache would disappear.

Micah was so angry he was trembling. He was too angry to just stand still and too angry to pace the floor.

How could he allow the same woman back into his life? Tamara was a master manipulator, willing to do anything—even sleep with him for a story.

He tried to get her to open up with him. Now he understood why she was so reluctant to discuss her past. There was nothing to tell. Tamara enjoyed playing the victim. She played well but no more.

Micah vowed from this moment forward that he would have nothing else to do with her.

He meant it this time. He was done with Tamara Hodges.

The telephone rang.

Micah checked the caller ID and saw that it was Sunni calling.

He was not in the right frame of mind to deal with Sunni and her pathetic attempt at manipulation. Unlike Tamara, she wasn't very skilled at it.

He spent most of his day outside by the pool, lost in thought and struggling once again to pick up the pieces of his broken heart.

Love is truly blind, Micah decided.

That was the only reason behind his falling for Tamara's antics. She was looking to further her career and it didn't seem to matter to her that she was using him to do it.

I'm a fool when it comes to Tamara.

Furious over his own weakness, Micah strode briskly across the room and went out on the patio.

It was a beautiful clear day in Los Angeles. Usually Micah enjoyed the beauty of nature, but now, he held no appreciation for anything and hadn't for weeks now.

He thought back to the promise he made Tamara's grandmother shortly before she died and felt a thread of guilt.

"I didn't lie to you, Mrs. Davis. Things changed after you left us. Tamara is not the girl we thought she was.

I think she had all of us fooled," he whispered. "Your granddaughter played me big time, and despite the fact that I love her, I'm done with her for good."

The telephone rang again.

He had to admit that he was a little surprised he hadn't heard from Tamara by now. He half expected her to call and plead for the interview—especially since that's all she wanted from him.

It was clear to Micah that Tamara wanted her career more than anything else—even more than she wanted him.

Tamara decided she needed some girlfriend time so she called Kyra and invited her to see a movie. After they agreed on a time for the next day, she hung up.

Each time Micah tried to force his way into her thoughts, Tamara pushed him into the far recesses of her mind. She didn't want to think about the man who had used her and then tossed her out like discarded trash.

Tamara found ways to stay busy in order to get through the day without dwelling on her failed romance with Micah.

She woke up early the next morning and went to the gym to work out some of her frustration. What bothered Tamara most was that she had no idea why Micah treated her so badly.

After Tamara's kickboxing class, she felt somewhat better, but the rest of the day, she continued to battle her heartsickness over Micah.

That night when she saw Kyra in the parking lot, she waved.

They walked up to the theater together.

"How was your trip?" Kyra questioned Tamara. They

had just purchased their movie tickets and were standing in line for popcorn and sodas.

Although she was dying inside, Tamara pasted a smile on her face. "It was fine. I had fun on the tour with Justice."

"I can't wait to read all about it. Actually, the reason I wanted to talk to you is because I have an idea for a story if you're interested. What do you think of writing an article about Terrence Franklin being courted to sign on as Hollington's head coach?"

"I wondered what he was going to do after retiring from the NFL," Tamara stated. "I remember how much he loved football."

"I'm hoping he will take the job." Kyra took a sip of her iced tea. "If he does, I'm definitely looking forward to next season."

Tamara agreed. "I think Terrence will make a great coach."

"It would be nice to generate as much buzz as possible."

"Can you give me his contact information? I'd like to interview him for the article."

"Now that we got that business out of the way," Kyra stated as they neared the counter, "did anything happen between you and Micah?"

Tamara tried to keep her face void of any emotion. "Nothing worth talking about," she responded.

"I'm surprised because that boy has always wanted you, Tamara. I could tell that Micah was crazy about you."

Well things have changed, she thought to herself. *He hates me now.*

Kyra ordered small popcorn and a soda while Tamara

ordered a root beer. She wasn't hungry so she decided against the popcorn.

Truth be told, she really was not in the mood for a movie, but Tamara decided that she needed to get out of the house.

Three hours later, she was grateful to be back at home. The chick flick only served to sink her deeper into depression. It was a beautiful romantic comedy, only she couldn't fully appreciate the story because of her own lack of a love life.

She just couldn't seem to get it right.

Tamara stared at the phone. She struggled with whether or not to call

Micah. It did not take her long to decide that calling him would be fruitless. The man wanted nothing more to do with her. He'd made love to her and then tossed her out. That spoke volumes.

She removed her clothes and padded barefoot into the bathroom. Tamara turned on the shower.

As soon as Tamara felt the soothing hot water on her skin, she allowed her tears to flow. She stayed in the shower until she was all cried out.

Tamara dried off and slipped on a pair of silk pajamas. She sat down on the edge of her bed and opened her journal.

September 10
I thought about calling Micah today just to get some clarity on what transpired between us, but I really don't know what to say to him. Besides, I'm not sure that he will even take my calls. He certainly hasn't tried to reach me at all. I had hoped

that once I was gone, Micah would miss me or feel bad over the way he threw me out of his house and that he would call to apologize.

I chose to think that he's angry with me because the other alternative is that Micah wanted to pay me back for what happened in college. I find it hard to think of him being so cruel.

During the tour, I thought we had gotten closer and that we had truly laid the past to rest. Still, I'm left with the question of why he has such a low opinion of me. Why would he think that I'd try to manipulate him in some way just to get a story?

I try not to think that Micah used me for sex because it would hurt too much. I don't want to think of him in that way. Feeling used in that way is such an ugly emotion.

I'm not going to keep dwelling on this. If Micah wanted nothing to do with me, so be it. I don't want drama in my life.

I am going to finish my story and then forget that I ever knew Micah Ross.

Tamara closed her journal with a soft sigh.
If only it were that easy.

Micah sat at the piano in his music room.
His fingers danced over the keys, creating a mournful piece that captured his mood perfectly. He played, stopping every now and then to record the notes on a piece of paper. Some of his best songs were born out of his pain.

He had no idea of time. Micah was engrossed in his

song. It pulled him along with its steady, jazzy melody. He continued to play, wrapped up in the music, the notes embracing him like a cocoon.

Micah's fingers struck the keys until his long fingers ached.

He stopped playing and just sat there, staring off into space. Micah turned around on the wooden bench, his eyes bouncing around the room. He had a twelve thousand square foot house, more money than he could ever spend in his lifetime, a very successful company and no one special to share them with—it did not seem to make much sense to Micah.

He got up, ventured into the kitchen and poured himself a glass of wine.

Micah took it with him upstairs to his bedroom.

Although he didn't want to see Tamara ever again, he couldn't deny that her absence left an extraordinary void in his life.

He sipped his wine; the golden liquid ignited a drowsy warmth deep in the pit of his stomach. Micah sat down on one of the chairs in the sitting room, enjoying his drink.

The clock read 11:41 p.m.

Micah was tired but he wasn't sleepy. He had to fly to New York the next day for business. Since his flight did not leave until six, Micah put off packing until the next morning.

He drank the last of his wine and then stretched out on the sofa. Micah had a hard time keeping his eyes open.

His last waking thought before he drifted into sleep was of Tamara. He hated himself for his inability to stop loving her.

Chapter 11

Tamara reluctantly met her mother for a day of shopping on Saturday. She had planned to just stay home and relax, but Jillian was redecorating her bedroom for the third time in less than a year and insisted on her daughter's help.

"I was beginning to think you were avoiding me," she stated as they strolled through the bedding department, looking for a new comforter. This was the third store they had gone to. Tamara was frustrated because her mother couldn't seem to make up her mind.

"Mama, I told you I was on a huge deadline." She fingered the delicate lace sewn along the edge of a bedspread. "Just because I'm home all of the time and not in an office doesn't mean that I'm not working. I don't have all day to just shop like you do."

"Maybe if you had a husband, you wouldn't have to

work so hard," Jillian pointed out. "Or if you'd just take the money I've put away for you—"

"Mama, please don't start…. I love what I do and I don't mind working for a living." She prayed her mother would move on to something else. Tamara was struggling to keep her frustration out of her voice.

Jillian would not let up. "Tamara, I'm just saying that it would be nice to have someone to come home to—wouldn't you agree?"

"I'm happy with my life," Tamara stated. "I wish you would just accept me as I am."

"All I want is the best for you. Why can't you understand that? Like this money I fought so hard to get for you. After everything that's happened, you deserve every penny."

"Mama, I don't need blood money," Tamara snapped.

Jillian's face paled. "I made sure you had a good college education and I secured your future. That money belongs to you, Tamara. Lucas Devane was a horrible husband and worse as a father. *He owes you.*"

"Mama, please be honest with me for once," Tamara implored her. "You're the one who didn't want to work or give up a life of luxury. You didn't do this for me and Callie. It was all about you."

"How can you say that?"

"I know what you did, Mama," Tamara stated. "I heard you that night on the telephone with him."

Jillian didn't respond immediately.

After a tense moment, she said, "I know how it must have sounded to you, but you need to understand that everything I did was for you and Callie. Do you know what this would do to your sister if she knew what happened?"

Tamara leaned forward. "I would never say anything to her, Mama," she said in a low voice. "I don't want Callie to know the kind of man her father really is. It would devastate her."

"My mother was right about him as much as I hate to say it," Jillian uttered. "She could see right through him. I was a young widow with a small child. I thought that he loved me. He did in the beginning...."

"I really don't want to talk about Lucas," Tamara stated.

"Did you ever find that necklace your grandmother gave you?" Jillian asked. "I've been meaning to ask about it, but with the wedding plans, I simply kept forgetting to mention it."

"I lost it in college, Mama. I'm never going to find it. I hate it, too. I really loved Grandmother's locket."

"I still think it's in some of your boxes. One day we should go through all of them. You need to get rid of some of that stuff. I'm taking my old bedding along with some other things to a Goodwill donation office. You should donate whatever you're not using, too."

Jillian pointed to the bed on display in front of them. "What about this one? It's gorgeous and very feminine."

"It's nice," Tamara agreed. "I could see that in your bedroom."

She wanted to do a praise dance when her mother decided to purchase the comforter set. Tamara was tired and wanted to get back home so that she could take a nap.

Jillian offered to buy her lunch, but Tamara begged

off. After promising to call her mother later, she got into her car and left Sak's Fifth Avenue department store.

During the drive home, Tamara's thoughts traveled to Micah.

The article on Justice Kane was finished and e-mailed to her editor. Samantha would forward a copy on to Micah for his approval. Tamara had been tempted to send the article directly to him herself, but it felt like she was trying to force her way into his life.

As much as Tamara loved him, she did not want to be with a man who didn't want to be with her. The thought that he had used her for sex kept creeping into her mind, but Tamara fought off the belief that Micah was that type of man.

She felt like they were in some type of crazy cycle. Ten years ago, she'd mistakenly believed he would do something like that and had been wrong.

It's time to move on. I'm never going to get the answers I need because the one man who can give them to me, won't talk to me.

"This is so crazy," she whispered. "I need to get this man out of my head."

At home, Tamara curled up with a pen and her journal on her sofa in the den.

September 15
Mama drafted me to help her redecorate her bedroom. As always, our talks come down to finding a husband or accepting that blood money from Lucas Devane. I don't like losing my patience with her, but she just won't give up.

I still have not heard anything from Micah, but

it's not like I seriously expected to hear from him. He's good at holding grudges real or imagined.

I thought that I would get over Micah eventually, but it has not happened yet.

I still love him as much as before. There are times when I feel nothing but anger toward him because of the way he dumped me, but then again, it doesn't really matter.

If Micah doesn't want to be with me then—I don't want to be with him either. Life is way too short to waste it. I decided a long time ago that I would enjoy whatever time I have left in this world.

I've finally put the disappointment and pain from my past behind me, and I've opened my heart to love.

I want to be happy.

That's not asking too much, is it?

Despite Sunni's constant, self-absorbed chatter, Micah could not get Tamara off his mind. He had been trying to flush her out of his system since the day he threw her out of the house.

As promised, Micah received an advance copy of the feature story Tamara wrote on Justice Kane. It would not be on the stands for another couple months. He had to admit that it was actually an excellent piece of work. Micah couldn't deny that she was a very gifted writer.

Before returning to his office, Micah decided to stop at the jewelry store to pick up a watch he had repaired. "I need to stop at Wyndham Jewelers," he announced to Sunni. "I need to pick up my watch."

"Not a problem, honey," she stated.

Sunni picked him up in her brand-new Mercedes luxury sedan. It was her gift to herself. She told him that she enjoyed being pampered, but if she couldn't get a man to buy it for her, then she would just buy it.

He supposed her comment was to be a hint for him; however, Micah chose to ignore it.

Sunni parked her car in front of the store.

While inside the store, a necklace caught Micah's attention. It looked familiar to him. He searched his memory, trying to recall where he'd seen it before.

Micah stole a peek over his shoulder where Sunni stood, checking out the engagement rings and her cell phone glued to her ear.

Micah wavered a moment, trying to comprehend what he was about to do. "Could you please box up this necklace, earrings and the matching bracelet?" he asked in a low whisper. "I'll be getting those, too."

The salesclerk eyed Sunni, smiled and nodded.

Micah could not believe what he was doing. *Why am I buying something like this for her? She doesn't deserve it.*

Micah couldn't explain his actions but for once allowed his heart to lead. Maybe it was time that he finally took action. It was time for him to just go after what he wanted—make his intentions plain and clear for the last time.

The clerk handed him the bag containing his purchases and his newly repaired watch.

"Honey, come look at this," Sunni said, gesturing for him to join her. Her excitement set off warning bells in his brain.

Micah walked over to where she was standing.

"Isn't this gorgeous?" she asked with a big grin on her face.

He glanced down at the huge diamond engagement ring she was pointing at and said, "Yeah, it's nice." Micah made sure to keep his tone noncommittal.

"It would look beautiful on my hand, don't you think?"

Micah shrugged. "I guess."

Out of the corner of his eye, he caught sight of a photographer standing outside the store.

"I need to get back to the office," Micah blurted. "We need to get going."

Sunni rolled her eyes. "I just want to try it on. It won't take long."

Micah kept his frustration to a minimum. He could see the headlines tomorrow—Micah Ross and Sunni shopping for an engagement ring.

When she saw that he was not interested in rings or her for that matter, Sunni released a long sigh and grunted, "Let's go."

The photographer outside the store began snapping pictures as soon as they walked outside. Sunni went into model mode while he kept a blank expression behind dark designer sunglasses.

Once they were in the car, she said, "Now I see why you were acting so mean in the store."

"I wasn't being mean, Sunni. I just don't want to be tomorrow's headline."

"Most people would kill for the kind of press that you get, Micah. I don't know why you get so bothered by it. None of your artists would be the people they are without the media, you know."

"I'm not saying that it doesn't help. I just don't want to be the one in the headlines. That's all."

"You need to get over yourself, Micah."

He recalled seeing her on the phone earlier and asked, "Sunni, did you call that guy to tell him that we were at Wyndham's?"

"Why would you ask me something like that?" she asked without looking in his direction.

"Because I know that you've done it before," he stated. "Sunni, I told you before to never do that when you're with me."

"I didn't call him," she said.

"Good," Micah responded. "I hope we have an understanding."

"We do."

Sunni dropped him off at the Ross Red offices and left to meet with her agent.

Micah had a strong suspicion that she had indeed given the photographer a tip as to their whereabouts. He was tired of being manipulated, and this time he was going to make sure Sunni understood or she would risk losing his friendship.

Just like Tamara.

However, he had some unfinished business with her. Micah planned to attend the college reunion in order to lay to rest his feelings for Tamara. Once he had the opportunity to say what needed to be said, Micah would be free to move on with his life.

He did not want to talk to Tamara over the phone. He'd speak his mind in person.

* * *

Tamara suddenly became dizzy and felt as if she were about to pass out while shopping for groceries. She left her items in the cart and went to sit down for a moment near the exit doors.

She glanced up at the clock. It was almost noon and Tamara skipped breakfast this morning, so she assumed that was the cause of her dizziness.

When Tamara felt strong enough to stand, she got up and walked over to the deli area. She purchased a sandwich and went back to the bench where she sat earlier.

She felt a little better after she ate.

Tamara returned to her cart, quickly scanning to see if anything was missing. Satisfied, she pulled her list out of her pocket and resumed shopping.

Her cell phone rang.

She saw that the caller was Callie.

"Hey, Sis," she said in greeting. "I guess you and Bryant have finally come up for air. I haven't talked to you in what? Three weeks or so. I guess married life is wonderful, huh?"

Callie laughed. "You should try it, Tamara. It's great!"

Tamara groaned. "You're not going to become Jillian Junior, are you?"

"No, you didn't just say that," her sister responded. "I was calling to see if you wanted to join me and Bryant for dinner tomorrow night. We can eat in or go out to a restaurant."

"That will depend on whether or not you or Bryant is cooking," Tamara replied.

"Ha-ha," Callie uttered. "Bryant can do it."

"Your husband is not going to work those long hours and then come on and cook dinner—not for me anyway. We can go out."

A wave of dizziness swept through Tamara once more.

"Callie, can I call you later?" she asked. "I'm in the grocery store, and my signal isn't strong. I'll give you a call when I get home."

She decided to finish her shopping another day. Tamara pushed the cart to the first available cashier and paid for her items.

When Tamera made it to her car, she climbed inside and sat there as she waited for the sensation of passing out to disappear as quickly as it had come.

What is going on with me? She wondered.

Tamara prayed that it wasn't some type of virus going around. *Luster* magazine had a function on Friday night that she needed to attend, so she couldn't afford to get sick two days before.

She hadn't felt well for a few days now that she thought about it. Tamara was moody and tired a lot more than usual. She made a mental note to make an appointment with her doctor if her symptoms persisted.

Tamara met Callie and her brother-in-law at Ruth's Chris Steak House restaurant in Buckhead.

"Thanks for inviting me to tag along with you two lovebirds," she told them.

Callie gave her a hug. "Stop being so sarcastic. The only reason why you don't have a man is because you're so picky."

Tamara glanced over at Bryant. "She doesn't know what she's talking about."

They were seated immediately.

"Are you feeling okay, Sis?" Callie inquired. "You look a little pale."

"I'm fine," Tamara said. She didn't want to worry her sister, especially if it were just a twenty-four hour type of virus.

Callie scanned her menu. "Do you know what you're getting as your entrée?" she asked Tamara.

"The petite filet with jumbo lump crab cake," Tamara replied. "What about you? What are you ordering?"

"I think I'm going to get what you're ordering. It sounds delicious. I know my husband will be getting the ribeye."

Bryant nodded in agreement. "I love my ribeyes."

The waiter arrived to take their drink orders.

While they waited for him to return, Tamara asked, "What are you guys doing this weekend?"

"We're going to Hilton Head with Daddy. He wants to spend some time with us."

At the mention of Lucas, her stomach turned and Tamara felt nauseous. She pretended to be engrossed in her menu.

"He asks about you all the time," Callie stated. "He told me that he feels bad about the divorce and everything. I really hope that one day you will be able to forgive my father for divorcing Mama."

The waiter returned, giving Tamara a reprieve. He gave them their drinks and then wrote down their order.

When he left, Tamara eyed her sister. "I hope this

is not why you wanted me to meet you and Bryant for dinner. Lucas is out of my life, and that's the way I want to keep it. I know he's your father, but I want absolutely nothing to do with him." She was tired of being manipulated.

Callie looked visibly upset. "What I want is for the two of you to get along. He's my father, and you are my sister. What's wrong with me wanting unity in my family?"

"I'm not saying that there's anything wrong with that, Callie. The reality is that your father and I aren't even in each other's radar, Sis. Getting along doesn't apply to us. He's *your* father. You have the relationship with him."

"You have no idea how it makes me feel knowing that you and Mama hate my father." Callie looked like she was about to cry.

"I don't hate Lucas—I don't have any feelings about him whatsoever."

"Tamara, that's cold."

Shrugging, she uttered, "It's the truth." Tamara took a sip of her sparkling water. "Why don't we change the subject to something we can all agree on?"

Bryant reached over and took Callie by the hand. "Shall we tell your sister our news?"

Tamara piped up. "News? What news?"

"Bryant and I are having a baby," Callie announced with a grin. "We're pregnant."

"Does Mama know?" Tamara asked. Her mother was going to be thrilled to be a grandmother. She could hear Jillian now, barking orders for a baby shower.

Callie shook her head no. "We don't want to tell her until after the first trimester."

"I thought you two were going to wait a couple years," Tamara stated. "What changed your minds?"

"I wanted to start a family right away," Bryant contributed. "I'm twelve years older than your sister, and I want to be able to play with my children without arthritis and gout setting in," he added with a chuckle.

Her eyes traveled back to Callie, who said, "I'm happy about the baby."

Tamara studied her sister's face to see if she was telling the truth. She knew that Callie was deeply in love with Bryant. She looked really happy and in love.

Their food arrived.

"Mama told me that you spent some time with Micah while you were in Los Angeles. She thinks that you're in love with him."

Why couldn't Jillian mind her own business?

"You know our mother," Tamara stated. She stuck a forkful of crabmeat into her mouth, chewing slowly.

"So you're not in love with him?" Callie inquired. "I thought he was your boyfriend in college."

Tamara met her sister's curious gaze. "We were just friends. He was my math tutor our freshman year, and we became friends after that. Callie, do me a favor and stop listening to Mama. When the time is right, I'll find my man. In the meantime, I don't need or want any help."

Tamara was getting tired of her family thinking that she needed someone in her life in order to be happy. Images of Micah drifted through her mind and filled her with certain sadness.

As they finished their meal, Tamara steered the conversation back to Callie and her baby. So far, her sister had experienced no morning sickness or any other symptoms associated with pregnancy. She actually looked radiant.

"I hope pregnancies like that are in our genes," Tamara stated. "With my luck, I'll be the one who's sick all nine months."

Callie chuckled. "Don't say that."

Tamara hoped that her mother would become so enthralled with being a grandmother that she would forget about her state of singleness.

At home, she made another entry into her journal. Tamara wrote about her feelings regarding her sister's marriage and pregnancy. She thought it was all nice and wonderful. Tamara wasn't jealous of Callie's happiness—she just wanted some of her own.

Tamara wanted a family. She wanted the house with the white picket fence and filled with love. She was beginning to tire of coming home to an empty house. Jillian would be so pleased if she knew this was how Tamara really felt.

She would probably throw a party.

Tamara chuckled a little at the thought.

The trouble with finding a husband was the fact that her heart already belonged to another man. However, that same man hated her with a passion.

Chapter 12

The week before homecoming, a trembling Tamara sat in her car for a few minutes; trying to digest the shocking news she had just received from her physician.

Despite how she and Micah had left things when she was in California, Tamara knew that she had to reach out to him once more.

She called and left a voice mail message on his cell phone. She also placed a call to his office and spoke with Bette, his secretary.

"Please call me back," she whispered. "I really need to talk to you."

The next day, there was still no word from Micah.

Tamara opted not to call him again. She had too much on her mind to have to try and chase after a man who didn't have the decency to return a simple phone call.

One thing she had learned about Micah was that the man could really hold a grudge. He could use a lesson or two on forgiveness, she thought to herself, then felt like a hypocrite. Tamara carried a load of unforgiveness in her own heart, although she kept telling herself that she had a valid reason.

In the five weeks that she had been home since that night she spent with him, Tamara felt a rush of emotions. She loved Micah, and if she could, she would be with him right now.

Tamara still held on to her questions about that morning—mainly why Micah didn't trust her anymore. They no longer mattered, she supposed. The fact remained that something happened the night before that affected and changed her life for all eternity.

As much as she wanted to do so, Tamara would never be able to forget that night she and Micah made love. It would forever be imprinted on her heart in many ways.

Dazed, she made the drive home in the midst of the distraction of traffic noises, the radio and her turbulent thoughts. Tamara had a headache and just wanted to lie down and sleep.

At home, she put on some soft jazz, made some hot tea and sat down in her den in an attempt to force her body to relax.

Tamara finished off her tea as the music playing in the background soothed her. She never made it up to her bedroom because she fell asleep on the sofa. Her last thought before Tamara closed her eyes was of Micah.

She slept for almost two hours, waking up when the telephone rang. Tamara sat up, stretched and yawned. She swung her feet off the sofa and stood up.

Tamara felt light-headed for a moment so she sat back down. She had an upset stomach to add to the dizziness. Groaning, she lay back against the plush cushions with her eyes closed.

Fifteen minutes passed.

She made a second attempt to stand up and made her way to the kitchen where Tamara prepared a pot of chicken noodle soup.

I'm not sure I can keep this down, but I need to put something in my stomach.

Tamara's eyes filled with water. She wiped her eyes with the back of her hand. "I'm not doing this," she uttered. "I can survive this. It won't be easy, but I'll manage."

Her eyes traveled to a nearby calendar.

Homecoming was next Friday. She had heard that Justice Kane was performing at the reunion dance, so Tamara was fairly sure that Micah would be in town for the weekend.

She felt a tinge of apprehension at the thought of seeing him again. Regardless, she needed one final conversation with Micah. After that, the ball was in his court and Tamara would follow his lead.

Friday, October 16

It's Friday and tonight is the cocktail party the university hosts for the largest contributors and VIP alumni. I'm going to cover the event for the magazine. I look forward to homecoming every year, but this one is special because it is my ten-year reunion.

The committee members have some events

planned to celebrate in addition to the regular homecoming activities. We have an alumni dance tomorrow night and we're having a picnic on Sunday.

As soon as Micah arrives, I am going to pull him off to the side so that we can talk. I need to know what made him so angry or if that was just part of his plan to humiliate me. I need to know so that I'll know what I need to do next.

If he wants nothing to do with me it will break my heart, but I have survived worse. I love Micah, but I refuse to make him my entire world. He and I need a real discussion because the truth is that I don't know if I can deal with his mood swings and tantrums.

I just really need to talk to Micah.

Tamara put away her journal.

She went downstairs to the kitchen to make a light lunch of tuna salad and crackers before heading back to her desk to work on the article that was due in a couple weeks.

Around two o'clock, Tamara found that she could not keep her eyes open or concentrate on her writing. She gave up and went to lie down on the sofa. Lately she found that she tired easily and needed to take naps during the day.

Tamara did not wake up until 3:30 p.m.

Nauseous and nervous over the thought of seeing Micah again, Tamara almost changed her mind about attending the private party, but if she wanted to be taken seriously as a writer she couldn't miss this opportunity.

Besides, she promised Chloe that she would write an
article on the event for *Luster* magazine. Tamara wished
fervently that she felt better, however.

She made her way to the master bath where she
showered and flat-ironed her hair straight, bumping the
ends with a large barrel curling iron. Still feeling sick to
her stomach, Tamara took her time getting ready, pausing every now and then to take tiny sips of ginger ale.

Tamara chose to wear the black Carmen Marc Valvo
designer lace and sequins dress with a lace bust, sequins around the empire waist that flowed into layers
of pleated chiffon. Strappy high-heeled sandals with
an ankle wrap, black diamond earrings, matching ring
and bracelet completed the look.

She stole a peek at the clock.

It was 4:45 p.m.

The event started at six, and she did not want to be
late. Tamara would be traveling in rush hour traffic. She
grabbed her purse and headed out the door.

Tamara got in her car, slipped in her favorite Mary
J. Blige CD and drove out to the freeway, humming to
the music.

Her thoughts traveled to Micah. What if he decided
not to come for homecoming after all?

A wave of apprehension washed over her as the
thought tore at Tamara's insides. She hadn't really considered it until now that he could've changed his mind
about coming.

What would she do then?

She didn't have an answer. If he didn't come, she
still had to straighten things out with Micah and soon.

Never speaking to her again wasn't an option anymore.

* * *

Micah gave the valet his keys before strolling into CORK, a wine bar located in downtown Atlanta, with Sunni.

"Honey, I have to go to the little girls' room," she told him. "I'll be back shortly."

A couple of women recognized him and began a conversation.

"Do you remember us?" they asked in unison.

He studied their faces. "June? We had a history class together, right?"

She giggled and nodded.

Micah glanced at the other woman and said, "Your face is familiar but I'm sorry. I'm at a loss."

Her lips turned downward. "It's Christine. We didn't have any classes together, but I dated your roommate for about six months."

He remembered her then. "It's good to see you again, Christine. Have you and Ron kept in touch over the years?"

She smiled and nodded. "He and I just started seeing each other again. Ron will be in town tomorrow morning. He had a business meeting and couldn't get here in time for the reception tonight."

Sunni blew out of the bathroom as if someone was after her. She flung her hair over her shoulder as she sauntered toward Micah and the women.

"Are you ready?" she asked him before greeting the two females standing beside him.

He introduced her to the women.

When they left, Sunni asked, "So when do I get to meet some of your friends?"

"How do you know those two women weren't friends of mine?" he demanded.

She turned and surveyed his face. "You've been in a weird mood since we arrived here in Atlanta. Micah, what's going on with you?"

His mouth tightened a moment before he answered her. "I'm fine."

Micah and Sunni navigated through the wine bar. He walked up to his longtime friend, saying, "Hey, Kevin, what's up?"

The two men embraced.

Micah introduced Sunni to his friend. He was beginning to regret bringing her to Atlanta. Actually, she invited herself, and he didn't bother to talk her out of it. Sunni could be great company when she wanted to be.

She accepted a glass of wine from a passing waiter and took a sip.

"Man, it's good to see you," Kevin told him. "Thanks for bringing Justice Kane to my club tomorrow night, man."

"Hey, this is how we roll, bro," Micah stated.

Kevin nodded. "The place is gonna be jumping tomorrow night."

Micah chuckled. "I hope so."

While they talked, Sunni strolled away to pose near the bar. Micah assumed she must have spotted a photographer or TV reporter hanging around.

His eyes traveled the length of the room, searching. Turning his attention back to Kevin, he said, "Hey, I was surprised to hear that you and Chloe are dating. When did this happen?"

"We've been together for about three months and we click. What can I tell you?"

"That's great, man," Micah stated. "I'm happy for you both. She's a nice lady."

"I have something special planned for her tomorrow night," Kevin stated. "I hope you plan on sticking around for a while. How are things between you and the supermodel?" Kevin inquired, his eyes traveling over to where Sunni stood surrounded by fans and admirers.

"Kevin, she and I are just friends. I told you that."

"Man, what's wrong with you?" he wanted to know. "That woman is *fine,* and it's obvious that she loves you. What's holding you back?"

"She and I want different things out of a relationship," Micah replied. "We do have a good time together, though."

With those words, Micah's eyes surveyed the room, looking for the one person who had dominated his thoughts night and day for the past couple months.

Tamara Hodges.

Tamara made a pit stop to the restroom as soon she walked through the doors of the wine bar. She rushed into the nearest stall and emptied the contents of her stomach. When she came out, she found that she wasn't alone.

"Are you okay?"

Tamara eyed the woman's reflection in the mirror, recognizing her. "Hey, Beverly. I'm fine," she responded. "At least I will be in a few minutes."

Beverly Turner was crowned the homecoming queen their senior year in college.

"Tamara, it's so good to see you again," she stated with a sincere smile. "It's been a while, huh?"

Tamara nodded. "Time goes by so fast. You were my first interview for the *Atlanta Daily* after we graduated." Tamara worked with the newspaper for six years before leaving to write for *Luster*.

"You did a great job on the article, by the way—I don't know if I ever told you."

Tamara smiled. "You sent me a nice note thanking me. In fact, I believe I still have it."

They continued to make small talk, catching up with current events.

She soon became gripped by another bout of nausea. Tamara put a hand to her stomach and rushed back into a nearby stall. She prayed for the sensation to pass.

"Are you sure you're okay?" Beverly asked a second time when she walked out.

Nodding, Tamara responded, "My stomach is a little upset."

"I hope I'm not being too nosy, but are you expecting a baby?"

She responded by asking Beverly, "Do you have children?"

Beverly gave a slight nod, then responded in a voice filled with sadness, "One."

Noting the pain etched all over Beverly's face, she did not push her to say anything more.

"I just found out," Tamara said in answer to the question Beverly posed earlier. "I'm still reeling from the shock when I'm not hanging my head over a toilet."

They talked for a few minutes more.

"I guess we should make our grand entrance," Tamara stated.

Beverly smiled and agreed.

They did one final check in the mirror before leaving the bathroom and going their separate ways.

Tamara walked upstairs, following the music and enjoying the quiet ambiance of the bar.

Her heels tapped across the dark wood floors as she walked past the wall of wine barrels, a large mahogany bar with a backdrop of rows and rows of wine bottles and an array of hors d'oeuvres on the countertop.

A waiter approached her carrying a tray of wine.

"No, thank you," she responded.

Tamara made her way around the center of the room, pausing to chat with old friends. She eventually ventured to one of the tall tables located off to the side and sat down on a stool.

Tamara spotted Beverly Turner, the woman she had encountered in the bathroom, and wished she had gotten her contact information. Beverly designed clothes and owned a boutique. She made a mental note to get her business card before leaving. Tamara had an idea for another feature story.

Her gaze traveled to Chloe who smiled and waved. Kyra walked over to where she was sitting and said, "You look pretty, soror."

"You do, too," Tamara responded, fighting the urge to get sick again. Her nose was more sensitive than normal, and the mixture of food smells, perfumes and wine were all doing a number on her.

"Do you want a glass of wine?" Kyra asked after chatting for a few minutes.

Tamara shook her head no. "I'm strictly on ginger ale tonight. My stomach's upset." She prayed that her friend wouldn't get curious enough to start asking questions.

"I hope you feel better," Kyra told her. "Have you eaten anything? Can I get you something?"

Tamara replied, "No, thanks, soror. I'm not hungry right now."

"There's Terrence," Kyra stated. "I need to go over and talk to him for a minute."

She looked over at the former football star and gave an understanding nod. "See you later."

Tamara enjoyed the quiet elegance and the ambiance of the club's color theme of deep reds and browns.

She found it soothing until Micah's face loomed before her.

"You look like you're a million miles away. Are you finding inspiration for another story?" he asked.

"Hello to you, too," Tamara responded, becoming increasingly uneasy under his scrutiny. Awkwardly, she cleared her throat. "Micah, I'm glad to see you actually. We really need to talk."

"I came over here to tell you the same thing," he stated. "There's something I should've told you a long time ago."

Tamara flinched at the tone of his voice and stirred uneasily in her chair. "I see you brought Sunni with you. Are you sure you'll have some time to spare?" She knew that she sounded like a jealous woman, and there was no denying it.

"I'll make time."

She nodded. "Micah, I don't know what's going on with you or why you're treating me like this. I wish you'd just tell me what I did. Do you think that maybe we could go downstairs to the sitting room and talk—"

Micah cut her off by saying, "We can talk right here."

Tamara sighed in resignation. "Fine," she uttered. "I'll go first, if you don't mind. Micah, I don't want to keep you from your date so I'll make this quick. Remember the incident with the condom?"

Without waiting on a response from Micah, she announced, "I'm pregnant. I just thought you should know that you're going to be a father, and before you accuse me of trying to trap you, I don't want or need anything from you. Oh, I'm willing to take a DNA test, if you want one done."

She stood up. "That's it. I really don't feel well, so I'm leaving. Enjoy the rest of your evening and your date."

Tamara walked as fast as she could. She just wanted to get as far away from Micah as possible. She held her tears in check, refusing to let him or anyone else see how much he had hurt her.

Lifting her chin defiantly, Tamara did as she had always done. She plastered a smile on her face and pretended all was well with her world, while on the inside, her heart was breaking into a million little pieces.

Chapter 13

Micah followed Tamara, gently grabbing her arm to keep her from running off.

They stood near the bar on the main floor. Keeping his voice low, Micah told her, "Tamara, you can't just drop something like this on me and then walk away."

She folded her arms across her chest. *"Really?"* Tamara questioned. "Do you think I wanted to tell you something like this in this way? Micah, I've been trying to contact you for weeks, but you wouldn't return any of my calls or my e-mails. When I found out about the baby last week, I didn't bother because I knew that you wouldn't talk to me. And I definitely wasn't going to leave the news with your secretary. Seeing you here was my only chance."

Sunni strolled over to where they were standing. Wrapping an arm around Micah, she met Tamara's gaze straight on and said, "Here you are, honey. I've been looking all over for you. Hello, Tamara."

"It's nice to see you again, Sunni. You look beautiful as always."

"I was about to say the same thing about you," Sunni responded with a smile. "I love your dress."

"Sunni, can you give us a moment, please?" Micah asked. "I really need to finish my conversation with Tamara."

The way that Sunni cut her eyes at him showed she was not happy about being sent away. After a long break in conversation, she responded, "I'll be at our table."

"I have to get out of here," Tamara stated. She pressed a hand to her stomach.

"Are you okay?" Micah asked out of concern.

"I'm fine," she managed. "I'm just a little nauseated."

"Why don't you sit down for a few minutes?" Micah suggested.

Tamara shook her head no. "I just want to go home. It was a bad idea for me to come in the first place. I knew that I wasn't feeling well, but I wanted to see you." She met his gaze. "To tell you about the baby. I've done that now, so I'm leaving now."

"Tamara…"

She shook her head. "I can't do this now, Micah. I really don't feel well. We can talk later…if you want to talk." She walked away from him, her heels tapping a steady rhythm across the floor.

"I assume you two have finished talking business," Sunni stated when he joined her at the table. "Is she okay?"

"Why do you ask?" Micah wanted to know.

"Tamara looked really upset about something." Sunni gave him a mischievous grin and asked, "What did you just do? Did you just break her heart?"

Micah didn't respond.

"Honey…" Sunni prompted as she surveyed his face. "Oh my… I don't know why I didn't see this before. It's *her*. She's the one."

He frowned in confusion. "What are you talking about?"

"I need you to be really honest with me right now, Micah. You're in love with Tamara, *aren't you?*"

"Sunni, we need to talk."

A flash of hurt crossed her face. "Micah, why did you bring me here? Especially when you knew that the woman you loved would be here, too. Were you trying to make Tamara jealous?"

"Sunni, it wasn't like that," Micah uttered. "Tamara and I… Let's just say that we were never meant to be, but now there is a situation." He paused a moment before continuing, "She's pregnant with my child."

Her thick, heavy lashes that shadowed her cheeks flew up. "What did you just say?"

"Tamara's carrying my child." He and Sunni were friends, and at times, she was his confidante. Micah knew that he could trust her with this secret.

"That would mean that you recently slept with her…" Sunni's voice died as the truth of her statement sunk in. Her eyes grew wet with unshed tears. "You slept with her during the tour, didn't you?"

He did not bother to answer her question. Micah didn't think he needed to confirm or deny when he and Tamara made love.

"Please don't tell me that you believe her?" She wanted to know. "How can you be so sure that the baby is yours? How do you know there really is a baby?"

"Because I know Tamara," he responded. "She's not the type of woman who would lie about something like this."

"People change," Sunni uttered. "She knows that you're a powerful and very wealthy man. You don't know what she's been doing in Atlanta."

Micah stated, "Tamara comes from an extremely well-to-do family. Believe me, she doesn't need my money."

Tears glistened in Sunni's eyes. "I can't believe this," she whispered. "I knew that she was after you. I knew it."

"This is not Tamara's fault. Sunni, I'm sorry. I just wanted to be honest with you."

"You have always made it clear that you didn't love me." Sunni gently wiped her eyes. "But I hoped that one day you would get a clue. I love you more than my own life, and I allowed myself to believe that you would eventually fall in love with me."

"I'm sorry."

"Don't be," she uttered with a shake of her head. "You never lied to me—I love you for that, Micah. We have been friends for a long time, and I hate to see that end, but I don't think I can do this anymore. I want marriage and a family."

Micah nodded in understanding.

"Before I leave, I want to offer you some advice, friend. You need to find Tamara and straighten out this stuff. You love her, and I have a feeling that she loves you, too. Work it out before your baby is born."

"Sunni, where are you going?"

"I'm going back to the house and pack. I'll stay at a hotel tonight and catch the first flight back to Los Angeles tomorrow."

"You don't have to leave the house. It's fine for you to stay."

She shook her head no. "It's best that I leave. If you're going to try and work things out with Tamara, you definitely don't need me in your house. I know if it were me, I wouldn't want her anywhere near you."

Micah embraced her. "Sunni, you deserve a man who will love you completely."

"I know that," she responded with a smile. "That's why I'm walking away instead of giving you a much-deserved beat down."

"That's right. You are a black belt in tae kwon do."

"Micah, I really wish you the best. I hope that Tamara will wake up and realize just how lucky she is, but if she doesn't call me."

"I don't know what's going to happen between me and Tamara. I'll just have to take it one day at a time."

"Micah, she loves you. I'd bet money on that. Go talk to her." She put a hand to her temple. "I need a glass— no, a bottle of very expensive champagne. Better yet, I think I need some whiskey straight."

"I will," Micah said with a chuckle. "Don't overdo it with the alcohol."

"I'll be fine."

"I need to make a few more rounds here, but as soon as I can get away, I'm going to talk to Tamara."

"You know I'm only a phone call away if you need me," Sunni stated. "I won't hold my breath though."

"I care a great deal about you," Micah confessed.

"In a best friend kind of way," she responded. "Which I hate but I'll deal with it. Tell reporter girl that she won after all."

"Sunni…"

She held up her hand to ward off his comment. "It's my last zinger, okay? Now move on, so I can scout for your potential replacement before I take off."

Micah released a short sigh of relief. It had gone better than he thought it would. He made a mental note to have Bette send Sunni some flowers on Monday.

Kevin signaled for him to join them at a nearby table. Straightening his jacket, Micah headed in their direction. He was ready to leave because he wanted to catch up with Tamara.

"Where's Sunni going?" he asked Micah.

"She's leaving shortly. She's going back to Los Angeles."

Kevin gave him a puzzled look.

"I'll explain later," Micah uttered.

An hour later, he walked out of CORK and got into his Land Rover SUV. Micah silently debated whether to call Tamara to let her know that he was coming over but decided the element of surprise was the best way to proceed in this situation. This way she could not tell him not to come.

There was an innocent child involved. He would not leave until he and Tamara laid everything on the table.

"Micah, what are you doing here?" Tamara asked when she opened her front door to find him standing outside.

She glanced around to see if Sunni was lurking somewhere outside. "Where is your date?"

"She's not with me," he said in response. "I know it's getting late but I had to come here to see you. Tamara, we need to finish our discussion. I would rather not do it out here, but I will if I have to." Micah's tone brooked no argument.

She stepped aside to let him enter into her apartment.

They sat down in the living room.

Tamara spoke first. "Micah, I don't know why you're so angry with me, but I don't really care anymore. I have a baby to think about, and if you're not ready to open up to me then just leave. I can raise my child on my own. I'm not gonna let you stress me out."

"Tamara, I didn't come to stress you out," Micah stated. "But I'm not going to let you keep me out of my child's life. I will go to court if I have to—I'm serious about this."

"Do what you feel you must," Tamara retorted. "I don't care about your threats. I've had enough threats to last me a lifetime."

Puzzled by her comment, Micah asked, "What are you talking about? Tamara, when are you going to tell me why you have this wall erected all around you? I've been thinking all along that you were nothing but a taker. You get what you need from me and then kick me to the curb, but now...I'm not so sure."

He held his hands up in resignation. "The truth is that I don't even know you anymore. There are so many conflicting things about you."

She gasped in surprise. "That's what you really think

of me?" Tamara wanted to know. "Why would you think something like that?"

"You needed a tutor, and I was there for you. When you needed a friend, I was there. But then when I ask you out, you told me in no uncertain terms that I was beneath you. When we were in Los Angeles, you wanted to snag an exclusive interview with me. We made love and I thought that we had shared something really special until that next morning. The first thing you can think to say to me is to ask if we can do the interview now. How do you think that made me feel?"

"Micah, it was nothing like that," Tamara responded. "You totally misunderstood everything. I've never tried to use you. We were friends and I valued our friendship. There was a lot going on with me."

"You keep saying that," Micah retorted. "So what was it, Tamara? What was going on with you? You keep talking about this great friendship that we shared, yet you've been keeping all these secrets. Why is it I never knew that you wanted to be a writer? I feel like we were involved in two very different relationships."

Her hands twisted in her lap. "It's true that there are some things that you don't know about me. Micah, I need you to believe that the only reason I never told you is because I didn't want you to think badly of me. Something bad happened to me before we met."

Micah surveyed her face. It was something in Tamara's eyes that prompted him to say, "Please tell me what happened to you. Help me understand."

"On the outside we looked like the perfect family. Micah, my stepfather…he was an awful man to me," Tamara stated. "Lucas was nice enough when he and my mother were dating, but after they married he wanted to send me away to boarding school. My mother refused. Anyway, whenever she wasn't around, he would say hurtful things. He verbally abused me, and when I would try to stand up for myself he started hitting me and threatening me if I said anything to my mother."

"Babe, I'm so sorry," Micah murmured. "I had no idea."

"This went on for a couple years. He would always tell me that if my own father didn't love me, how could I ever expect anyone to love me? I believed him."

"Tamara…"

Her eyes filled with tears. "Please let me finish. I need to get this out."

Micah got up and crossed the room to sit beside her. He took her hand in his.

"Go on, sweetheart."

"One day, he just started being nice to me out of the blue, I think I was sixteen or seventeen at the time. He started buying me little gifts, and he acted like a dad. He even apologized for the way that he had treated me in the past—blamed it on his drinking too much and stress from company business. Sometimes he would come to my room at night and we would talk for hours."

Tears streamed down Tamara's face. "All I ever wanted him to do is love me like he loved Callie. I just wanted him to be my dad, too." She put her hands to her face and sobbed.

Micah handed her a tissue.

When she had stopped crying, he asked, "Baby, what happened? Tell me."

Tamara focused on the intricate designs of the

wrought-iron fireplace screen as she talked. She was too ashamed to look directly at Micah. She didn't want to see the look of disgust on his face when he heard what happened between her and Lucas.

"I thought we were on the way to being a real family, but then one night he came to my room and started to touch me. He made me touch him in return."

The muscles around his mouth tightened, and Micah's hand curled into a fist. His heart ached for the woman he loved and the pain she was forced to endure. How could a man do something like this to a child he was supposed to protect?

Tamara wiped her face. "I wanted his love, but I never wanted him to love me in that way. That's not what I wanted from Lucas."

"Did he…" Micah couldn't even say the words.

"It only happened once," Tamara stated without emotion. "He was planning on doing it again, but when he came to my room a few nights later, my mother burst into the room just as he was removing his pants. He started blaming me, saying that I seduced him and that I'd been coming on to him for weeks."

He had never been a violent man, but he was ready to put her ex-stepfather into the grave. "Did your mother believe him?" Micah questioned. "Is that why you went to live with your grandmother?"

"To her credit, Mama didn't believe him for a minute, but it didn't stop her from using what happened to blackmail him into giving her half of his millions. She took me to a doctor and had everything documented. She knew that Lucas was deathly afraid of going to prison. We moved in with my grandmother and Mama filed for divorce. She signed a prenuptial agreement when they married but she used what happened to me to get it invalidated. She got the house, two of the cars and a hefty settlement. She and Callie moved back into the house but I couldn't— That place held so many bad memories for me. I just couldn't go back."

Tamara glanced over at him. "Micah, I never meant to hurt you. I was going through hell back then. I didn't trust anyone, especially a man. That's why I reacted the way that I did when I heard those people talking about us. As for the article, I won't lie—I really wanted the exclusive on you, but that's not why I made love to you. I've been manipulated all of my life and I hated it, so I would never try to manipulate another person, including you."

Micah felt lower than something he scraped off the bottom of his shoe. His guilt intensified when he thought of how he had treated Tamara, the woman he claimed to love. He was no better than Lucas was.

"I'm so sorry for assuming the worst, Tamara. I feel like such an idiot. I had no idea that you were dealing with something this heavy. I wish you'd felt safe enough to confide in me back then."

"There really wasn't any way that you could've known," she responded. "I was determined to keep my secret by any means necessary. It was just too shameful to tell you something like this."

"Does Callie know? I can't imagine she'd even let him near her after what he did to you."

Tamara shook her head no. "He gave Mama everything she wanted on the condition that she and I never mention what happened to my sister. He loves his daughter and doesn't want her to think badly of him. Callie adores Lucas, and they have a close relationship."

"How do you feel about what your mother did?" he asked. "I know things were pretty intense between you two in college."

"Back then, we didn't really get along at all," Tamara admitted. "I blamed her for using what happened as a threat in the divorce. She didn't want to go back to being poor so she used blackmail to keep her social standing in the community and her lifestyle. I don't care about all of that—he should have paid for what he did to me."

"Tamara, she didn't blackmail him," Micah interjected. "I think you mother was making sure that she received what was rightly hers. I think she deserved it all. I do agree with you that your stepfather should have gone to jail. But what would you have said to Callie?"

"That's why I never pressed charges," Tamara told him. "Part of their agreement was that Lucas had to undergo therapy, and he wasn't allowed to see Callie without supervision until she was sixteen. He was furious about that. Mama even insisted that Callie study karate in the event she needed to protect herself."

"Didn't you study, as well?" Micah asked.

She nodded. "It was too late for me. My virginity, my dignity and my security had already been taken away."

He wrapped his arms around her, wanting to offer her some comfort.

"As for the writing, I didn't have a lot of confidence in my ability so I never talked about it. I felt that if I didn't mention it no one would ask to read my work. Working at the *Atlanta Daily* helped me develop my skills. Now you know all of my secrets, Micah. You can leave if you want to. I won't fight you on visitation. I don't need your money, though."

"I fully intend on supporting my child, and I want you to understand something, Tamara. I'm not going anywhere. I intend to be a very active parent in my child's life. Now, if you're done talking, it's my turn to speak," Micah stated. "I have something I need to say to you."

It was time for him to come clean with her about everything. When Micah was done, there would be no more secrets between them. Everything would be out in the open—the way it should have been all those years ago.

"Micah, before you say anything more, I need to make this clear to you. I don't want you hanging around because of the baby or because you feel sorry for me."

"Why would I feel sorry for you?" Micah asked. "Tamara, I happen to think that you're the bravest person I know. Not many people could have gone through something like that and be the person that you are now. Even back then, you were always smiling. None of us had a clue that anything was wrong."

Tamara met his gaze straight on. "I'm not sure I understand. How was I brave? I let my mother convince me not to press charges or go to the police. She told the doctor that I had been raped, but she didn't tell him that it was Lucas. There's no bravery in that."

"Yes, there is," Micah countered. "You silently carried the weight of your stepfather's abuse to protect your sister all these years. You're still protecting her from the truth. Callie has no idea what kind of man her father really is and that's thanks to you. Lucas is afraid of you, Tamara, because you hold all the cards. One word from you and he could lose his daughter."

"I used to worry every time she would go over to visit him," Tamara confessed. "I was afraid he would do the same thing to her."

"Are you sure that he hasn't?"

Tamara nodded. "Callie would have fallen apart. That's not something she would be able to deal with. I just found out last week that she's going to have a baby." She glanced up at Micah. "I just pray this baby is a boy. He didn't touch Callie, but I don't know about a grandchild. I couldn't be quiet about this if I thought my niece was in danger."

"He should have gone to prison," Micah uttered. "Sweetheart, you have a quiet strength— I've always said that about you. It's one of the things that I love about you. Life can get crazy at times but during those times, you can't crumble. You have to stay strong."

"It's not an easy task," Tamara confessed. "I have just never been one to give up, but I will tell you that. I'm tired, Micah. That is one of the reasons I'm alone and not in a relationship. I just don't have time for drama." She put her hands to her face. "I'm really tired emotionally."

"I'm sure I added to the stress and for that, I'm sorry," Micah told her. "Honey, you don't have to face all of this alone anymore. I'm here for you. Tamara, you can tell me anything. I want you to know that."

A tear rolled down her cheek. "Right now, I just want you to hold me, please."

Micah wrapped an arm around her. "I am really sorry

about the way I've been acting. I had no idea that you had this kind of chaos in your life."

"There wasn't any way that you could have known, Micah. I wouldn't let you see my pain. Then we both just assumed the worst about the other when it came to our hearts. I'm not saying it's a good thing. We're just scared of getting hurt."

"I did the same thing to you that I accused you of— that's not cool."

"Micah, I don't hold it against you," Tamara assured him. "I just didn't know what I'd done wrong. I had no idea what upset you at the time, but I do see your point, and if it were me, I would probably have felt the same way."

"Well now that we've gotten all of this out—it's time for us to bury the past and look to the future, so I think we need to talk about the baby. Tamara, are you absolutely sure you're pregnant?"

Tamara looked him straight in the eye because she had nothing to hide. "I went to the doctor, and he confirmed it last week, Micah. I went in because I thought I had a virus but found out that it was a baby."

"I'm confused. I know we had the issue with the condom breaking the night we made love," he stated. "I thought you told me that you were on the pill or did I misunderstand?"

"I was on the pill, Micah." Tamara replied.

"Then how did this happen?" he asked.

"A few months ago, I had to get a lower dosage than what I was using before. I guess in my case, they weren't a strong enough dosage. I started having a reaction to the ones I was taking."

Micah agreed. "I take it that you're going to keep the baby."

"Of course," Tamara responded. "There aren't any other options as far as I'm concerned."

Micah held up his hands in defense. "Hey, don't hit me…. I had to ask— No more assumptions, right?"

"Right," Tamara agreed. "We're not making any assumptions. We didn't plan to conceive a child and I know this is as much a shock to you as it was to me. I also know that we're not a couple, which is why I won't force you to play a role in—"

Micah cut her off by saying, "I intend to be a part of my child's life. I want to make sure that you're hearing me on this, Tamara. You're right that we didn't plan to have baby, but we did create one and I'm not going to run away from the situation. I'm not that kind of man."

"I never thought that you were, Micah. That's why I wanted you to know that you had a child and to give you the option of being in his or her life. Like you, I didn't grow up with a father, so I would really like for this baby to have two parents." She yawned. "I'm sorry. I get tired pretty quickly these days."

Tamara glanced over at the clock on the mantel of the fireplace. "We can talk some more tomorrow because I'm sure Sunni must be wondering when you're coming home."

Micah shook his head. "Sunni's going back to Los Angeles tomorrow. I told her about the baby. I needed to make her know that there's no future for us. There never was."

"How did she take it?"

"Pretty good, I thought," Micah responded. "She knew it all along that there was only one woman for me."

She glanced up at him. "What are you saying? I know that you've been wanting to tell me something and I've cut you off. What is it that you want to tell me?"

Micah took her hand in his. "I want you to know that I care a great deal for you, Tamara. I tried ten years ago to let you know how I felt about you. You shot me down and as much as I wanted to forget you I couldn't."

Tamara's eyes never left his face. "Micah, what exactly are you telling me?" she asked.

"That what I feel for you is much more than friendship," Micah confessed. "It goes much deeper than that. Tamara, I love you. I always have."

Her eyes filled with tears as she smiled. "Micah, I love you, too. I can't believe that we've wasted so much time."

He kissed her. "Well, we're here now, so let's not waste another minute more."

Micah lay in bed beside Tamara, propped up on his arm as he watched her sleep. Stunned by Tamara's revelation, he felt the urge to protect her. He prayed he was never in the same location as Lucas Devane. Micah wasn't sure how he would react.

He couldn't imagine how hard it was for Tamara to keep such a dark secret from him and the rest of her friends. Having learned all this, Micah better understood why she reacted the way that she did graduation night. Any woman fighting inner demons, such as what she lived with, would respond the same way.

Micah was still stunned over how well Tamara was

able to hide this from him. He had always assumed she was a happy-go-lucky girl with this sunny personality; all the while she was suffering in silence.

"I won't let anyone hurt you ever again," he whispered. "I will protect you and our child with my life. I promise you, sweetheart. I'm going to keep you safe."

She moaned softly and turned over to her side.

Micah eased out of bed and walked over to the window, staring out at the heavens. Atlanta nights were always a vision of beauty, but this night seemed especially beautiful. The stars painted across the heavens and the moon seemed brighter than usual.

I'm going to be a father.

He and Tamara were going to have a child together. The thought thrilled Micah to no end. He had loved her all of his adult life, and the fact that they now shared a child that bonded them forever.

Micah wasn't complaining. He had always desired something permanent between them. If it had been up to him, he and Tamara would have gotten married years ago. He had always known that she was his soul mate.

His heart raced as he recalled her declaration of love. Tamara loved him in return. It surprised him to find out that she had loved him for as long as he loved her. Too many years were spent in misunderstandings and wrong assumptions. Micah didn't want to waste another precious minute. He and Tamara would talk tomorrow about their future to make sure that they were on the same page.

I'm not going to lose her again.

Chapter 14

Tamara woke up to the mouthwatering aroma of sausages cooking. Yawning, she climbed out of bed and padded barefoot into the bathroom to take a quick shower.

Fifteen minutes later, she walked out wrapped in a towel.

Humming softly, Tamara slipped on her robe and headed downstairs to the kitchen.

"Good morning," Micah said when he saw her standing in the doorway. "I hope you don't mind that I made breakfast. How are you feeling?"

Tamara smiled as she sat down in one of the chairs at the breakfast bar. "I'm fine in the mornings. I don't get nauseated until the afternoon or in the evening."

Micah's presence in her home gave her great joy. This was a dream come true for her.

"Since when did you start cooking?" she asked.

He gave a short laugh. "I had to learn if I wanted to eat. Did you think that I ate out all the time?"

Micah handed her a glass of orange juice.

"Thanks," she murmured.

Tamara took a sip before saying, "I thought that maybe you had a chef on staff or something."

He shook his head. "No, I do my own cooking."

"Do you need any help?" she asked.

Micah shook his head no. "I have everything under control. You just sit there and look beautiful."

She talked to him while he finished cooking.

Micah fixed their plates and placed them on the breakfast bar. He came around and sat down beside her.

"Tamara, you know that my mom was a single parent," Micah stated after blessing the food. "It wasn't easy for us, but we managed to have a good life. I know that this is a really confusing time for both of us and with our penchant for misunderstandings, I want it to be clear to you that I don't want that for my child. I'm not talking about the money aspect of it—I missed out on having a father. That's what I wanted most."

"Micah, I already told you that I won't keep you away from your child," Tamara said. "I mean that. If it'll make you feel better, we can have some type of legal document drawn up for visitation."

He met her gaze straight on. "Sweetheart, what I'm trying to tell you is that I don't want to be a part-time father, either."

She lay down her fork and wiped her mouth on the

edge of her napkin. "Micah, what exactly are you saying?"

"I've always been crazy about you, Tamara. Now that I know you love me as much as I love you, I'm saying that I want you to be in my life. We made love last night—it wasn't two people having sex."

Micah sliced off a piece of sausage with his fork and stuck it in his mouth. "I have always wanted to be in a committed relationship with you."

Tamara finished off her scrambled eggs. "I don't want to rush into a relationship just because I'm carrying your child, Micah."

"That's not what this is," he responded. "Tamara, we've known each other for fourteen years, remember? Look, if you're not interested in—"

"That's not it at all," she quickly interjected. "It sounds to me like we want the same things, Micah. I definitely want you in my life and not as just my friend. I want a relationship with you but we have to consider the fact that you live on the West Coast and I'm here in Atlanta. All I'm saying is that there's a lot to talk about—like if you're moving here or if I'll be moving to L.A."

"You're right," Micah stated. "I know that we won't be able to figure it all out this weekend, but we have to start somewhere. Right now all I want to do is pamper the woman carrying my unborn child. Now that I've fed you, I want you to go upstairs and get back into bed. We've got a lot going on today, but before that, I have some people coming over."

Tamara reached for the jar of apple jelly. She loved putting some on her toast and was touched that Micah remembered. "What people? Who's coming to the house?"

"Relax, sweetheart," he told her with a small chuckle. "I have a massage scheduled for you. You're going to get a manicure and pedicure, facial—whatever you want. Oh and a hairstylist will be here, as well."

"You don't have to do this, Micah. I don't need to be pampered."

"Yeah, you do," he countered. "You deserve to be treated like a queen. As long as we're together, I intend to spoil you and our child."

Tamara reached over and took him by the hand. "Micah, all I want is your love. I don't need anything else. Love is all I've ever wanted—not money, material stuff or anything like that. *I only want your love.*"

The telephone rang.

"It's my mother," she announced, glancing over at the caller ID. "I'll call her back later."

Micah leaned over and kissed her. "You have to forgive your mother, sweetheart. I know that you find her motives suspect, but I believe she was well intentioned. She only wanted to secure you and your sister's future."

Tamara nodded and replied, "I know you're right about the forgiveness part, but I'm just not as sure as you are about my mother's motives."

"Look at how much time we missed because of our assumptions," Micah pointed out. "Talk to your mother and really listen to her without judgment. Listen to her heart. That's where we went wrong in the first place."

"Micah, I'll think about what you've said," she responded.

He sent her upstairs to wait for the massage therapist to arrive and set up.

Tamara felt like a new woman.

The therapist used a floor cushion and utilized foot pressure and techniques along the musculature of Tamara's body. She felt a total release as tension left her body.

"This was a wonderful idea. They also have prenatal massages. I'm going to schedule some, but I have to wait until after my first trimester," she told Micah afterward. "Thank you."

He smiled. "You're glowing."

She hugged him. "That's because I'm deliriously happy. I never thought I would ever be this happy. I love you, Micah."

He reached out and took her face in his hand. "I love you, too, sweetheart."

Tamara's eyes brimmed with tears of happiness. She would never tire of hearing him say those words or the little catch in his voice as he said them.

Without another word spoken between them, Micah picked her up and carried her up the stairs to the bedroom.

"We need to get ready," Tamara reminded him as he sat her down gently on the bed.

Micah shrugged. "It's a tailgate party. We'll be fine."

He untied her robe as he told her, "You are my dream come true, Tamara."

They kissed.

She eased under the covers and watched him as he undressed.

Micah joined her in bed and pulled her into his arms. "Sweetheart, are you sure you're feeling up to this?"

She nodded. "I want you, Micah Ross."

His hands explored the soft lines of her back, her waist and her hips searing a path of desire through her. Tamara surrendered blissfully to the deep feelings drawing them together.

Micah kissed her repeatedly, courting her senses with sweet and fiery sensations. Tamara matched him kiss for kiss. His love-filled gaze traveled over her curves. She was so exquisite and sexy that Micah shivered with passion for her.

His lips seared hers aggressively as he pulled her closer to him. Tamara clutched him tightly because she never wanted to let him go.

Together, they rode the waves of passion, crying out their pleasure when their desire peaked out of control.

When their pulses returned to normal, Micah and Tamara spent a few moments cuddling before getting up and showering together.

He was dressed and ready before her, so Micah went downstairs to make some phone calls.

Tamara dressed in a pair of skinny jeans with matching jacket. She paired the outfit with a white lace shirt. She fingered through her hair and then paused briefly to place a hand to her belly where the child she created with Micah was growing.

After all these years, she and Micah were finally together. Tamara could hardly contain her joy.

"Are you almost ready?" Micah shouted, his voice carrying through the apartment.

"I'll be right there," she stated.

When Tamara came down, she found Micah sitting in the living room giving instructions to Bette.

"Schedule a meeting for me here in Atlanta," he stated. "I'll extend my stay here for a few more days."

Micah glanced over at her and winked.

Tamara walked over to a nearby mirror to give her look one final perusal.

"You look beautiful," he said from behind her.

She turned around. "Mr. Ross, you don't look too shabby yourself." Tamara liked the jeans and crisp linen shirt he wore.

An hour later, they were ready to leave the townhouse.

"I told you that we were fine on time," Micah stated as he opened the passenger door to his Mercedes luxury sedan for her. He had her pack an overnight bag because she would be spending the rest of the weekend with Micah at his home in Buckhead.

Micah stopped at a nearby grocery store so that they could pick up hot dogs, buns and sodas for the tailgate party.

Back in the car, Micah reached over and took her hand in his. "I really love you, and I'm happy about the baby. The timing is off, but I already love this child."

"I had just found out that Callie's pregnant the week before. You can imagine my shock when I found out that I was having a baby, too," Tamara commented. "I kept telling my doctor that it was a mistake. He explained that most likely my dosage was much too low. I had to get them changed because the side effects were awful."

"Tamara, I'd like for you to be honest with me about this. How do you really feel about being pregnant with my child?" Micah asked.

"I would've liked to have been married first," she admitted. "But, Micah, I want this child, and I'm glad that you want him or her, too. I guess the big question is how we're going to raise the baby together. We haven't really discussed it."

"We've had ten years to make up for," Micah responded. "Tamara, I'm not trying to avoid the issue or anything. I just don't want to overwhelm you. We love each other. All I know is that we are going to work this out."

When they pulled into the parking lot located north of Hollington College, Micah commented, "The stadium looks nice. Too bad we didn't have it when we were here in school. Cushioned seats and backrests in the VIP section—nice."

"It's very nice," Tamara agreed.

Micah smiled. "I flew down last year for homecoming. I thought I'd see you there."

"I didn't go because I was sick that weekend. I've only missed two homecoming games since we've been out of school. It's the one game I don't like to miss."

"I need to get a sweatshirt," Micah stated. "I bought one last year, but I have no idea what happened to it."

"I have a couple, but they're packed up somewhere," Tamara announced. "I looked last weekend for them."

"How long have you lived in your apartment?"

"Almost six months. I haven't finished unpacking

because I've been so busy with writing assignments, and I mentor a group of girls at church. I'm not complaining though."

"How do you like working with the girls?" Micah asked.

"I love it," she responded. "These girls need to know that someone cares—that they are loved. Most of them don't have fathers in the home. A couple did but were going through the same thing I went through. I've been able to heal by helping them."

He wrapped his arms around her.

Kyra walked by them and then backed up, grinning from ear to ear.

Tamara smiled. "Hey, soror."

"Wow," she murmured. "It's good to see you two together like this, but I'm a little confused. When did all this happen?"

"It doesn't matter," Micah stated with a chuckle. "As far as I'm concerned, it's about time."

He kissed her.

Kevin gave him a thumbs-up as they walked over to the area where the rest of their class members gathered.

Tamara caught sight of Beverly and waved. She sat down with a few of her sorors while Micah took the hot dogs to the men standing around the grill. He stood with them for a moment to chat.

She could feel the eyes of everyone on them when Micah joined her, but she didn't care. Tamara was with the love of her life and that's all that mattered for now, other than Hollington winning the game against the Greenville Rangers.

"I am so ready for this game," Tamara stated when he sat down beside her.

"You still love football?" Micah asked as he handed her a plate containing a hamburger and chips.

"You know it."

"Got any favorite NFL teams?" Micah inquired. "I hope the Falcons aren't one of them."

"I love my Atlanta Falcons. I like New Orleans Saints, the Panthers and the New England Patriots." Tamara bit into her burger. "What about you?"

"I like the ones you mentioned, but I'm a big Dallas fan."

Tamara shook her head. "Ooh, not me."

Micah took a long sip of his drink. "So what do you think of our team this year?"

"They had a pretty good season so far," Tamara stated. "I think Terrence Franklin as head coach will be a good move on Hollington's part. Everyone really wanted to see Coach Neal succeed but emotion wears off. Football isn't an easy game—it's like construction work. Those boys have to put in work to get this done, and they need a more hands-on coach. A lot of the talk about the game today surfaced around the offense, but during the last game, the Lions defense staged a stellar goal line stance late in the fourth quarter for a 14–8 win."

Micah broke into a smile. "Have you considered a career in sports journalism?"

She nodded. "I thought about it, but I like what I'm doing much better. I'm not sure I could always be objective."

Tamara bobbed her head to the music playing in

the background. "Do you remember this song?" she asked Micah.

He grinned. "I sure do. I sang it in the talent show my junior year."

"And you won first place." She took a sip of her soda. "I love to hear you sing. You have a very sexy voice."

He grinned. "You think so?"

She nodded. "I do, so I expect you to sing to our baby all the time," she whispered.

After they finished eating, Micah and Tamara went into the stadium to claim their seats.

As soon as the game started, Tamara was on her feet, cheering on the Lions.

When she sat back down, she told Micah, "I have a good feeling about this game. I really believe that we're going to win."

"The Rangers have a pretty good team this year," he told her.

"So do we," Tamara countered. "I'm telling you the truth—the Lions are going to walk all over the Rangers this day. If you don't believe that, then maybe you need to sit over there."

"Baby, you're fired up, huh?"

"Don't mess with the Lions," she uttered. "You know how I feel about my team."

Micah laughed.

The first two quarters flew by, and it was time for the halftime show. The Marching Lions put on a stellar performance, playing musical hits from the mid-to-late nineties.

Micah and Tamara stood up and began dancing to the music along with several of the alumni.

In the third quarter, the Rangers scored their first touchdown. Two plays later, the Lions scored on a four-yard touchdown.

A Ranger fumble gave the Lions the ball at their forty-two but were successful in stopping the senior linebacker from Hollington for a two-yard loss.

The Lions ended up with a 27–11 win over the Greenville Rangers.

Tamara jumped up and down, squealing with delight.

Micah smiled to himself as he watched the mother of his unborn child enjoying herself. Her love for football still rivaled his love for sports. When the Lions scored that final touchdown, he had never heard Tamara scream so loud. She was ecstatic.

At one point, Tamara turned around to find him watching her. "What's wrong?" she asked.

"Nothing," Micah uttered. "I was just thinking of how much you love this game. I'm glad we won't have to fight over the remote on game days."

Tamara laughed. "We definitely won't have to worry about that," she stated.

Micah surprised himself when he kissed her.

"Wow," she murmured. "You're not one for public displays of affection. I guess you must really love me."

"I do," he whispered in her ear. "I love you more than I love my own life. I have always loved you."

"It never should've taken us this long to get together," Tamara stated. "I've loved you for a long time, too."

"Maybe we just weren't ready," Micah commented.

Tamara stifled a yawn.

"Are you tired?" Micah asked.

"Getting there," Tamara replied. "I've gotten used to taking a nap every day."

Micah rose to his feet. "Let's get out of here. We'll go to my place so that you can get your nap in before the dance tonight."

"I thought you wanted to spend some time with Kevin and Chloe," she pointed out. "Micah, you really don't have to stay home and babysit me. Go on with your friends and enjoy yourself. You haven't seen most of them in years."

"I'll be fine," he replied. "It's more important to me that you get some rest."

Hand in hand, they made their way out of the stadium, caught up in the crowd of students, alumni and others in attendance.

Tamara fell asleep in the car during the ride back to Micah's house.

"Wake up, sleepyhead," he whispered.

She awoke with a start.

"I'm so sorry," Tamara mumbled. "I really didn't mean to fall asleep in the car."

"It's fine. Why don't you go on upstairs and lie down for a while," he suggested when they entered his house. "I'll give you a tour of the house after you wake up."

"Sounds good to me."

Micah led her upstairs to the master bedroom. "You can lie down in here. I'll be downstairs if you need me. You can just use the intercom."

Nodding, she sat down on the edge of the king-size bed and removed her jacket. She then kicked off her shoes.

"Would you like something to drink?" Micah offered. "There's bottled water, juice and some soda, too."

"Yes, please," she responded. "Bottled water is fine. Thanks."

Micah left the room and went down to the kitchen.

When he returned to the bedroom a few minutes later, Tamara had fallen asleep.

Pleased, he eased the double doors closed and descended the stairs. Micah navigated to his office to make a couple of phone calls.

While he was on the phone with Bette, he opened a drawer and pulled out the bag from Wyndham Jewelers.

Micah eyed his purchase and smiled.

He came up with an idea that propelled him out of his seat. He needed to run an errand before Tamara woke up. Micah scribbled a quick note and left it on the counter in the kitchen.

He grabbed his keys and headed out through the garage.

Micah left Tamara a note but he hoped to pick up one last gift and get back to the house before she even realized he was gone. He knew that deep down she still had some doubts about them, and it was his plan to erase them from her heart.

Chapter 15

It was almost seven o'clock when Tamara woke up from her nap.

Tamara assumed Micah was downstairs in his office.

Since she didn't want to disturb him, Tamara reached for the remote control and turned on the television.

As she scanned through the channels, her mind was on Micah. Tamara was deeply in love with him, but she couldn't stop from wondering if Micah truly felt the same way.

Sure, Micah had said the three words she longed to hear, but did he really love her or did he just say them out of obligation to his child?

She generally tried not to be so pessimistic, but when it came to matters of the heart, Tamara faltered.

I won't accept less than I deserve.

She would not allow herself to stay bound to a man just because she was pregnant.

Tamara felt loved by Micah; there was no denying that. However, she was now filled with the fear that this was just too good to be true. Something would go wrong, especially with her being on the East Coast and Micah on the West. Tamara didn't want to worry about women like Sunni going after her man. She wanted her pregnancy as stress-free as possible.

Now she understood why Callie wanted to wait until after her first trimester. Jillian would stress her out enough once she found out that Tamara was pregnant.

She decided not to say anything to her mother until she and Micah sorted out their relationship.

My mother and I need to work on our own relationship, as well, Tamara thought silently. *I know that I have to forgive her.*

Deep down, she knew that Jillian loved her daughters and only wanted the best that life had to offer them.

Tamara knew that her mother loved Lucas and had been hurt by his actions. In her anger, Jillian wanted to fight back in the only way that she knew how, and that's what she did.

She made sure that her daughters would never have to suffer financially. Jillian could've spent the money like it grew on trees, but she didn't. She sought out advice from professionals and invested wisely. Callie was in possession of her money while Tamara refused to have anything to do with her trust fund.

Now that she had a child on the way, Tamara reconsidered. She would have most of the money placed in trust for her children. With the other, she planned to donate to the center for sexual abuse as well as a sizable donation to her church in memory of her grandmother.

Micah peeked into the room. "I was just checking to see if you were awake."

"I am," she stated. "I was in here thinking about my mother and the money. Micah, I realized something— I could've taken the money and done something positive with it." She told him about the trust for the child and donations.

"I think that's a great idea," he told her.

"I'm going to talk to my mother on Monday. Actually, I'm going to apologize for the way I've treated her over the years and ask for her forgiveness."

"She loves you, Tamara. That much I know for sure."

"I love her, too."

"Hungry?" Micah asked.

Smiling, she nodded. "Always."

"I made scallops and pasta with a creamy garlic sauce."

Tamara climbed out of bed. "Okay, now you're just showing off, Micah. I see now that I'm going to have to enroll in a cooking class or something."

He laughed. "Don't hate...."

She stood up for a minute, her hand to her stomach. "Do you have any crackers instead?"

Micah was instantly by her side. "You okay?"

"I'm nauseated." She groaned as she sank down into a nearby chair. "You made one of my favorite meals, too."

"I'll save it for you," Micah promised. "I think there's some soup in the pantry. I'll heat that up for you."

"You're being so good to me." Tamara was touched

by Micah's obvious concern for her. He made her feel loved until he said, "You're the mother of my child."

Her insecurities rose as Tamara began to suspect that he was acting this way because of the baby. Hurt, she looked away from him and said, "I'm not real hungry right now."

"Maybe you should lie back down," he suggested.

Tamara shook her head no. "I need to start getting ready for the reunion dance." She tried to keep the disappointment from her voice.

Micah was watching her. "Tamara, is something wrong?"

She pasted on a tight smile. "No. Everything is fine. I'm just waiting for the nausea to pass."

"You lie down. I'm going to grab a bite, and I'll be back up in a few minutes."

"Take your time," Tamara stated. She wanted a few minutes alone to gather her thoughts.

Despite the vomiting, Tamara was a vision of beauty when she walked out of the bedroom. She had chosen a chic drop waist dress with an ostrich feather skirt in black. She paired it with black opaque hosiery, open-toe patent leather shoes with a matching clutch purse. She undid her twists and wore her hair loose and full of waves.

He could tell that something had changed between them after they arrived at his house. Micah didn't press her because he wanted to be sensitive to the fact that she wasn't feeling well at the moment, and it was possible that she was feeling a bit moody.

The dance started at eight o'clock but Micah and

Tamara did not arrive until shortly after nine. She had another bout of nausea right before leaving the house.

Micah initially tried to convince her to stay home, but Tamara wasn't going to miss it or Justice Kane's performance.

This was around the tenth or eleventh time that he had come to Bollito, the trendy nightclub in South Atlanta owned by his best friend Kevin Stayton. The popular club was comprised of several levels housed in a large, warehouselike building.

They walked through the large double doors.

Kevin greeted him and Tamara seconds after their arrival.

They paused for a moment so that he and Kevin could discuss business. Micah liked that each level featured different colored accents on each dance floor while the club was decorated in the school colors of navy and white. Each floor was devoted to a different genre of music, making it a club that appealed to almost everyone.

Micah escorted Tamara down to the main floor where the stage was positioned against the back wall. They sat down on a plush velvet loveseat in one of the private balconies.

"This is very nice," Tamara murmured. "How many of your artists will be performing tonight?"

"Two," Micah responded. "Justice and Blue Silk are singing tonight."

He wrapped an arm around her. "How are you feeling?"

Tamara looked up at him and said, "Much better."

More of the class of 1999 arrived. She got up to

chat with some of her sorors and former classmates while Micah went down to check on his performers. She seemed happy, but he couldn't escape that feeling that something was bothering her.

Micah already knew she was capable of hiding her emotions behind a smile.

He would find out what was going on with her when they returned home.

Tamara glanced over her shoulder to see if Micah had returned.

When she couldn't locate him in the growing crowd, she returned her attention to the women grouped around her.

Beverly arrived wearing a form-fitting black dress that looked stunning on her. She and Tamara embraced.

"You look absolutely beautiful," she told Tamara. "I hope that you're feeling better."

"I am," Tamara stated. "I have to tell you how much I love this dress you're wearing, Beverly."

The chatted a few minutes about fashion before Beverly moved on. Tamara waved at a couple she hadn't seen since college. It was nice to see that they were still together. She was shocked to hear that they were also proud parents of seven children.

Micah came up a few minutes later and escorted her to the dance floor. The DJ played all of her favorites. Putting a large hand to Tamara's waist, he drew her body toward him. The warmth of his muscled arms as they danced was so bracing; she felt like she was dreaming.

Being this close to Micah made Tamara weak in the

knees. She couldn't remember when she'd felt this way in her thirty-two years. They danced to the next couple of songs. She couldn't remember when she'd had a such a good time.

"Did I tell you how beautiful you look?" Micah asked her.

She smiled. "I believe you did. Thank you."

The DJ slowed down the music, prompting him to pull Tamara into his arms, holding her close as they moved to the sultry rhythm.

When the music stopped, they reluctantly parted a few inches. It was time for Justice to perform so they returned to their seats.

Leaving the dance floor, Micah asked, "Would you like something to drink?"

"I'm fine," she responded.

Tamara was exhausted but didn't want to leave before Justice finished performing. She could feel the heat of Micah's gaze on her.

"We can leave if you're not feeling up to this," he whispered in her ear. "I told Justice that I might have to leave early."

"I'll be okay," she assured him. "Micah, please stop worrying about me. The baby is fine. So am I." Tamara hoped he didn't hear the thread of irritation that was in her tone. She was tired, and his constant attempt to make sure all was well really got on her nerves.

Micah must have gotten the hint, because he didn't say anything else to her during the performance.

Justice took his final bow shortly after ten o'clock. Tamara couldn't take it anymore. "I'm ready," she whispered in Micah's ear. "I'm exhausted."

While Micah and Tamara were saying their good-byes, Kevin walked onstage.

"What's going on?" she asked Micah.

He looked as puzzled as she did. "I don't know. Kevin never said anything to me… Wait a minute, he did mention something about a surprise for tonight. I think it has something to do with Chloe."

She gave him a knowing look. "We can't leave yet. I want to see this."

Tamara's eyes filled with tears at the unique and very romantic proposal from Kevin to Chloe Jackson.

When Micah wiped away her tears, she told him, "You have to excuse me. It's my hormones. They're going crazy right now."

"Let's get you home."

She nodded. "I'm so ready."

Tamara did not say a whole lot during the ride back to Micah's house. She didn't really know what to say, and Tamara didn't really want to spoil the evening by bringing up something Micah might not be ready to discuss.

However, she couldn't delay this any further. Tamara was suddenly afraid that they were moving too fast, trying to force a relationship because of her pregnancy.

She couldn't fully give Micah her heart until she knew that what they were both feeling was real.

Micah had his own surprise for Tamara waiting at the house.

"You were quiet on the way here," he began. "Tamara, I need you to talk to me, sweetheart. Tell me what's wrong, please."

"I'm confused, I think," she responded. "Micah, I know how I feel about you—there's no confusion there."

"Okay, then what is the problem?" he asked.

"I need to be absolutely sure of how you feel about *me*." Tamara took a deep breath, then released it slowly. "Micah, I need to know if you're with me because I'm having your baby or if this is something you really want. I know the sacrifices you would make for your child."

"I love you, Tamara," he told her. "I love you with my whole heart. I wouldn't tell you this if I didn't mean it." Micah raised his hands in resignation. "I don't know what else to tell you."

Tamara's eyes filled with tears. "This is a dream come true for me, Micah, but I have to be realistic. We love each other, but I just don't see how this is going to work. I know you have this house here in Atlanta, but really, how often are you in town?"

"That will change because we're together," he told her.

"How? Are you planning to move here?"

"I would," Micah replied. "If my business wasn't in Los Angeles."

Tamara twisted her hands nervously in her lap. "That's what I thought."

"What about you moving to Los Angeles?" he questioned. "You can write anywhere."

Tamara wiped her eyes with the back of her hand. She hadn't really considered that option.

"Well?" Micah prompted.

"This seems to be moving really fast, don't you think?" Tamara responded. She was feeling a bit overwhelmed. Less than a week ago, she'd discovered that she was pregnant; she and Micah weren't speaking to each other and now he wanted her to consider packing up and moving to California.

"Micah, we haven't seen each other for ten years until a few months ago and now I'm carrying your child. Then you just asked me about moving to Los Angeles."

He frowned. "Are you having second thoughts about us?"

Tamara shook her head. "I love you and I want to be with you, but I…I'm scared."

He pulled her into his arms. "Sweetheart, we don't have to rush into anything. I don't want you to feel like I'm pushing you into this."

"That's not what I'm saying," Tamara interjected. She placed her hands to her face. "Micah, I really need to clear my head. If you don't mind, could you call me a cab? I think that I really need to go home tonight."

"You can take one of the cars," he told her. "But you don't really have to leave, sweetheart. If you want, I'll sleep in one of the guest rooms."

"I think I need to go home. Micah, please don't think that I don't love you. Everything is just happening so fast, and my hormones are on overload. I just need some time alone. I hope you understand."

"I'm trying," he confessed. "Call me when you get home."

"I will." Tamara hugged him. "I'm so sorry."

"I don't want to lose you, so I have no choice but to take your lead on this."

"I do love you, Micah. I just need to try and figure all this out."

Tamara kissed him before walking out of the door.

It wasn't until she was in the car that Tamara broke down into sobs. She wiped her face and drove away from the man she loved.

"I really want this to work out," she whispered. "Are we moving too fast? Lord, I really need You to help me out with this. Help me find the answers, please."

Chapter 16

Micah clenched his fist in frustration and shook his head as he removed his jacket. *Why can't Tamara and I get this right?* He never once doubted that they belonged together, and he refused to start now.

The thought resonated in his head. They were in love and had been for years. So what was the problem?

He removed his shirt before sinking down on the sofa to remove his shoes.

Micah believed that Tamara loved him—he could see it in her eyes. However, he also saw that she was running scared, and he was powerless to stop her. She would have to find a way to deal with her fear. All he could do was love her and only if Tamara allowed him entry into her heart.

He was about to head upstairs when he heard the garage door go up. Curious, Micah made his way toward the door leading outside.

He cautiously reached for the handle and opened the door. Micah was surprised to find Tamara standing there.

"I couldn't figure out which key opened the door," she said sheepishly.

"I didn't think you would be coming back here tonight."

Tamara followed him into the family room. "I know that you're probably wondering if I'm losing my mind, but I'm not, Micah. It's hormones," she said with a nervous chuckle.

Micah gave an understanding nod. He did not want to say anything until he had a sense of what was going through her mind right now.

She paced back and forth. "I'm thinking much clearer now, and I know exactly what I want."

"And what is that?" he inquired.

"*I want us, Micah.* I want us and everything that means." Chewing on her bottom lip, Tamara added, "That is if you haven't changed your mind."

He pulled her into his arms, kissing her until she pleaded for him to stop. "There's something else that I need to tell you."

"I don't want to talk anymore," Micah stated, shaking his head.

"This won't take long, and I know that you'll want to hear this," she promised.

"Okay," he said. "I'm listening."

"Micah, I'm not afraid anymore," Tamara blurted. "I realized when I left here that there are only a couple of times I've truly felt safe in my life and that's when I was with Grandmother and *you*. I love you, and I want to spend the rest of my life with you even if that means I have to make this move to Los Angeles."

Micah broke into a big grin. "Really?"

She nodded.

He took her hand and led her upstairs to the master bedroom where they planned to spend the rest of their evening.

Micah held Tamara in his arms.

"That was wonderful," she murmured. "I love making love with you."

He smiled. "I'm glad to hear that."

She laughed.

Micah sat up and swung his feet out of bed. "I have a little surprise for you," he announced. "I'd planned to give it to you earlier but then you ran out on me."

"I told you it was hormones."

He padded across the room to the huge walk-in closet. Micah reached in and pulled out a gift bag.

Tamara set up in bed, pulling the covers up to cover her breasts. "What is this?" she asked when he sat down beside her.

"Open it and see," Micah responded.

Tamara pulled a medium-size fluffy, white teddy bear out of the bag.

"Micah, he's so adorable," she murmured. "I'll have to put him away for the baby." Stealing a peek over at him, she said, "I have to tell you that I'm a little disappointed. I thought this was a gift for me."

"Look closer."

She gave him a questioning look. "Huh?"

"Take another look at the bear."

Tamara stared at the stuffed animal and then she saw it.

Around the bear's neck was a beautiful necklace—its design was very close to the one she lost in college.

Tears formed in her eyes. "Micah…it looks like the one my grandmother gave me."

"I remember how upset you were when you lost it," he responded. "You used to talk about passing it on to your son or daughter one day."

"Grandmother always made me feel loved and safe. When she died, that necklace was all I had of her. Of course, it wasn't as expensive as this one, but it was like gold to me because it belonged to her. Her mother had given it to her on her wedding day. My mother eloped with my father, and when she married Lucas, she wore a Devane heirloom so Grandmother passed her necklace to me."

Tamara wiped away an escaping tear. "Thank you so much, Micah. I can't put into words how much this gift means to me." Her fingers lightly traced the locket. "This is so beautiful, and I'll cherish it forever."

"I also have these for you." Micah handed her a black velvet box.

Inside was a pair of earrings and a bracelet that matched the necklace.

"I know that necklace isn't the original one that your grandmother gave you, but you still have your memories," Micah said as he put them on her. "No one can ever take those away from you. I hope that we can make new memories to pass on to our children. I want you to feel just as loved and as safe as you felt when you were with your grandmother. I promise to protect you and our child with my life."

Tamara was choked up with emotion and couldn't talk now. Any doubts that she had about them suddenly vanished.

Micah kissed away her tears. "We are going to have a great life together."

Wiping her face with the back of her hand, Tamara nodded in agreement. "I have never been happier than I am right now."

"This is just the beginning, Tamara," Micah stated, his voice filled with emotion. "If you'll trust me with your love, I will make sure that you never regret it."

Chapter 17

Sunday, October 18

The next morning appeared much too soon for Tamara. She and Micah had been up late sealing their commitment to each other.

He was up at 6:00 a.m. as usual but did not bother to wake her until 8:00 a.m., allowing her to get as much rest as she could before they had to leave for the reunion brunch.

Micah leaned over her and whispered, "It's time to get up, sweetheart."

"Nooo," she moaned softly.

Micah suspected that Tamara was not fully awake and gave her a gentle nudge. "C'mon. You know how long it takes for you to get ready."

"Then you shouldn't keep me up so late," Tamara grumbled.

"I tried to get some sleep—you were the one with the insatiable appetite," Micah teased. "You couldn't get enough of me."

Tamara opened one eye and then the other. "I think that was the other way around."

He laughed. "Actually, it was both of us."

She crawled out of bed. "This weekend has really worn me out. It's either because I'm pregnant or I'm getting old."

Micah eyed her naked body, loving her with his eyes. "You're definitely not getting old, baby. Not from where I'm sitting."

Smiling, she stole a peek at him from over her shoulder. "You always seem to say the right things. That's one of the reasons I love you."

"What are some of the other reasons?" he asked with a seductive grin.

"Meet me in the shower," she responded. "I'll show you."

Afterward, Tamara slipped on a pair of blue jeans and a white tank top. She draped a Hollington College scarf around her neck. Tamara pulled her natural curls back into a ponytail.

They left an hour later, driving across town to the campus for the annual brunch, an event geared toward the alumni and their families, regardless of graduation year. However, the class of '99 had a designated section near the food tent.

Large tents had been erected around the center lawn known as The Square. The caterer set up a large buffet of breakfast foods as well as sandwiches and Southern specialties.

White tables and chairs were spread out around the

grassy area. Some of the alumni brought their own blankets and searched for empty spaces to settle down.

Micah and Tamara found a spot near Kevin and Chloe and sat down. She congratulated them on their engagement.

Kevin smiled. "You two look real good together," he told them.

"We think so, too," Micah stated. "It took me fourteen years, but I finally got the woman of my dreams."

Tamara could not keep from yawning.

"I guess you were up late with a certain someone," Kyra whispered in her ear. "All right, soror."

Tamara could feel her face heat up. "You need to quit, Kyra."

Micah brought her a plate piled with more food than she could handle.

"Who did you make this for?" Tamara questioned.

He leaned down, close enough for her ears only and said, "You're eating for two so I figured you'd need—"

"What?" Tamara interjected. "Twice the food?"

"I'll eat what you don't," he told her, grinning. "I know how much you like to enjoy your food."

"If I eat like this the entire pregnancy, I'll be big as one of your houses." Tamara smiled up at him. "You're not going to be like this the entire time, are you?"

"Like what?" Micah asked. "Protective and caring? Yeah, I am. I'm like this about the people I love."

She resisted the urge to kiss him.

He was so good to her, and while all of this attention got on her nerves from time to time and irritated her to no end, she was not going to complain. Tamara was looking forward to a future with Micah and their child.

* * *

The homecoming parade would begin at the college stadium, wind around the small local streets and end at the center lawn.

Tamara stood in front of Micah as they waited for the parade to start. She had always loved parades, even as a child.

Several Atlanta high-school bands, local and university clubs would also be participating. Tamara had planned to help her sorority work on the float for the parade but her bouts of nausea prevented her from doing so.

The parade began.

Former homecoming queen, Beverly Clark, rode on the class of '99 reunion float. Tamara cheered and waved as she passed by them.

Micah and Tamara stayed to see the award-winning Hollington College Marching Lions perform as the parade ended.

Micah had his arms around her with one hand resting on her belly. She leaned against him and reveled in the closeness.

"How are you holding up?" he asked.

"I'm okay," she told him.

Some of the others were going to a sports bar for drinks and fellowship, but she and Micah opted to head home. Tamara was near exhaustion although she tried to put on a brave front. She knew that Micah saw through the facade and that's why he insisted on going back to the house.

"Did I ever tell you what a great job you did on Justice?" he asked while walking across the parking lot to his car.

Tamara shook her head. "Did you really like it?"

"You are an amazing writer, sweetheart."

"Thank you. I love what I do, and I'm trying to learn everything I can because it's my dream to own my own magazine one day."

Micah nodded his approval. "I can see that."

"I'd still like to do a feature on you for *Luster*," Tamara stated. "But it's totally up to you, Micah. If you're not comfortable with the idea, then I won't do it."

He gave her a big smile. "I trust you, sweetheart. We can do the article. Pitch it to Samantha, and see what she thinks."

"I can tell you right now that she is going to be thrilled. I have a feeling she's going to want you on the cover, too. We need to do this before our relationship is public record though," Tamara stated.

"I was thinking along those same lines," Micah said.

"I'll send Samantha an e-mail later on tonight. I won't let you down, Micah. And you won't ever have to worry about me discussing our relationship with anyone in the media."

Micah laughed. "Worrying about you keeping secrets is not an issue for me. I already know that you are skilled in keeping your mouth shut."

Tamara elbowed him in the arm. "I deserved it, but you do know that you're wrong for that, don't you?"

They laughed as they made their way across the stadium parking lot.

Tamara and Micah were in the car driving back to his house when she asked, "Do you mind if we make a quick stop before we go back to your place? It's not too far from here. It's the—"

"The cemetery where your grandmother's buried," Micah interjected. "Today is the eleventh anniversary of her death."

She could not contain her surprise. "Micah, I can't believe you actually remembered the day my grandmother died. Wow."

"I remember it because we were supposed to hang out together homecoming weekend, but instead we were with your family," Micah explained. "You kept trying to get me to leave but I couldn't—you were devastated by your grandmother's passing."

"I didn't want to ruin homecoming for you."

He said, "It wouldn't have been the same without you. In truth, I think that is why I didn't bother coming all these years. I enjoyed spending those times with you."

They stopped at a florist shop so that Tamara could purchase flowers to put on her grandmother's grave.

A few minutes later, they were on their way. Micah drove through the entrance and pulled into an empty space near the road that led up to where Mrs. Davis was buried.

"Do you want me to go with you?"

"I can do this," Tamara stated. "For a long time, I couldn't come out here, but I need to do this today."

She got out of the car and headed down the path to her grandmother's gravesite, the roses in her hand.

Tamara easily located the grave.

"Grandmother, I miss you so much," she stated. "A lot has happened since I was here the last time. I'm in love, and I'm going to have a baby. You met Micah when we were in college. He was that cute lil' tutor—that's what you used to call him. Well we're together now, and I want you to know that he makes me feel safe and loved. He treats me like a queen."

"Mrs. Davis, I just wanted to tell you how much I love your granddaughter," Micah said from behind her. "She means more than anything else in this world. Tamara is the love of my life."

He dropped down beside her. "I promise to keep her and my baby safe. I told you a long time ago that I would marry Tamara, and I fully intend to keep that promise. I would've proposed already, but your granddaughter is the one holding things up."

Stunned, Tamara glanced over at him.

"You told my grandmother that you wanted to marry me?" she asked after a moment.

He nodded. "I think she knew that I was in love with you long before I knew it myself."

Tamara grinned. "That was Grandmother. She suspected things weren't right at home for me, but I would never open up to her. Maybe if I had, things would've turned out differently. For so long, I felt dirty and ashamed, but my grandmother—she would always make sure I understood that I had done nothing wrong. That it wasn't my fault."

"Mrs. Davis was a wonderful lady, and I enjoyed talking to her."

"When did you and Grandmother have these discussions?" Tamara asked out of curiosity. "I was always around you two."

"Not always," Micah told her. "I would call her from time to time to see if she was okay or if she needed anything."

Tamara stared at him in amazement. "I never knew. Grandmother didn't tell me anything."

"It was our secret."

She folded her arms across her chest. "So you were keeping some secrets, too. I didn't think it was possible, but now I love you even more."

"Are you ready to go home?" Micah asked.

"Yes," she responded. "That's what being with you feels like to me. *Home.*"

Micah helped Tamara to her feet.

"Rest in peace, Grandmother," she whispered before leaving. "You don't have to worry about me anymore. I have Micah, and he's very protective. He's going to take good care of me and the baby."

Later at home, Tamara and Micah discussed the events of homecoming while they settled in for the evening.

At one point, there was a break in their conversation. Tamara stared off into space, lost in thought.

"What are you thinking about?" he asked.

Tamara turned to face him. "I was just thinking how you changed my life the day that you came to tutor me. I don't know if I ever told you that you were a great teacher."

Micah reached for Tamara. "Now it's your turn to teach me tonight."

* * * * *

REQUEST YOUR FREE BOOKS!

2 FREE NOVELS
PLUS 2 FREE GIFTS!

KIMANI™ ROMANCE

Love's ultimate destination!

YES! Please send me 2 FREE Harlequin® Kimani™ Romance novels and my 2 FREE gifts (gifts are worth about $10). After receiving them, if I don't wish to receive any more books, I can return the shipping statement marked "cancel." If I don't cancel, I will receive 4 brand-new novels every month and be billed just $5.19 per book in the U.S. or $5.74 per book in Canada. That's a savings of at least 20% off the cover price. It's quite a bargain! Shipping and handling is just 50¢ per book in the U.S. and 75¢ per book in Canada.* I understand that accepting the 2 free books and gifts places me under no obligation to buy anything. I can always return a shipment and cancel at any time. Even if I never buy another book, the two free books and gifts are mine to keep forever.

168/368 XDN F4XC

Name	(PLEASE PRINT)

Address	Apt. #

City	State/Prov.	Zip/Postal Code

Signature (if under 18, a parent or guardian must sign)

Mail to the **Harlequin® Reader Service:**

IN U.S.A.: P.O. Box 1867, Buffalo, NY 14240-1867
IN CANADA: P.O. Box 609, Fort Erie, Ontario L2A 5X3

Want to try two free books from another line?
Call 1-800-873-8635 or visit www.ReaderService.com.

* Terms and prices subject to change without notice. Prices do not include applicable taxes. Sales tax applicable in N.Y. Canadian residents will be charged applicable taxes. Offer not valid in Quebec. This offer is limited to one order per household. Not valid for current subscribers to Harlequin® Kimani™ Romance books. All orders subject to credit approval. Credit or debit balances in a customer's account(s) may be offset by any other outstanding balance owed by or to the customer. Please allow 4 to 6 weeks for delivery. Offer available while quantities last.

Your Privacy—The Harlequin® Reader Service is committed to protecting your privacy. Our Privacy Policy is available online at www.ReaderService.com or upon request from the Harlequin Reader Service.

We make a portion of our mailing list available to reputable third parties that offer products we believe may interest you. If you prefer that we not exchange your name with third parties, or if you wish to clarify or modify your communication preferences, please visit us at www.ReaderService.com/consumerschoice or write to us at Harlequin Reader Service Preference Service, P.O. Box 9062, Buffalo, NY 14269. Include your complete name and address.

KROM13R

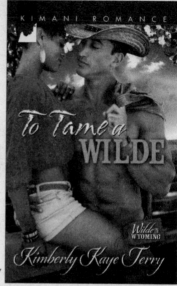